MW01135702

Subscribe to my newsletter to learn about promotions, competitions, and new novels:
www.milaolsenbooks.com/newsletter

TRAPPED

UNTIL YOU LOVE ME

MILA OLSEN

PROLOGUE

I can still picture him perfectly, the way he looked on the day he kidnapped me. The memory is like a delicate, winged creature, trapped for eternity in a mantle of amber.

He was standing in the parking lot of the visitors' center, with a dark band of towering sequoias at his back. It was already early evening, and his dark eyes shimmered in the light of the setting sun. Sparks danced within them like tiny will-o'-the-wisps from an enchanted world, seeming to promise secrets, maybe even adventures. Back then, I wanted both.

How else could I have been so deaf and blind to all the warning signals? The glances over his shoulder to check whether the back-packers had gone inside yet. The way the keys jangled anxiously in his fingers, the laughter that echoed through the silence a shade too loudly. I didn't notice, or didn't want to. All I heard were the silent questions behind that shimmer in his eyes.

Do you want this?
It could have meant anything.
Do you want to come with me?
Do you want to sleep with me?
Do you want me to kidnap you?

I balance on the edge of the curb, humming, arms outstretched as though I'm flying.

Today, I finally managed to dye the school mashed potatoes bright blue without Mr. Smith, the cafeteria server, noticing. I grin to myself. Not because I'm picturing the look on Madison's face, or anyone else's, but because I've officially passed the admissions test for the most important club in the whole high school. Which makes me the first person in our grade to make it in, and only the third person in our town.

Although "town" is an exaggeration when it comes to this tiny village in the Nevada desert. Not even a hermit would want to live in Ash Springs. It sits forgotten in the middle of nowhere, lifeless like a shed snakeskin. I should probably be grateful that this wasteland even has a school bus stop. A veil of sullen thoughts descends over my mind, but I push it aside immediately. Nothing can ruin my good mood today—not the extinct-looking streets, not the heat that seems to burn the life out of everything around me. Today, I'm only focusing on the positives.

The sun prickles my skin; my hair tickles my shoulder blades through my backless top, and my colorful bracelets jingle softly.

How will joining the Hades in Love club change my life? Will I automatically become one of the popular kids? I mean, the members are considered the high school creme-de-la-creme—it's an honor just to be nominated for the admissions test. I bet this is finally going to turn my life around completely!

At the intersection, I turn off the main road and onto a sparsely populated side street Jayden has fittingly dubbed the Road to Nowhere. From there, I take the worn footpath to our house, dodging sagebrush every few feet as I walk. Today, even its herbal smell is like some enticing perfume.

No sooner have I reached the picket fence than I spot my third-oldest brother. Liam. He's standing under the apple tree with his eyes closed, balancing on one leg with the sole of his other foot nestled against his thigh. His palms are pressed together above his head, forming a triangle with his arms.

Ever since he came back from India, he's spent every afternoon in the prickly grass, contorting into bizarre positions he calls the Swan, the Crane, or the Crow.

"Is that the Vulture?" I ask, tapping Liam on the shoulder as I walk past, but lightly, so he won't lose his balance.

"It's the Tree, goober," he replies quietly without opening his eyes.

I pick a puny-looking apple and take an energetic bite. Chewing, I watch him for a moment. Liam's the brother I feel closest to. When I was little, he always came up with the best games for me.

"Go catch the rhinoceros!" he'd exclaim to wake me every Sunday morning, and I'd immediately jump out of bed and run into the yard to rope the beast with my invisible lasso. While Ethan and Avery set the table on the veranda, I'd polish my imaginary animal's horn until it gleamed and "feed" it raspberries before popping them into my own mouth.

"Someday Louisa's going to go crazy, and it'll be your fault," Ethan would tell Liam every time, but Liam would just laugh and bring me a bowl of water for my pink rhino. Liam claimed I was more likely to go crazy from doing too much math homework.

"Jayden home yet?" I ask Liam now, even though I know I should quit bugging him while he's trying to meditate.

"Already in there working on one of his million stories."

I have to smile. "Of course." I picture Jayden's slim fingers flying across the keys on his laptop. Living in Ash Springs obviously doesn't bother him, since he can travel to any world he wants through his stories. Liam doesn't mind anymore, either, not since he hiked across India and up into Nepal in order to find himself. When he returned from Kathmandu, he was as emaciated as an ascetic and his matted hair was crawling with lice, but his soul was filled with inner peace. Somehow I seem to be the only one on bad terms with Ash Springs. Avery and Ethan don't want to leave, either. They both work on the same farm that Dad used to.

On a whim, I stretch up on tiptoe and blow into Liam's face. I'd kind of like to share my joy with him, but I don't think the name Hades in Love will make him explode in rapturous excitement. "Wind in your treetop, you knotty old oak," I say, hefting my backpack, and head for the rickety stairs leading into the house. It's a one-story wooden building on short stilts that's always reminded me a little of an old longhouse. The front door is open because of the heat, as it always is when at least two of my brothers are at home.

The wooden floorboards creak beneath my feet as I walk toward the kitchen. There's a plate of sandwiches on the counter beside the gas stove. Jayden probably took it out of the fridge and forgot to put it back. Nothing left of the ham-and-cheese rolls but crumbs. Typical. I take one with salami and flop into a chair in the breakfast nook. I could have eaten at school, of course, but after the whole mashed-potatoes thing, making myself scarce seemed like a wiser course of action. Too bad Jayden's home already. He could have told me how everyone reacted.

As I eat, I fumble my phone out of my backpack and check Facebook. Twelve new messages jump out at me immediately.

Congrats, Madison's written. She's not one to waste words, especially not on gushing praise. She's like Ethan that way. *Welcome to godhood*, Ava's message says. My stomach starts fluttering in anticipation. Hades in Love means tons of fun, tons of parties, even weekend trips to Vegas clubs with the older boys. Provided, of course, that I manage to convince Ethan that I'm spending the night at Elizabeth's. I scroll through the rest of the congratulatory messages and accept my new friend requests, all of them from club members. Even one from Damon, one of the hottest guys in the senior class. I blow a few sweaty strands of hair away from my face and smile to myself as I accept the request. Every girl at school has a little bit of a crush on Damon, and I have to admit that he's the first boy I've seen that the thought of kissing him doesn't gross me out.

"Where is she?"

Ethan's voice whip-cracks through the open kitchen window, and I jump. Oh, man, he sounds pissed. I hear Liam reply with his usual serenity but don't hear what he says, because I'm busy rummaging through the apocalyptic chaos of my backpack to fish out some books and pens as fast as I can.

Ethan's footfalls thunder across the floorboards. By the time I open the book, he's already in the kitchen doorway, staring at me with narrowed eyes. He's still wearing his work clothes: the plaid shirt with the sleeves rolled up, the mud-caked lace-up boots. Not a good sign. Apparently he was in such a rush to get here that he didn't change at the farm the way he normally does. Hopefully he wasn't hurrying on my account.

"What were you thinking?" he snaps.

Oh no! Suddenly it's even hotter in here. I pretend to continue doing my homework. "What was I thinking when?" I ask cautiously.

"Do you have any idea what kind of consequences this will have?"

I hate when he doesn't just come out and say what the problem is. Especially because I can think of several possible reasons he might be mad right now.

I adjust the ruffles on my pink lace top and then look back up at him. "Ethan, I need to finish this homework, and I really don't know what—"

"Homework?" His gaze shifts to my textbook, and one corner of his mouth twitches derisively. "You should probably turn the book right-side up, then."

"I was just about to get started."

"Your math teacher called me."

A sinking feeling spreads through the pit of my stomach as I flip the math book around. "Ms. Fitch?" I can only think of one reason why she would want to talk to him, but it's even worse than the blue potatoes.

"Oh, so you know her name? That's comforting." He scowls at

me, folding his arms. He's only twenty-nine, and I know a lot of girls at my school think he's cute, but to me he's always seemed like he came into the world old and uptight. Even his hipster ponytail does nothing to remedy it.

"Louisa. She. Saw. You."

My heart somersaults in alarm, but then I remember: Ms. Fitch can't have seen me. Nobody but Mr. Smith was in the cafeteria, and he didn't notice me, because he was busy sorting silverware.

"Of course she saw me," I say evasively. "We had math today."

"You dyed the school cafeteria mashed potatoes blue and caused mass hysteria. Don't you dare deny it." He looks so furious that I really don't dare deny it. He's standing in the door broad-legged, almost like he's trying to block my escape.

"She *would* call a little prank 'mass hysteria,' wouldn't she..." I murmur in a lame effort to defend myself. But goddammit, why did he have to be the one to find out? Why couldn't it have been Avery? Because Ethan's the one Ms. Fitch always calls, obviously. It's like they're united in a losing battle against me. She probably has a secret crush on him. I mean, she was totally thrilled to hear that he'd managed to get custody of us—at barely eighteen years old—right after Dad died.

"So you admit it?" Ethan shakes his head in exasperation.

"I thought I'd already been tried and convicted."

He takes a deep breath. I stare at the words and numbers on the page in front of me, mentally bracing myself for the impending lecture, but he's silent. I look up. There's a lot more than just irritation in his eyes. Frustration. Worry. Grief.

"That's not all, Louisa."

True! I smooth the textbook page with my palm, just to have something to do.

"You lied to me." His tone is serious, and he sounds like he's struggling to keep it objective. "You told me you got a C+ on your math test, but you got an F."

My cheeks start burning. I'm ashamed of the grade, ashamed at my own inability to think logically. Liam says I perceive the world using feelings rather than reason, which has its advantages. Ethan, unfortunately, sees it differently.

"Nothing to say for yourself?"

15

The disappointment in his voice is boundless, which I assume is more due to the lie than the grade. I know it was shady of me, but then again, he's always putting me in these emotional headlocks, acting all injured, and it's completely infuriating. "I have dyscalculia, I can't help it."

"That's not what I mean."

"I didn't want to make you mad."

"So you faked my signature? Don't give me that wide-eyed look, I know you did. And anyway, having trouble with math is no excuse for getting bad grades. It means one thing: study, study, study. More than anyone else. But you never even opened the book, did you?"

"Studying doesn't help me. I don't *get* math!" I straighten the dog-eared corner at the bottom of the page. "And besides, I wanted to—"

"You wanted to go to the movies with Ava, so you decided to just bump your grade up a notch." Ethan snorts with indignation. "Louisa... I won't tolerate you lying to me!" He's still standing in the doorway. The heat is hanging in the air, sticking to my skin, and all at once I feel like a cornered animal. Ethan's not letting me off easy this time. But in a way, this situation is his fault, too.

"If you'd let me do more, I wouldn't have to lie," I blurt out angrily. "You're stricter than any dad I know. Why can't you be like Ava's dad?"

"Ava's dad works twenty-four hours a day. He has no idea what his daughter gets up to."

"At least Ava's allowed to go out with her friends if she wants!" I slam the book shut. "And I always have to ask your permission. To do anything! Even if I just want to go over to Emma's. It's so unfair. I'm not three anymore!"

Ethan regards me for a while, his gaze softening slightly.

I look back at him, at the face that's so like mine and my other brothers'. An oval face with a high forehead, wide-set turquoise eyes, and nicely curved lips. Five different variants on the same basic idea, except my features are softer. I have fuller lips, and my blonde hair is one shade lighter.

I can barely remember my dad anymore—he died in an accident when I was five, while he was out baling hay—but everyone in the village says we Scriver kids all look just like him. Especially Ethan. It's pretty obvious from the photos, too.

The problem is that I know he means well. But it doesn't change the fact that sometimes he acts less like my brother and more like my personal dungeon-master.

"Why did you do that today?" he asks now.

I realize I probably do owe him some kind of explanation, and I can't lie to him again. "It was an admissions test," I tell him. "For the Hades in Love club."

"The what?"

He knows perfectly well what I said—the club existed back when he was in school. He's just saying it to show his disapproval as clearly as possible. He raises a reproachful eyebrow. "Aren't those the stuck-up chicks who wear a ton of Tommy Hilfiger and the look-at-me-I'm-so-tough guys?"

"You mean 'bad boys'?" I ask in a snide voice, although I know there's a grain of truth to his description. Of course only the popular kids are in the club. That's the whole reason I want to join. It's not like I don't have any other friends, but Emma and Elizabeth are like Ethan and Avery: deeply rooted in our village. And I'm sick of vegetating—I want to get out there and start living, before I end up as dried out as the sagebrush.

"You wouldn't fit in with them." Ethan ignores my snarky tone. "We're not super-rich, and you're not super-talented."

That stings, but I don't let it show. I try to remain calm and collected, like Liam. "And yet Ava and Madison asked me if I wanted to join, imagine that!"

"Sure they did. But it was probably the boys that wanted you in. Maybe having a pretty face counts as a special talent. It certainly wasn't your amazing math skills that caught their attention."

I press my lips together to keep myself from hurling some cheap shot back at him, which would only mean even more punishment.

Ethan walks over to me and stops beside my chair. I keep my eyes stubbornly focused on the nick in the kitchen table—left there by a blade years ago, the time Jayden and I were playing knife-throwers. "To get anywhere in life, you need more than just a pretty face."

I roll my eyes. Not this again.

17

"Under the circumstances, I'm not sure I can let you do that modeling camp. It's not too late to cancel the reservation."

"What?" I exclaim in outrage. Model camp is going to be the highlight of my summer, and it took me a million years to convince Ethan to let me go. "Madison's mother is coming with us and staying right nearby. It's totally safe!"

"You're only five-five, you're too short to model anyway. And besides the fact that neither Ava nor Madison are model material, they're a bad influence. Madison drinks too much, and Ava jumps into bed with any guy who gives her the time of day."

I leap from my chair so forcefully that it scrapes across the ground. "You always ruin everything for me," I snap at him.

"You know we talked about this. You have to get your grades up first." Ethan is perfectly calm, which is not good at all. "Ms. Fitch tells me that you'd rather paint your nails in biology class than participate. You never do your math homework at all, and you're conspicuously absent from physics." He looks me over from head to toe, and then points to my pink-flowered sandals with the silver pearls. "Yesterday I got a bill from Stylight. For five things I doubt I'd wear even if I were a size extra-small and wore a women's eight and a half."

Crap. I totally forgot to tell him. I open my mouth to mount my defense, but Ethan keeps right on talking.

"My issue isn't with the two hundred dollars. It's with the fact that you used my credit card without asking and pretended to be Ethan Scriver."

"I'll pay you back, promise," I say hurriedly. "I just needed a cool outfit for Hades in Love, like, just in case—" I regret it the minute I say it.

And Ethan promptly sighs. "Hades will have to wait."

I stare daggers at him. "What do you mean, wait? You can't just forbid me from joining the club!"

"Lou." I hate it when he does that soft Mister-Nice-Guy voice. It leaves me defenseless, makes it impossible to argue with him. But he's not getting me that easily today! "I don't know what's going on in your life these days," he continues. "I look at you and I see a girl heading in the wrong direction for getting what she wants. What she really wants, you know what I mean?"

"Oh, like you've *ever* been interested in what I really want," I snap at him. "All you care about is whether I 'make something of myself,' whether I get good grades so I can get into college and live the life that you wish *you* had. But you could care less what *I* think about anything!"

His eyes bore into mine as he fishes his phone out of his jeans pocket, but then he turns his gaze to the screen and scrolls until he finds what he's looking for. "Hi, everybody out there," he reads aloud and glances up at me. I chew on my lip, already half-sure what he's reading. The next sentence confirms my suspicions. "Here in Ash Springs, the asphalt's melting in the sun again, and I'm hanging around and don't know what to do. Does anyone else ever feel like their life is like the monotone road from Ash Springs to Rachel? Like, nothing but dry sand and branches roasting in the heat? Don't you wish something would happen? Something that would grab you like an eagle and carry you into the air, until you can see the whole world from above? Something that makes you soar so high that the rays of the sun light up your heart? Something that turns you inside out and leaves behind a person you don't recognize? Do you dream about that too?"

When he finishes, I swallow. I posted that publicly to my Facebook wall, and when Ethan reads it, it sounds like a prayer demanding to be heard. By someone, somewhere out there.

"Trust me, I know how you feel," he says quietly. "I understand what you want." He slips the phone into his back pocket again. "But this isn't like the movies, it doesn't work like that. We should just be glad that Avery and I have jobs, and that we all have each other. Life can be worth living even if it isn't dramatic."

I study the doorframe intently. "So you're criticizing my dreams now?" I ask in a small voice.

"Mom and Dad would have wanted me to look after you, Lou. I can't just let you do whatever you want all the time."

"You always bring up Mom and Dad when you want me to feel guilty." My throat is closing up, and the words are hard to get out. "When you run out of arguments. But they're dead. They have no idea what my life is like, or yours. None. So who cares what they would have wanted? They'll never know you're here playing Mother Teresa!"

Ethan takes a deep breath, and I can see he's struggling to keep calm. Unlike him, I don't remember our mom at all. She died giving birth to me, and sometimes I wonder whether Ethan subconsciously blames me for it. Maybe that's why he's always so strict. He was twelve when it happened, so to him Mom is more than just a woman's face in a picture frame and a couple of anecdotes. And Dad, he practically idolized. When I think about Dad, I remember a sad man who didn't talk much and almost always smelled like horses and hay. Who rarely had time for me because he worked day and night. But Mom and Dad were everything to Ethan, and I don't know why I said those mean things to him. Maybe because he was comparing my dreams to movies, acting like they're worthless.

I start to apologize, but the way Ethan's shaking his head, with his lips pressed together adamantly like that, keeps me from saying anything.

"You can hurt me all you want, Louisa, but it doesn't change the situation," he says. "Even if you don't honor Mom and Dad's memory, I do. And I sure as hell am not going to let you go chasing a ridiculous dream." He nods toward the door. "I'm going to drive up to your school now. Not everything is just about you this time, for once. Mr. Smith is going to be in a lot of trouble with the administration. If he's really unlucky, they'll call in the Board of Health, and he'll lose his job."

My jaw drops. "That's not true!"

Ethan turns to go, but then pauses and looks down at me. "Did you know he was color-blind?"

"Yeah."

"And you took advantage of it." He gives me a look of contempt.

I try to hold his gaze. "I didn't mean to get him in trouble. Really, Ethan. I'm sorry." Poor Mr. Smith. Ava makes fun of him sometimes because he's such a dumb old coot. I picture them grabbing him and hauling him out of the cafeteria. I feel bad for laughing at the things Ava said about him, even though I actually like Mr. Smith.

"You never mean to do anything," Ethan replies coolly. "And you're always sorry afterward. Maybe next time you'll think twice before you risk a man's job for a bunch of self-obsessed douchebags."

Quickly, I grab my phone and put it in my bag. "Let me come with you, Ethan, please! I can explain that I—"

"That won't do him any good anymore now. The point is, it shouldn't have happened in the first place. What if some nutjob had put poison into y'all's food?" Ethan sounds like even he can't entirely forgive Mr. Smith's inattention, although he knows perfectly well what happened.

"But it was just food dye," I protest weakly.

"It doesn't matter what it was, he neglected his duties. Don't worry, you can make your case to the principal tomorrow." Ethan points to my book. "You're staying home for the rest of the day. Do your homework, and help Jayden fix the rotten boards under the house. We'll talk about the consequences for your actions after dinner."

I nod, and he leaves. The creaking floorboards sound like they're sighing out his disappointment in me with every step he takes. Although I'm still furious at him, I run over to the kitchen door. "Ethan."

He stops at the front door and looks over at me.

"I'm sorry I said that about Mom and Dad," I tell him quietly.

He nods, but the expression on his face is distant. "I know."

I do actually do my homework, or at least I try to, but months of slacking on algebra means the gaps in my knowledge are more like craters. Plus, I keep getting distracted thinking about Mr. Smith—and about all those rude things I said about Mom and Dad. For the first time, I start thinking maybe they would be just as disappointed in me as Ethan is. That they would think I was a superficial, irresponsible daydreamer whose only good quality was a pretty face. The idea hurts in a way I hadn't expected. Right now, I'm almost glad they're dead so they don't know about any of this.

After an hour of staring at the same equation, I give up. Maybe Jayden can help me later. Instead of moving on to bio, I empty the dishwasher. Motivated by my guilty conscience, I gather the colorful pile of clothes on my bedroom floor and dump it into the laundry bin in the bathroom, and then vacuum the entire house. Then I clean the bathroom as a surprise for Ethan, even though it's his turn to do it, and pick up all the empty yogurt containers and half-full chip bags in the living room.

Cleaning distracts me from sulking. And maybe when Ethan sees it, he'll go easier on me, as in not ground me until the end of the school year. The word "grounded" is so childish that it turns my stomach. Who actually gets grounded anymore?

As I knot the trash bag in the kitchen, I think about what the worst possible scenario could be. He threatened to cancel modeling camp, but he was probably just saying that because he was so mad. "Hades will have to wait"—yeah, okay, he might make me wait until next year to join the club. That would be sort of medium-catastrophic, mostly because I would have to tell Madison and Ava what happened. Hopefully the offer will still be on the table next year.

I mop the floor, too. Better safe than sorry. If I know Ethan, he'll just leave it at a lecture and a week or two of grounding. He can never stay mad at me for too long.

Jayden walks into the kitchen just as I'm pulling the overflowing trash bag out of the wastebasket. "What happened in here?" He runs a hand through his mussed hair, blinking like he just woke up. He always looks vaguely disoriented when he first steps away from one of his stories, like he's still remembering where he is. "The bathroom and the living room are, like, hospital clean," he says, motioning vaguely toward the hallway with his chin. "You could perform open-heart surgery in there." He regards me for a moment, and breaks into a grin. "What'd you do this time? I mean, besides the baby-blue potatoes? Judging from the cleanliness of the house, it must be something horrible, right? Did you poison Ms. Fitch?"

"You heard already?"

"What, you really did poison her?" His grin widens in amusement, though he obviously knows that wasn't what I meant.

"I hate to disappoint you," I mutter, pushing past him, "but Ms. Fitch is just fine. How did you hear about the potatoes?"

"Avery texted me."

"Traitor."

Jayden laughs. As withdrawn as he is around everyone else, he always seems perfectly relaxed in my presence, though I'm never totally sure what's going on in his head. "He's on his way home right now to cook you your favorite meal."

An uneasy feeling begins to spread in my stomach. Ethan probably called Avery and told him what I did. Maybe he even told Avery how he's going to punish me, and Avery thinks he needs to cook my favorite meal to make me feel better. That would be just like the two of them: Ethan's strict, Avery's a softie. Sometimes I feel like they're trying to replace Mom and Dad for me. If so, Avery's definitely the mom.

I take the trash down to the Dumpsters outside our fence. Liam's standing on his head now. If the President of the United States came on the air and announced that the world was ending, Liam would probably go right on doing yoga.

Later, after I've watered the young tomato plants and the string beans behind the veranda, I squeeze in beneath the house with Jayden. We lie there on our backs, shoulder to shoulder, with the wooden floorboards over us and the warm, red earth under us. There's barely three feet of headroom under here, and I feel like I've been buried alive. Thick swaths of cobwebs hang from the support beams. Not the slightest breeze gets through down here, which is why I keep having to put my forearm over my nose and breathe into my sweaty skin to get away from the musty smell.

"This one spot under the bathroom is almost totally busted." Jayden tugs at a plank he's just finished unscrewing with the battery-powered screwdriver in his hand. It snaps in half. "Good thing the floor has two layers—otherwise we might fall right through here while we're sitting on the toilet! We really need to figure out some better ventilation."

The thought of Ethan crashing straight through the floor with his pants around his ankles makes me grin. "Like a better bathroom vent?" I ask.

Jayden groans and laughs at the same time. "The vent in the bathroom doesn't do any good under the floor. I was thinking more like a ventilation system for underneath the house." He uses two fingers to peel away another hunk of rotten wood. "We need to get the air circulating down here."

I feel like a moron. How does he know things like that? He just turned eighteen three months ago, so he's only a year and a half older than I am.

"I looked it up for a novel," he explains as though reading my mind. "Board!"

I reach over to grab one of the boards beside me and pass it to him. "Do you think Mom and Dad would be disappointed in me?" I blurt out.

He stops short and turns his face toward me. Someday I'll probably see it in the New York Times, when he makes it onto the bestseller list. Jayden's totally on another level. He's not like Liam, whose whole life is one long journey to "find" himself. He's known what he wanted to do with his life ever since Avery read him his first book, and he's been working tirelessly to make it happen ever since. He's probably the most ambitious of any of us. A kid Mom and Dad would be proud of. I get another sharp pain in my heart at the realization.

Jayden fixes me with a penetrating gaze. Tiny mosquitos cling to the sweat on his forehead. "That's ridiculous," he says after a moment, a shade too gruffly. "Why would you even think that?"

I confess everything. When I'm done, he whistles through his teeth, which doesn't make it better. "Ethan will get over it," he says then.

I know he's just trying to cheer me up. "Do you think I'm egotistical?" I ask him.

"Obviously."

"I'm serious, Jay. Tell me what you really think of me."

"You're my sister, what am I supposed to think? I think you're annoying."

"Jay!"

"Okay, okay. You're all right, overall."

I'd throw the pack of screws at him if I had room. "Overall?!"

"Like, in general, as a complete package. I mean, I don't think you're available as individual parts."

It makes me think of our old game, where one of us would describe something in three words and the other had to guess what it was. Nowadays, we do it the other way around sometimes.

24

Describe Ash Springs in three words. Describe American history in three words.

"Describe me in three words," I say. "Pretend you're trying to characterize me for your novel, and you can only use three adjectives."

"Nobody would buy that novel." His eyes still light up at the challenge, but he takes his time about answering. First he screws the new board into place and loosens the screws on the next one. The boards creak up above somewhere behind us. Avery's probably home, starting the spaghetti. Or maybe it's Liam, coming in from his yoga session.

"Well?"

"Fun-loving, emotional, insecure." Jayden smiles to himself as he twists a screw into the hole. Hopefully he's not trying to imagine what kind of character I'd make in a book.

"Insecure? Why?"

"Because you need other people to tell you who you are."

"Ethan says I'm superficial, irrational, and difficult."

"And you believe that?"

"Isn't it true?"

Jayden shrugs his shoulders, which looks weird on a person lying on his back. "The negative way of saying fun-loving, emotional, and insecure."

He's given me a lot to think about. He goes on working—silently, which is normal for him—and I just lie there. Afterward I take a shower to scrub all the dirt off. I make sure to pick a top that isn't too low-cut and shorts that aren't too short—my "revealing" clothes are another thing that Ethan and I fight about constantly. He thinks dressing sexy is like advertising to guys that I'm easy. Or worse, that I'm one of those girls that guys like to think "no" means "yes" with. I asked him what went through *his* mind when he saw scantily clad women, but he waved the question away. Whatever. Tonight I have to make nice, so I slip on a coral-colored blouse trimmed with lace and a pair of dark-blue shorts that go to just above my knees. Then I braid my hair so it'll be wavy in the morning.

When I emerge from my room, the house is already filled with the delicious scents of garlic and fresh basil. I join Avery in the kitchen and snag a couple of the diced sun-dried tomatoes. He gives me a comforting hug, even though I'm the one who's done something wrong.

"Did Ethan say anything to you?" I ask.

Avery makes an indistinct gesture. His face is most like mine, softer than our other brothers', which makes him look a lot younger than twenty-six. Most people think Liam's older, but he's only twenty-two.

"You're not allowed to tell me," I realize after a few more moments of silence.

"Ethan wants you to hear it from him." Avery stirs the pot of pasta, avoiding my gaze.

"That sounds bad."

"I don't think you're going to like it."

"Can't you just tell me? Come on, Avery, I have to be prepared!" I pluck at his sleeve and gaze up at him with a doe-eyed look that almost always works on him.

"You sure did it this time," he says evasively.

"Is that why you're cooking for me?"

"Oh, Louisa," he sighs, turning back to the stove. Maybe he's disappointed in me too. "Ethan just wants you to be able to go to college. You should get a proper degree so you don't end up on a farm."

"You guys enjoy working for Mr. Goodman, though."

"I never wanted to do anything else, but Ethan's not like me... I mean, he had to take the job because we needed the money."

"But I'm not Ethan!" I protest, pushing aside the thought that Ethan had probably sacrificed a lot in life because of us. "Maybe I don't want to go to college."

"What do you want to do, then?"

"I don't know yet."

"See? And as long as you don't know, you should be trying as hard as you can. When you don't make an effort, to Ethan it's like you're just spitting on all his hard work and sacrifices."

I pull some dishes out of the cupboard and start setting the table. "You've said yourself that he's too strict."

Avery turns back around, still holding his cooking spoon. "I'm just trying to explain how he feels."

Normally Ethan is the one explaining how I feel. The anxious feeling in my stomach has been growing ever since I first saw the food, and now it's a hard knot. I'm starting to suspect that he's planning to do something way worse than just ground me.

We eat in awkward silence. Ethan is at the head of the table, his face inscrutable, and the others don't seem particularly approachable, either. I guess they probably all know. The sound of forks scraping against plates is fraying my nerves, and I almost choke a couple of times because the spaghetti with tomatoes and pine nuts keeps getting tangled in my mouth. I feel Ethan's eyes on me. He didn't say one word about how clean the place was—he just asked me about my homework. When I confessed that I hadn't gotten past the first problem, he simply turned away, which was worse than getting yelled at.

After Avery and I have cleared the table and sat down again, my trial begins.

Ethan starts by listing off my many misdeeds with stoic calm: faking his signature, faking my identity online, using his credit card without permission, failing my math test, lying, skipping class, sneaking in through the back door of the cafeteria, dyeing the mashed potatoes blue—which was thoughtless, he adds, and will have consequences as yet unknown. And then there are my bad grades in biology and physics, and the "Ms. Fitch, The Bitch" graffiti Ava and I did on the gym wall... all of which Ethan just found out about today.

Even I have to admit that it's a pretty sizeable list, though to me it sounds like a bunch of minor stuff. "Ava was the one who actually sprayed that," I say meekly, and it's true: I just kept watch and acted like I thought it was cool so Ava wouldn't think I was boring.

Ethan doesn't acknowledge my protest any more than he did the clean house. "This wasn't an easy decision, Louisa," he begins, and then glances around the table like a king regarding his subjects before issuing a new decree. His gaze comes to rest on me. "Long story short, Hades will have to get along without you next year."

His words hang in the air between us. They can't possibly be true. "All next year?" Mind. Blown. He's actually serious. "You can't do that!" I ball my fists under the table in fury and try to hold back the tears forming in my eyes. "What's so bad about the club? You're always saying how important it is to have good friends."

"Do you seriously believe you're going to find real friends in that snobby clique? The sole purpose of that club is to belittle nonmembers to make themselves look better."

"Ava and Madison are okay."

"Besides, you have good friends. Emma and Elizabeth, for example."

Emma and Elizabeth are nice but boring, though I'd probably better not say that out loud right now. "Can't you think of a different way to punish me?"

"You really think that's it?" Ethan shakes his head in disbelief.

My eyes widen. "Isn't it?"

"I canceled model camp. You're coming on vacation with us instead."

Now I can barely breathe. "You expect me to go camping with you guys in the wilderness? You're out of your mind!"

Ethan goes right on talking, unmoved. "Enjoying nature, getting some fresh air, and being somewhere without commercialism or Facebook will all do you good. Oh, right, and speaking of Facebook: your account is being deactivated for the next six months, and you're only allowed to use the Internet for homework purposes. You're also grounded until the start of the next school year."

"Until the start of—that's in August! It's May!"

"That's correct."

"And the end-of-year party..."

"No parties. No sleeping over at friends' houses. Nothing."

I'm utterly speechless. My lips are trembling, but I definitely, definitely do not want to start crying. I never would have thought he'd go this far, that he'd ruin my entire life!

Avery lays his hand on my arm. "It'll be fun, Lou, you'll see. We're going to some national parks. We're going camping, and we'll see the giant sequoias, and there are lots of waterfalls in Yosemite... and we might even spot some elk or caribou."

I shake his hand off. A million thoughts are racing through my head, but before I can turn them into a sentence, Ethan starts talking again.

"From now on, every night when I get home, we're going to review a chapter of your math book. Hopefully by the end of summer break you'll be caught up to the others."

"I have to study during vacation?"

Ethan allows himself a smile that makes me want to strangle him. "It's not like you'll have anything else to do. If necessary, I'll bring your books with us on the camping trip."

"You're only doing this because I said that stuff about Mom and Dad," I manage to stammer, and a tear runs down my cheek. Impatiently, I wipe it away and jump out of my seat. I glance over at my other brothers. Jayden's staring at the table, Avery's trying to keep his expression as breezy as possible, and Liam is rolling some herbs he picked himself into a cigarette. Not one of them is taking my side—Ethan must have prepped them in advance. For my own good, of course! I feel betrayed and abandoned by them all.

"I'm sorry, Louisa," Ethan says as he rises to his feet and comes toward me. "You have to learn to show responsibility. Food dye has no business being in school food, just like your most personal hopes and dreams have no business being on a public Facebook wall. I genuinely think this is what's best for you."

He tries to put a hand on my shoulder, but I jerk away, shaking my head vehemently. "No, it's what's best for you, so that you can feel great about yourself!" I choke out. "Maybe I should just leave! Then all your worries will go away, and I finally won't have to be around you anymore! That would seriously be the best thing that ever happened to me!"

I storm out of the room. Before I slam the door, I hear Liam and Jay reasoning with Ethan.

None of them stuck up for me. I really do wish I could just start packing!

CHAPTER
TWO

I'm sitting cross-legged on the forest floor, staring into the glowing coals in the grill tray. Dry needles are pricking my thighs, and I keep having to flick ants off of my shins and back to their trail. *What a great vacation!*

We haven't even been here three hours and I already feel totally inept. After I broke the middle tent pole as I was putting it together and then accidentally tore the outside of Ethan's sleeping bag with the sharp end, he released me of all further duties. So that I wouldn't do any more damage.

I really was making an effort, though. I want to give this vacation a chance, like I promised Avery I would yesterday. Maybe it won't be as terrible as I'm expecting.

Our car and our tent are nestled within a ring of boulders and ancient sequoias, with wild hawthorn and massive branches filling the gaps in between, so we're fairly well isolated from our camping neighbors.

Earlier, as we were driving from the visitors' center to our campsite, I spotted a sparkling green mountain stream. With a warning sign about bears right next to it. Obviously, nobody told me that there are black bears here. Either my brothers didn't want to upset me, or they assumed that it was just common knowledge. At any rate, I'm going out first thing tomorrow to get myself some bear spray, just in case. The thought of black bears slinking around here makes me kind of nervous. I keep checking into the bushes, but all I see are the outlines of other people's tents and a couple of chipmunks.

I whirl around in terror when I hear a muted rustling behind me, but it's only Liam, setting up a camping table beside a picnic bench anchored into the ground. The few rays of sunshine piercing the canopy overhead cast a net of shimmering light around us, with ghostly shadows dancing among them like tiny insects. It'll be dark in about an hour, so we have to get the tent up and dinner ready by then. I could help Liam, of course, but Ethan did tell me not to touch anything else until dinner.

Out of boredom, I grab a stick and start poking the coals.

"Hey, Lou, quit it!" I hear Ethan call. "You'll make the embers go out!"

Even from inside that crooked tent, he seems to be keeping an eye on me.

I make a face at him behind his back. He always manages to make me feel like a toddler. Spitefully, I start jabbing the stick around the edge of the coals even more. Acrid smoke promptly billows into my face, and my eyes begin to water. Liam laughs. I throw the branch aside with a scowl. Ava and Madison are off hooking up with super-hot guys at model camp while I'm stuck here with my brothers. The one highlight of my entire vacation will probably be a couple of unshaven nature freaks in hiking boots that look like survivalist street vendors with all their gear. *Psst, hey, kid, wanna buy some bear spray?*

Thanks a lot, Ethan! I've barely spoken to him since that horrible night. Only during our tutoring sessions, and only when absolutely necessary. After a couple of days, I wanted to ask him to take away at least part of the punishment, but at the last minute my pride got in the way. Weirdly, apologizing to Mr. Smith was easier than any of the rest, especially since he got to keep his job and my little prank didn't have any other serious consequences.

Once that was certain, I asked Liam to talk to Ethan again for me. But Liam's opinion doesn't count in Ethan's eyes, so then Jayden was up. Ethan values Jayden's opinion quite a bit, but this time my youngest brother's pleas fell on deaf ears. And the day before yesterday, Avery sat me down for a chat.

So I'm going to try to make the best of the situation, for Avery's sake, Liam's, and Jayden's.

Which is why I clamber to my feet now and help Liam with the camping table after all. After that, I go to the car, pull the plastic tablecloth out of my backpack, and spread it over the table.

"Lou!" I hear Ethan call.

I ignore him and go back to fetch the dishes from the transport case. Despite everything, he still acts like everything is fine between us. Well, sure, he got his way, so as far as he's concerned, every-thing *is* fine! The fact that he's derailing my whole life doesn't seem to interest him in the slightest. On my last Facebook post, I wrote that I had to leave Facebook for a while. I didn't explain why—telling everyone that my own brother is punishing me with that would be way, way too embarrassing. Instead, I posted our travel route. Ethan, obviously, used it as yet another reason to get all furious at me. I don't know why, but I just needed to do it. If the rest of the world isn't going to hear anything from me, they ought to at least know where I am. Otherwise it's almost like I don't exist, strange as that sounds.

"Louisa!" It's Ethan again, more annoyed this time.

I act like I'm engrossed in my work.

"You can go ahead and grab the camping lanterns. It gets dark fast out here!"

I remember the promise I made to Avery. "Where are they?"

"How would I know? You were the one who was supposed to pack them. I specifically put them in your room."

"Dammit." Hopefully Ethan didn't hear me say that under my breath. I open the trunk and start rummaging around in my back-pack, even though I know I'm not going to find them in there. They're still sitting next to my bedroom door.

"I think I forgot them," I call to Ethan, just as Avery returns from the visitors' center with a sack of firewood, a bag of potatoes, and a six-pack of beer. He heaves the wood and the potatoes onto a bench, sets the beer beside them, and then flops down himself.

"You're kidding!" Ethan is beside me within seconds. He tears my bag away from me and starts yanking my clothes out. Shorts, lace tops, and ruffled T-shirts land on the dirty cargo liner.

"Watch out!" I grab a white blouse out of his hand.

"Don't tell me these are the only clothes you brought." He stares, baffled, at the particularly tight T-shirt he's holding, which has a brightly colored necklace caught on the hem.

I cross my arms. "That's all. So what?"

"No long pants? No sweaters? Where are your hiking boots?"

"I can hike in my Chucks."

"Or in those things, which you still haven't paid me back for," Ethan sneers, gesturing at my flowered sandals. He continues searching my bag, and curses to himself when he sees my arsenal of cosmetics and bracelets. "Where, exactly, did you think we were camping at? A spa hotel?"

"If I have to come, I'm going to wear what I want to wear."

"And where are the camping lanterns?" Ethan glowers at me.

"I forgot them, like I just said." I cringe inwardly, bracing myself to get chewed out.

Ethan takes a deep breath. "You really are completely useless." He says it loud enough for anyone within a hundred feet to hear. "It's not like I asked you to remember a hundred things. Just the two lanterns and the tablecloth. That's it. Three things. That shouldn't be too hard, even for you."

"Sorry," I snap, trying to mask how much that hurt.

"Maybe you left them behind on purpose," he sighs in resignation.

"I did not! I just forgot them!" My face heats up in rage.

"Like you forgot your math stuff?" Ethan pushes me away from the trunk and slams it shut. Then he reaches into his pants pocket and slaps a few dollar bills into my hand. "Go to the visitors' center and buy two new ones. Now."

He says it like I'm a total idiot, and it's completely demeaning. We really do need lanterns, though, and it's totally my fault that we don't have them.

"Can I get some bear spray too, then?" I ask, making every effort to sound friendly.

Ethan stares at me like I've officially lost my mind. "I wouldn't give you bear spray if there were a grizzly right in front of our tent. You would somehow manage to spray us all and leave us totally defenseless. Anyway, you wouldn't have the guts to use it in an emergency."

"But I'm scared of bears!" I insist stubbornly.

He gives me a look of pure contempt. "Just the lanterns. That's it. Got it?"

"Maybe I'll just get in the next bus I see and go home, then." The words are tumbling out before I can stop them. "Or somewhere else!" My voice sounds whiny, and I hate myself for it. I hate myself for letting Ethan provoke me into acting like a small child, instead of a sixteen-year-old, almost seventeen-year-old.

"Yeah, yeah, sure." He waves dismissively. "Make sure you don't get in the wrong bus." His grin is cruel. And patronizing. It makes me completely forget my promise to Avery.

"And you think you can replace Dad for me," I shout. "But Dad would never have been so mean to me. He would have never told me that I'm useless. Never! I hate you!" I turn around and stalk off.

I hope a sequoia branch falls on his head and kills him!

As I trot down the gravel road toward the visitors' center, I try to push the whole conversation with Ethan out of my mind, but his words keep circling around me like the blades of a windmill. *Shouldn't be hard, even for you. You really are completely useless.*

I *do* feel like jumping onto the next bus I see, just to get back at Ethan. I know it would be childish of me, but he'd be getting what he deserved for talking down to me like that. Then I count the bills crumpled in my fist and realize that thirty bucks isn't going to get me home anyway. Scowling, I shove the money into my shorts pocket, and then stick my hands under my armpits because I'm suddenly freezing, like the temperature just dropped twenty degrees from one minute to the next. It's gotten darker, too. And quieter. I hadn't realized just how loudly the gravel was crunching under the soles of my sandals.

I glance around. A couple of gigantic crows are sitting near the big Dumpster, picking at crumbs left behind by other campers. Uneasily, I peer into the thick trees looking for black bears, but all I see are green and brown tents, campfires, people in outdoor gear... and trees, hundreds and hundreds of trees. Everything else looks so tiny next to them, like a bunch of toys. The shadows around their bare trunks are beginning to swallow the flickering sunlight, as if they're strangling it with their evil claws... or maybe getting ready to leap at me from the darkness.

There. Wasn't something moving back there, between those two trees? Something dark, like a cross between a man and a bear? I freeze in place for a second and then retreat back to the center of the gravel road. I squint into the forest, but then shake my head at my own ridiculousness. Why wouldn't there be things moving in there? This place is full of people, even if there aren't technically any tents in the part I'm walking through right now. Maybe the public toilets they mentioned earlier are back there? I set off down the road again. The visitors' center isn't far now, maybe a quarter mile away, on the other side of the main road running through the park. I can already see the brightly lit entrance from here.

But I still can't shake the sense that someone or something is walking along beside me, and keeps slipping behind the nearest tree every time I look in that direction.

Heart racing, I tug my paper-thin blouse up to cover my shoulders. *Quit showing so much skin, Louisa,* I hear Ethan say. *Don't tell me you've never heard anyone say, "If she didn't want it she wouldn't have been dressed like that."*

I glance into the trees again, and this time I'm sure I saw it. Something long, wild, scurrying into a shadow as though it were part of the forest itself.

I start walking faster now, keeping my eyes straight ahead. It's not far at all now—I'm already in the RV park. To get there faster, I veer off onto a narrow path winding past the individual campsites. In my anxiety, I run smack into a clothesline spanned between two trees, and curse loudly as I break into a near-jog.

A branch snaps somewhere nearby. I glance toward it and feel a hand on my shoulder. I want to scream, but everything happens too fast. The hand jerks me around.

"Lou! Wait up already!"

I smack the hand away reflexively. "Jay," I wheeze. "You scared me to death. What are you doing sneaking up behind me?"

"I wasn't sneaking, I just took a shortcut." He grins, and for a moment I wonder whether this is some kind of test he's running for one of his stories. How would a teenaged girl react to a mysterious threat in the forest? But no—Jay may be ambitious, but he wouldn't go that far.

"Don't you ever do that again!" I snap. My heart is still hammering in my chest. "I thought you were a... oh, never mind." Suddenly, it dawns on me. "Ethan sent you to make sure I didn't run away."

Jay shakes his head. "He doesn't mean it like that. He just wants to protect you."

"Is that what you came out here to tell me?"

"I came out here to make sure everything was okay."

"Ethan hates me! He thinks I'm worthless!" I'm almost shocked at myself for saying it aloud. This is the first time I'm realizing that I genuinely believe it. There's a dull pressure in my chest. Anger goes away eventually, so does disappointment. But contempt is more intense, it runs deeper. It's harder to fight.

"Bullshit!" Jayden retorts energetically. "Ethan loves you. If he hates anyone, it's himself, because he can't help being so hard on you."

You really are completely useless. I'm not sure what to think anymore. I'm pretty sure I've just disappointed Ethan once too often, and at some point, his disappointment turned into contempt. Which is why he doesn't even care anymore if I say hurtful things to him.

I turn away. "Just leave me alone so I can buy the stupid lanterns in peace," I mutter. Maybe I can do this one thing right.

"Are you sure?" Jay sounds wary.

I turn back around and force myself to smile at him, so that he'll leave me alone. "I'm sure!" With that, I leave him standing there.

The visitors' center is warm and brightly lit, with wood paneling on the walls and ceiling that gives it a cozy feel. The whole room smells like the French fries and fresh-brewed coffee at the kiosk in the far corner. I wish I could just spend the night in here instead of shivering in the cold, listening to my brothers snore. Bringing me along was so dumb of Ethan, especially because now there'll be five of us squished into a four-person tent.

Thinking about Ethan brings back that funny feeling in my

stomach. Knowing someone's mad at me is bad enough, but I totally can't deal with people looking down on me. Maybe I should use this vacation as a chance to show Ethan that I'm not as irresponsible as he thinks. If I'm on my very best behavior all summer, maybe he'll even change his mind about letting me be in Hades in Love this fall. Anyway, I did promise Avery I would make nice.

I rub my arms, still shivering a little, as I look around the visitors' center. It's a one-story building divided into two sections. One side is full of tourist brochures; the other is where they make money off of campers who forgot stuff at home. Out through the other exit is where the park ranger said they have proper toilets and showers —thank God!

I saunter up and down the aisles, searching for the lanterns. The sales area is like a mini-grocery store, except obscenely overpriced. Eight ounces of Starbucks iced coffee for ten dollars. Sandwiches for eleven. Seriously? I thought camping was supposed to be cheap?

Eventually, I drift over to a rack of hoodies. A grey one with a green hood says Sequoia National Park in big letters across the front. Maybe I should buy that instead of the lanterns? I really didn't bring anything long-sleeved, and it's already freezing outside. I slide it over to look at the one behind it. *Keep calm and camp on*, it says underneath a picture of a grizzly bear. Very funny. I wander off again, and soon find myself in the alcove with the camping equipment. The bear spray is the first thing that catches my eye.

I reach for the can. *Animal repellent spray. Works up to 30 feet away. $50.*

Well, great. I wouldn't have fifty bucks if I asked Ethan for a month's allowance in advance. Plus I still owe him for the clothes. With a sigh, I put the can back, and my gaze drifts to the entrance, just as a guy in dark clothing walks in through the open glass doors. I stare at him as though hypnotized. Black cargo pants, black hoodie. It's not his outfit I'm fascinated by, though. It's something in his expression. I can't place it. I just know it's got my attention.

I take a deep breath and look away. If Madison were here, she'd say he was hot like fire and call dibs on him. Ava would probably be squeezing my wrist to death. Dammit, if Ethan hadn't taken my phone away I could have taken a sneaky picture of him.

In an effort to look busy, I pick up the bear spray again and act like I'm studying the ingredients, though in reality I'm watching Hoodie Guy from across the lid of the can. His dark hair is slightly too long to be neat, but it doesn't seem unkempt. More like... rakish. He looks like a guy who's not afraid to take risks.

With one quick motion, I slide the ponytail holder out of my hair and smooth it down. Maybe he'll notice me yet. You never know!

He's standing in front of the freezer case now, reaching for... are those fish sticks? Lord, I wouldn't have pegged him as a fish sticks kind of guy. He looks like a steak guy. Rare, I bet. As if in a trance, I watch him pull out iced coffee—not the Starbucks one—and a couple of frozen donuts. All things I love!

Suddenly, as if sensing me sneaking glances at him behind the bear spray, he turns around and looks at me from across the room. He has a questioning look on his face, almost like he's wondering if he's done something wrong. Or like he's astonished that I'm looking at him. Like he can't believe he's caught my attention.

I can't even move. I just go right on staring at him like a complete psychopath. *Goddammit, Lou, get your shit together already!*

Before I can make myself smile, I realize that he's already turned away and gone to the cash register. He pays with a bill he fishes out of his pocket and then turns to leave. But he's heading for the alcove, not the glass doors.

Help! He's coming this way! Maybe he wants to know why I'm gawking at him. Or he forgot something. Or he just wants to chat.

I grip the bear spray in both hands, gazing at it like I'm in spiritual communion with the ingredients list, wondering if he's actually walking in my direction. Half of me desperately hopes he is; the other half has basically shut down, and taken whatever's left of my rational mind with it.

I really, seriously think he's coming over here.

Quickly, I spin around and run my thumbnail between my front teeth to make sure there's nothing stuck in there if he does talk to me. What am I wearing again? Oh, right, the white blouse with the billowy lace sleeves, the long chain with a bunch of multi-colored pendants, and my jean shorts. No hiking boots, fortunately. Then again, maybe he's into that kind of thing.

Out of the corner of my eye, I see him step into the alcove and position himself in front of the shelf holding flashlights, lanterns, and batteries. He's using one forearm to hold the frozen foods neatly against his stomach—his slender, toned stomach, at least from what I can tell from his baggy clothes. He seems pretty athletic in general, based on the way he moves. Like a panther, whose deadly strength you barely notice beneath its elegant grace.

I could ask him whether he knows about camping stuff, and it wouldn't even be a pretense, because I don't have the first clue about camping lanterns. But I just stand there tongue-tied, feeling my cheeks starting to burn. Hoodie Guy looks like he's out of high school already. Twenty-two, maybe? Older? *Way too old for you,* Ethan would say.

Perfect, Ava whispers seductively in my head. I don't remember the last time a boy threw me this far off my game. Well, not a boy. Definitely not a boy.

"The bear spray is useless," he says out of the blue, without turning around. "Total scam." His voice is dark, gravelly, confident. It only amplifies my insecurity. I stare at his back, wracking my brain feverishly, trying to come up with a reply before he thinks I'm deaf or dumb or both.

"Or at least I don't know anyone that's successfully taken out a bear with it." He turns and gives me a brief smile.

I can feel my heart pounding in my throat, and all I can do is pray that he doesn't notice how nervous I am. He's even better-looking up close. His eyes are dark, nearly black, framed by long, thick lashes. Bedroom eyes, Ava whispers. My gaze travels around his face: thin, well-defined lips; a nose that isn't too big or too small. His cheekbones are unusual—they stand out so much that they actually have thin shadows underneath them. The shadows give him an unapproachable air. Unapproachable, but vulnerable. Which is probably the thing about him that got my attention so fast.

He gestures casually to the can in my hand. "All that stuff is going to do is provoke them. In fact, if you're super unlucky, it'll make them want to attack you. Especially if your aim is off." He takes a step toward me. He smells like firewood, salt, and woods, but there's another sweet, pungent smell mixed in that I can't identify. Some kind of chemical. Cleaning fluid, maybe.

I still can't get a smile out. He seems so perfectly controlled, so experienced. He's probably talked to hundreds of girls. Anything that comes out of my mouth is going to be totally stupid. If I ever manage to say another word again.

"You must not go camping much," he says, as if to help me get over my shyness. Which of course he knows how to do, because I'm sure this isn't the first time that a girl has gone speechless at the sight of him.

"But what if there's suddenly one in front of me?" I blurt out. "Um, a... a bear, I mean...?" I could seriously smack myself for stammering like this. Soooo embarrassing.

Hoodie Guy either didn't hear it or is very smooth about ignoring it. "Stand still. Keep calm." He smiles again, this time with a strange gleam in his eyes. Maybe he's happy to discover that I know how to talk after all. "Just wait until it goes away. If it keeps coming closer, you should sing or clap your hands—loud noises will scare most black bears off."

"Okay," I say in a near-whisper, setting the can back on the shelf. "I'm supposed to buy a camping lantern," I quickly add, not wanting him to leave. "Do you know anything about them?"

"To hang, or to put on the table?" He looks at me. His pupils are gigantic—nearly to the outer edge of his irises. I heard somewhere that people's pupils get bigger when they like the person they're talking to. The thought of him thinking I'm pretty gives me a tiny bit more courage. Maybe I really am pretty. Even Ethan says that.

"To put on the table." I clear my throat a little so that my voice will sound more confident, and toy nervously with my pendant. "I forgot our lanterns at home, and my brother sent me to buy new ones."

He nods like he already knows, and I wonder whether he heard our argument. Ethan was pretty loud. If he did hear anything, though, he doesn't say so. Instead, he plucks a lantern from one of the upper shelves that I wouldn't have been able to reach on my own. Wow, he's tall. At least as tall as Avery. Six-one, maybe six-two. I barely come up to his chin, if that. "Solarez are the best. They give off plenty of light without blinding you."

I act like I'm looking more closely at the lantern, but all I can really see are his long, slim fingers wrapped around it. There's a faint scar across the back of his left hand. For some reason, I like it.

"I'm Louisa," I suddenly tell him.

"Bren." His pupils have swallowed his entire iris now. Is he on drugs or something? I'm not sure how to tell. He seems too lucid to be high, though. His gaze seems to penetrate straight into my core, almost like he's trying to tell me something. Like there's something I need to understand. But what?

"Just Bren?" I hear myself ask from a million miles away.

He blinks, and the moment passes. "Brendan." Now he's the one speaking softly, as if his name's a secret he's only revealing to me. He glances over his shoulder, toward the cash register. The cashier's back is to us; he's organizing a rack next to the counter. Bren sweeps his gaze across the shelves.

My optimism shrivels to approximately walnut size. Probably searching for his girlfriend. What was I thinking? Of course a guy who looks like Brendan is going to have a girlfriend.

"I've gotta go," he says abruptly and presses the lantern into my hand. "Maybe I'll see you around."

I smile to hide my disappointment. "Are you staying a while?" I ask anyway.

His gaze drifts through the room again. "Couple more days."

"Same here."

"Yeah." He gives me a goodbye nod. "Later."

"Later." I watch him exit through the glass doors, still holding the frozen foods and the iced coffee against his stomach.

I stay standing there for a minute or two longer, feeling like I'm in some kind of dream. Finally, I look down at the lantern in my hand. It's fourteen dollars, practically the same as the iced coffee. Crazy. I ask the cashier to get me a second one from the shelf, but my mind is still on Brendan. I should have told him about model camp. I bet that would have impressed him, and then he wouldn't have taken off so soon. Although maybe he would have just thought it was me being a dumb, naive teenaged girl. Yeah, probably better I didn't mention it. He didn't look like the easily impressed type. What type *did* he look like? As I pay for the lanterns, I try to play the three-word description game on Brendan. Confident... daring... and...

Hm. Too many choices. Hot? Exciting? Wild? Vulnerable? Intense?

If there was one thing he had going for him, it was that he didn't talk or act like I was completely useless. He actually managed to distract me from Ethan.

Lost in thought, I walk back out into the visitors' center parking lot. It's already dusk; reddish-gold rays of sunlight are fanning out through the gathering blue-grey clouds. It'll be dark soon. The thought of having to walk the whole way back to our campsite makes me shiver—partly from cold, partly because the forest looks more sinister than ever. I wish I hadn't sent Jay away. I fumble with the switch on one of the camping lanterns, and then the other, but they stay dark. Ethan probably would have thought I was stupid for even trying, but sometimes batteries are included, right? Not this time, though.

With one lantern in each hand, I set off across the parking lot. From a distance, I see a dark figure approaching. His determined stride reminds me of Ethan's, but when he gets closer, I recognize Bren.

He seems to have put the stuff he bought away already.

"Hey, Louisa."

I stop in my tracks, surprised that he's talking directly to me. His expression is serious, almost contemplative. "Bad news," he says in a clipped tone and gives me a once-over, as though assessing me somehow.

"What?" Involuntarily, I grip the lanterns more tightly. Hopefully it's not about my brothers. Then again, how would he know about them?

"There's a mama black bear with her cubs right by the Dumpsters."

I feel the blood drain from my face. "That's exactly the direction I'm going."

"You'd better wait until they leave. Mother bears always get crazy aggressive if they think someone's threatening their cubs. Some idiot forgot to lock one of the Dumpsters. Same thing happens every year. It may be hours before they finish eating."

My thoughts begin to race. If I don't show up back at camp soon, they'll come searching for me, and then they'll run straight into the arms of that mama bear. "I have to get back."

Bren shakes his head, pursing his thin lips. "You can't get past there."

"But my brothers..." I glance over my shoulder toward the visitors' center. "They'll be looking for me. We should tell the rangers. I've gotta—"

Bren raises a placating hand. "Louisa, the rangers are already there, making sure everyone's safe. They're not going to let anyone get anywhere near the bears."

"Really?"

He nods.

"And they'll be on both sides of the Dumpsters?"

"Um, of course, why wouldn't they be?"

I breathe a sigh of relief. Rangers have guns, and they're allowed to shoot bears in emergency situations. And when my brothers see them, they'll realize that I'm waiting on the other side.

"There's always some idiot trying to take pictures," Bren explains now. "This one tourist in Canada even tried to get his daughter to ride on a grizzly's back."

"No way!"

"I swear to God! But nothing happened."

I have to laugh, and he joins in with a brief, loud "ha ha." It's barely a laugh at all, but it changes his face for a moment, softens those rough, unapproachable shadows, makes him look younger.

"I was headed back to the visitors' center." Bren takes the lanterns out of my hands. Why, I don't know, but somehow it feels natural. "Forgot tomatoes. But if you want to get back to your brothers, I can drive you around the long way to your campsite."

"There's another road?" I blink, baffled. "The ranger didn't mention that." Unless he did and I just wasn't paying attention. Again.

"There's three, actually, but the third will be blocked off, too, because it's too close to the Dumpsters. People don't take the other route much, because it goes a few miles through the forest, and it's got a million potholes." His eyes shift to my bare shoulder. The blouse has slipped down again, nearly to my elbow. Automatically,

I pull it up a little. He looks up, directly into my eyes. The intensity of his gaze hits me again. "You shouldn't walk that whole way by yourself. Really."

For half a second, I think about all the things Ethan is always warning me about, but then the sun emerges from behind a grey mountain of clouds and the entire sky seems to drown in the blood red of the setting sun. Everything is glowing, radiant. The towering sequoias behind Bren look like they're about to burst into flame.

"What about your tomatoes? Don't you want to go grab them first?"

He waves the question away. "I'm right over there, a little ways down the road." The sunlight flickers in his eyes, tiny pinpoints of red dancing across his black irises, or pupils, I'm not sure. And there's that feeling again, the one I got in the visitors' center. The feeling that he wants to tell me something. Or is it a question he's only asking me in his mind?

Do you want this?

A faint tingling sensation pulses through my veins. It could mean anything.

Do you want to come with me?

Do you want to sleep with me?

Do you want something to happen?

The key ring jingles in his hand like an invitation. Out of the corner of my eye, I see a man hoisting a backpack from the trunk of his car. Bren glances over at him, and I follow his gaze. The man shoulders the bag and heads straight for the visitors' center. Otherwise, the lot is completely empty.

Bren turns away from the man to look at me again. "It's not far."

I nod, and he moves around to walk beside me, between me and the center.

Ethan would kill me if he knew I was getting into a stranger's car. But he doesn't know the situation. Besides, Bren is too hot to turn down. I guess there's also a chance he's hoping something will happen if he drives me. Maybe he wants to get to know me. Or more than that. Which is what makes this so exciting.

Do you want this?

My heart is racing as I walk next to him. I take a deep breath. I feel like I'm sensing everything around me at once: the rhythmic

45

rustling of the treetops, the scent of pine needles and smoke, the wind on my skin, Bren's keys jingling, the sound of the camping lanterns clacking together in his other hand.

"You're shivering," he says suddenly.

"I'm fine."

He gives me a sidelong look, and then smiles like he knows better. We leave the parking lot and continue down the main street. Within minutes, the sky changes from reddish gold to grey. "We're almost there." Bren points straight ahead. I can barely make out a camper bus parked in a pull-off area a short distance from the road.

My stomach knots. Is he traveling with his wife and kids? Maybe he's older than I thought, and he's just being nice to me because he saw me holding the bear spray so he knows I'm scared of bears. Maybe he only offered to drive me because he's a responsible guy who doesn't want a girl walking around in the woods alone.

"So you're here with your family?" I can't stop myself from asking.

His face darkens for a second, but he smiles the shadows away as soon as I see them. "Just me."

"I pictured you with a car and a tent."

He raises an eyebrow. "Is there a difference between tent guys and RV guys?"

Is he making fun of me? I shrug uncertainly. "Um. You just... looked like a tent guy, I dunno." I hope he's not mad. "I guess I thought maybe because you know so much about... bears and stuff."

He smiles. Thank God. "The bus gives me more flexibility." His keys clink against his cargo pants.

"It's huge," I realize. "You could fit a family of five in there."

"I need space. Sometimes I spend the whole summer on the road."

"So what do you do in winter?" The question is out before I can bite it back. I'm too damn nosy.

"Work."

"Oh." Now I feel dumb. Like, obviously, if you spend the whole summer traveling around, you have to earn money sometime.

We've reached the camper. *Travel America*, it says in red-and-blue striped letters across the side. I wonder what it's like going on vacation all by yourself in this gigantic RV. Is Bren a loner? He doesn't look like one. But you can't tell that Jayden's a loner at first glance, either.

Bren walks to the passenger-side door, unlocks it, and pulls on the handle, but the door doesn't open. "Ah, fuck," he groans. "Stuck again." He yanks on the door grip as hard as he can, but nothing happens. He turns to me with a sheepish grin and shrugs. "Sorry. You mind getting in the back and then climbing up front?"

"No problem," I say, but all at once I'm starting to get a bad feeling. I don't know why, though. I mean, I'm standing here with the single most attractive human being in California. Ava would probably walk across broken glass for a chance to sleep with him. Everything's fine. The passenger-side door sticks, no big deal.

Bren opens the back door on the side, which leads into the living area. Over his shoulder, I see a small yellow kitchen island and a table with benches. It's pretty dark in here, though. When he steps aside to let me through, I hesitate, peering into the camper again. There's a dark jacket tossed carelessly across one bench, and a two-liter of Coke and a glass sitting on the table. A small dishtowel hanging on the fridge door handle. The tiny counter is cluttered with stuff.

Organized chaos. Exactly what I'd expect from a guy like him.

I look up at him.

He smiles, but it's different somehow. Maybe it's just that weird feeling in my stomach that I totally have no idea why I'm getting.

He seems to notice my anxiety. "Hey," he says, taking a step back. "I'm Bren, not Jack."

"Jack?"

He raises his hands as if to show he's not armed. My camping lanterns swing into the air with them. "The Ripper." Grinning, he lowers his hands and stuffs his keys into his pocket.

I let out a laugh. "Okay." But that weird feeling stays with me. Maybe I'm scared of my own courage. Maybe he wants to get right to it, like he'll offer me a Coke and then make his move. I wonder how I would react to that. Or will react. My stomach is still doing flip-flops, but I'm not sure anymore if I'm feeling excited or threatened.

"We could walk if you'd rather," Bren suddenly says. "It's kind of far, but I understand if you—"

"No, it's fine," I say, cutting him off, and take the stairs up. He wouldn't offer to walk with me if he was actually trying to do something bad. So I don't understand why now, of all times, Ethan's warnings come flooding back into my head again. Like that stuff he was saying about guys seeing my clothes and thinking maybe no means yes with me.

But Bren wouldn't have to force girls to do anything, I reason with myself. *With those eyes and that smile, he can get any girl he wants.*

Once I'm in the RV, I look to either side. The curtains are all drawn, I notice for the first time. Bren gets in behind me and jerks the door shut roughly.

Why didn't he go around to the front?

That weird feeling flickers to life again. He's behind me, close enough that I can feel the warmth of his body, although he isn't touching me.

He doesn't say anything. Doesn't go to the fridge to offer me something to drink.

Where did he put the stuff he bought earlier? He was coming from a totally different direction. He can't have walked the whole way to the camper and back in that short of a time. Something is off here. A wave of fear washes over me. The sweet scent I smelled back at the visitors' center is suddenly really intense. I'm too scared to turn around and look at him. I open my mouth, not sure whether I want to talk to him or scream or just run to the driver's side door.

At the exact moment that I decide to run, there's a loud crash, and glass splinters fly in every direction. A lantern rolls past my foot. Before I can react, Bren's arm shoots out. He presses my elbows against my body, squeezing me. At first I'm frozen in shock; then I start trying to wrench my arms free, but I can't, he's too strong.

I scream again and again, so loudly that it hurts my throat. "Help!" "No!" "Please!" but then his hand is on my face. He's pressing something soft against my mouth and nose, holding it down tight.

The sweet smell burns my lips, makes my eyes water. Immediately, the room starts to spin. I can't breathe this stuff in. *Don't breathe, don't*. Still holding my breath, I dig my nails into his thigh, but Bren's grip is like iron, like the bars of a cage. Blind panic fills me. I can't get away. Oh, God, I can't get out of here. I understand what's happening to me and yet I don't.

"Hold still, I'm not going to hurt you." He sounds perfectly calm, even as his arm is winding tighter and tighter around my body.

All I can see now is the white cloth. All I can think about is how I'm going to die. My pulse is throbbing in my ears. The pressure in my chest is unbearable. I have to breathe. Aimlessly, I kick out at him, land a couple of blows, but then he crushes me more tightly against him, lifting me so my feet are dangling in the air. My eyes start to water. My lungs are exploding. I can't hold my breath any longer. The sweet stuff flows into my mouth, scratches my throat. Neon-colored spirals dance before my eyes against a black background. I try to wriggle free, but my muscles have other plans.

"I won't hurt you, don't worry." Bren's voice pierces the thick, dark fog circling inside my head. I feel myself slump in his grip, tip forward. I know that I'm blacking out. And that it means I'm going to die.

Wild patterns envelop me. At the end, all that's left are words.

Hold still, I'm not going to hurt you.

You really are completely useless.

Do you want this?

THREE

The first thing I notice when I wake up is the rocking. I'm lying on something, and whatever I'm lying on is swaying back and forth, like on a ship.

I'm not sure why, but I don't want to open my eyes. What's stopping me? Fear? Was I having a nightmare? If so, I can't remember what it was about. I'm not really awake, am I?

Maybe I should just go back to sleep. But I blink a few times anyway, because I'm so disoriented. My eyelids are leaden and sticky; I can barely open them.

More anxiety now. Everything around me is completely dark. I can't see a single thing. Places this dark don't exist, at least not where we're from. There's always light coming from somewhere—streetlamps, moon, stars, whatever.

I blink again, but the darkness stays. Why is it so dark? My pulse twitches hard in my throat.

If I can just find something familiar, that will calm me down. Like my messy nightstand or the flowered curtains. But when I turn my head to one side to get my bearings, a stabbing pain hits behind my eyes. Red flashes flicker at the edges of my vision, and it hurts so bad that for a few seconds I'm afraid I'm going to pass out.

What the hell is wrong with me? I try to do some kind of self-inventory, but the fear is making it hard to think clearly. All I know is that it's crazy hard to catch my breath. My chest is sore, like maybe I have a lung infection. And I can still hear my pulse hammering in my ears. *Bam. Bam. Bam.* Maybe I have a fever?

"Ethan?" My voice sounds weirdly choked, and my throat is raw, like I've been screaming or crying. I try to remember what happened before I fell asleep, but there's this big, gaping hole where those memories are supposed to be. Nothing. No mental images, no information, nothing but dark fog.

Where am I? Where are my brothers?

Deep in my bones, I sense that something terrible has happened. The feeling gets stronger with every breath I take, permeates my entire being. I'm not sure if I want to know what it is, which may be why I didn't want to open my eyes earlier. Is this the first time I've been awake since it happened?

Cautiously, I feel around underneath me. I'm lying somewhere cool and dry. Now I notice that my fingers are trembling like crazy. Am I cold? Am I in pain anywhere besides my forehead and around my eyes? I try to listen to my body, but I keep coming back to my shaking hands. And my hammering heart. This throbbing sensation everywhere. In my chest, in my throat, in my temples. Even in my wrists. And there's something on my face, on my mouth and nose. That's why I'm having such a hard time breathing.

I want to pull it off, but I can't raise my arms. I let out a whimper. What's wrong with me? Why am I so weak?

I focus on my hands, curl and uncurl my fingers, and then try to lift my forearms.

It works, but my hands immediately hit some hard barrier directly above me.

Oh, God, what is that?

I can't fight back the terror any longer. My heart is racing faster and faster. Bam-bam-bam. As if running on autopilot, I run the tips of my fingers across the surface. It's cool and dry, like the floor. It's big. It's everywhere.

I'm trapped.

I hear myself gasping for breath. No, no, that's impossible, I would remember that. It feels like I can't get enough air to deal with this horror around me. Now I feel that thing on my face again, smell that sweet, chemical scent. Right against my nose. Is that what's making it so hard to breathe? A cloth of some kind?

I try to bring my hands to my head, but my arms are heavy, so heavy. My fingers flop weakly at my sides, slide along an edge or corner or something.

This is where the ceiling angles down around me, it must be right by my shoulders. I envision myself inside some sort of rectangle. With the last of my strength, I push against the walls at my sides, but they're like granite, they don't budge an inch.

All at once I'm so terrified that my head starts to swim. I hear a horrible sound, like the strangled sob of an abandoned animal, and realize it's coming from my throat.

I'm trapped in a coffin. For a moment, I believe the darkness, decide I must be dead. My pulse accelerates even more, becomes white noise.

No, no, no, I'm still alive, I'm alive.

It's not a coffin. It's a box.

My body is soaked with sweat. The noise gets louder. It reminds me of something. An image, a sensation, something that happened right before I conked out. It's floating around in there somewhere. I have to remember. If I can remember, I'll know where I am, and then maybe I can get myself out. But my head is muzzy with fear and this disgusting sweet stuff.

I take deep breaths through the cloth, trying to push the fear down, but it's not working. My arms and legs are trembling uncontrollably. *Calm down, Lou! Think! Where have you heard this noise before?*

I can hear my blood rushing in my head. That terrible sweetness fills my lungs. It must be in this cloth on my face. Or else it's all around me. Consciousness is slipping away from me like a wet fish I can't keep hold of.

I sense it sliding from my grasp, feel myself sinking back into the darkness. As I start to fade, I catch a fleeting glimpse of something. A sense of being alive. I see treetops swaying back and forth like reeds beneath a blood-red sky. The scent of pine needles and smoke flows through me. It feels like freedom. It swells within me until it's so real that I can almost grab it—but before I can latch on, the darkness swallows everything.

· · ·

53

The next time I come to, the rocking is the first thing I notice again. The rocking and the darkness. Bam. Bam. Bam. I'm still in the box. As soon as I realize that, my heart starts thundering wildly again, sending muted shock waves through me. I can't think at all anymore. It feels like I'm in the belly of a monster, being digested alive. My whole body is shaking. I remember the three-headed monster living behind my dollhouse that I was so afraid of when I was little. Every night, Ethan had to come in and say a magic spell so that it wouldn't come out. But Ethan's not here. I'm alone. Nobody can see that it's swallowed me. In the darkness, the thought becomes more and more real. Even the sound of my own breathing is suddenly strange and frightening. Wheezing, rattling... maybe that isn't me? Weird, nonsensical thoughts are tumbling through my mind. But all at once, I realize that my brain is in perfect working order. The monster thing is just my subconscious playing tricks on me because it thinks the truth will freak me out way more than my childhood fears.

I force myself to breathe evenly. In, out, in, out. Longer out than in, the way Liam taught me to do so that I wouldn't get so anxious about math tests. In. Out. I can breathe a lot more freely than I could earlier.

The cloth is gone.

Did it slip off, or did someone come take it away? Who? New terror builds within me. Twenty feet tall. Massive.

What happened to you, Lou? Think! You have to remember!

Talking to myself seems to help, even if it's only in my head. It's like having someone else there who cares about me, and it also proves that I'm still alive. *Someone's locked you in here, but left you alive. Why didn't they kill you?* My memory is still one giant black hole, as impenetrable as the thing I'm lying in. Darkness inside me, darkness around me.

Remember, Lou!

But I can't find anything to grab onto. And the last question hangs in the air, unfolding into a labyrinth with hallways of terror.

Why didn't they kill you?

I focus on my lower body, trying to figure out if anything down there hurts, but I don't feel anything. All I know is that I absolutely cannot, must not answer that last question, because as soon as I let my imagination step into that labyrinth, I'll get lost in my own fear and I'll never find my way back. Then I'll pass out from panic...

Quit thinking about that, Lou, please! Don't go there! Try to remember...

But I can't...

Why am I in this box? How much oxygen do I have in here? Am I going to suffocate, or will they get me out in time? And what are they going to do with me then? Torture me? Rape me? Images of meat hooks and knives and electric shocks flicker in my head. A man in a mask. Am I going to end up dead in a landfill somewhere?

The thought of my brothers finding me like that—cold, lifeless, contorted—presses the air from my lungs. Ethan's face, the devastation in his eyes, knowing that all his lecturing was for naught... that I didn't listen to him yet again.

A single sob bursts out of me with almost violent force before I can swallow it. I can't stop picturing Ethan's face. He's looking at me there in the darkness, from far away. I want to reach out and cling to him.

I'm so sorry, I'm so sorry...

He looks down at me with a solemn expression in his blue-green eyes, and part of my memory abruptly returns, as though it had been there in his gaze the whole time.

We had a fight, Ethan and I did. He yelled at me because I forgot the camping lanterns at home. I remember shouting that I hated him and then running off, and then being afraid of a long shadow that was moving through the forest.

Right, the shadow. There was something evil there.

Another wave of fear rolls out from the darkness and into me, filling me until there's no space left for rational thought. I'm trapped inside a monster, I'm going to die... *Lou, please...*

I breathe deeply to fight it back, try to conjure up details, but I can't latch onto any of them. They're all in tatters, little shreds of memory fluttering around in my head until panic shoos them away. Ethan, the lanterns... the rustling of the trees... I heard the rustling trees after I fought with Ethan. For some reason I'm positive of that.

To keep myself from losing my mind, I run my hands over the surface above me. Definitely the lid of a box. I feel around for an opening, silently praying that I'll wake up even though I know this isn't a dream.

Eventually, I close my eyes, though that doesn't change anything. It's dark one way or the other. But I tell myself it's better not to actually see the darkness around me. With my eyes closed, I can focus in on my own darkness, on the gaps in my memory. I go back over what I know. Ethan and the lanterns, the shadow... and then Jay was there... and the rustling trees. I felt free, I was laughing. Talking to someone. But who?

That question suddenly looms over the others, circling and echoing in my head. Who? Who was I talking to? Who? If I remember that, I'll know what happened to me afterward.

I went with someone!

The realization hits me out of nowhere. Followed by more panic. I went with someone, and that someone is holding me prisoner, caged up like an animal. Why is everything rocking like this? Are we driving? Is he driving me to some remote place? If so, that means he really does plan to do something horrible. Something he needs to take me far away for, because he doesn't want to be disturbed...

This time, I can't make myself calm down. I wheeze, scream, hammer on the wall above me with my fists. My head explodes with pain, my knuckles are on fire, but I can't stop. I'm going to scream until I pass out. Maybe I just want to know. To know for sure whether I'm going to live or die. I push against the lid with my hands and knees—and then suddenly a hard jolt slams me against the side wall. I lie still, woozy.

Something's changed. My pulse throbs hotly at my temples. I listen into the darkness.

The rocking has stopped.

It feels oppressive, like a response to my outburst.

Icy dread crawls up my spine, though I'm pouring sweat. I don't know which is worse: not knowing what's happened to me, or knowing that I'm about to find out.

FOUR

Desperately, I try to make out a sound, but all I can hear is my heart, thumping so fast that I can barely breathe. I stare at the lid in a daze, but then the side of my prison swings open, not the top.

The brightness is like a punch in the face. I squinch my eyes shut and roll onto my side, pressing my back against the wall behind me. Even through my closed eyelids, I can still see the shadow that steps in, covering the blinding flood of light. Someone is standing in front of the box, in front of the wall that swung open a moment ago.

Is this when I die?

My teeth are chattering, and I realize that I'm soaking wet. Head to toe.

"Shh, quiet," I hear a man's voice say. "I didn't have a choice."

I know that voice. I'm not sure where, but I don't trust it. My hands clench around the chain of my necklace, practically crushing it. The tiny cross Ethan gave me once bores into my skin. I think I would rather just pass out again, but my body refuses.

"I'm going to get you out now."

I can't make myself keep my eyes shut any longer. I look directly at his face.

Brendan!

He's kneeling on the ground, observing me with his head tilted to one side. For half a beat I don't know what the hell is happening.

Has he come to free me? But no, the look in his dark eyes is too narrow, too searching, too calculating. Too knowing. As I'm lying there, trying to work out what his presence means, the gaps in my memory begin to fill in. I see the *Travel America* signage, his jacket on the bench, the stuff on his counter, his questioning look. I even feel his arm around my torso, the way he's restraining me to keep me in check.

Reflexively, I press myself more tightly against the wall behind me.

He raises a hand like he's trying to soothe a shy deer. "I'm not going to do anything to you, Louisa."

I'm Bren, not Jack.

He's lying. He was lying to you the whole time. He's lying to you now. He's going to kill you.

His arms stretch into the box. To me they look like tentacles, coming to grab me and throttle me. I start screaming. I hear him talking to me, trying to calm me down, and I scream louder to drown him out. I slap his hands away, over and over again.

Cursing, he grabs my upper arm so tightly that I whimper in pain and stop fighting him. He uses the moment as a chance to slide his other hand underneath my hips. "I don't want to hurt you. Stop fighting me." His tone is calm, but determined. He's going to get his way, and he knows it.

I try to kick him, but my legs are like pudding. He heaves me out of the box in one quick motion. My head starts throbbing again; a gyroscope of colors rotates around me. Black, red, white. His hands are still gripping me tightly. I try to get away, but my body ignores my commands, like maybe the nerves connecting my legs to my brain have been severed.

I'm not going to escape him. I'm completely at his mercy.

The moment I understand that, really and truly get it, I gag and spit a wad of bile onto my fingers.

He grips my hair, holding it away from my face, and I can't stop him. He waits. "That's from the chloroform," I hear him say almost casually. "It won't last long, don't worry."

I focus on a point on the ground to make the world stop spinning so fast. It looks like a half-moon, but the spinning is making it fuller and fuller. I retch some more bile onto my hands. My throat is raw, and my lungs are on fire. I wish I were dead. Then I wouldn't be afraid anymore.

After a while passes without me puking again, he clears his throat. "I'm going to put you on the bed now. That's all."

I don't know how he takes hold of me, only that he does.

I flail around again, but I can tell my resistance is futile. I feel myself swinging down and landing on my back, onto something soft. The ceiling overhead is rocking back and forth.

Where is he?

I turn my head to the side and see him at the foot of the bed. I stare between his thighs at a hallway leading to the driver's cab.

I'm still in the RV! That explains the rocking. He's hauled me away somewhere so that he can do whatever he wants with me and then dispose of me afterward.

I clench the material under me as tightly as I can. Of course he's going to say he doesn't want to hurt me. He wants to lull me into a false sense of security. Probably more fun for him that way—first get my hopes up, then watch them shatter when I realize he's killing me. I can almost feel his piercing gaze on my skin, blazing and burning, as he pictures everything he's going to do to me. How he's going to torture me.

Inside, I curl into a ball, try to get away from him. I want to lift my hips and scoot to one side, but whatever he gave me, I'm still numb from it.

"Do you need to use the bathroom?"

I flinch. The question rips me away from my fear immediately, as if the fear had just been a dream. I shake my head, but the next thing I notice is the pressure in my bladder.

"Tell me when you do and I'll help you."

I look up, working my way up his black cargo pants with my eyes. His T-shirt is completely soaked through with sweat. Even though I'm close to passing out again, I can tell that it's unbelievably hot in here. I focus on his face. He's regarding me closely. His pupils are huge, his eyes wide. They have an unnatural glint in them, the way they did in the parking lot of the visitors' center. I remember that look. He keeps staring and staring, swallowing me with his gaze. It's so much worse than the darkness from earlier.

Why didn't I see what that look really meant when I first met him? That he wants to devour me until there's nothing left of me? How could I have thought those ominous dark shadows beneath his cheekbones were attractive?

"I've put you on the toilet a couple of times. Don't you remember?"

I shake my head again and close my eyes in defeat. I don't dare think about him dragging my unconscious body from the box, undressing it, and setting it on the potty. The fact that I can't remember any of it only makes it worse. Who knows where he touched me, or what he was thinking about.

Still, he's given me one piece of information: if I've used the bathroom twice already, I must have been out for an awfully long time. If I knew how long, I might be able to work out how far we've driven and where we are. But I don't want to have to ask him. I don't want to talk to him at all.

A soft rustling sound makes me open my eyes again. He's standing a little closer to the bed now—he must have taken a step forward. Now he's looking down at me from above. "I'd give you something to drink, but I can't for twenty-four hours after the anesthesia. It would be too dangerous. You might pass out again and then choke on your own vomit."

I roll my head in the other direction so that I don't have to see him. Now I'm facing the back wall of the camper, which the double bed is directly against. There's a wall cupboard near the top, extending maybe a foot and a half over the bed. Everything here is totally cramped.

"Lou, I know you're probably scared, but I'm not going to hurt you. I promise."

He chloroformed me and stuck me in a goddamn box. Does he have any idea how grotesque he sounds right now? My upper arm is still burning where he grabbed me and dragged me out. I don't know what his definition of "hurt" is, but it seems to be quite a bit different from mine. Maybe he doesn't think it will hurt me when he chokes me, squeezes my breasts and forces himself on me.

I press my fist against my mouth to suppress a whimper. I taste my own sour bile on my fingers, but I don't care.

Behind me, I hear him sigh. "Okay, I'll leave you be for now. You'll just have to see for yourself that I'm going to keep my word."

Heart pounding, I listen to his footfalls as he walks away. They sound hard and heavy, and the floor creaks under his weight.

"Why me?" I whisper into the fist at my lips.

The creaking stops. Everything is still for a while. A bird twitters outside.

"Because you're so full of life," he says quietly.

My throat closes up, but I'm so horrified that I can't even cry.

I nod off, wake up, nod off again. Every time I come to, I'm terrified that Brendan will suddenly show up and attack me. He's actually there two or three times, standing there at the foot of the bed with his dark gaze fixed on me... but this time when I wake up, I don't see him.

I'm lying on my side with my cheek mashed against the bedsheet, sticky with drool. I'm drenched in sweat from head to toe. Something is different, though. I lie there for a moment and realize that I feel better, less exhausted... more *full of life*. That phrase has been echoing in my head since the moment he first said it. I think I even dreamed about it. I can't figure out what the hell he meant by it. Did he kidnap me because he'd rather see me dead? Am I *too* full of life for him?

I tell myself to stop thinking about that. Too terrifying.

I lie completely still for a while, letting my head clear. What is he planning on doing with me? Where are we? Can I get away from here somehow? Hundreds and hundreds of questions, but I push them aside, focus on my own body.

I turn my head from side to side a couple of times. My head is still pounding, but not quite as badly. Tentatively, I wiggle my toes and rotate my ankles, and then manage to lift my knees and roll onto my back. After another minute or two, I somehow muster the strength to pull myself into a sitting position and scoot against the back wall.

I rub my swollen eyes a little and then look down at myself. I'm still wearing my shorts and my white blouse; even the chain is still there. It's weird seeing myself in these clothes. It seems like weeks have passed since I put them on this morning.

I pluck at the blouse, which is so soaked that it's clinging to my skin—which means it's totally see-through, but I'm too exhausted to care. I smell absolutely rancid. Sweat, puke, terror.

Here in the rear of the camper, there's just the double bed, with barely enough space for a person to stand in front of the tall, narrow wardrobes built into the back wall. There's another wall-mounted cupboard directly above me, high enough that I won't hit my head on it. When I look straight ahead, I can see into the hallway, which is about thirty feet long and leads to the cab with the two front seats. I still don't see Brendan, which is a tiny bit comforting.

A wave of bitterness washes over me. God, he lured me in here so easily with his pretend-vulnerability, with those dark eyes of his. He won the minute he spoke to me. Did he know I'd walk straight into his trap? Could he tell how naive I was just by looking at me? If so, he's amazingly good at reading people, which doesn't make anything about my situation easier.

I scoot forward a bit to examine my surroundings more closely. There are metal plates on the walls at different heights, each one with a grip bar on it, a little like the narrow handles on our kitchen cupboards. And there's a window on either side. I'd been too focused on myself to notice them. Silver blinds block the view outside, but I have to know what it looks like out there, wherever we are. Maybe Brendan's taken me to a different campground, and I can escape and get help.

Don't be an idiot, I scold myself sharply. *If you really believe that, you're completely underestimating this guy.*

I scoot forward an inch at a time and then cautiously let my legs drop over the edge of the bed. Brendan might be lurking outside somewhere, so I don't dare raise the blinds with the cord and risk drawing his attention, but I slide my fingers in between two slats and bend them apart a crack.

The first thing I see is a metal bar running left-to-right across the window. I saw them on a few RVs in Sequoia National Park. It's designed to protect against break-ins, but obviously it's also preventing me from crawling through the window and escaping. Brendan really did think of everything. I try to ignore the dull ache in the pit of my stomach.

On the other side of the bar, I see a cluster of pale birch trunks, and then nothing but dark pines. The trees aren't nearly as massive as the ones at Sequoia, so we're obviously in a different forest. I tilt my head to look from a different angle. The trees are standing in rows, thick as prison bars. A thin cone of sunlight is shining from behind their tops, creating elongated shadows on the needle-strewn forest floor. I try to guess the time based on their length, but I'm not sure if it's early or late.

I clamber across to the other side of the bed, but there's a bar across this window, too, and the view is the same: trees, trees, trees. No people. No tents. No other campers.

On the other side of the blinds, I spot the window handle. I could pull the window open. Then the screen would be the only barrier between me and the outside. I listen toward the hallway. Everything's silent. I don't know what Brendan would do if he caught me opening the window. My stomach knots up. Just thinking about that, I'm not sure I have the courage anymore. With trembling fingers, I reach in past the blinds, fold the handle down as silently as I can, and ease the window open a crack.

My heart starts pounding in hopeful anticipation. A distant conversation or the sound of children laughing would be enough. Then at least I would know that there are other people nearby. Besides Brendan, I mean.

But no matter how quietly I breathe, I can't hear anything. Apart from chirping birds and the soft rustling of leaves in the underbrush, everything's quiet. Too quiet. Like we're at the end of the world. No cars, no humming machines, just... forest. Is this where Brendan's going to bury me? Somewhere nobody will ever find me? Is he already out there digging my grave?

I press my hand against my mouth like I'm physically holding the horror back, keeping myself from giving voice to it, as though not letting it out will make it go away. It's in every part of me, though. And the longer I sit here at the window thinking about my grave, the worse it gets. And the worse the pressure on my bladder gets, too. I can't sit around here any longer.

I scoot to the foot of the bed, facing the narrow hallway. A wave of dizziness hits me as soon as I stand up. The walls feel like they're coming at me, and I have to put one hand against the wall on either side to keep from falling over. There's no way I can escape in this condition. Brendan would find me right away. I don't even want to think about what he'd do to me then. Maybe I can lock myself in the bathroom? Then at least I could pee.

I wait for a few seconds. Stare at my bare feet. The half-moon-shaped spot on the floor I was focusing on hours ago is near my left heel, which means that horrible box must be right underneath the bed.

I try to picture him sticking me in there and then driving away like it's no big deal. Driving on and on, bringing me further and further away from my brothers, one mile at a time. My throat closes up. Probably better to not think about my brothers. It makes everything a million times worse.

Cautiously, I put one foot in front of the other. I feel like some kind of junkie staggering toward her next fix. I'm certainly shaking like one. There are doors to either side of me. Up ahead is the table and the kitchen unit. I shove the right-hand door open and discover a tiny shower and one small shelf, but that's it. The room behind the left-hand door is maybe ten square feet, barely enough space for a toilet and a sink. It smells wretched in here, like an outhouse. A handful of fat, black flies are circling beneath the bottom-hung window near the ceiling.

I half-swing, half-flop from the doorframe to the sink, and then from the sink to the toilet. I drop down onto it and take a few deep breaths, and then stand up exactly as far as I have to in order to push the door shut. There's no lock. I sit there for a minute listening for noises on the other side, but everything's still silent, so I tear my shorts down my hips with one hand while clutching the toilet lid with the other for support. I can't at first, I'm too tense, terrified that Brendan will fling the door open, like maybe he's been lurking nearby, waiting for this exact moment. But he doesn't, and eventually my bladder relaxes.

Once I'm dressed again, I turn the sink on and run water over my hands and forearms. It's fresh and cool, and I wish I could drink it, but it smells like it's about half chlorine, which is just as gross as chloroform. I pick up the pale blue soap on the edge of the sink and use it to wash my face and hands. Immediately, the smell of sea salt and lavender fills the tiny room, and suddenly it's like I'm back in our bathroom in Ash Springs. I turn the soap over and over in my hand, lathering it up, anxiously rubbing one hand across my cheeks again and again, feeling the soft suds melting against my skin, still clutching the bar in the other hand. I don't want the scent to go away. I want to smell more of it, as much of it as I can. I want to draw it into me. I keep rubbing my face more and more frantically. I can't stop. It's like I've snapped. I glop the suds onto my arms, my neck, my hair, until I'm completely covered in white crowns of foam.

The scent reminds me of home. The realization hits me like a bolt of lightning. It's the first rational thought I've had in here. My brothers and I use this same soap. Wild Ocean Dream, some discount store brand. *Now we can dream wildly about the ocean here in the desert.* Avery laughed as he said it. Liam rolled his eyes.

I hear myself gasping for air.

At that moment, the door jerks open.

Brendan stares at me with narrowed eyes.

From one second to the next, I turn to ice.

"What are you doing there?" His voice is tight.

I must look strange covered in soap suds, with only my eyes peeking out from behind a cloud of lather.

Brendan extends a hand very slowly, like *I'm* the psychotic one here. "Give me the soap, Lou," he says. From his tone of voice, you'd think it was a butcher knife.

"Don't call me Lou," I whisper in a strangled voice. "You don't know me."

"Of course I do. Give me the soap, Louisa."

"No!" I press the wet chunk of baby blue soap to my chest like it's a piece of my heart he's trying to take away.

"I told you to call me when you wanted to use the toilet." He sounds accusatory, but there's not much heat in it. "Did you drink any water?"

I press my lips together tightly and shake my head.

"Good. Wash that off."

"No!" I want to keep the smell. I don't want him taking it.

He gives me an appraising once-over, like maybe he's trying to decide whether he should let me win this round. Finally he shrugs in indifference. "Okay, then stay that way." He nods toward the bed. "Come on back. I suppose you're done using the toilet, right?"

I don't move. I stand there clutching the soap. It's totally dumb, but I can't help it.

"We need to get going." He moves in to take my arm, but I jerk away, and then slip on the wet floor and land butt-first on the toilet.

"Going where?" I manage.

His smile is sickeningly triumphant. It makes me want to punch him in the face. "Further. Further away from where I picked you up."

Picked me up. Like I was hitchhiking or something.

My grip on the soap relaxes as he speaks, and he plucks it gingerly from my fingers and places it on the top shelf where I can't get at it. Then he grabs my arm with such determination that I don't dare resist.

He stops near the foot of the bed, and a horrific suspicion comes over me. My toes cramp against the floor. "Are you going to lock me in the box again?" It comes out as a whisper.

He gazes down at me, and for a second it's almost like I can see the horror I felt in that black hole written on his face—as though he'd already been in the belly of that beast, not knowing whether he was dead or alive. The expression in his eyes gives me chills way more than that all-devouring look he normally has.

After what seems like a million years, he shakes his head, slowly and mechanically, as though bringing himself back from somewhere else. "This road will be empty enough that I can let you stay out here. I only needed the box in the beginning." He lets go of my arm; I can't shake the feeling that he was hanging onto me for support. Which is obviously totally ridiculous.

I rub the spot he was clutching as inconspicuously as I can, and feel the blood shoot from my arm into the tips of my fingers.

Brendan's at the window now, which is at stomach height for him. He pushes two of the slats apart on the blinds, the way I did before, and then leans over and peers outside.

Then, in a terrifyingly soft voice, he says, "Unless, of course, you try to run away from me."

CHAPTER
FIVE

I know what those metal plates with the grip bars are for now. Brendan's chained me to them so that I don't do anything stupid while he's driving—that's how he phrased it, anyway. He's put one pair of handcuffs at each end of a thin iron chain. One pair's attached to the bar; the other's for me. He's only cuffed my right wrist, though, and the chain is long enough that I can lie on the bed while we drive. The blinds are still shut, and he's expressly forbidden me from opening them. Though that would be pointless, since the windows are tinted so dark that nobody would be able to see me outside anyway.

As soon as the camper started moving, I got super dizzy again, but fortunately I nodded off two or three more times. By this point, I've lost all sense of time. I can't see out the front windshield, because there's a folding door between the sleeping area and the hallway, and Brendan has it shut. What little light comes in through the blinds is twilight grey, so I'm guessing it's late afternoon.

Thinking about nighttime makes icy dread spread through me. In horror movies everything terrible happens at night. It's like the darkness somehow brings out the evil—the wild, untamed, uncontrollable, irrational side that people manage to keep under wraps during the day. That's how Jayden explained it to me once months ago, when he was researching it for whatever reason. Maybe Brendan's some kind of Jekyll-and-Hyde character.

He said he knew me, and I can't figure out where from. I bet I would understand him better if I did.

I lean back against the rear wall of the RV and thump the back of my head against it in a monotone rhythm like I'm trying to shake the memory loose, but I just can't come up with how we might be connected. I briefly wonder whether he's a friend of one of my brothers', but I doubt it—I'm pretty sure I know all their friends. Besides, I would have noticed Brendan, the way I noticed him immediately at the visitors' center.

How can he know me when I don't know him? Or was he saying that to confuse me? I don't think I was just a random victim. If I were, he'd have answered my question differently. Although he might have been lying. Maybe he lies all the time. Maybe he's preying on my fears.

That dull throbbing pain in my eye sockets flares again, and I quit hitting my head on the wall. I press the tips of my fingers against my eyelids, and then wipe my sticky fingers on my thighs. The soap lather is dry now, leaving a slimy feeling on my skin. I pat my hair. It's stiff and dry like straw at the ends, but it smells like Ash Springs and my brothers.

My hand drifts to my long necklace almost automatically, and I look down at the collection of pendants hanging from the thick silver ring at the end. Each one is special in its own way. I shouldn't do this, but I also can't stop myself. If I don't keep busy somehow, I'll lose my mind.

I lift the silver cross Ethan gave me for my sixteenth birthday. *So you never lose your faith, no matter what happens,* he said. A big, hard lump starts to form in my stomach. I wait for the tears to form in my eyes, but they don't. I'm too tense to cry.

My fingers tremble as I pluck the pink heart out from the bunch —another sweet-sixteen gift, this one from Avery. *A heart for our family's heart,* the card said. I was surprised, because I'd always thought that if anyone was the heart of the family, it was Ethan. He'd always been the one who kept us all together, especially after Dad died. Apparently, Avery doesn't see it that way.

I give the heart a tight squeeze and then turn my attention to the silver Buddha hand with the all-seeing eye. Liam's Christmas present to me. Maybe his last. The hand has a Buddhist saying engraved on it. The letters are so tiny that I can't make them out now, but I know what they say. It's the same saying he has tattooed on his back: *It is better to travel well than to arrive.*

Oh, Liam… I think about that dumb invisible rhino. I remember how miserable I was when he suddenly took off for India, how I cried myself to sleep at night. He was eighteen then, and I was twelve. I thought he didn't love me anymore. At least not enough to stay with me. And I remember how Ethan and Avery tried to cheer me up. Ethan tried to play the rhinoceros game with me even though I was way too old for it by then, and Avery made me gigantic portions of all my favorite foods every day, pasta with tomato sauce and fish sticks with mashed potatoes and ketchup. And they let me eat myself sick on peanut butter, lemon cookies, and chocolate donuts.

I stroke the cold metal hand before letting it slide back to the others, and then pick out the round turquoise charm with pink polka dots. This one's from Jayden. *A little sister,* it says on the front. On the back: *is more than a forever friend, she is joy to the heart and love without end.*

I let go of the round charm and press my hand to my mouth. My throat hurts, because that's where all the tears are stuck, but they just won't come out. My eyes are even burning, hot and salty, but they're dry.

If only I hadn't gone with Brendan and gotten into his camper. If only I hadn't tried to make him like me. If only I'd asked Jay to wait. If only I hadn't forgotten the camping lanterns at home. If only I'd been better in school, and hadn't dyed the potatoes blue...

You never mean to do anything, I hear Ethan saying mournfully. *And you're always sorry afterward.*

Maybe they think I ran away. They're probably driving back home right now to look for me. Back to Ash Springs.

I lie down on my side and draw my legs in, wrapping my arms around them. Then I press my face against my knees, so hard that it hurts. But I need the pain.

I hear Brendan's footsteps in the hall. Fortunately, he's not trying to sneak, so I have time to retreat to the head of the bed, to the rearmost part of the RV. He folds the door open like a harmonica and stops, standing there between the two walls.

"You didn't turn the light on," he says. "The chain's long enough." He nods to the light switch.

I stare past him, clenching the links of the chain tightly. If I can't stop the inevitable from happening, what good does light do me?

He waits a moment before pushing his way in to one side of the bed. I shift to the other side, but he stops at the window and pulls open the blinds. I can't not look out. It's pitch dark outside, and I can't make out any of our surroundings, but almost directly overhead in the raven-black sky is an oversized, white full moon, shining as pale as a death shroud.

"Brought you a drink." Brendan holds out a small bottle. "Just water for now, it's less likely to make you sick. That's how it was for me, anyway."

"For you?" I blurt out. I ignore the bottle, even though my throat is like sandpaper.

He smiles. His gaze has lost that penetrating edge—he seems as confident and self-controlled as he did in the visitors' center. "I tested the chloroform on myself," he says. "I mean, I was trying to knock you out, not kill you."

He is clearly totally insane.

"Water was always easier to keep down afterward."

"You did it more than once?"

"Four times." He shrugs like it's nothing, and then offers me the water bottle with an emphatic gesture. "Drink!" It's not a request.

"If I don't, are you going to force it down my throat?" I ask through clenched teeth.

He withdraws the bottle. "If it helps keep you alive."

I close my eyes. "So I'm supposed to stay alive?" I'm not actually sure if that's a good or bad thing, because I don't know what he's got planned for me.

"Of course." He sounds perfectly casual. "What, you thought I would go to all this trouble just to kill you?"

"Maybe you're going to do it later."

"Or maybe never. Now drink!" He hesitates for a moment. "Please," he adds.

I open my eyes in surprise. He looks harmless, as harmless as he did in the parking lot. There's a stale taste in my mouth, and my body is screaming for water. But who knows what he's put in it? Who knows where I'll wake up next? How I'll wake up? Whether I'll wake up?

"You first," I whisper.

That's all I have to say. He shakes the bottle, unscrews the cap, and takes a long swig. I watch him swallow, and then he hands me the water. "No more than half for now."

I suppress the disgust at the thought of drinking from the same bottle as him. The water is cool and tastes clean, not like chlorine. With every swallow, I become more acutely aware of how thirsty I am.

After I've managed a few gulps, Brendan takes the bottle out of my hand. "That's enough. You can have more later." He nods to the door on the right-hand side. "Do you want to shower?"

"No."

"It smells like a puma cage in here."

"Don't care." I definitely do not want to undress with him anywhere nearby. Besides, it's his fault that I stink.

He sighs in resignation. "You're still afraid I'm going to hurt you."

I draw in my knees and hug them again. "Why else would I be here?"

"So that I don't lose you again." When he says it, he looks as innocent as a newborn babe.

"You never had me, what makes you think you can lose me?" I do my best not to let on just how disturbing this conversation is to me.

He shrugs, and the innocent expression turns distant, unapproachable. "You're not all there yet. You're still out of it from the chloroform. And you're still way too afraid. Your head needs to be clear before we talk about this."

I close my eyes. If he was planning to do something terrible to me, he wouldn't go out of his way to explain everything to me, would he? He could have gone ahead and done it right then and there. Then again, what do I know about how crazy people think? Maybe this is his idea of foreplay.

"Tomorrow you can have some food," I hear him say. Everything's silent for a while. Then the floor creaks like he's stepping in place. He takes a deep breath. I can picture his pupils widening. "I had to do it," he says suddenly. "I didn't have a choice. There was no either-or. Never." Another creaking sound, and then footsteps. "If it's okay with you, I'm going to go take a shower."

I hear the water running. If I can get free now, I'll have a head start. As silently as I can, I slide to the edge of the bed. The metal plate he's handcuffed the other end of my chain to is screwed into the wall in front of me. My gaze shifts outside. I hadn't realized how bright the night is. We're still in the middle of the forest, at least I think we are. Millions of stars cast their silvery light down on the trees, enveloping them in pale fog. For a fraction of a second, I consider pounding on the windows with my fists, but then I realize there's probably no point. It looks like there's not another living soul out there—there's just that milky, shimmering light. It's like we're on an undiscovered moon that happens to have a patch of forest on it. If I start making noise now, Brendan will jump out of the shower, and my shot at escape will be over before it begins.

I try to force my hand through the metal ring of the handcuff, but it's so tight, it's like Brendan measured my wrists. The thought that he might have actually done that makes me nauseous. I tug at the ring, make my hand narrow, but I can't even begin to wedge it past my thumb joint. After a few minutes, my skin is lobster red, and the back of my hand is bleeding. Tears of pain and frustration spring to my eyes. I don't have much time—Brendan's not going to stay in the shower forever. In a fit of desperation, I brace my feet against the wall and pull like crazy on the grip bar on that metal plate, until my heart is hammering wildly and I'm nearly sick from overexertion. I have to get out of here. Now.

I pray, I curse, I jerk, but the metal plate doesn't give. Not an inch. It's screwed tightly into the wall with four screws, and each of the screws is apparently stronger than I am.

I start pulling again, but then I hear the water turn off. Abruptly, I release the bar, just as the door swings open and Brendan appears, wearing only a towel slung across his hips.

"The whole camper's rocking. What are you doing?"

My pulse is racing; sweat is running down my face. "Nothing," I whisper, hiding my hand behind my back.

He comes toward me, around the bed, brows knitted darkly. "Forget it. Not even I can tear the plates out."

I stay sitting there stiffly; he stands directly in front of me, so close that his legs are almost touching my knees. "Did you try that too?"

"Of course. I think you'd need a cordless screwdriver and a ton of patience to get those things down." That triumphant gleam returns to his eyes. "And the handcuffs, forget it. Double-lock. The trick with the needle or the paper clip won't work." He gestures with his chin toward my necklace. "Or with one of those things."

I bite my lip and lower my eyes. The thought had occurred to me, it's true.

"You're not going to escape me, Lou. With or without the cuffs, you're not going anywhere. Get used to it."

"Louisa, my name is *Louisa*," I spit back, keeping my eyes focused on the black towel covering his hips so I won't have to look at his torso. I don't want to see how perfect he is. How can pure evil be so flawless? It makes everything even more confusing. I don't want to remember how attractive I thought he was at first, with those strikingly dark eyes of his, that infinitely penetrating gaze. The question gleaming and flickering in his eyes like a falling star: *Do you want this?*

Do you want me to kidnap you? Do you want me to lock you in a box? Do you want me to rape and murder you?

And, oh my God, he saw the goo-goo eyes I was making at him, saw the way I got tongue-tied just looking at him. He knew I would like him. Another wave of nausea washes over me at the realization.

He turns away. "You'll want to dress warm," he says. "It gets colder here than it does in Sequoia."

Here? Where is "here"? Are we all alone "here"? Isn't he afraid I'll start banging on the windows to get someone's attention? I should have tried that earlier instead of wasting time pulling on his DIY prison construction like a lunatic. Then again, if there really had been anyone within shouting distance, Brendan would probably have bound and gagged me before he showered... or put me back in the box. The thought makes me sick all over again.

I scoot back onto the bed. My limbs are heavy, as if I had the flu. I still don't know how long he's had me in here, but I'm guessing I was in the box for at least a day. Judging by how I feel now, I must have been unconscious for quite a while. When I had to get my appendix out when I was eight, I recovered from the anesthesia pretty quickly. Now, I feel like he didn't just kidnap me with the RV, he ran me over with it.

I can't sleep. Brendan is outside now, enshrouded in his hoodie. He's made a fire, and he's sitting on a rock near the flames, staring into them like he's reading the future. For a few horrible minutes, I wonder if he kidnapped me so he can sacrifice me, like maybe he's bringing me to an altar somewhere so he can slit my throat. Maybe he's one of those super crazy types with voices in his head telling him to do stuff. Or maybe he just does a ton of drugs. There are too many maybes here, not enough definites.

I wrap the blanket around my body more tightly, and then lean forward to rest my cheek against the window, to feel the coolness of the pane as though it might somehow comfort me.

Does he see me watching him? Probably not, the windows are tinted, and I still have the lights off.

He smokes a cigarette, then stands up and disappears from view. The floor rumbles underneath me—he must be doing something underneath the camper. A moment later, he reappears and sits back down on the rock. I squint my eyes. He's got something in his lap. A notepad? And it looks like he's writing. I blink a few times, but it's too dark to make out any details.

I scoot to the back of the bed and curl into a ball, staring out at the hallway. I want to know when Brendan comes back in. I wait and wait for what feels like hours. Suddenly I hear a muted thump, almost like the sound of a trunk lid slamming, and then the side door opens and Brendan comes up the stairs.

Through half-open eyes, I watch him take off the hoodie. He stands there for a moment, perfectly still. His bare back gleams unnaturally pale in the moonlight streaming in through the window. Each individual muscle is visible beneath his skin as though in sharp relief, and seems to come alive with every breath he takes. It's spooky, almost animalistic. Same with the dark tattoo winding across his right shoulder blade. From here, it looks like an evil dragon or a writhing snake. I can't help picturing some vicious monster breaking out of his back as he rapes me. Underneath the blanket, I clench my fists and pray he doesn't get into bed with me.

He starts walking in my direction. I squeeze my eyes shut. But nothing happens. I hear him turn on the water and brush his teeth. My fingernails dig into my palms. He's going on with his life like everything is perfectly normal, and it's fraying my nerves. When I hear his footsteps moving away, I exhale in relief and open my eyes a tiny bit. He removes his cargo pants and slips on a pair of sweats and a light-colored T-shirt. Then he hoists himself into the loft bed above the driver's cab and lies down.

I keep listening. Eventually, after what seems like *so* long, I hear him breathing evenly.

Bit by bit, I realize what that means. For tonight, I'm safe. He's not going to do anything to me tonight. I almost start crying in relief. I'm so desperate for a break, for a couple of hours of not being terrified. I can finally allow myself to sleep.

Tomorrow, I think as I give myself over to the exhaustion, to the darkness settling over me like a sheet. *Tomorrow I have to try and get away, no matter how. Tomorrow I'll be stronger.*

But before my eyes fall shut, I remember his voice, so dangerously and terrifyingly soft.

Unless, of course, you try and run away from me.

CHAPTER
SIX

S till groggy, I roll over from my right side to my left.

The aroma of freshly brewed coffee hits me, along with the hearty scent of eggs and bacon. Avery must be cooking. Avery's the only one who can get bacon just right, so that it's crisp but not charred. When Ethan makes scrambled eggs, they always come out half burnt. I'd like to doze a little longer, but if I don't get up, Jayden will snag the crispiest strips of bacon, and that would be a bad start to the weekend. Anyway, I'm sort of looking forward to having breakfast with everyone this morning, even if Ethan trots out another big to-do list for Saturday: fixing rotten wood slats, shopping, watering the garden, laundry, cleaning the kitchen...

I blink sleepily and straighten up.

I'm not at home. The realization is like a punch in the gut, jolting me wide awake. I hear dishes clattering near the front of the RV, but I can't see what's going on, because the folding door's only partway open.

I slide to the edge of the bed and discover that Brendan's unchained me—or at least he's removed the long iron chain. I still have the handcuffs. They're just like the ones in the movies. One cuff is on my left wrist now; the other is dangling uselessly. It's probably there so Brendan can chain me up quickly anywhere, anytime. Great.

There's a thick, white bandage around my right wrist.

When did Brendan put that on? The fact that I didn't notice is frightening. I look down at the gauze, spread my fingers a few times to shake off the numbness, and then peer past the folding door.

Brendan's in front of the stove in the hallway, shaking a pan. The smells of scrambled eggs, bacon, and coffee were the only real parts of my dream.

I slide to my feet, propping myself against the bed for support as I stand up.

"Oh, you're awake!"

I flinch. He sounds so perfectly normal, like we're a young couple on our honeymoon or something.

"Breakfast will be ready in a minute."

"I have to pee."

Brendan points to the bathroom door with his spoon. "You don't have to ask permission."

I slip into the bathroom. Walking is a lot easier than yesterday, and the throbbing pain in my head is barely an echo of what it was.

I use that disgusting-smelling toilet and then wash my hands and face—without soap, since it's still sitting out of reach. The dangling handcuff clinks against the edge of the sink with every movement, plus the bandage gets wet and the wound underneath starts to burn. I don't unwrap it, though, because otherwise Brendan might insist on putting a new one on me, and I definitely do not want him touching me.

I shut off the water and then impulsively fling open the mirrored cabinet, searching for something I can use to defend myself against Brendan. The results are pretty disappointing, unless I can somehow choke him out with a gauze bandage or smother him with a washcloth. As silently as I can, I flip the toilet lid closed and climb up to check if there's anything on the top shelf... but it's as empty as it looked from underneath. No nail clippers, no files. I briefly toy with the thought of retrieving the soap, but then Brendan would know that I searched the cabinet.

Resigned, I clamber down from the toilet lid and shut the cabinet. I catch a glimpse of myself in the mirror and barely recognize myself. I look like the kind of person you'd see on the street and then cross to the other side. My face is as pale as winter, with rings under my eyes like blue-black war paint. The paleness makes my eyes seem oversized, like a manga girl's, but without the gleam. They're like blue-green glacier ice, as if my unshed tears have diluted the color.

I stare at my own reflection for a while, until finally I realize that I'm just stalling for time, not wanting to go out to Brendan. I can't stay in here forever, though.

You can do this, I tell myself silently. *With or without a weapon. You're not chained up anymore, so maybe you can even get away today. Back to Ash Springs.*

Talking to myself still helps.

I open the door, but as soon as I see Brendan, my courage evaporates, and I feel like my own shadow. A pale little winter shadow, deprived of light until the darkness finally smothers it. Brendan's so big, so much stronger than me. And I'm afraid he's probably smarter than I am, too.

"Sit!" He gestures to one of the short two-person benches. It's across from the side door, but the side door is shut. Of course.

Mechanically, I slide in and take a seat on a bench. The sight of breakfast makes me ill. There's a stack of chocolate donuts beside a platter of scrambled eggs and bacon. Next to that are some lemon cookies and a jar of peanut butter.

"Coffee?" Brendan holds out a mug. I feel like slapping it out of his hand, but I don't want to make him mad, so I take it. "Black with two spoons of sugar," he adds.

Which is how I always drink it. Which he knows.

He sits down across from me. To hide my confusion, I sip my coffee, and promptly burn my tongue.

"I didn't know what you'd be hungry for, so I just made everything." He leans back slightly, radiating total self-confidence. He's got his hair back in a little ponytail, which brings out his eyes and makes him look older. God, maybe he's actually Avery's age. That would make him ten years older than me. Maybe he's a total pervert who only likes young girls, even though he could have any woman he wanted. "You want some eggs? Lemon cookies?"

I nod robotically, accepting whatever he offers. All I care about is him leaving me alone. I stare at the eggs as he piles them on my plate. They're fluffy and golden, exactly the way I like them.

"Make sure to eat slowly and chew every bite, or you won't be able to keep it down. And maybe no peanut butter yet, now that I think about it." He pushes the jar away slightly with the back of his hand. I notice his braided black leather armband with a silver coin dangling from it, the size of a hazelnut. It's got an image engraved on it—birds in flight, maybe? I didn't quite get a good look at it.

I look back at my plate. Brendan doesn't say anything. He's probably watching me. Nervously, I knead my fingers.

I think he's waiting for me to start eating, so I do, even though I feel totally sick. *One bite at a time*, I tell myself. *Whatever you do, don't get him mad. He's a complete psychopath who chloroformed himself to see what it felt like.*

The fork shakes in my hand. The first bite of scrambled egg falls off three times in a row. Out of the corner of my eye, I notice that Brendan is suddenly intensely interested in a chocolate donut. He's peering at the bottom of it, like maybe checking it for mold.

I pause for a moment. If I want to get away, I need to calm down. I need to watch him, wait for him to make a mistake. He can't possibly have everything under control all the time. Sooner or later, something will go wrong. *And then you smash him in the balls and run away as fast as you can*, I hear Jay say.

I put the fork aside without having actually eaten anything. "How do you know what I like?" It comes out sounding more confrontational than I feel.

"Don't you know?" He blinks in surprise.

"No."

"Think about it, then!" He sets the chocolate donut back down on his plate and folds his hands on the table.

"Were you spying on me? Sitting in the yard with binoculars watching us through the window?"

"Nope. But I still know." He smiles, seemingly enjoying my uncertainty. It almost sounds like he's trying to mess with me.

A memory comes back to me, a mental image of him buying fish sticks, iced coffee, and donuts at the visitors' center. All things I like, I thought at the time. But he couldn't possibly have brought them back to the camper; he must have thrown them away somewhere.

Another mental image replaces the first. It makes me even more anxious. "You followed me. When I was walking to the visitors' center, you were tailing me in the woods, parallel to the gravel road."

He gives me a penetrating look. "Possibly."

"You were the shadow," I whisper to myself. It wasn't Jay at all. Jay's "shortcut" probably wasn't even through the forest. "Which was why you knew about me and Ethan fighting about the camping lanterns. You heard. You were listening."

He looks out the window. Nods.

I bite down hard on the inside of my cheek, distracting myself from the fear with pain. "You heard me telling him that I wanted to run away." Suddenly it's all coming together.

"It was convenient, yeah." Brendan looks back at me. His eyes gleam as he smiles. "It could have turned out differently, though. I'd been expecting a long wait, but you were easy to catch."

Picturing him stalking me, waiting for an opportune moment, nearly makes me physically ill. I press my hand against my stomach. "How long... was I unconscious?"

"About five days. But it wasn't only chloroform. That would have been too dangerous."

Five. Days.

I feel like he just pushed me off a cliff. My brothers have been searching for me for *five days*! Knowing how worried they must be makes me ten times more miserable. "What else, then?"

"Atropine, dimenhydrinate, gamma-butyrolactone, barbiturates..."

"What?"

"Belladonna, knockout drops, sleeping pills... the dimenhydrinate was for the nausea. To keep you from puking." He gazes straight into my eyes, like he can sense my rage and wants to nip it in the bud.

"You gave me knockout drops?"

"A small dose. Don't you remember?"

What a stupid question! Bewildered, I shake my head. He's crazier than I thought.

"You woke up a couple of times. I explained everything to you and gave you some water. Not much, just a few sips at a time."

"Why five days?" I can't believe it. This nightmare is getting worse and worse.

"The first part of the trip was dangerous. I couldn't risk anyone searching the RV and finding you. That's the only reason. And I knocked you out so you wouldn't be scared in the box. On the last day, I gave you some more chloroform so I wouldn't give you too much of the other stuff."

I need to get away from him. I think I'm losing my mind. I pull myself to my feet using the back of the bench for support, but then my knees give out and I flop back onto the upholstery.

That's why I've been so weak, that's why I can barely remember anything. Five days!

"There were never any bears on the path, were there?" My voice comes from far away, yet also thunders in my ears. "You preyed on my fears to lure me away. You... you're..." I force myself to swallow the insult, but contempt is probably written all over my face.

Brendan's expression hardens, and he sets his jaw. "Think what you want of me, I'm still keeping you with me."

"But..."

"You're staying with me. Forever. There's nothing you can do about it. Crying isn't going to help you. Crying never helps. Not with me." He averts his eyes when he says that last part.

I wipe my eyes, but the tears keep flowing and flowing and falling on the lemon cookie and the scrambled eggs.

He glances through the window again, which is at table height. "Where I grew up, might makes right, and here, that's me, not you. Sorry." He pushes himself up from the bench and looks down at me. "I know how hard this is for you."

Hard?

"I'll do everything I can to make it more bearable. When you're angry, be angry. When you're sad, be sad. I'm not going to forbid you to have feelings. I can handle them until things get better. If you think you want to spit on me or whatever, then do it, but don't overdo it. There's only one thing I absolutely forbid you from trying."

Every second I spend listening to him talk is making me more confused and agitated. "What's that?"

"Escaping." That word is my only hope, and he snaps it in such a steely voice that it's like the sound alone is enough to break every bone in my body.

"What would happen then?" I whisper.

Brendan's face stiffens, mask-like, completely lifeless. His hands ball into fists, and it terrifies me so much that I grab the butter knife next to my plate. It's short and dull, but I hold it like a dagger anyway. He doesn't seem to notice, though, or else he doesn't care. He takes a few deep breaths.

"Just don't try," is all he says.

With that, he walks out and slams the door behind him. I'm alone. Alone, unchained, and I still don't dare move.

I'm still sitting at the table, clutching the butter knife, staring at my plate. Brendan is outside, doing something with the camper. I don't know what. I hear thumping and rattling every so often, and then the whole RV rocks for a few seconds, and once or twice I hear water running through the pipes. After a while, it stops. I look through the window. He's leaning against a tree, smoking. He's standing there so perfectly still that, for one strange moment, it's like he melts into the tree. I get a ridiculous urge to set the camper on fire. He wouldn't get far without a vehicle. Then again, he'd probably kill me for it. *Because you're so full of life... I know you...*

I set down the knife and bury my face in my hands. I haven't eaten a thing—all I had was a sip or two of sugary coffee. My escape fantasies are torn full of holes now. Holes I see Brendan rising from and strangling me. With his hands, with a scarf, with the iron chain. I'm afraid he'd probably be a hand-strangler. Which seems like it would be the worst. Why, I don't know.

But if I have to stay with him, I may as well go ahead and kill myself. I know I can't live like this. Where is he even planning on taking me? He can't keep driving around with me forever, right?

When Brendan returns, he starts clearing the table, not looking at me. "You want to wash up?" he asks casually as he runs water in the sink.

I stare out the window.

"To distract yourself, maybe." He dribbles some dish soap into the water. "When you use the toilet, there's a box of little orange sachets in there, make sure you always throw one in afterward."

"Why?"

"Disinfectant."

Can he tell I'm imagining poisoning him with them? Then I remember the drugs he used on me. They must be around here somewhere. The RV isn't that big.

"Are you going to do the dishes or not?"

"No."

"Probably just as well with the bandage anyway." Brendan shrugs and regards me thoughtfully. Today, he's wearing deep-green cargo pants and a black Jack Wolfskin T-shirt with a pawprint on the right side of the chest. The shirt is faded, which makes Brendan's dark eyes gleam with an unnatural intensity. They creep me out. At times it's almost like he's already seen literally everything. Every facet of life, every detail. Maybe that's why he's so confident.

He turns and switches on the television, which is attached to a kind of telescopic bar on the wall next to his loft bed. Then he picks up the remote and flips through the channels. The millionth reruns of *How I Met Your Mother* and *The Big Bang Theory*. Soaps, more soaps, game shows, documentaries, the usual afternoon stuff: *Hero of the Week*, *Find me* …

He clicks past that last one super-fast, probably hoping I didn't see it.

"You want to watch anything in particular?"

"Find me!" Maybe they're reporting on me? I haven't watched it much, but the episodes I saw were all old missing-persons cases with happy endings.

"Besides *Find me!*"

"Hero of the Week," I hurriedly reply. It's Avery's favorite show.

Brendan gives me a look of astonishment. "You like that show?"

Don't you know that? is what I'd like to shriek at him, but I'm too scared. I'm scared to do pretty much everything in his presence. Movie kidnapping victims always seem to be defiant and mouthy and great at snappy comebacks. But this is real. I don't want Brendan to hit me or do something else to me. I never thought I would be in a situation where avoiding physical harm became a top priority for me, even to the point that I'd swallow my pride.

Brendan flips back to the show and leaves it on while he washes the dishes. He keeps glancing over at me, and then at the TV, like he's just learned a new fun fact about me and is trying to categorize it.

I try to focus my full attention on the show, to pretend I'm sitting on the couch with Avery and Liam with a bag of tortilla chips clamped between my thighs. And Jay's peeking in every so often, more so he can gather material for his stories than because he's actually interested in who ends up being Hero of the Year.

I feel Brendan's eyes on me again. I stare stubbornly at the screen, trying not to let on how uncomfortable it makes me.

Today's Hero of the Week is a 22-year-old Harvard student named Andrew Franklin. He recognized a homeless man as an old friend of his dead father's, and now he's going to pay the guy's rent for the rest of his life.

The moderator, David O'Dell, was last year's Hero of the Year. On a bone-dry day in August, he saved nine children from the top floor of a burning orphanage. He was our favorite, because he always seemed totally authentic, like being in the spotlight was more embarrassing to him than anything. Even now, as he's interviewing Andrew Franklin, he looks like he'd rather be grilling hot dogs in his modest back yard than standing in front of a camera. Next to him, the much-younger Andrew Franklin looks like a stockbroker. I know Avery and Liam would hate him, Hero of the Week or not, because of the way he's got his hair parted and way-too-gelled.

"Okay, so, tell the nation how you came across Henry Clark," the moderator says.

Andrew smiles in a preening-peacock way. "Well, David—can I call you David?" David nods, but Andrew has already gone on talking. "David, a few weeks ago I saw that picture in the paper, where some teenagers had assaulted a homeless man. Yet another photograph of a subway station and a *literal* whipping boy. I mean, we *all* know those pictures, don't we, David? It's literally *always* the same story. Not that I would describe myself as jaded, but it is what it is. Nobody knew the man, and *something* made me want to look more closely, and I mean *really* closely, David. God knows why. Anyway, I looked at him and I thought, wow, that old man *literally* looks *just* like a good friend of my father's. God rest his soul."

For reasons I can't quite explain, I really hope this Andrew guy doesn't end up the Hero of the Year. Everything about him seems fake, plus he talks like he's fifty. And if he says "David" one more time I'm *literally* going to throw up.

"So I recognize him, but it's been so long that I have no idea what his name is."

"So what did you do?"

Andrew looks straight at the camera, not deigning to glance in David's direction. "I started putting the word out on Facebook and Do You Know? And eventually I managed to find a friend of a friend of a friend—you know, the usual route—who was able to identify him."

"And now you're going to pay Henry Clark's rent for the rest of his life?"

"Absolutely, David. I mean, it's a matter of honor, isn't it? Our fathers were both Marines."

"That is truly heroic."

"Hah!" Brendan snorts behind me. "That Henry Clark guy is probably dying of lung cancer and only has two months to live. This kid's doing it for the attention."

"Do you know him as well as you know me?" I can't stop myself from asking.

"You seriously think he gives a shit about the old man?" Brendan asks, ignoring my question. He saunters from the sink to the bench. "He wants people to think he's important. He's probably a mediocre student, and he thinks this will help him land a better job."

"Maybe he just wants to help," I protest exactly as loud as I dare.

"If he really wants to help, he should let this lonely old man live with him, if he was actually his father's best friend." Brendan gives me a sharp look before snatching the remote from the counter and switching off the television, even though the show isn't over. "Go on, go to the back room, we're leaving in a minute."

I do what he says without protest, and he follows me.

"Sit on the bed... now scoot to the left." He attaches the loose handcuff to the chain again.

"Where are we headed?" I manage to ask.

"Onward and upward."

"Onward, where? You must have a destination."

"You won't like it, so why do you want to know?" he retorts gruffly.

"Where are you taking me?"

Brendan fixes the blinds so that I can look out the window.

"Away," is all he says before turning and striding out.

I don't have anything to do, apart from maybe go through the charms on my necklace again. There are others on there, like the little red lipstick from Ava, the silver high heels from Madison, the four-leaf clover from Elizabeth and the yellow sun from Emma... but looking at them will only make me more miserable.

Instead, I gaze out through the slats of the blinds at the desolate landscape. We're driving continuously in one direction, on what seems like a real-life Road to Nowhere. Brendan has the folding door shut, blocking my view toward the front, but on either side, I see patches of pine and spruce forest interspersed with endless stretches of scorched-looking grassland. Behind them are strings of grey foothills, one after another, like elephant feet. If I lean right up against the blinds and look up, I can see the radiant blue sky. I start doing some mental math, trying to work out where we might be. If Brendan drives 200 miles a day, we might already be in Canada. Or in Mexico, if he's driving south. To the east would be... Arkansas? Oklahoma? Kansas? I'm not sure. I'm guessing it's not Mexico, anyway, because the landscape doesn't fit. It *is* still hotter than hell, though. My blouse has practically melded with my torso and my sweat to form a second skin. I've been wearing this thing for six days now. Same with my underwear and my jean shorts. I feel utterly disgusting, but I still don't want to shower. Maybe I can wash in the sink this evening, so I won't have to take everything off at once. Or I'll shower with my clothes on, at least as well as I can. I wonder if Brendan has clothes for me? Maybe he'll just give me some of his. Or nothing at all.

I scoot closer to the window, not wanting to miss any of the few cars going by in the opposite direction. So far there have been five: three compact cars, a truck, and a black station wagon of a make I didn't recognize. They flitted past the window like spirits before I'd fully registered that they were real. Sometimes this still feels like a bad dream I can wake up from. I press my face against the glass, straining to see out, hoping someone else will drive by. I feel invisible, forgotten. Nobody sees me anymore. Except Brendan. And if he has his way, that will never change. I refuse to let that thought take root in my head, because otherwise I'll fall apart completely. One way or another, I have to get away from him.

I spend a while longer waiting for a car, staring down at the cracked, brittle asphalt. Then I scoot back onto the bed. And try not to think about anything, including Ethan, Avery, Liam, or Jayden. It doesn't work, of course. I paint their faces on an imaginary canvas. I can still picture them exactly. Ethan with his stern mouth and his serious eyes. Avery with his soft features and laugh lines. Liam with his long hair and sunburn and that inward, glowing smile of his. Jay with his mussed hair and wise, knowing expression. I'm the only one missing from the picture. I've put them all side by side. Where would I be standing? In the center, no doubt—the heart of the family. I stretch my hands out like I'm trying to touch them, feel my shoulders grow heavy with the weight of missing them. I miss them so much that my throat closes up and my heart is like a lump of lead in my chest. Like I've been scoured from head to toe with longing.

I don't become aware of my surroundings again until the bed suddenly starts shaking, jostling me from side to side. Immediately, I clamber to the window and peer through the slats. Brendan is driving on a rough forest road with dozens of potholes. A chill runs down my spine.

The dark spruce trees seem to close ranks more and more tightly as we trundle onward, interspersed only with the occasional cluster of birches or aspens. Those are sparse enough to let a tiny bit of sunlight through, but between the spruces it's as dark as night.

At one point, we pass a turn-off, and I spot a rusty, broken-down tractor-trailer just sitting there on the side of the road. Forgotten, like me. Clearly nobody comes out this way anymore. Maybe people used to do some logging in this area, but now it looks completely abandoned.

Brendan follows the road a while longer, but I couldn't guess how far we've driven. Ten miles? Twenty? It seems like a distance I'd be able to walk if I had to, if I managed to escape. Brendan turned onto this forest road from a street at some point, so that's how far I'd need to get.

Once Brendan has parked the camper in a small clearing, he comes straight back to me and unlocks the handcuff attached to the chain. As usual, he drops the key into his pants pocket.

"I'm going to go build a fire," he says. "We can grill out later if you want."

I nod, mostly so that he'll be busy and I'll have time to look around and work out an escape plan.

His eyes start to light up. He must think I'm starting to accept the situation. "If you like, you can come out and help me."

I look down at myself, shake my head. It's still hard to talk to him. His presence is like a hammer blow, crushing me effortlessly like dry bread, again and again.

"You could shower," he suggests.

I nod again.

"But be careful with your wrist."

Unconsciously, I run my hand across the bandage, which is dry now.

He maneuvers past the bed and opens the door to the narrow wardrobe. "There are clothes in here for you. You're an XS, right?"

I gape in astonishment at the giant stack of blouses, shirts, pullovers, and pants. I'm all the more stunned because it never once occurred to me to open the wardrobe. Most of the clothes are pink, coral, yellow, and white—my favorite colors. An anxious fluttering sensation starts spreading through me.

Brendan pulls a drawer open. "Socks and underwear are in here. Shoes are over there"—he points to a different cabinet—"and up there is everything else you'll need." He gestures to the overhead cabinet, and then gives me a glance that's almost sheepish. "Shampoo, shower gel... tampons and stuff."

I must be staring at him like a cyclops. Maybe talking about this is uncomfortable for him. Then again, if you're fine with drugging someone and putting them in a box for five days, what could possibly make you uncomfortable?

"Okay, I'm gonna go start that fire." He reaches the folding door, but then stops for a moment. "Towels are in the overhead cupboard."

I sit there perfectly still, like I've been turned to a pillar of salt. Seconds later, he's back outside, messing around with the camper. The firewood must be stored underneath it in some kind of storage hatch, but I only half-register the thought.

I blink, still staring at the clothes. The fluttery feeling that started in my stomach when I discovered my favorite colors intensifies. No way. My knees are like jelly as I stand up and take the topmost blouse. It's pastel yellow with lace sleeves, and there are two pull strings in front to adjust the neckline. My heart starts beating faster. Ethan bought me this blouse two years ago.

No. Way.

I toss it onto the bed and take the next shirt from the stack. White with wide sleeves, the one I bought on sale at H&M, the same one I'm wearing now. It practically falls from my fingers. As if in a trance, I lift the next one. It catches on the handcuff, and I have to jerk it free. It's the coral-colored blouse with the lace trim, the one I had on when Ethan played judge and jury on me for my sins. Under that is my pink ruffled top. I'm dizzy. I feel like I'm being smothered. One by one, I yank the tops out and throw them onto the bed. I recognize almost all of them.

How did Brendan get my clothes?

Calm down, Lou! Think!

I take several deep, long breaths, the way Liam taught me.

Is this actually *my* stuff?

The white blouse can't be yours—you're wearing yours. He must have bought these things new.

Yeah, that must be right. My hands shake as I pull out one pair of bottoms after the next: my hot pants with the lace waist, also H&M. My dark-blue capri jeans, my 7/8-length pants with the tight cuffs.

The blood pounds in my ears. He must be even more insane than I thought. Completely batshit. Now I realize that the soap in the bathroom wasn't a coincidence, either.

The pants slip from my hands. How does he know what clothes I wear? How long has he been watching me?

Dazed, I open the cabinet with the shoes in it and discover two pair of my pink-flowered sandals. Of course. The ones I was wearing, and the ones he bought. And there are my flip-flops with the stars on them. And my bright-yellow Chucks.

I slam it shut. I'm terrified to open the overhead cabinet. I know what I'm going to find up there: my orange-blossom shower gel and my blonde shampoo. I crawl across the bed toward the hallway. My brain is sparking, every synapse is firing, I think I may black out. All I can think about is running. Now. I can't wait any longer.

CHAPTER
SEVEN

I hold my breath as I sneak into the hallway, stopping at the open window above the sink to peek out. Brendan is a safe distance away from the RV, arranging large rocks into a circle. Between him and the RV is a bundle of firewood like you'd find in any grocery store. The seam of dark trees runs along the far side of his fire-pit-in-progress, but he's kept a safe distance to them.

The sound of the rocks scraping against each other as he arranges them is fraying my nerves. I keep picturing him smashing my head in with one of them. Half of me is paralyzed with panic; the other half wants to burst through the door in the living area and start running.

My gaze shifts from Brendan to the side door. It's locked, plus it's on the side facing Brendan, so he'd see me immediately.

It feels like someone is choking me very, very slowly. Dazed, I look back at him. He straightens up, walks over to fetch the bundle of firewood, and then kneels in front of the stone circle. He pauses for a moment to smooth back a strand of dark hair that's come loose from his ponytail. The afternoon shadows of the trees tremble in the summer breeze, making them seem more alive than he does. Every movement he makes is like the minimalist version of itself. Even now, as he lays thick hunks of wood between the stones, creating a barrier between the fire and the moist earth. My brothers used to do that in the yard in Ash Springs, even though the ground there is practically never damp. They made it into a competition, though, pulling pieces out and rearranging them again and again. Brendan positions each piece perfectly the first time. Once he's got the base down, he piles smaller chunks on top with an expert precision that suggests he's done this hundreds of times already.

I take a deep breath and take a look around the inside of the camper. All the windows have those burglar-proof bars across them, except for the one in the driver's cab.

Maybe I can get out through the driver's side door. It's facing away from the campfire. If it's not locked, I can sneak out, cross the forest road, and disappear into the trees before Brendan notices. I peer through the window by the dining-room table, gauging the distance between me and the spruce trees. Thirty feet, maybe. And Brendan's probably thirty feet from the camper in the other direction. If I can get to the tree line before he realizes I'm gone, I'll have a sixty-foot head start, which should be enough time to hide.

I glance between Brendan and the door a few more times. My legs are like toasted marshmallows, but I still take a step forward, and then another. Now I'm almost up front in the driver's cab.

"Go ahead and pick out what you want to eat later!" Brendan suddenly calls.

I freeze in place, racking my brain feverishly, trying to decide what to do. Then I squat down and crawl back to the sink, handcuffs clinking. Carefully, I straighten up.

"Okay," I call back. Did he hear how shrill my voice sounded?

He glances toward the camper, but not to the open window I'm standing beside. Maybe this is my lucky day, and he can't see anything clearly through the window screen.

"It's all in the fridge. Pick me out something, too!"

"Right." I clench my fists in agitation.

Brendan returns his attention to the wood. If he's planning to start the fire right away, he'll probably be busy for a while. He might even have to go gather tinder.

I can't wait any longer. This time, I crawl up to the driver's cab on all fours, and then wedge my body through the narrow gap between the seats, across the gearshift. I ease myself into the driver's seat as quietly as I can and glance at the ignition. The keys aren't in it. Of course not. Then again, I wouldn't have any idea how to drive this beast anyway. Ethan's only given me a couple of driving lessons, and that was months ago.

With trembling fingers, I feel around behind me for the door handle without taking my eyes off the passenger-side door, sick with terror. Finally, I find it. How loud will the click be when the door opens? I scoot to the left, preparing to make an immediate run for it if Brendan hears. Thirty feet, I just have to make it thirty feet, and then I can disappear into the underbrush.

I pluck the handle like a guitar string. Nothing happens. I pull again, harder. Still nothing. He's got it locked. Tears spring to my eyes, but then I notice the window crank. It's a crank! Not electric! I can barely believe my luck. With sweaty palms, I roll down the window. If only I knew where Brendan was. Is he still working on the fire, or has he started sneaking around the camper? With every second that ticks by as I crank the window down, I expect him to fling open the side door. Once it's completely open, I listen hard for quick footfalls or suspicious cracking-twig sounds. Birds sing somewhere overhead, and far away, across a horizon I can't see, thunder rumbles. It's only now that I realize how cool and humid the air outside is. If Brendan heard the thunder too, he might change his mind about grilling.

I shift into a squatting position on the seat and grip the top of the window frame with both hands. First I slide one leg outside to straddle the bottom of the frame, and then I pull the other leg around so that I'm sitting side-saddle.

Now!

I drop to the ground, scraping my back against the door as I fall. I grit my teeth to keep myself from screaming in pain.

The muted thump of my feet hitting the ground makes my heart freeze in my chest. It takes me several seconds to jolt myself out of my shock, but then I start sprinting toward the trees in a blind panic. My legs are nightmarishly heavy. The forest seems to be receding in the distance. Stones bore into my bare feet, ripping the skin.

"Louisa!" Brendan shouts behind me. My name, and some other words that I don't hear, don't care about. I just have to get to the forest. To hide. To be invisible to him.

I'm about to reach the tree line when I trip on a rock and go flying. I hear myself wheezing; everything is swimming. At the last second, I manage to break my fall with one hand.

But then I see Brendan. Like a flickering shadow at the edge of my vision, faster than I would have ever thought possible. He's running not from behind, but from the side, his eyes wild and smoldering. Before my mind has even processed what I'm seeing, the full weight of his body hits me.

EIGHT

He flies directly onto me, slamming me to the ground. I can't catch myself, I scrape across the stones. Every bone in my body seems to break. For a second, all I see are stars and a bright light. He's on top of me, screaming random words I can't make sense of, squeezing my arms down hard against my sides, gripping my neck with one hand.

"I said *no escaping*," he growls, yanking my head up. "I said no leaving me! Don't. Leave. Me." He squeezes more tightly with each word.

I try to yank my arms free, try to fight him off, but it's like fighting a steel wall. I can't move a muscle. I want to say something to calm him down, but I can't get a sound out—his weight is pressing the air from my lungs. For several terrifying seconds, I'm sure he's going to snap my neck, but then he abruptly releases it and yanks me to my feet instead.

Through the fog, I'm dimly aware that he's dragging me back to the camper. I kick his shins, scratch him wherever I can manage to make contact, ram an elbow between his legs, gasping and screaming, but his grip only tightens.

When we reach the side door, he stops, wraps his arms mercilessly around me from behind: my back against his torso, his arms crossed around my chest. His breaths are like slaps against the back of my neck. I hear him gasping for air now, though I'm completely still myself.

"Goddammit, Lou, do you want to get yourself killed?" he whispers, which is infinitely more terrifying.

For several seconds, he stays there completely motionless, almost like he doesn't trust himself. Like he has to stop himself from hurting me.

"I'm sorry, I'm so sorry." The words come bubbling out of me like water from a spring. "I got scared... the clothes... I'm so sorry... please..."

He's saying something over and over again, so softly that I can't hear it. It sounds like the murmuring of a priest. He's still squeezing me the way he did when he first chloroformed me. He keeps on talking, getting gradually louder, until finally I can hear him.

"I have to keep you safe. I have to..." Abruptly, he breaks off and lifts me to carry me up the steps inside. I don't even fight him anymore—I'm too scared he'll flip out completely. His grip on my forearms is so tight that I'm whimpering behind closed lips. When we get to the hallway, he stops again and lets out a dreadful sigh. "You have to get away... away from me..."

He yanks me toward an overhead cabinet, flings it open, and starts rummaging around frantically inside. Several pieces of paper sail to the floor. Suddenly, he stops short and makes a relieved noise. He withdraws another iron chain, then attaches handcuffs at each end.

"I was scared, Brendan." I have to try again. My heart is racing. He's only holding me by the arm now. He seems almost absent, like his mind is somewhere else entirely.

Without a word, he pulls me back outside and takes a quick glance around. "Safe," he murmurs and leads me around the side of the camper. "Stop... okay, on the ground." He presses my shoulders firmly, and I sink to my knees beside the RV.

"Bren..." I can't make myself meet his eyes, so I stare at the pockets of his cargo pants.

"You shouldn't have run..." He bends down, takes the wrist with the handcuff on it, and attaches the loose cuff to the underside of the vehicle.

"Brendan..."

"Too late!" he snaps in a choked voice tinged with horror. "Getting dark... it's getting dark..."

Now I'm positive he's going to kill me. Tears stream down my face. I don't want to die. I cross my other arm over my head protectively, hunching over to make myself as small as possible, and squeeze my eyes shut. I hear my own rapid breathing. Thunder nearby. Footfalls, moving away from me. A clinking sound somewhere to my left.

I open my eyes again, blinking, and wipe them on my blouse to clear my vision. Cautiously, I turn to look in the direction of the clinking noise, and discover Brendan about twenty feet away.

He's got that chain wrapped around the trunk of a spruce tree.

Now I see that he's completely soaked with sweat. His pants, his shirt, his hair. His face is ashen.

I scoot closer to the camper without taking my eyes off Brendan. He picks up the handcuffs at each end of the chain and clicks one onto each of his wrists. The chain is still encircling the tree behind him, so he's trapped. A brief smile appears on his face, and for a moment he looks like the Brendan I saw in the visitors' center, the one I was so fascinated by.

"Louisa." His voice cracks on the last syllable. Rivulets of sweat run down his face. "Whatever happens, don't be scared, nothing bad can happen to you." He tugs on the handcuffs. "See?"

"Yeah," I wheeze, high and helpless. What can possibly be so bad that he's got *himself* in chains?

"Everything's dark." He starts moving toward me, but then the chain digs into the tree trunk, jerking him back.

"No, it isn't." My whole body is shivering. "There's a thunderstorm coming, that's all."

"Lou."

This time I'm weirdly happy to hear him call me by my nickname.

He's staring in my direction, but blindly, like he's not really looking at me. "Lou... Promise me something."

"O-okay," I stammer.

"But first, take this." He holds up a tiny key. He's shaking so hard that he can barely keep a grip on it. "You have to take it."

"How?"

Brendan leans in as close as the chain will allow, and then tosses the key in my direction. It lands right between my knees. It's on a metal ring with a black marble-sized sphere on it.

"Keep it safe."

I fumble the key ring into my pocket, shoving it down as far as I can.

"Now listen! The key only unlocks my handcuffs, not yours. I want you to—" He breaks off, gasping, and flails in his restraints like he's being slapped. His face contorts in a grimace of pain.

"What's wrong?" I'm trying to hide my terror, but I'm pretty sure my voice gives it away.

Brendan leans forward, propping his hands against his thighs. "To hide underneath the camper," he finally finishes. "You... should be able to do that with the handcuff on."

I shake my head. "Why should I hide?"

"Just do it," he says in a tight voice. The veins in his temples are so swollen, they look like they might burst at any second.

I turn away. In the distance, the first flashes of lightning dance in the sky, pale spirits with hundreds of spindly arms. The clouds overhead are thick and grey; only their edges gleam metallic violet.

"You can throw the key back to me in the morning, got it? Tomorrow morning, not before!"

"Why? Brendan? What's wrong?"

"It's getting dark... and when it gets dark, death comes." He sounds like a small child in a horror movie. A chill runs through me. He walks backward, slowly, step by step. "Keep the key safe. Otherwise, we'll never get out of here." With that, he starts circling the tree in a wide arc. His hands are balled into fists, his shoulders rounded, like he's getting ready for a fight. He disappears behind the spruce and into the thicket.

Oh, God, what's he doing?

I listen, but hear only frightening stillness. I start to wonder whether this is all some kind of sick game. At the next thunderclap, he's going to jump from behind the tree and strangle me with the chain. Maybe he's got a spare key.

Suddenly I remember what he said about hiding. I get down flat on my stomach and worm my way under the camper—slowly, so that I won't put too much pressure on my shackled wrist. The other cuff is attached to a steel eye that there's no way I'll ever break loose. The tips of my fingers throb. The metal cuff digs into my wrist. I can't stay on my stomach without cutting off my circulation, so I roll onto my back, clenching and unclenching my hand to get the blood flowing again. After that, I look over at the tree again, but I still don't see Brendan.

I wriggle out a few inches, just enough that my left side is peeking out from under the camper. A low-flying swarm of mosquitoes buzzes around my nose, and several of them land on my upper arm. I couldn't care less. They can suck me dry as long as I live through tonight somehow.

"Brendan?" I call, but in a muted voice. "Where are you?"

Silence.

Lightning creases the sky, and the lead-grey clouds light up in a sea of white for several seconds, which makes everything seem much darker afterward.

It's getting dark.

What did he mean by that?

"Brendan? Say something!"

The underbrush crackles somewhere between Brendan and the alpine rose bush, to the right of the spruce tree.

A shadow races out of the forest toward me. I scream, but it's just an ermine, zigzagging through the small cove Brendan's parked in, its tail fluttering behind it like a feather boa. With an elegant leap, it dives back into the cover of the trees. I exhale in relief, but then thunder fills the air.

Brendan isn't the only problem here. I slide further back beneath the RV, which hopefully will protect me from lightning. Hopefully. But what if Brendan gets hit by lightning? I'll starve to death under here. Months or years from now, some lonely hiker will find me here—a decomposed corpse whose bony hand has slipped out of the handcuff. Or maybe I'll get so thin that I can slide my own wrist through the ring and save myself?

Another burst of lightning illuminates the sky again, but I only see the tail end this time. The air is so heavy with the coming rain that I can taste it. The thunder follows soon after. There's still no sign of Brendan.

A ghostly veil of grey settles over the clearing. Finally, the pattering overhead begins, like fingers drumming on a table, faster and faster. And then from one second to the next, the clouds burst so violently, it's like someone's pouring pails of water onto us. I slide completely under the camper, but keep close enough to the edge that I can still peek out—not that I would be able to move much further with the handcuff anyway.

The sky above me is a raging battle between ghostly white light and raven-black darkness, between rain and wind. The echoing thunder makes the cove seem endless. Rivulets of rainwater run down the sides of the camper; a few droplets follow the pipes and drip onto me from the undercarriage.

It's like the ground has opened up and swallowed Brendan.

To keep my mind occupied, I count the seconds between lightning and thunder.

Twenty-one... twenty-two... twenty-three...

An ear-splitting howl shatters the night into a thousand pieces. I jerk upright and smack my head on a pipe. The screams sound neither human nor animal—more like a mix between the two. A dying animal and a man being beaten to death.

Shuddering, I peer into the thicket. It takes a moment for the fragments of night, howling, rain, and tree trunks to fit together like puzzle pieces.

There's a shape near the spruce tree Brendan has himself chained to, a horrible shadow dancing back and forth, like a boxer who keeps taking hard left hooks to the face and then winding up to strike back. The shrieking is so loud that it drowns out the thunder. I plug my ears as best I can, but it doesn't help. The sound penetrates into my bones like it's trying to tear me apart.

Abruptly, the horrifying noise stops. In the empty space left behind where the wild howling was, the rain is even eerier, like there's a hole in the night itself. I stare at the spruce, transfixed.

When the next burst of lightning hits, I recognize Brendan, standing there as though turned to stone. In the darkness, his face shines as pale as the moon; his eyes seem hollowed out. He's looking at me. I think he is, anyway. He's staring at me without seeing me.

"I'll kill you!" he suddenly thunders in a voice that seems to shake the air around him. "Do that again and I'll kill you!" He runs toward me.

I clamp my hand over my mouth to keep myself from screaming. The chain stops him, though, just feet from the camper. He jerks on the metal handcuffs like a madman; blood and rain are streaming down his palms, but he doesn't stop. He pulls against his restraints with all his strength, roaring. The tree bends. The branches sway back and forth, creaking. A thin twig snaps.

Another peal of thunder directly overhead makes him stop. He stands utterly still in the pouring rain, his hair whipping his face in the wind. His lips are moving, he's whispering, I can't hear him. Abruptly, he clamps his hands over his eyes like a scared little boy.

I just lie there. Wet, trembling. I have absolutely no idea what's going on.

Eventually, the rain subsides a little and his voice gets loud enough that I can hear him, but he's not talking to me anyway.

"How could you possibly think she loved you? That she'd come back? How could *anyone* ever love a worthless piece of crap like you? You're nothing. A bastard. A weakling. Nobody wants you. *Look* at you! There you go, crying again. Didn't I tell you to quit sniveling like a little girl? Didn't I tell you what would happen, you pathetic little shit? You want to play dead again?"

Thunder and lightning chase each other across the sky, hunting one another. Bren sinks to his knees.

My heart hammers wildly, full of panic and dread.

"Tell me what you are, I want to hear you say it!" he screams, and then his upper body tenses up. "I'm nothing," he whispers, so softly that I can only hear him because he's so close, and because the rain has let up. His fingers dig into the ground. "She left me. Anybody would have. I'm nothing. Nobody can love me. I should be dead. Buried in the ground, in the darkness... I'm nothing..."

I wriggle through the muck on my back and crawl out from underneath the camper so that I can sit on my knees. I can't let myself think about what's wrong with him. If I do, I'll freak out.

"Brendan," I say urgently, not too loudly, not too quietly. The rain has died down to just the occasional fat raindrop, but the wind is howling through the treetops like it's sweeping across earthen jars. Hopefully it doesn't bring any branches down on us.

"Bren-dan!" I stretch out an arm in his direction.

He looks at me, but I'm positive that he still isn't seeing me. He's still caught in some kind of hallucination.

"Everything's okay." I fight the quaver in my voice. "I'm still here. See? I didn't leave you." Slowly, so as not to startle him, I lower my arm. Obviously I know that he must be talking about someone else leaving him, but I don't know what else to say. "I'm not going to leave, okay? I promise. I'll stay sitting right here the whole night. Until morning. And then I'll give you the key back."

I'm not sure whether it's what I'm saying that calms him down or just the sound of my voice, but he stops clawing at the ground obsessively. It's a small victory, but it gives me the courage to keep talking. "But I can't aim very well, you know. I've always been bad at hitting targets from a distance—like throwing rocks at cans or whatever, you know?" For a moment, I wonder if he really does know that. "My brothers are good at it." I'm glad he's hearing me but not actually hearing me. "Especially Jayden." A lump forms in my throat. This is all too much. I feel like crying. About everything. Crying for myself, crying for my brothers, crying over the lies that led to me ending up here, with him. Maybe even crying for him, or for whoever he used to be.

But there will be time to cry later, so I force myself to keep talking. "I was afraid of the dark for a long time, too. After my dad died. Darkness and dying, I sort of associated the two for a while. I slept in Ethan's bed for the first couple of months, and I made him bring my nightlight into his room, the blue star. Even though it made it hard for him to fall asleep. Ethan always did everything for me..." My voice falters. I can't keep talking about my brothers if I don't want to burst into tears. Instead, I turn my face toward the sky for a moment. The wind is blowing the clouds along like a herd of black sheep. The rain has stopped completely now, though it's still thundering in the distance.

"When I throw you the key tomorrow," I continue, "I'm, like, definitely going to screw that up. We should come up with a strategy, like what we can do if I miss. You could go find a stick in the underbrush..." I ramble on and on about how long and how thick the stick should be. And then about how in track I can jump farther than I can throw, and about how I wanted to join the cheerleading squad, but my grades were too bad. "I'm actually a really good dancer, though." It may even be the only thing I'm genuinely talented in, but Ethan never thought it was important. *Dancing doesn't help you at job interviews,* he always said.

Later, the wind changes, and it starts to sprinkle again. I keep talking, but a clap of thunder interrupts me mid-sentence. Brendan leaps to his feet and stares at the sky with wide eyes. It's like he can't cope with his own fear.

"You should be dead, buried in the ground!" he suddenly roars again. "I'll kill you!"

I press my back against the camper, which twists my left hand painfully. Hearing him yell like that, I suddenly have a horrible fear that he's going to rip the tree right out of the ground and come at me.

But Brendan disappears behind the spruce once more, like a sick animal hunkering down to die. I hear him mumbling again. "So dark, so dark... in the ground... why did you leave? Don't stop breathing. Don't stop breathing. Keep your hands still. Don't cry. Don't stop breathing..."

I don't move a muscle. I promised I would stay there, so I'm not going to hide under the camper, whether he comes back or not. No matter how scared I am.

After a couple of minutes—I think it's minutes, anyway—I shift into a more comfortable position, facing more toward the side so I don't have to bend my hand around. I hug my knees with my free arm to keep warm. Every inch of my body is soaking wet, even my underwear.

This too shall pass, Lou. Tonight will be over eventually, just like last night was. Everything passes. Someday you'll be back home again.

I wait. I wait for the thunder to stop, for Brendan to reappear, for the night to end. It doesn't get as cold as I feared, but eventually my whole body goes completely numb, to the point that I don't even feel the sharp stones under my butt anymore. I just sit there, leaning against the side wall of the camper with one shoulder, collecting rainwater in one cupped hand every so often to still my thirst.

My eyes fall shut occasionally in exhaustion, but the thunder keeps jolting me awake. Probably for the best—I'm afraid to dream.

I keep mulling over what Brendan said. *I should be dead. Buried in the ground, in the darkness.*

What happened to him? Why would he think that? Who did this to him? Maybe when he was shouting, "I'll kill you!" he didn't actually mean me? Did someone say that to him? It sounded to me like he was being two people at once.

It's weird how some things change in such a short time. Until a few hours ago, Brendan was just the horrible kidnapper psychopath that lured me into his trap. The person I was terrified of. The evil, evil guy who gave me knockout drops and stuck me in a box. Who apparently stalked me for months. Until a few hours ago, he didn't have a past—he was my kidnapper, and that was that. Now, all of a sudden, he's a human being with feelings. Someone who's been hurt. Like, really hurt. At least, that's what I'm getting out of everything that's happened tonight.

I think about his eyes, about how they look like they've seen everything. Maybe they have. Maybe I don't want to know. Knowing might frighten me more than I am already.

I rest my head on my knees, but then I see movement from the corner of my eye, so I turn my head to one side. Brendan is sitting with his back against the trunk of the tree, head tilted back like he's stargazing. The sky is still too cloudy for that, though, even if the storm's mostly passed by this point.

Right now, he seems perfectly calm. I'd love to toss him the key so that he could unchain us both and I could return to the warm RV. But he said to wait until morning.

I close my eyes. Raindrops patter softly against my skin. I picture myself at home, in Ash Springs. I see my brothers. They tell me they love me.

I can't hold back the tears anymore.

CHAPTER
NINE

I haven't slept at all. For the past hour, I've been sitting here looking up at the sky, waiting for it to change color. It's dark at first, with only a few lingering clouds separated by wide stretches of clear sky, like grazing land for stars... but the stars aren't really shining tonight. They seem further away, and colder, like they're made of glass.

Bit by bit, the first hint of grey develops, a seagull grey that spreads in feathery swaths and eventually swallows the stars.

Brendan had another bad attack earlier. I kept talking and talking, and he actually calmed down again. Now I'm hoarse, and I haven't seen him for two hours.

Everything's still. Night transitions into day, accompanied only by the raindrops falling to earth from the treetops. The grey brightens, and soon the sky is streaked with fingers of salmon pink and peach, stretching out further and further. A bird starts singing, a mournful song that seems to fill every corner of the forest. After a few minutes, it's a choir. Later, the ermine races past again, without looking at me.

Tentatively, I rotate my stiff wrists and ankles. Every movement hurts, and I notice for the first time that the hard landing on the forest road left marks. My knees are scraped, and when I run my hand over the painful spot on my forehead, I feel a lump. No wonder, the way Brendan threw me to the ground. I pull the neckline of my wet blouse down to inspect the blue-green bruises on my upper arms, from where he grabbed me. And there are still patches of fading yellow near my elbows, too—must be left over from his first chloroform attack.

I don't want to look at them. I pull the neckline up again and take a few deep breaths of cool, resin-scented morning air, before fishing the key to Brendan's restraints from my shorts pocket.

I roll it back and forth in my hand, and then try to unlock my own handcuff with it.

"I told you," I hear Brendan say out of nowhere. "It only unlocks mine."

His voice startles me so much that I nearly have a heart attack. He's standing as close as his chain will allow. For the first time, he doesn't look perfect. He looks weakened and tired; there are bluish rings under his eyes, and the skin on his palms is ragged.

I bite my lower lip. Is there any way of knowing what he'll do when I give him the key? He might still be planning on locking me in the box, as punishment for wanting to run away. Right now, when he's acting so normal, it almost feels like last night was a bad dream.

"What happens when I give you the key?"

"I unlock our cuffs."

"And then?"

"And then you should shower." A faint smile flits across his face, as fleeting and jittery as the ermine.

I follow his gaze down my own body. I'm flecked with mud from head to toe. But the word "shower" makes me remember the clothes, the whole reason I panicked. I'm scared to bring it up, scared of the answer I'll get, because it may make him seem more insane than ever. Then again, what could possibly top last night?

"Are you going to punish me by putting me in the box?" I ask in a challenging tone.

"Lord, no, Lou!"

"But you threatened me with it."

"I thought maybe locking you in there would be for the best if I... I mean... if that kind of thing happened." He raises his shackled hands in a strangely helpless gesture.

I force myself not to look away. "What are you going to do then? You're going to do something, right?"

"I'd be lying if I said I wasn't." He squats down, at eye level with me, and regards me for several seconds with an expression I'm not sure how to interpret. "I don't remember what happened last night."

I stare at my feet.

"Flashbacks, they're called. Reliving an old traumatic experience. Ever heard of them?"

"On TV," I say quietly. "But I changed the channel." At least there's a name for what happened. Back then, the story hadn't interested me, it hadn't had anything to do with me or my life.

"There are different forms of flashbacks. Afterwards, I never remember what I did during them. They start with everything turning black-and-white. Everything gets darker, and seems like it's moving away from me. Eventually, it's like I'm trapped inside myself, I'm not aware of my surroundings anymore."

He doesn't say anything else, and after a minute or two, I raise my eyes. He's staring at his scraped palms. "Must have been a bad one," he says. "I tried to break free, didn't I?"

I nod.

"Once during a flashback I beat someone unconscious because I thought he was..." He hesitates. "Someone else. That's why I chained myself up. I didn't want to hurt you."

"You never want to," I murmur, narrowing my eyes. "And yet you do. Constantly."

He hangs his head. "I'm sorry, Lou." His voice sounds so ashamed, I nearly believe him. Reflexively, I run my hand over my arm; even that soft touch is enough to make my bruises hurt.

"Then why do you do it?" I hiss over at him.

He jerks his eyes up again. "You just can't run away. There's no point anyway. I'll always catch you. The old cat-and-mouse game."

I'm about one second away from swallowing the key, marble ring and all, just to see the look on his stupid face.

"There are a couple of things that... bring that out in me. Triggers, we call them."

Aha. So me running away is a "trigger." Okayyy. "Um, are there any others? Seems like something I probably ought to know."

He stands up, lips pressed into a white line. "Yeah, but I don't want to talk about them. Now give me the damn key already."

"You sound so mad. I'm not giving them to you when you're this angry."

He sighs impatiently. "You're still scared."

I look at him with what must be wide eyes, because his expression softens, his features smooth out. "I could never do anything bad to you. What can I do that will make you believe me?"

"Let me go," I grunt.

Another fleeting, ermine smile flickers on his face. "One-zero for you. But you know perfectly well that that's not going to happen. Now throw the keys here so that I can reach them."

I wonder why he's so impatient. I could stall for time, because maybe, just maybe, someone will actually come by. The thought makes my heart beat a little faster. "What if someone finds us here?" I say in a tight voice. "People are looking for me. Maybe the cops will fly over in a helicopter."

"Maybe. Maybe not. The police think you ran away. Same as hundreds of other teenagers every year. So I don't think they're going to go to all the trouble of searching these deserted woods."

"You're lying," I snap. "Of course they're looking for me. That's why you wouldn't let me watch *Find Me*!"

"I'll let you listen to the news if you want. You're not in it anymore. What do you think your friends told the cops?" He gives me a sharp look, and doesn't wait for me to reply. "Your brother's so strict, he doesn't let you do anything... you said yourself that you wanted to take the bus home. Or somewhere else. Trust me, the police have better things to do than run around looking for a rebellious little teenage girl. Give me the key, and I'll let you read the papers from the first couple of days after you disappeared."

Helpless, furious tears spring to my eyes, but I don't want him to see them. I stare at the side of the RV, at the letters spelling out *Travel America*. "That's blackmail," I say in a strangled whisper. "That's not fair, and you know it."

I hear the chain clinking as he moves. "I shouldn't have mentioned it. But you can go on waiting, of course. Until we're both too exhausted to move. Which will be quicker for you than me." I look back at him. He's sitting stick straight, shoulders back, like he's suddenly completely recovered from the long night. "This territory is almost 200,000 square miles and has a population of 30,000. Nobody's going to save you here."

Exhausted, I rest my head on the camper, squeezing the key in my hand. I'm so miserable I could die. The worst part is, I believe him, and there's no sense lying to myself about it.

I turn back toward him and scoot as far forward as possible. He's maybe twenty feet away now—it shouldn't be too hard to throw him the key. Or it wouldn't be for someone less tired and hungry and wet and exhausted and depressed. I can't bring myself to throw.

My hand is trembling. *Come on, Lou!*

But what if he's lying? What if he locks me in the box after all? For days, weeks... a memory shoots through my mind. *You should be dead, buried in the ground!*

"You're really not going to put me in the box?" I ask again.

"Nope." His dark eyes shimmer gently, almost caringly. But he looked the same way when he was warning me about the bears. I have no way of knowing when he's lying and when he isn't.

"But you're going to do something else. You said so earlier!"

"True." He's still looking at me.

"What?"

He sighs. "I won't lie to you. I hadn't planned on keeping you chained up permanently, but I suppose I'm going to have to for a while."

I toy with the keys in my hand. I'm freezing, I'm starving, I'm ungodly tired. And I really, really have to use the bathroom, and I'm not sure how much longer I can ignore it—and I certainly don't want Brendan watching me pee. Maybe stalling is only going to make things worse. Maybe it'll piss him off so much that he'll hurt me after all. Or maybe he's just pretending, waiting for the moment he gets his hands on the key.

I lean against the camper again with my shoulder and look up. A couple of crows glide over the pine-green treetops. Way overhead, I see the jet trail of an airplane. Everything's quiet. No sound of helicopter blades anywhere, no car engines, no voices. Nothing but forest and sky, Brendan and me.

Against all reason, I wait. Brendan doesn't say anything; after a while, he sits down on the ground and starts rotating a pair of rocks around and around in his hand. Time floats by like a bird, silent and weightless. The sky turns to steel blue as the sun rises. The heat licks the moisture from the ground. I squeeze my thighs together, because the pressure in my bladder is almost unbearable.

When I can't take the heat anymore, I roll underneath the camper. I briefly consider peeing my pants down here, but I think I can still hold it for a while.

I keep waiting. Tiny bugs crawl over my arms and legs. I flick them away at first, but after a while I give up. My lips are starting to crack. I try to work out how many people per square mile there are here, if it's 200,000 square miles and 30,000 people. I divide 200,000 by 30,000, but the result doesn't start with a zero, so it must be wrong. I try 30,000 divided by 200,000. Then I rotate onto my stomach as best I can with the handcuff and draw the equation in the dirt, but when I get a zero after the decimal point, I quit in frustration. Zero point zero something. The 30,000 people probably all live in one or two towns, and everywhere else is pretty much uninhabited. I think back to that rusted-out tractor that nobody even bothered to tow away so it wouldn't block the forest road.

Canada. This has to be Canada. The US has states, not territories. Especially not such sparsely populated ones. I'm pretty sure, anyway.

But why would I believe anything Brendan says? That thing about the population might not be true at all. I close my eyes.

"If you're trying to provoke me," Brendan says abruptly, "it's about to work." I see him kick a rock through the air with one dark biker boot.

"I'm waiting for someone to come rescue me," I call from underneath the camper.

"Not gonna happen."

"We'll see about that."

"Yeah, we will."

I keep waiting, but Brendan's creaking footsteps and the rustling underbrush when he briefly disappears into the woods are the only human sounds, besides the ones I make myself. Other than that, all I hear are the light and dark twittering of the forest birds, the drawn-out cawwws of the crows, the buzzing bees, and the spruce trees groaning in the sunshine. Once in a while, I see something small and soft dashing back and forth in the trees. Could be the ermine again, or maybe a marten or a chipmunk. Hundreds of white butterflies flutter amid the strips of lilac-colored willow herb scattered at the feet of the spruce trees.

If we really are in Canada, there are grizzlies here, too. It's weird: I didn't think about bears once last night. There were so many other things to be afraid of. Now the idea's in my head, but they seem a lot less scary than they did a few days ago. Maybe because I was underneath the camper, so I know the bear would have attacked Brendan first.

The light gets thinner; the shadows lengthen. A woodpecker jabs at a tree somewhere nearby, a monotone hammering sound that comes and goes. Still no sign of other human life out here. I begin to accept the fact that nobody will ever find me. Not alive, at least. Every bone in my body hurts; my bladder is aching, and hunger is eating a hole in my stomach. I've barely eaten anything in seven days now. I didn't touch a bite at breakfast yesterday. The only thing I ate was a sandwich Brendan brought me when he took a short break. I haven't had much to drink, either.

I've never felt so alone in my entire life. The waiting is shriveling my hopes, leaving an emptiness that fills my every pore. And yet my whole body is leaden, like I've inhaled iron. I could keep stretching the wait out, of course—I've heard people can live for two days without water. Maybe even three. But I wouldn't make it that long, not under these conditions, the drugging, the fasting. I remember that endless, lonely stretch of road, where only five cars passed us the whole day. Five! And I think about Brendan, whose pacing sounds more and more impatient with every passing hour. I hear him cursing softly. If I don't give him the key back until the very last moment, right before I die of thirst, I'll definitely feel his wrath. Besides, I really don't want to pee my pants.

It's late afternoon when I crawl out from underneath the camper, stiff-limbed. I don't even ask Brendan whether he's going to do something to me, whether he's going to lock me in the box. I don't want to think about anything anymore.

Brendan is silent as well, though his expression is one of relief.

I crawl as far forward as I can. This time, I don't think before I throw, I just do it. Without looking at him.

The key flies past Brendan, but he picks it up. I stare at the ground, listen to the locks clicking. Once, twice. Heavy footfalls in my direction.

Suddenly I'm terrified after all, pressing myself against the camper, shaking, yanking at the handcuff.

"I'm not going to hurt you," he barks furiously. He squats down beside me and unlocks the handcuff. A winged patch of sweat is spreading across his T-shirt. It reminds me of the water-color butterflies Jay and I used to make by putting globs of paint on the paper and then folding in half. Except it's black, not colorful.

When Brendan stands up, I briefly imagine the butterfly spreading its wings and lifting Brendan into the air. Carrying him far, far away. Then we'd both be free.

"Come on, up! You need to drink something." He grabs my arm. I can't help gasping in pain.

He releases me immediately. "What's wrong?" he asks, brow furrowed.

"I can do it myself." I scramble to my feet, using the side of the vehicle for support. I definitely do not want him to see what he did to me.

"What's wrong?" he repeats. "Are you hurt?"

"No!" I fold my arms. He has no right to know how I feel. Everything about me that he doesn't know already, I don't want him to find out. I want to protect that information from him. Even the injuries that he gave me.

He grabs my wrist; his jaw juts out. "I don't believe you. Let me see."

"I banged my arm," I say evasively. "It's no big deal."

"Banged your arm, hm." He rolls up the sleeve of my blouse. I don't fight him, since I know he's going to win. There's no point in resisting pointlessly over and over, just to remind myself of how helpless I am.

"Oh, shit," he breathes when he reveals the blue-green bruises; a couple of spots are nearly black. "Both arms?"

I nod and stare past him at an alpine rose bush with dark rosehips.

"That won't happen again," he says through gritted teeth. "Never. You have my word, no matter what happens."

"Don't make any promises you can't keep." I yank my arm away and unroll the sleeve again. "But even then... do you seriously think these bruises are worse than everything else you're doing to me? Trust me, you could beat the crap out of me, rape me, whatever, I wouldn't care as long as you dropped me off by the side of the road afterward."

He flinches like he's been slapped. For a moment, I think he's going to punch me in the face. I suppose that's when he remembers the promise he made two seconds ago.

"You don't know what you're saying. You're completely out of your head. Go on, get inside." He points to the side door with his chin, hands balled into fists.

I don't need to be asked twice. I cut a wide berth around him as I climb back into my dungeon.

I wait until I'm in the shower to peel myself out of my clothes. My shorts get caught on my scraped knee, tearing the skin open all over again. Blood runs down my leg in thin rivulets, and the wound burns a little, but it's almost like it's happening to someone else.

There's no driving away the emptiness in my soul. At this point, I wouldn't even care if Brendan came in and saw me naked. Anyway, he already has, if it's true about him putting me on the toilet. I toss my clothes out of the shower onto the floor, slide the plastic door closed and turn on the hot-water tap. Soon, the tiny room is filled with steam. I let the water run over my head. It's hot, almost scalding, but the pain helps.

I soap up with the shower gel and the shampoo Brendan gave me. The shower gel smells like herbs; the shampoo, like moss. I wonder whether there's a way to get water hot enough to burn grief out of your insides. Or memories out of your head. I want to wash everything out of me, but most of all, I want to wash the images of my brothers from my mind. Not the ones I'm always picturing, but the ones I won't let myself picture, and they still won't go away. The images of their faces when they realize that I've disappeared. Like, really disappeared, not run away. I know they don't actually believe that. They may have considered the possibility at first, but once they realized I wasn't at home, they must have known something bad happened to me. They know how much I love them. Even Ethan knows that, despite what I said to the contrary. I would never run away. My eyes fill with tears under the spray, which is getting progressively hotter. I picture Ethan checking his watch and looking worried when I don't return from the visitors' center. Walking through the dark campground, calling my name. Cringing in fear at the thought of what may have happened to me.

Deep sobs well up from within me and wrack my body. I can't hold them back. I don't think I've ever cried so desperately in my life.

I pull the showerhead down and hold my face right against the hard spray, wishing the water could dissolve me. The heat is breathtaking, chokes off my sobs. I want to drown.

I'm so sorry, Ethan. I'm so sorry I told you I hated you. I'm sorry I went with him. I'm sorry he's got me captive and you're worried to death back home. I'm sorry I can't give you some sign of life. I'm sorry I always gave you so much trouble...

There are so many "I'm sorry"s in my life. So many.

The spray abruptly shuts off. The sudsy grey water on the floor of the shower is past my ankles.

I stare as though hypnotized at the barely dripping showerhead, sure that this is Brendan's way of forbidding me from burning myself.

"You used all the water in the tank," he calls from the other side of the door. "It'll be a minute before I can fill it up again."

His words pass straight through me. I take the towel I hung on the doorknob and wrap it around myself.

"You all right?"

I nod, although he can't see it.

"Louisa. Everything okay?"

Nothing will ever be okay again. I take a few long breaths. My skin is lobster red. It's weird: I'm in pain, like terrible-sunburn pain, but I don't feel anything. Everything seems backwards.

Brendan flings the door open and stares and me like I'm a mutant. Then he shakes his head, but doesn't say anything. I notice a scratch across his forehead. Probably from me. It should make me happy, but it doesn't. Finally, he returns to the kitchen.

I walk to the back part of the RV on autopilot, fold the door closed, and sit on the bed. A stoic calm settles over the emptiness inside me. I rummage through the pile of clothing I ripped from the closet, fishing out shirts one by one until I find something that isn't a replacement for a top I own back home. A black boat-neck T-shirt. He may have picked it because he likes that style, I guess, but even that makes no difference to me anymore. I keep poking around until I find some knee-length jean shorts. With shirt and shorts in one hand, I climb onto the bed and open the overhead cabinet. I give the underwear a quick once-over. Simple stuff, no lace, no ruffles. Most of the bras and panties are plain white and exactly my size. I pluck out one of each at random, unwrap the towel and get dressed.

Then I just sit there, staring straight ahead. All my senses are deadened.

At some point Brendan comes in holding a tray. He makes sure I eat a bowl of oatmeal and drink two glasses of water. After that, he rubs some kind of brown tincture on my right wrist and then re-dresses it. I have no idea when or how the old bandage came off. I didn't notice how badly it hurt until now. But even this pain doesn't affect me. It's happening to someone else.

"Hopefully it doesn't get infected," I hear him murmur. He bandages my left wrist, too. Just to be safe, he says. I understand what he means. Just to be safe, because I'll be wearing the shackles from now on. And the skin around my left wrist is already reddening.

Once he's done with my wrists, he rubs a salve on my upper arms and elbows. It smells like pine needles and rosemary. After that, he disinfects the scrapes on my knees.

I guess he doesn't have anything for my soul.

When he finishes, he returns the first-aid stuff to the kitchen. Then he comes back, removes the cuff from my wrist, and puts it on my ankle. He attaches the other side to the iron chain, which is still hanging on the wall, firmly anchored.

He gives me a questioning frown from the frame of the folding door. "You weren't serious about that earlier, were you?" His arms are crossed.

Instead of answering, I mess with the fabric of the T-shirt. It's kind of therapeutic to twist and squeeze the material, pretending it's Brendan's neck.

"That you wouldn't care if I raped you and beat you half to death if I would drop you by the side of the road afterward?" His pupils are pinpoints. I see the color of his irises for the first time: dark brown, not black. He shakes his head in disbelief. "I must really be a monster."

I close my eyes and try to ignore him.

"I just want to have you with me. That's all."

That's all. Yeah, right.

"I won't touch you again—especially not in the way you think I would. Not as long as you don't want me to."

I would love to ask him if he actually buys his own bullshit. If he's seriously planning on keeping me with him forever, eventually he won't be able to stop himself. Eventually my grace period will run out, that's a given. Tomorrow. The day after tomorrow. Next week. Next year. Depending on what his testosterone levels are like.

"I'll wait until you're ready. I promise."

I look at him. His eyes are shimmering, a mixture of longing and skittishness, as if he's been waiting for this day to come with both anticipation and dread. It's an expression I've never seen in his eyes. But before I can figure out what it might mean, the shimmer fades, and he's as confident as ever.

"That's never going to happen." My voice cracks. "Ever."

He gives me that same intense look, the one that squeezes the air out of my lungs every time.

His pupils flow outward, like midnight-black ink in a glass of water. Without taking his eyes off me, he uncrosses his arms and holds his tattered wrists up in front of my face. They're both completely red and raw, but the left one still has that braided armband with the silver coin on it.

It dangles down sadly, like a tear that refuses to fall.

"This time," he says in a dark voice as I stubbornly stare at the coin instead of at his wounds, "you were lucky. I was able to chain myself up in time. I might not make it next time. So think carefully about whether you want to try and run off again."

He glances at the chain. "Assuming I ever give you a chance to try."

CHAPTER
TEN

The next few days drift past as if I were sitting in a train watching them through the window. Everything's far away. The morning after Brendan re-did my bandages, he refilled the tank. Grey water, he called it. I don't know where he got the water, and I don't care. Nothing is important anymore. I don't even mention the newspaper reports—I don't want to ask him for anything at all.

We hit the road every morning after breakfast, and usually keep traveling until the sun is low on the horizon. The temperature's been dropping steadily, which makes me think that we really are heading straight north. Maybe we're in British Columbia, maybe Alberta, maybe the Yukon or the Northwest Territories. The fissured landscape looks about how I would picture Northern Canada, anyway: craggy mountain ridges with endless green valleys, wild rivers, lots and lots of trees.

The birches and aspens are fewer and further between here; it's a primeval forest of pines, firs, and spruces, atop a carpet of dead wood, ferns, and willow herb. Here and there, a lake stretches out to one side, glittering and blank like the turquoise eye of a giant.

But wherever this is, it's at the end of the world, a place whose sheer expanse makes me shrink a little more each day. Maybe I really will be just a pale shadow before too long.

Sometimes I find myself thinking about Jay's stories. One of them was about a Native American who was born with grey skin.

He turned into a shadow in the forest, too. An outcast, unseen, abandoned, until finally he only talked to the animals. But he got a happy ending, because Jay wrote the story especially for me, and I love happy endings.

Too bad it doesn't look like I'm getting one of my own. Brendan doesn't make mistakes—after that night we both spent chained up, I can see that more clearly than ever. Whoever caused him so much suffering also made sure that Brendan turned out unrelentingly tough. Tough, strong, and calculating. He listens to a lot of Nickelback and Green Day as he drives, which always takes me back to memories of my brothers.

I've never felt so hopeless in my entire life. Even in the evenings, when the iron chain and I are theoretically allowed to join him at the campfire, I stay inside and peek out at him every so often —maybe just so I can see another human being. He mostly sits around staring into the flames, smoking an occasional cigarette, and every other night he spends some time scribbling in that notebook.

When dinner's ready, he brings me grilled meat and vegetables, or occasionally fish. I barely touch any of it.

Once in a while, I try to calculate how much time has passed since I was kidnapped. In movies, the victims carve notches in wooden chairs to mark the days, but I don't even have the energy for that. I was unconscious for five days, and I remember two days after that, and it's probably been another week since I tried to escape. If I were a doctor, maybe I could work it out based on how much my wounds have healed, or the color of my bruises. As it is, I can only guess.

I barely notice my surroundings anymore, because I spend almost all my time sleeping or thinking about the life I used to have.

After a few, I stop eating entirely, and stop leaving the bed. My memories are a magnet drawing me inward; my brothers' voices dance around me like wind chimes. They shout my name, hold me tight. I try to call every little inflection to mind—their words are clearer than their faces.

Today, I find Liam's voice first.

Go on, go catch the rhino! He's eating our raspberries again, that bad little rhino!

He laughs. I swing myself out of bed. The soles of my bare feet hit the warm wooden floor of my room—a familiar, comforting sensation. I hear myself giggling, feel myself running without seeing myself. Quick, pattering little footsteps into the yard. The herby smell of sagebrush wafts in through the open veranda door. Warm wind caresses my skin. Dishes clatter in the kitchen.

Liam, come help me with breakfast, Ethan calls.

I'm playing with Lou-u.

You should be practicing multiplication with her, not putting more silly ideas in her head!

I keep running through the dry grass; a thistle pokes my toe, making me squeal. I grab the invisible lasso out of the air, feel the rough leather against my fingers, hear it whistle in the wind.

I caught it! I caught it!

It takes all of my strength to drag the rhino to Liam. It's pulling against me, and I have to brace my feet against the ground. I'm giggling like crazy.

What should I do with him now, Liam?

Rope it to the post!

You mean like tie it to a stake?

No, just tie the rope around the post so it doesn't run off. You could tame it!

I lead the rhino to the end of the veranda and tie it up. It takes a lot of knots to keep it in place.

Heavy footfalls thudding on the wooden floors behind me. Dishes banging down on the table. I hear Ethan and Liam talking. I'm still hard at work—tying up a wild pink rhino properly is a difficult job—but eventually their conversation reaches my ears.

The kids at school are going to make fun of Lou when they find out that she's still playing with imaginary animals at her age. Is that what you want?

I just want to make her laugh, I hear Liam say. *It hasn't been that long since Dad...*

Silence. They've remembered that I'm there. I forget the rhino and run back, reach for Liam's warm hand. It's so large, it swallows mine up. I want to tell him that I can still laugh even though I miss Dad. That I have everything I could ever want. And that I wouldn't trade my brothers for anything in the world. But before I hear myself say anything, I startle upright, and I'm back in the present.

The next time, it's Avery's voice floating down to me. It's soft, nearly a whisper.

We'll bring you home as soon as they'll let us.

Quiet murmuring. Hospital smell. Swallowing is painful, and one part of my stomach hurts really bad. I want to cry, but I don't want Avery to think I'm a crybaby. It's bad enough having Jay tease me about it all the time.

The doctor says the operation went well.

Tender fingers stroking my forehead.

Is Ethan here, too?

No, sweetheart. He has to work. He'll be here later. And Liam's coming tomorrow.

I wanna go home. When can we go home?

Soon. Very soon.

The next time, the voices are different. My classmates' voices. Wild chatter.

Hey, Lou, is it true that Ethan and Avery are gay?

No, they aren't.

Elizabeth says they never bring girls home.

So?

So that's weird.

Is not. If every one of my brothers brought a girlfriend home, there'd be five girls there. Which would be hell!

You're sure Ethan's not gay?

Positive.

Does he have a girlfriend?

No. Of course not.

Why of course not?

He doesn't have time for that stuff.

Maybe you could introduce me...

He's twelve years older than you, Liv. He likes women, not girls.

. . .

132

I wonder if I'm the reason my brothers didn't bring girlfriends over. I can't remember Ethan ever having one. Avery had a Claire and then a Marie, but they never came over, or at least not that I saw. Jay's had a bunch of girlfriends, but only ever for a week at a time. And Liam supposedly had some brief, passionate relationship in India, and has been celibate ever since.

Maybe that'll change now that I'm gone. As they start forgetting about me.

My head is silent and empty.

Empty and silent.

It scares me.

The thought of their love for me becoming as pale and invisible as I am grips my heart like an iron fist.

Someday, everything will be gone. The hunger, the memories, their voices... and all that'll be left is me.

And him.

"You have to eat. If you don't do it voluntarily, I'll force you." His tone isn't a friendly reminder. It could cut glass.

I stare at the ceiling and don't see it.

The mattress gives as he sits on the edge of the bed beside me. I lie there as though turned to stone.

"I always loved how full of life you were. It was like nothing could bring you down."

I have the urge to swallow, but don't.

"I know exactly how you feel right now. It's like you're lying in a glass coffin, dead but not buried. You can see and hear everything around you, but everything is muted. The sky could be bright blue, but for you it's grey. When you reach out to touch something, all you feel is cold glass."

I turn my head in his direction, shocked at how well he just summarized it.

"I wish there were a way to make this more bearable for you. I wish I could be the one to shatter that glass for you. But I was the one who put it there." He lowers his head and wipes his face as though drying secret tears. "I should have taken a different girl and spared you."

Normally, hearing that would have made me either furious or deeply sad, but I don't have the energy. Even breathing is exhausting.

"I'm going to bring you some food now, and then you're going to come sit by the fire with me." From one second to the next, he's gotten himself back under control again. He doesn't sound like he's going to tolerate any protest, and I'm too tired to put up a fight anyway.

Eyes fixed on the ceiling, I listen to him work in the kitchen. He switches the TV on and puts on a music station. Nickelback, Satellite. After a few minutes, a tea kettle whistles, and I hear soft, scraping sounds.

Shortly after that, Brendan returns to the back room. I rotate my head in his direction. He's standing in front of the bed, bearing a tray with a bowl and a glass of milk.

"I made you some oatmeal with grated apples—anything else would probably hurt your stomach. And, Louisa, I'm not leaving until you finish it."

Something stops me from sitting up. I just... can't. Finally, Brendan pulls me upright like I'm a vegetable. He stuffs the blanket behind my back and then sets the tray on my lap.

"Eat!" His gaze is even more piercing than his voice. When he looks at me that way, I don't dare do anything but follow orders.

My fingers shake as I reach for the spoon, and I withdraw my hand, not wanting him to see it.

But Brendan doesn't let me out of his sight. He walks around the bed and then sits on the other side. "We'll be staying here for a while," he says, "so you won't have to spend the whole day in the back room anymore."

I try again to put the spoon into the bowl. It hits the edge a few times, but I manage to eat. I swallow mechanically, without chewing. Knowing that Brendan won't leave until I clean my plate is motivation enough. I want to be alone, I don't want to stay anywhere for too long, because that will mean that he doesn't have to drive, so he'll have time for me. I glance over at him from out of the corner of my eye, and he meets my gaze. That same question is in his eyes, the one I saw back at the visitors' center.

Do you want this?

Hastily, I avert my eyes. My hands are still trembling. It just doesn't stop.

Brendan's taken the handcuffs at the other end of the chain, the ones that were holding it to the grip bar, and attached them to his own wrist.

"Now we're connected, you and I," he says with a smile. "I can imagine worse fates."

He threads the key onto a carabiner on his belt. He's started doing that regularly—maybe he thinks it's safer or more practical that way, I dunno. He uses the chain to pull me outside, like a pet keeping him company.

I stop for a second on the steps of the camper and glance around at the spot he's decided to stay put in.

The sun is already down, so at first all I see is the pale red glow of the campfire. We're completely surrounded by trees, of course, but I figured as much, since Brendan never parks for the night without spending hours following a bunch of narrow, bumpy off-roads through the woods. I follow him, cautiously, almost as if I'm afraid one false step and I'd break my leg. It feels like I've had the flu for three weeks.

He sinks contentedly into a camping chair by the fire and gestures to the other one. I scoot the chair slightly away from him and then perch on the edge of the seat, ready to jump to my feet at any moment.

A cold breeze blows underneath my sweater, making me shiver despite the fire. The flames and the smoke twitch back and forth in the wind; sparks leap from it and fly off like red glowworms. A few of them land on my shirt, but go out immediately.

"The night air will do you good," Brendan says. "You look like a ghost."

I stretch my fingers toward the licking flames. Warmth flows over my skin like water.

"Shh, be quiet for a second." Brendan leans slightly toward me as though he's about to tell me a secret.

I was quiet already, so I'm not sure why he would say that. Maybe just as an excuse to talk to me.

I listen, since I don't exactly have a choice. The logs in the fire are cracking like hazelnuts. Behind that, I notice something else. A soft splashing sound, like a murmuring brook.

"Water." Brendan nods, as though reading in my expression that I'm hearing it. "Water is good. We can use it to fill the tanks, so we can stay independent for longer."

Hearing the word "independent" makes my stomach cramp. I don't want to be independent. I don't want to be here at all. I hold my hands closer to the flames and stare past Brendan toward the forest, though I can't make out anything but darkness. The heat of the fire is nearly burning my fingers, but I don't pull them away. I need the pain. Somehow the fresh air makes me feel worse than the camper did. On the bed, I can convince myself that I'll wake up eventually. Out here, the nightmare is way more real.

"You don't want to talk to me, then?" Brendan fumbles a pack of cigarettes from his jacket pocket. He fingers one out and lights it with a Zippo.

A couple of wolves are howling in the distance. It sounds a little like wind whistling through an old chimney, multivoiced. We heard coyotes every so often in Ash Springs, but this howling is deeper and wilder, it's nothing like dogs.

Brendan regards me appraisingly. In the darkness, he looks like a wolf himself. Black fur, black eyes. Eyes made for hunting. Hunter's eyes. Probably has a hunter's heart, too. It's only a matter of time until he bags his kill.

"Why me?" I whisper. It sounds deafeningly loud in my ears, even with the howling in the forest.

"Why not you?" He takes a drag with relish, as a provocative gesture. I don't know why he sometimes pretends he wants to make this bearable for me, and then one second later he's back to acting all superior.

Meeting his eyes takes every ounce of my willpower. "You said you should have kidnapped another girl, right? So I wasn't the only girl you were considering? Did you have a list or something?"

Smoke billows out of his mouth. No other muscles in his face move. "I think you misunderstood."

I pull my hand back a little. "What is there to misunderstand?" I

136

ask in a quiet, but cool voice. "You stalked a few different girls, and finally you picked me." God, I hate him so much!

"I checked out a few different girls, but I never planned on kidnapping one. Until I found you."

"Found? Where did you find me?" Now I'm completely confused. His voice echoes in my head: *I checked out a few different girls...*

"You'll have to figure that out for yourself. It's actually not that hard, though, if you think it through." He takes another drag. I suppress the urge to stuff the cigarette into his mouth, lit end first.

"Anyway..." He leans back, and I feel a slight jerk on the chain connecting us. "There was never another option besides you." He tosses the butt of his cigarette into the fire and gazes into the dancing flames, watching them hop back and forth vivaciously. "I saw you and wanted you. I would have done whatever had to be done. Anything. I know that sounds ridiculous, and heartless, and frightening. And I'm not going to try and convince you that I'm a good person or anything." His gaze shifts from the fire back to me, enveloping me in shadow. "Because I'm not."

An icy shudder runs down my spine.

He runs his hand across his forehead. "I just want you to understand why I had to do it."

"Well, I don't," I grunt.

Brendan slides forward slightly, so that he's sitting on the edge of his chair, too. "When you concentrate on your heartbeat, what do you feel?"

"My heart, what else?"

"Just try it."

"I don't want to."

Brendan slides his hand underneath his leather jacket and lays it flat against his chest. For a moment he looks like he's holding his breath... or like he's afraid. "All I feel are the spaces in between. Emptiness. Darkness."

So dark, so dark... under the ground... why did you leave? Don't stop breathing, don't stop breathing...

"Which is why you kidnapped me," I snap to push the depth of his words as far away from me as possible. I don't want him to touch me. Inside or out.

"Yeah," he says solemnly, and there's a strange look of liberation in his eyes. "It's not as bad with you here."

I can't look at him any longer, so I stare into the fire instead. He seems so different when his mask of confidence falls away. I don't have any idea who he is. That may actually be the thing about him that frightens me the most: I can't figure him out.

"You said earlier that you would have done whatever needed to be done. To kidnap me, I mean." I struggle to keep my voice steady.

He nods, almost eagerly. Maybe he's glad to see me showing an interest in him. All I'm doing is trying to determine how much danger I'm in, though.

I scoot a little further forward, until I'm barely on the seat at all. "Would you have killed one of my brothers to get at me?"

His eyes turn to black stone; color drains from his face. This probably isn't quite how he pictured our little fireside chat, but it's too late to turn back now.

It takes him a moment to reply. "That's not a fair question, Louisa. There's no way to answer it. If I say yes, you'll be scared and you'll hate me more than ever. If I say no, you won't believe me. So what do you want to hear?"

"The truth."

"The truth is that I've never even considered that question. And you shouldn't have, either. I can't answer it after the fact."

"You're making it easy on yourself," I say in a whisper.

"I could have said no and risked you calling me a liar."

I grip the edge of the chair tightly. "Have you ever killed anyone else?"

He was already pale, but now his face is a death mask. Abruptly, he jumps up and turns his back to me.

For a while, the only sounds are the crackling fire and the rustling of the underbrush. Even the wolves are silent. My heart is pounding so hard, it's making me nauseous.

"Is that a yes? So y-you really..." This changes everything. "I... I want to go inside."

He spins around. "No," he says in an icy voice. "You asked me a question, and I'm going to answer it. Sit down. *Now.*"

I drop back onto the edge of the chair as if on autopilot, without taking my eyes off him. Hundreds of horrible visions explode in my head like splinters of glass. Maybe I'm not even the first girl he's done this to.

"It was almost three years ago..." Brendan starts pacing back and forth behind his chair, dragging the chain across the ground behind him and making the cuff around my own wrist scrape across my freshly healed skin. It burns and itches underneath the metal ring, but I try not to let on. Weirdly, pain I cause myself is somehow liberating, but this I can barely stand.

"It wasn't how you think," he says now.

"What do I think, then?" I wish my hands would stop shaking.

Abruptly, he stops in place. "The worst, of course. That I killed someone out of envy, greed, or rage. You're probably picturing how you think I did it. Something especially barbaric or underhanded, I suppose." He lets out a snort of laughter. "Am I right?"

Not wanting to look at him, I stare into the pale-red flames. "How did you do it, then?"

"It was an accident."

Right. Of course.

"It's kind of a long story."

"I only need the short version. And then I'd like to go back inside." Pretending to be strong is exhausting when my whole body is quaking in terror. I'm sure he sees it. He has to. He probably just doesn't care—or he's feeding off it.

"The short version is: we fought, he didn't survive."

"You beat him to death."

"Don't twist my words. There was a fight. We both knew what we were getting ourselves into. There were no rules and a whole lot of prize money."

"So you *did* kill for money."

Brendan comes toward me with a cold look on his face. He stops directly in front of me and leans down. "I hit him and he fell down," he hisses at me. "He broke his damn neck! It wasn't supposed to be a fight to the death."

I stare at his face. At his hard, implacable mouth, his straight nose, the infinite abyss of his dark eyes. There's so much arrogance in that expression, a protective shield of self-confidence. But I've seen other things behind it—as fleeting as fog over the desert around Ash Springs. Too briefly to understand them, but long enough that I can't forget them. It's like he has two faces.

"Maybe your punch is what killed him, how can you be sure?" I know I'm asking to provoke him, to draw something out of him that will tell me who he is.

Brendan props his hands on the arms of my chair and leans closer. I turn my head to one side, trying to avoid him. "Yeah, a lot of other people thought the same thing. Especially the guy's dad and brother." His breath is hot on my ear.

I sit perfectly still. "If there were no rules, it was an illegal fight, and nobody looked into it. Lucky you."

Brendan takes a deep breath. "Go ahead and keep needling me to see whether I'll break my promise. You're going to be disappointed, though. I never hit people weaker than me, even if they try to make me do it."

"You kidnap them instead," I mutter through my teeth.

He makes a noise I'm not sure how to interpret and pushes himself up from the chair arms.

"What are you going to do to me?"

Brendan scoffs impatiently. "I've told you a million times. I'm taking you with me. That's all. You just refuse to believe it."

I jump up, fists clenched. "I do," I say, quietly and coldly. "I do refuse to believe you aren't planning to do something terrible to me. And you know what? I wish you would get on with it already, whatever it is. Do it now. Then it'll be over and you won't have to keep up these nice-guy theatrics."

"I'm. Not. Going. To. Hurt. You." Each word is a growl.

"*Liar!*" I get right up in his face, much closer than I would normally dare. I'm not sure why. Maybe I just want to know whether he's serious or not. "Why are you drawing it out? Because you enjoy watching me suffer? You really are sick. Sick and perverse." I spit in his face.

He stares at me in utter disbelief, pure madness flickering in his eyes. My heart hammers in my throat as I watch the spittle slide down his cheek. Moving even more slowly than the spit, he raises his hand and wipes it off with the sleeve of his jacket.

"Come on!" I scream at him. "Do it already!"

"Yeah." A dangerous whisper, so sharp that I stumble back

reflexively. "Yeah, it's time. Something needs to happen." He takes a long step toward me and reaches toward his belt. A moment later, he's clutching a hunting knife.

All at once, I can't move. I'm staring at the blade in a daze, watching the glow of the flames reflect in the surface, golden and red, red like blood.

I was right... I knew it... now he's going to kill me!

Everything's swimming. I barely register that he grabs me by my long hair and drags me toward the camper. Not violently, but emphatically.

"Bren..."

He pushes me against the side wall of the vehicle—almost casually, well aware of his own strength. He'd only need a fraction of it to kill me. He's standing so close that I can't get away. I feel his body. His thighs on my butt. His scent envelops me. Tobacco, firewood, wet earth. I let out a whimper.

"Won't take long," he says with quiet grimness. "And if you hold still, it won't hurt, either." He pushes the back of my head, pressing my forehead against the steel body of the RV. Then he pulls my hair up, twists it in his hand. That one hard jerk is enough to force me to keep still. I can't turn my head. Any moment now, he'll tear my jeans off or slit my throat. I'm dizzy with terror, I can barely breathe. *Just get this over with!*

All at once, he's pulling my hair even harder. My head jerks back and forth a couple of times; my forehead bumps softly against the steel.

Before I can figure out what's going on, I'm yanked away from the wall by the chain. The ground sways beneath my feet, the dark earth comes toward me, but I manage to catch myself at the last minute. I stumble along behind Brendan. What did he do? I look at him. Then I see it.

His right hand is still gripping the leather handle of the knife. His left is clutching a blonde ponytail.

Automatically, I reach up and touch my own hair. The strands are fringed, and end somewhere between my chin and shoulders.

He cut my hair! My beautiful long hair that I was always so proud of!

"So do you believe me now?" With a decisive, almost triumphant swing, he throws the ponytail into the fire, which immediately stinks of singed keratin and sulfur. "Do you think a guy who was only interested in *that* would chop off the girl's hair?"

I watch in stunned silence as the flames consume my hair, crackling greedily. It simply melts away, becomes invisible like me. In a matter of seconds, there's nothing left but ash. Still in disbelief, I pat the feathery ends of my hair a second time.

"Do you believe me now?"

A defiantly spoken question that rotates and rotates. Faster and faster. Right now, I have absolutely no idea what to think or feel. This is too much. Too much homesickness, too much fear, too much despair, too much Brendan. Even too much Louisa. I wonder how I can possibly be invisible to the world when I'm feeling so much that I can barely take it. My suffering is so enormous, I don't get how nobody else can see it. My heart is too small for this.

I wrap my arms around myself as though my emotions will all come streaming out of me otherwise.

"Do you believe me?" This time, Brendan's voice is quiet and solemn.

I cast a brief, sidelong glance in his direction. He's staring into the fire again, at the place where my hair has finished burning. When he feels me look at him, he turns his head toward me, and I hurriedly avert my eyes.

"You're crying."

"Am not!" I wipe my eyes, furious at myself.

"Because of your hair? It'll grow back."

He doesn't understand anything. How would he? He wasn't torn away from everything he knew and loved. He can't possibly understand that I'm crying because I feel too much. Because I have no way of changing anything. Because I don't feel like I'm me anymore. Me, Louisa Scriver.

"Things couldn't go on the way they were. I needed to make you less scared somehow... well, I tried to, anyway."

"You made me think you were going to kill me."

"I told you I wasn't going to hurt you. All you had to do was trust me. It's not my fault. I wanted... I wanted to make the situation here clear, once and for all."

"So you did what had to be done. As is your nature." My words are tinged with bitterness. Now I know more about him than I wanted to.

He laughs, but it sounds lost and infinitely lonely in the dense forest. "I told you I'm not a good person. Good people do good things."

"And what do you do?"

He regards the blade, and then slides the knife back into its leather sheath. It dangles on his belt, right next to the keys.

He shrugs. "Today, I cut hair. Tomorrow, I'm building rabbit traps. The day after tomorrow, maybe I'll tell you where I found you—if you haven't figured it out by then. Would that be a start?"

It feels more like the end, but I don't tell him that.

CHAPTER
ELEVEN

T hat night, I dream of Ethan. We're sitting on his bed, and weirdly, my blue star night light is plugged into the wall. Ethan takes my hand and places it on his chest. "Feel my heart," he tells me. "What do you feel?"

I focus on the pulse, but there's nothing beneath my fingers. Just coldness.

"Do you feel the emptiness between the beats?"

"Yeah," I whisper.

"That's the place where you're missing. Come back, please come back. It's so dark without you..."

I cry in my dream because Ethan's heart isn't beating anymore. The silence is like a flatline.

Eventually, he shakes my hand off and stands up; his cheeks and the tip of his nose are pale as a dead man's. "When all that's left there is silence," he says, "I've forgotten you. Hurry!"

I startle awake. My back is so sweaty that my shirt is sticking to my skin. I glance around in confusion. The blinds are up, and the moon is shining straight down onto the white bedding. The light in the hallway is on. Brendan must still be awake. I slide toward the window and see him sitting in the camping chair, head propped on his hands, eyes closed like he's sleeping. The campfire has burned down to a pile of pale grey ashes and hunks of charred wood, with the wood moisture-barrier underneath.

The notebook he's always scribbling in is sitting by his feet. The top few sheets are waving in the breeze like white sails. I'm not sure why, but I climb out of bed and walk down the hall until the chain stops me when I reach the sink. Still acting on some strange impulse, I slide the checkered curtains open and squint at the fluttering pages, trying to get a better view. It doesn't look like writing. It's... pictures. He's drawing.

I stretch up on tiptoe and press my forehead against the window. The white sheets of paper are filled with dark blotches—figures, bodies, heads, but all completely black. One looks like a disembodied hand reaching out with distorted or broken fingers. Before I can make out the rest, the top pages flip back to cover it. A shiver spreads over my skin like an icy mantle. I don't particularly want to see what he's drawn, but instinct tells me I need to know. Like maybe it's important, maybe it'll tell me more about him. I blink to focus my eyes, but then Brendan raises his head.

Anxiously, I pull away from the window and step back. My heart thumps in my chest. Hopefully he didn't notice me. I stand frozen in place for a few seconds, but he's apparently too deep in thought to pay the camper much notice. He rests his head in his hands again and closes his eyes. Sitting there like that, he seems as vulnerable as a child.

My hand reaches automatically to my hair. I pluck at the uneven strands. *Do you believe me now?* He sounded like he meant it.

With a strange feeling in my stomach, I close the curtains.

Maybe he really isn't going to rape me. And maybe he's not going to hurt me, either. But maybe this is even worse. If his only goal is to keep me around, he'll do whatever it takes to make that happen. Knock me out for five days, for example. Which means I'll never be free again. My brothers will forget me. I'll forget my brothers. Eventually, the silence between us will be too great.

The next morning, Brendan wakes me before the sun is fully up. He unclicks me and goes to the kitchen. The generator is humming, and I hear the coffee machine burbling.

"After breakfast, I'll show you how to build a rabbit trap." He sounds like he's eager to get started.

"I don't eat rabbits," I reply and walk toward the toilet.

"You might have to one day," he retorts. "When our supply of food runs low, for example." He hesitates a moment, and I shut the door behind me. "Oh, right," he calls loudly enough that I can hear him through the door. "I nearly forgot you're on a hunger strike."

As I wash my hands and face, I catch a glimpse of myself in the mirror almost by chance, and I nearly jump. I really do look like a ghost: ashen and hollow-cheeked, with blackberry-colored rings under my eyes. My thick, blonde hair hangs down perfectly straight; here and there, a couple of longer strands peek out and tickle my shoulders. I still don't know what to think about the fact that he hacked my hair off so brutally, but I decide to risk believing that his intentions were just as he said. I have to. Otherwise this constant fear of being tortured and killed will drive me insane. I look weird. The short hair makes me look younger, but my thin features make me seem older. This isn't me.

I open the overhead cabinet to search for a ponytail holder, so that my face will look how it used to when I put my hair up. To my surprise, the cabinet is nearly full now: aftershave, several bars of blue soap, lotion, disinfectant, cough syrup, aspirin, Band-Aids, tape, and of course the gauze and the washcloths... I pick out some gauze, fiddle the package open, and then rummage around for scissors, but there still aren't any. No razors, either. Nothing sharp, nothing even close to being usable as a weapon. Instead, I tear off a piece of gauze savagely with my bare hands and use it to tie my hair back. A few strands don't make it into the ponytail and hang loose on either side of my face.

Brendan notices immediately. "You got into the cabinet?" he asks the minute I emerge from the bathroom.

"Is that a problem?"

"No." He smiles.

I retreat to the back room and push the folding door closed before peeling off my dirty jeans and sweaty shirt. Then I open the narrow closet. I still haven't mustered the courage to ask Brendan how he knew to get all these clothes. Maybe he'll tell me once he reveals where he saw me for the first time.

As I sift through the blouses, a wave of burning homesickness hits me with such force that I have to suppress the urge to pound my head against the wall. I need to put something familiar on today so that I can be me again, even if I don't feel like me. Instinctively, I reach for my favorite shorts with the crocheted hem, but then I change my mind. Too short. Definitely do not want Brendan seeing too much of me. Instead, I pick out the dark capri jeans and the coral-colored blouse with lace trim. After hurrying to put them on, I stand there for a moment, indecisive. My fingers slide along the smooth material of the blouse and close around my pendant.

When all that's left there is silence, I've forgotten you.

I clench the charms more tightly. *Ethan. Avery. Liam. Jayden.* I repeat their names in my head like I'm afraid I might forget them.

"Are you coming or what?" I hear Brendan call.

He can't even let me remember in peace! I take a deep breath, slip my flip-flops on, and go back to the kitchen. Without a word, I slide onto the bench and watch emotionlessly as he takes my left wrist and clicks the free end of the handcuff onto an iron chain. I follow the links of the chain with my eyes until I spot the anchoring plate on the wall underneath the table. He probably has these things all over the camper, and who knows how many chains. I ball my fist automatically, but then open it again right away—I refuse to let Brendan see any more reaction from me.

He plunks a coffee in front of me. It's so sweet I can actually smell the sugar in it. "Want some blueberry pancakes?"

"No." I lift the cup and practically dunk my face in it. The chain clinks with every movement I make, no matter how slight.

"Okay."

I hear him opening drawers near the counter. Zing—two waffles pop out of the toaster. From the corner of my eye, I watch Brendan put them on a plate with several more. He cautiously sprinkles them with powdered sugar, then slides in across from me and places the plate in the middle of the table.

"You look cute with your hair up," he says out of nowhere.

I tense up so quickly that the coffee slops over the side of the cup. *Dammit!*

"Sorry." He sounds exasperated. "Shouldn't have said that."

I peer over at him. After wiping the coffee up with a kitchen towel, he sinks his teeth into a waffle and chews energetically. Our eyes meet, and I look away quickly.

"You need to eat."

"I'm not hungry."

"I believe it. But you still have to eat."

"Or you're going to force me to?"

"I'd find a way to get you to eat, trust me." He says it breezily, and it irritates me that he can afford to be so relaxed.

My stomach knots up. "I really do feel sick."

He sighs deeply. "You're eating tonight, promise?"

"Okay. But no rabbit."

He lets out a short laugh that sounds artificial and out of place, as if he's trained himself to laugh in certain situations so that nobody will notice how deranged he is. Like he did in the parking lot at Sequoia.

I stare out the window as he works his way through at least four of the enormous waffles. It's light outside now, and the air around the trees is shimmering. It's not hot, though, so that must be a swarm of tiny mosquitos.

"Can I open the window?"

"You don't have to ask permission on every single thing."

I slide the window open; a cool morning breeze wafts through the screen and envelops me. The woods are full of birdsong, making them seem livelier than they did last evening. A wasp smacks into the screen and speeds away, buzzing.

Maybe I could pretend to like Brendan, pretend I can imagine a future together with him. Maybe then he'd leave the chains off and I could make a break for it. But the idea of being nice to him, of talking to him any more than absolutely necessary, sits in my stomach like a rock. There must be another way.

I regard the trees thoughtfully. They're all conifers about the same height, no more than a couple feet apart—one big, happy family. "Where are we?"

"Canada."

"Where in Canada?"

"Doesn't matter. The important thing is that it's never as hot here as it is down south, and temperatures can get near freezing at night—last night was comparatively mild. That's all you need to know."

I spot a little bird hopping from branch to branch, making the thin twigs near the ground sway. When my gaze slides to the foot of the tree, I see a small group of chipmunks. I long to be out there with them. They're free, and they aren't alone. "What other animals are around here?"

"Besides those obnoxious chipmunks?" He leans in and casts a contemptuous glance in their direction. "Rabbits, weasels, different kinds of rodents, elk, wood bison, caribou, red foxes, deer, black bears, grizzlies... and wolves, you heard those last night."

"I like chipmunks."

"Well, you're a girl." He straightens up. "I'll give you the grand tour later. You'll like it here."

Yeah, no doubt! As I watch him wolf down another waffle, I marvel that someone so slim can eat so much. I look at his bicep, or at least the part of it that's peeking out from beneath his white T-shirt. It's smooth, sinewy, lightly tanned. I wouldn't have guessed that he was that strong. He did seem athletic to me when I first saw him at Sequoia, but I had no idea.

I find myself wondering what kind of guy it was that he was fighting against. Did he underestimate Brendan, too? Did Brendan know the guy was underestimating him? Why would either of them agree to a fight with no rules, where death was a real option? Brendan is still a complete mystery to me. Part of me wants to figure him out; the other part is afraid of what I'll discover.

I go back to staring out the window while he clears the table and washes up. As usual, he turns the TV on, but the reception is pretty bad today, and *Hero of the Week* is mostly snow. I zone out.

Later, he chains us together again. Probably so that I'll feel less like a dog he's walking. Solidarity with the hostage appears to be part of the plan.

As we step outside, I'm immediately greeted by the scent of the woods, of clean air and spruce needles. The sky above the treetops is a brilliant blue, without a cloud in sight.

"Gonna be a warm one today." Brendan's boots crunch on the gravel as he walks once around the camper, and then opens a storage hatch that extends almost the entire length of the vehicle.

"Put on some hiking boots so you can walk in the forest more easily." He reaches into the storage space and then holds out a pair of lace-up ankle boots. "I hope you like them, I made sure to get yellow and pink."

Not wanting to provoke him, I silently put on the socks sitting inside the patterned boots, and then slip the boots on. They fit perfectly, of course.

Brendan tosses my starred flip-flops into the hatch. A couple of neatly stacked cans catch my eye.

"What's in there?" I hurriedly ask before he closes the hatch.

He stops in surprise, but then hooks the cover open so that he doesn't have to keep holding it.

"Supplies. Tons of extra food."

I blink into the opening, baffled. The space is gigantic—it's like the camper's digestive tract, packed tight with boxes, cans, and cartons.

Brendan points around to the different boxes. "Peaches, pineapple, potatoes, peas, beans, corn, sausages, tuna, canned ravioli—sorry, I've always loved that stuff..." He turns to look at me and falls silent. I'm not sure what face I'm making, but he furrows his brow for a moment before continuing. "I brought a bunch of dried pasta, too, no worries, I know you like spaghetti. Plus red sauce and white sauce. And a jar of chopped garlic. The fresh basil may be tricky, but I've got pine nuts... there in the back, on the left." He gestures vaguely toward the corner.

The last shreds of optimism still buried deep inside me begin seeping out very, very slowly, like the air in a balloon someone's holding at the end but hasn't knotted. I blink at the cardboard boxes, dazed. They're all labeled in black lettering: *Medicine, Winter Clothes, Bathroom, Games, Hunting*. I spot two gas canisters secured near a wooden box.

"Propane," Brendan explains, following my gaze with his own. "We cook with it. And the fridge runs on propane. The two canisters should last us through the winter."

I feel the blood drain from my cheeks. "You want to spend the entire winter here?" Apparently he's not planning on heading for a city any time soon. Or a village. Or any other place humans live in.

"Sure." He gives me a steadfast look. "I plan to stay forever."

He's completely insane. "Won't it be way too cold?" I ask weakly.

"I've thought of everything, Lou, don't worry." He smiles, probably mistaking my horror for worry about my own well-being.

"Nothing bad's going to happen to you out here. And besides, civilization is far away, but not completely unreachable."

"So why do you want to catch rabbits if you've got this whole thing packed with food?" I do my best not to let on how shocked I am. I'm barely managing to hold back tears. I wish I'd never seen that storage space.

Brendan shrugs. "Fresh meat is important. Plus we can save food this way."

"But I don't want to eat rabbit." It comes out in a choked whisper.

Sighing, he unhooks the hatch door and lets it fall shut. "I could catch squirrels instead. Or chipmunks." He locks the storage hatch. "Oh, don't give me that look, Lou. I might even bag a deer here and there. Anyway, you don't *have* to eat it. I brought plenty of multivitamins and iron supplements along."

I turn my back to him, wondering whether he enjoys torturing me with his perfect planning.

"C'mon," he says in a cheery voice and tugs the chain almost teasingly. "I'll show you around."

As if he didn't know full well how miserable I am.

Directly beside the camper, behind the row of spruces Brendan built the fire near yesterday, there's a clearing with a small, emerald-green lake. A narrow waterfall feeds into the lake, glittering like diamonds in the sunlight as it tumbles over a rock ledge.

Step by step, I make my way to the water, over mossy stones, past willow herb, around fir-tree roots. The trunk of a fallen spruce lies directly beside the shore in a bed of ferns, its branches and needles long since rotted. I climb over it and stand close enough to the shore that the soles of my hiking boots are underwater.

A cool breeze rises from the surface, and my bare skin immediately breaks out in goose bumps.

"It's a quiet place," Brendan says from behind me. Of course he's behind me—we're chained together, after all. "Can't hear anything here but the bubbling water and a couple of cheeky birds. Spend a little time here, it's like your spirit dissolves into the ether. You become one with the air and the water."

I try to ignore Brendan. The lake is barely bigger than our property back in Ash Springs. The sky and the trees tremble on its green surface as delicate, transparent reflections.

"This lake always felt like my safe place, like I was protected here."

"What could *you* possibly need protection from?" I ask sarcastically, although the night of the thunderstorm definitely left me with the sense that someone hurt him terribly in the past. My mind automatically shifts to those dark drawings in his notebook.

Even so, I keep walking along the shoreline to show I'm not interested in hearing his response. I know I shouldn't be.

A couple of boulders are scattered along the shore, like game pieces tossed carelessly aside by some long-extinct creature. Some of them extend deep into the lake. I wade past them, muddying the ice-cold water, which swirls around my ankles and seeps into my shoes.

"You can swim here if you want," Brendan suggests now, without acknowledging my question.

"I can't swim," I mumble and eye the waterfall cascading in front of the wall of grey stone.

"You can't swim?" he echoes in disbelief.

"Don't tell me you didn't know that already?" I ask, not bothering to look in his direction. For some reason, we didn't get around to swimming lessons in Ash Springs. Ethan never had time to teach me, and eventually the idea just stopped coming up.

"The water isn't deep. Three feet, maybe." He ignores my snide remark. "You'd be fine, plus I'd be there." He rounds the boulder behind me. "Or I could teach you how."

I have nothing to say to that. It's completely out of the question. I go on staring at the waterfall.

"Look at me, Louisa."

His voice is completely determined again, so much so that I can't bring myself to defy him. It takes me a minute to raise my head.

The longer he looks at me, the more his eyes shimmer. They're mirrors, like the surface of the lake. Bitterness, sadness, impatience —I'm not sure which of them is most prominent. He lifts his hand as if to touch me. Horrified, I stumble back and nearly land in the water. When I've recovered, I see that he's clapped the hand over his own eyes.

"You don't have to fight me all the time," he says and lowers his hand again. "You're only making it harder on yourself. Nothing's going to change about your situation, so you might as well try to get along with me."

I turn back to the waterfall and bite my cheek until I taste blood, pushing his words aside and concentrating on what I see.

The rock wall towers into the heavens, a grey mountain fringed by trees that get smaller toward the top. It's got to be several stories high, but it's angled, and the stone is full of deep ridges—an expert climber could probably climb up there. For a beginner it would be difficult, very difficult, maybe even impossible, but I'd be desperate enough to try.

What's at the top? A forest path, maybe? I glance down at my own shackled wrist, and then over at Brendan, who's regarding me with narrowed eyes.

"Forget it," he says in a frosty tone, seeming to guess what I'm imagining: myself, hanging on that wall. "The water makes the rock smooth and slippery. You'd fall and break your neck."

"I can think of worse fates," I murmur in a flat voice.

"Then I guess I'd better not tempt you!" Demonstratively, he lifts his shackled wrist to eye level. "But if you ever want to come here without me, I can always chain you to a tree." With that, he yanks me away harder than necessary. Maybe I ruined the peacefulness of the place for him.

He leads me alongside the lakeshore, where the water has carved a small creek bed through the forest. There are even a few lush broad-leaved trees here. But Brendan takes another route, pulling me straight through the dense woods. It's demoralizing. It takes us at least fifteen minutes to walk maybe a quarter of a mile. The spruce limbs extend nearly to the ground. blocking my view. I keep having to duck or push heavy tree branches aside; after a minute or two, I'm sticky with resin. We clamber over dead tree trunks poking out from amid the ferns and brush like deer antlers. My calves start burning after brushing against something that looks very much like an oversized stinging nettle.

I get the sense that Brendan isn't doing this to show me how beautiful this area is—he just wants to demonstrate that I'm not getting out of here on my own.

After a while, I simply stop dead in my tracks. He doesn't notice until the chain jerks him back.

"What's wrong?" There's still an icy edge to his voice.

"I want to go back." There's a spruce tree between us, its trunk covered in pale green lichen that looks like fat ocean coral in the patchy sunlight.

"I was going to build the trap first." As he rounds the tree, the chain catches on a branch. He tears it free, cursing.

"Can't you bring me back and then build the trap?"

"No. You're coming with me." With that, he simply drags me onward.

He finally stops after a few minutes. "Here's the animal crossing," he says, gesturing vaguely behind himself. "The creek can't be far from here. Perfect place to set traps." He takes a blue scarf from his pocket and knots it around a tree limb at eye level. "So we'll find the traps later."

After that, he stamps a little further through the underbrush, brutally hauling me along with him, and glances around. Eventually, he pulls a thick, arm-length tree limb from a tangle of dead wood. "Long enough," he murmurs to himself. He reaches for his belt and unclicks something he'd had tucked underneath his shirt. A rope. It's rolled up, but it turns out to be several meters long. More than enough to tie me to a tree. I suppress the mental image and watch him cut the rope in half with his hunting knife After that, he ties the tree limb to two tree trunks, near ground level. The knots he uses are strangely complicated, crossed over and over in ways I can't follow. Finally, he sticks several smaller, forked twigs into the ground underneath the construction, using them as supports.

"Just need the snare now," he muses before plucking a bag out of another pocket, then reaching into it and withdrawing some wire. He creates a loop and twists the ends. He's obviously done this hundreds of times. I'm not sure why, but I picture him building traps like these for me. To keep me from running off.

Brendan uses his fingers to measure the distance between the horizontal tree limb and the ground, and then attaches the wire so

155

that it dangles down. "We'll have to check these several times a day. If the snare is too big, the rabbit's paw will catch in it, and it will take hours for it to die. A painful death."

I glance at the hunting knife, which is hanging on his belt again, beside the key to my handcuffs.

"I want to go back," I say softly. His agility at building deadly traps with knives, rope, and wire snares is chilling. He truly does have the heart of a hunter. "I don't want to watch a rabbit get caught in that," I add.

Brendan taps the wire snare with the tip of his toe, and it swings easily back and forth. "I'm going to set three or four more traps, and then I'll bring you back. You don't have to join me when I check them."

That evening, there's a dead rabbit hanging head-first from a spruce branch not far from our campfire. Brendan puts one snare around each of its hind legs to hold it in place while it bleeds out through the slash in its throat. He catches the blood in a bowl—because of the wolves and the bears, he says, and then suggests using it to make soup. He laughs at the look of disgust on my face before taking the bowl to the lake to pour it out.

He leaves me chained to the camper when he goes. This time, he uses two chains hooked together, so that it's long enough to reach the camping chairs by the fire.

When Brendan returns, he pulls out his hunting knife and skins the rabbit. I look away, grimacing, and go back to staring into the flames.

Later, I watch Brendan attack the cooked legs like a voracious wolf. I can't bring myself to touch the meat. I don't think I can eat anything, even though I promised I would.

He brings me a plate of buttered toast with cheese and lemon cookies, but I'm pretty sure I'll throw up if I take a single bite.

When he finishes eating, he looks over and sees that my toast and cookies are still untouched. He rises to his feet, cursing loudly, and fires a rabbit bone into the flames as he stalks into the RV. A few minutes later, he emerges again, mellow and self-satisfied, almost like a businessman who's just made an especially great deal.

He's holding a folder under one arm, and he brings it over to his camping chair with him, where he sits down in a deliberately casual way.

"These are the newspaper articles I told you about," he says, but without opening the folder. It sits flat across his thighs. "The ones from after you disappeared."

I suppress a noise of astonishment. He never mentioned the articles again, so I've been assuming he was making up what he said about having collected them.

"You didn't believe I really had them."

"No," I say tonelessly. I want to jump to my feet and yank the folder away, but I stay right where I am, frozen in place, incapable of moving.

"There are pictures of your brothers in the paper." His eyes glisten in the dancing flames like dark torches. "One of them looks a lot like you. Avery, I think."

I swallow hard. *Avery…* Rage wells up inside me. I hate it when he talks about them as if he knows them.

"Eat today and I'll let you read the first article. And then you can have the next one tomorrow… if you eat three meals."

My heart is beating so loud that I'm afraid he can hear it. I have to have those articles! Now that he's offering them, which means they really do exist, I'm not about to let this chance slip away again. I have to see the pictures of my brothers! I know they're going to break my heart and that afterwards I'll wish I hadn't ever laid eyes on them—just like this morning when I discovered the supplies—but I don't care, it doesn't matter, I think I would probably walk across hot coals to get those articles. All I want is a few words about my family, an excerpt from the reality that seems centuries away. I would never have guessed that I'd be so desperate for a few seconds of happiness that I'd take them despite knowing my soul would bleed from my body afterward.

"Blackmailing me with those articles isn't fair," I say, trying to hide how excited I am. And probably failing. Jay and Ethan always said I was bad at hiding my feelings. I have too many of them. A deluge of emotions, Ethan called me. My eyes are glued to the folder. "You know how important they are to me."

"I'm not expecting a whole lot in return," I hear him say in a gruff voice. "Not even a smile."

"It's still blackmail."

"I'm not a good person, I told you. Hell, I kidnapped you—blackmail is nothing by comparison."

I start eating. No, wolfing. I'm gulping down the food so fast that Brendan holds me back.

"If you puke everything up again, it doesn't count." There's concern in his eyes. I guess it's possible that he's genuinely worried about my health, but it's still underhanded of him.

I stuff a lemon cookie into my mouth whole and swallow huge chunks of it one after another, until one piece goes down the wrong way and Brendan jumps up to slap my back.

"Choking doesn't count, either," he says almost gently once I've recovered.

There's a weird pressure in my stomach. Furtively, I cover it with my hand.

Brendan opens the folder. "Do you want the first article I have?"

I nod, and he holds out a folded sheet of paper. I reach for it, but he doesn't let go right away. "I don't have the very first article," he says. "I was too busy with you, with keeping you unconscious. This is the second one."

"Doesn't matter," I whisper. *Give it to me already!*

He releases the page with an admonishing look in his eyes. "Don't forget, you have to earn the others, too." With that, he saunters back to the camper, folder in hand, and switches on the outside lighting.

I'm glad he's letting me be alone for this. My hands shake as I smooth the newspaper page open.

TEENAGER STILL MISSING

The all-caps headline jumps out at me. A picture of me fills the entire top half of the page. My heart seizes up. It's the picture Avery took of me last summer, standing beside the apple tree that Liam always does yoga under. They've zoomed in on the picture so it's just my face, smiling cheerfully into the camera, and part of the neckline of my coral-colored blouse. My cheeks are glowing nearly as red as the apple hanging from the branch beside me. My long, blonde hair is mussed from the wind; my eyes are as clear and blue as the sky.

I look happy. Happy, young, and vivacious. Anyone who saw this photo would be shocked to read of my disappearance. That's how it always is: when people disappear, they use the best pictures of them, as if the editors are trying to emphasize the life and joy that's been lost. It's the same with milk cartons—they never show kids sulking.

I stare at the picture, incapable of reading the text. There's a flutter inside me, an indistinct feeling of recognition. A suspicion. I can't quite grab hold of it. Sinister shadows emerge from the darkness. There's something there, whispering softly. Part of me wants to reach out for it, feel my way to it...

No, I have to read this article. Brendan could come out any second and take it back. I hastily shoo the feeling off, but I sense that it merely steps away, like an uninvited guest that won't be denied entry for long.

Tensely, I begin reading.

Sequoia National Park, California

The search for sixteen-year-old Louisa Scriver continues. Yesterday, a large contingent of police officers, fire and rescue personnel, and volunteers searched the area around Lodgepole Campground in Sequoia National Park, but failed to uncover any new leads.

The teenager was first reported missing three days ago. Park officials say Louisa was last seen on the evening of June 25th, when she purchased two Solarez camping lanterns at the Lodgepole Campground Visitors' Center. Park rangers have not ruled out the possibility that she lost her way in the dark, and is now alone in the wilderness somewhere.

According to Sequoia Park Ranger Thomas Baker, cases like these are not unheard of, though the missing person is usually found unharmed within forty-eight hours. With every hour that goes by, he says, the likeli-

hood of the teen having suffered some sort of accident increases. Baker worries that the cliffs and rock ledges in the area around Moro Rock would pose a particular safety risk in the darkness.

The article reads like a report about someone else. Factual, distant. Is this really about me? I take a deep breath before reading on.

One of the girl's brothers, however, insists that she could not possibly have gotten lost. Jayden Scriver says he followed his sister to the visitors' center, and that she knew her way back—especially considering that only a single gravel road leads from there to the tent area.

The teen's brother went on to lament the police's handling of the situation, saying it was "scandalous" that the search did not begin immediately. According to Mr. Scriver, the police instead "wasted precious hours" focusing their attention on outsiders who heard the girl arguing loudly with her brothers that evening, saying that she wanted to go home.

Police Spokeswoman Carmina Loper tells the Daily News that "every option is still on the table," including the possibility of Louisa having fallen victim to a crime.

"We're investigating in several directions at once," she says, "but of course we're still hoping that Miss Scriver simply ran off and will show up at her family's doorstep in a day or two, healthy and happy." In fact, police still consider that scenario the most likely of all.

After that, the article describes the clothing I was wearing that day, and gives a phone number for people to call if they have any information regarding my disappearance.

I read the story over and over again. My head is one big swirling mass of chaos. Half-dazed, I study the pictures at the end of the article. There's a travel brochure-style photo of the entrance to the Lodgepole Visitors' Center. Beside that is a huge picture of Moro Rock and the surrounding area. *Park rangers wonder if this beautiful rock formation may have spelled disaster for young Louisa,* the caption underneath reads.

I read the part about Jayden several times. He doesn't believe I got lost or ran away. And if he's so sure about that, he and the others will do everything in their power to make sure that the police don't quit searching for me. The thought gives me a faint glimmer of hope, but it dies again right away when I remember what Brendan said earlier: *The police have better things to do than run around looking for a rebellious little teenage girl.*

Unlike me, he's already read every one of these. So they probably really have given up on me. I don't even know today's date. I was kidnapped on June 25th—it must be nearly mid-July by now.

I look at the picture of me again: my radiant eyes, my open smile, the coral blouse I'm also wearing now. That terrible feeling of recognition washes over me again, a wave of darkness that threatens to drown me. I posted this picture on Facebook, visible to the entire world because I thought I looked pretty in it. Especially my eyes and my windswept hair. Ethan kept telling me I should change the privacy settings to "friends only," but I always ignored him. Because I felt trapped in Ash Springs. Because I wanted the world to see me. Because I thought that, if the world saw me, my life would have meaning. I may have even thought that I would only truly start living at that moment—once I meant something to the rest of the world, I mean.

That miserable feeling cuts deeper. I posted so many videos and photos of myself. They all start flashing past in my mind, image upon image of summer, sunshine, color, laughter.

Me and Elizabeth eating ice cream, sitting back-to-back in the dandelion meadow, me wearing the pastel-yellow blouse Ethan gave me, my lips smeared with matching lemon sherbet. Me and Ava arm-in-arm in our new crocheted-hem H&M shorts, making duck-lipped faces into the camera. I see the white blouse I was wearing in that one, the way it slipped down to reveal my tan shoulders. Another image flickers past: Madison and me, Rollerblading on the Road to Nowhere near my house, both of us holding cake pops, me wearing the pink ruffled top and the dark-blue capri jeans. A picture of my feet in the bright-yellow Chucks; another in my pink-flowered sandals. Me and Emma lying on the veranda, heads touching, eyes closed dreamily, a package of lemon cookies between us. A picture of a radiant blue sky with a huge, bright sun. A picture of my favorite food: garlic spaghetti with pine nuts, tomatoes, and fresh basil. Me in front of the bathroom mirror, with the blue hand soap beside the sink, still in its package.

I know you.

I clutch my throat, gasping for air, when I realize what that means.

CHAPTER
TWELVE

I checked out a lot of girls, but I never planned on kidnapping one. Until I discovered you.

Brendan found me online. He must have been watching me for months, every post, every picture, every video. That's the only way he could have known to get these clothes.

Hot rage bubbles within me, until my entire body is shaking. It's partly at him, partly at myself. I clamber to my feet and circle the camping chair like a stalking predator, clutching the article tightly in my fist. I wish I could choke Brendan out with this chain, wrap it tight around his neck until I hear him wheezing the way that poor bunny in the trap probably did. I made everything so easy for Brendan. I even posted our entire route before Ethan froze my account. At the time, I thought it was cool—if I had to disappear from the Internet and the world, I wanted everyone to know where I was. Plus it was a small victory over Ethan.

All Brendan had to do was wait around at the park. He had plenty of time to sit back and weave his trap. If he hadn't succeeded that day, he probably would have done it some other day.

But now I'm done for. Hardly anyone thinks anything seriously bad has happened to me, and no one will ever suspect I'm in Canada. They can search the campground a hundred times with dogs and sticks and whatever else, and I'll go right on being a missing person. They won't officially close my case, but others will start taking priority, and the police will stash my file away somewhere.

In all these weeks, the reality of my situation has never been so painfully clear as it is now. I'm so miserable it's making me light-headed.

It's exactly the way Brendan described it. I'm lying in a glass coffin, and I know I'll never get out, never. I'll never see any of my brothers ever again. No matter how often I throw myself against the glass, knowing that my life is right there on the other side, I'll never break through. And every time I try, the pain will be worse, the heartbreak will be harder to take. Each time will hurt more. I'm only exhausting myself with this futile hope.

How long can I keep doing this? When will I stop trying to break the glass? When will I finally lie still because my body and soul are failing, my strength is gone?

I stare at the crumpled page in my hand. My cheeks are wet, and my shoulders are shaking. I won't tell Brendan what I found out today. I just don't have it in me. I'd end up bawling and begging and pleading, trying to make him change his mind.

With a strangled noise, I toss the newspaper article into the flames, watch the fire char my face and consume everything that's left of me.

I'm not going to throw myself against the glass any longer.

Days and days and days go by. Each one is ten weeks long. I spend most of my time sitting on the bed in the camper or near the fire, staring into space. In the beginning, whenever I happen to get some time alone, I keep going through the cabinets and drawers over and over. But I don't find anything that might help me defend myself against Brendan, and everything I *do* find only makes me feel more hopeless. He's got everything organized perfectly.

In the meantime, even he seems to have figured out that he can't cheer me up.

I break each day down into individual actions, because it's the only way to get through them. Get up, shower, get dressed, watch *Hero of the Week,* wait, eat, wait, eat.

Brendan gives me another article each evening, but I don't read any of them. I fold them into squares and put them in the closet underneath my clothes, because Brendan doesn't want them back. The temptation to look at them is huge, but my willpower is stronger. I can't allow myself to hope anymore.

When Brendan asks me a question, I answer. I've stopped talking to myself, stopped repeating my brothers' names. And I don't look at or touch the charms on my pendant anymore. I pretend I'm someone else, watching my life from outside. This horror is happening to someone else, not to me. I'm not that girl in the forest.

Brendan's making an effort, but he's the whole reason I'm suffering. I can't smile at him, can't waste words on him. I don't want to feel anything, I just want to be. To exist one day at a time. I wish I were like the wind, so that I could simply blow away without taking anything with me. I want to dissolve into nothingness, but I don't want it to be painful.

Sometimes Brendan sits down next to me and doesn't say anything. I get the sense he's trying to share part of my burden. Once in a while, he'll try to start a conversation, but I always shut him down, and after a few minutes he leaves me alone again.

I'm vaguely aware of what he does during the day. He's still building traps, and he often returns with dead rabbits. Sometimes he goes out picking raspberries or cranberries, and not long ago he returned from the woods with a bowl full of blueberries. That alone leads me to believe that his supply of fresh and frozen fruit is starting to run low. He takes our clothes to the creek to wash them every few days, and hangs them up to dry on a clothesline he's strung between two trees. He hangs his heavy cargo pants and jeans over separate tree limbs, because otherwise he wouldn't have enough clothesline for the rest. And he leaves quite often to fetch canisters of water from the lake, which he uses to refill the RV's water tank. Once in a while, he empties the water tanks. Grey water and black water. The black water is the toilet water—he didn't have to explain that, I smelled it for myself.

Recently, he's taken to starting the camper a few times a day and running the motor. He says it keeps the battery from discharging. From what I understand, he needs the battery for the generator, plus he's always putting in different CDs and cranking them loud to scare the bears away.

My days are defined by his activities. Of what he does or doesn't do. He's stopped forcing me to join him anywhere; he just makes sure I keep eating and drinking.

Yesterday, he said, "It would be better if you cried again to get your grief out of your system."

Only then do I realize that the last time I shed a tear was as I was burning the first article. I simply don't allow myself to do it anymore, though my throat is constantly raw from the tears trapped inside it. Even at night, when Brendan is fast asleep and can't hear me, I still swallow the grief over and over again until it's locked away in the pit of my stomach again. Because I know that the next time I cry, I'll never be able to stop.

This morning, I realize that the nature around me has changed, though I couldn't say exactly how.

Maybe the needles on the trees are darker. Or the birds are singing a little more brightly. Or more butterflies and bees are fluttering around the tall willow herb.

It's still early in the morning, the air is cold and clear, and I'm sitting near the faintly glimmering remnants of last night's fire. Besides eating, the only other thing Brendan insists I do is get at least two hours of fresh air.

He disappeared into the woods a while ago to check his traps, so he left me chained to the camper. I've taken to wearing scarves around my wrists so that my skin isn't constantly infected from the metal rings.

I'm scratching at an oozing scab when I hear a loud crack in the underbrush behind me.

"Lou!" It's Brendan. He's coming through the trees from the direction of the lake, returning much sooner than I expected. "You have to see this!" His voice nearly cracks. He breaks through the brambles full of dark berries and stumbles clumsily toward the campfire. Only then do I notice that he's holding something in his arms. It's not a rabbit, though—he always carries those hanging head-first, and not without a certain look of pride on his face.

Mystified, I stand up. It isn't like him to tromp around so loudly and excitedly—normally he moves as silently as the forest itself.

My gaze shifts to the tiny little something in his arms. It's a grey bundle, and now it lets out a high, pitiful whine. I stare as though hypnotized at the tiny ears, the adorable paws that seem oversized.

"Here, take it!" Without waiting for an answer, Brendan holds out the bundle, and I clumsily accept.

"Wolf pup," Brendan explains as he strides back toward the camper. "I found him near a cave."

I feel the short, wooly fur under my fingers and involuntarily hold the pup a bit closer. Something's happening inside me, but I'm not sure what.

"I heard him whining." Brendan opens the rear hatch and disappears halfway into the belly of the camper.

I trot after him, making sure to tread softly so I won't scare the pup. "You didn't steal him away from his mother, did you?"

Brendan glances over his shoulder and makes a face at me like I've just accused him of wanting to roast the pup over an open fire. "Of course not! Who do you think I am?" He turns back to the hatch. I stand to one side, listening to him rummage around. "Come on," he mutters to himself. "I know I brought you..." Clattering sounds. "I figure his mom rejected him. Or she died, and the other pups were eaten. Any number of possibilities..."

"Poor thing," I whisper, cuddling the pup. He's still for a second, but then his wet nose burrows into the crook of my elbow, and his front paws start moving rhythmically against my forearm. The pup has me all mixed up. It's like he's melting a layer of the ice surrounding me. "I think he's hungry," I say, uncertain.

"What do you think I'm doing here?" Brendan growls from inside the storage hatch. "I'm trying to find the powdered milk. I'm positive I brought some, in case we ran out of canned."

"You brought powdered milk?" I don't know why that surprises me.

"Of course." Brendan emerges with a triumphant smile, clutching a blue package. "Got it." He glances at the ball of fur in my arms. "I hope he drinks this. If not, I'll have to drown him."

"What?" My eyes widen in horror.

"So he won't suffer, I mean."

169

"You're insane," I snap, not even caring whether my tone makes him mad. "That is completely out of the question."

"Lou, be reasonable. If he doesn't drink any milk, he'll starve, he'll die a miserable, painful death. Is that what you want?"

I take a few steps back, stroking the pup softly. "He'll drink it," I say quietly, but with determination. "I know he will."

Brendan disappears into the camper, carrying the package of powdered milk. My chain and I go in after him.

"Can he come in?"

Brendan looks surprised—maybe he didn't realize I was following him. He regards me for a second, holding a tea kettle in one hand. Then he smiles. "Sure, why not?" He fills the kettle from a plastic bottle. "It doesn't matter whether he's outside or inside. The other animals will smell him either way."

Cautiously, I climb the stairs into the camper and ease myself onto the bench, holding the wolf pup under one arm. He's taken his face out of the crook of my elbow now—apparently he's figured out there's no milk in there. Now he's trembling all over, and he starts whining miserably again. *Where did everyone go?* I imagine him saying. *I'm hungry and thirsty, and it's really cold and lonely here without that thick fur to snuggle up to.*

Still cradling the little wolf, I stand up and angle Brendan's dark-blue fleece pullover down from the driver's cab loft he sleeps in. Then I sit down again and wrap the pullover around the wolf, sliding my hand inside so he can feel my body heat.

"We have to weigh him so we can monitor whether he's growing." Brendan turns on the stove, and small blue tongues of flame spring to life beneath the kettle. It smells like gas, even though Ethan always says gas doesn't have a smell. Brendan pokes through several drawers before finally holding up a box of plastic sandwich baggies. He takes one out. "This'll be our milk bottle."

"That? How?"

"I'll cut off one corner, and he can suckle milk out of it like a teat." He measures spoonfuls of powdered milk into a measuring cup. "The first domesticated wolves were nursed by human women, did you know?" He smirks at me. "I doubt that would work with you, though." Mockery flashes in his eyes.

I swallow a sharp retort.

Brendan retrieves a flat kitchen scale from one of the bottom cupboards and sets it on the table. "Go on, put him on there before we feed him."

I lift the pup out of the pullover and carefully set him on the scale. Seeing him lying there helplessly on the steel plate, I realize for the first time just how small and scrawny he really is. His short fur is grey with a streak of cognac brown, sticking out from his body on all sides. His ears are tiny, and his little eyes are barely open.

"Hurry, he's getting cold," I say, wishing I could scoop the pup into my arms again.

Brendan pushes a button. "Seventeen and a half ounces," he mutters grimly. "Way too scrawny. Wolf puppies normally weigh that when they're first born, and this one must be three or four weeks old."

"How can you tell?" Without asking permission, I pick the pup up and wrap him in the fleece pullover, so that only his head is sticking out.

"His eyes are open, so he's more than two weeks old. Plus he reacts to sounds. Watch." Brendan makes a throaty noise that sounds a lot like a wolf howl. Immediately, the small animal on my lap starts whining. "See? They don't start doing that for at least three weeks."

"You're scaring him," I protest, twisting to one side protectively.

Brendan laughs. "This guy? Nah." He turns away again, because the kettle's whistling. The whining gets louder. It's like the pup is putting all of his strength into calling for help. Maybe he thinks the kettle is his mother.

Brendan takes the kettle from the stove and prepares the milk in the measuring cup. "Believe it or not, there are people and animals in the world that aren't scared of me."

I scritch the tiny wolf's soft fur, and his whining gets quieter, but doesn't stop entirely. "Don't worry," I murmur, "you'll get your food in a minute." He has to drink, he has to. "Do you think he'll tolerate the milk?" I ask Brendan.

"Hopefully. The first question is whether he'll drink it at all. He's pretty weak." A shadow flickers on his face, so briefly that I wonder if I just imagined it. "Sometimes wolf mothers bury their young. Actually, though, they only do that when they think the pup is dead."

"Maybe she was about to bury him but something startled her."

Brendan shrugged. "Maybe. Or else the mother wanted to move to a new den." He adds cool water to the mixture, pours the milk from the cup into the plastic bag, and knots it at the top. "Hold this for a second." He hands me the bag and removes a key from the carabiner on his belt, which he uses to open the cabinet above the side door, so far overhead that I'd have to climb on the counter to reach it... which would be a real challenge with the chain, so it's one of the few cupboards and cabinets I haven't tried to search.

Curious, I peer over Brendan's shoulder and spot a couple of brown bottles along with an arsenal of tools. Is that where he stashes the knockout drops? Or anything else that would help me keep him in check so I can run? My heart starts beating faster. I haven't thought about escape for so long, or rather I've been assuming it'd be impossible because he never makes mistakes. But maybe I can manage to break that cabinet open. Yeah, right, I'm sure he wouldn't notice a thing like that! I force myself to suppress that faint glimmer of hope, that tiny spark dancing around within me... but the more I try to squelch it, the stronger it gets. Suddenly I remember that one of the cartons in the storage space was marked *Hunting*. Maybe he has more weapons in there?

I'm so lost in thought that it takes me a moment to realize Brendan's looking at me. His eyes are full of shadows, dark and unfathomable, like the depths of the ocean. He knows I saw those bottles, plus he's holding a pair of scissors now, which I assume he also got from the cupboard.

"Give me the bag," he says, but the look on his face says something else entirely. *Don't you dare even think about it.*

My fingers tremble as I hand him the milk and watch him bore a tiny hole in one corner. He sets the scissors on the table and pinches the opening closed. "That should do it," he murmurs. He gives me a questioning glance, though his expression is still darker than usual. "Do you want to feed him?"

I look from Brendan to the whimpering ball of fur and then back again. "Can I?"

"Why not?" He smiles briefly, as though trying to drive the

shadow out of his soul, but he doesn't quite succeed. "If you're doing that, you can't exactly run away, can you?" The flatness of his tone gives me chills.

"No," I mumble, taking the bag with both hands—and then I'm not sure what to do, because I need one hand to hold the corner closed.

"Want help?" Without waiting for a response, Brendan sits down beside me. It's the first time he's done that, and instinctively, I scoot away. He acts like he doesn't notice. "Put the open corner to his mouth and drip the milk onto his upper lip. A few drops should be enough."

I put the bag to his tiny, still mewling muzzle and release the opening. Milk drips out. Brendan quickly reaches for the pup's head and turns it, so that the milk flows onto his upper lip from the side. Immediately, I feel tiny paws moving against the pullover, and the whining gives way to sucking motions so hectic that the milk ends up dripping all over his face.

"Try this." Brendan flips the pup onto his belly. "Hold the bag at an angle."

I lift the baggie again. The little wolf is frantic with excitement. He suckles and suckles, and when he realizes he's really, actually getting food, he starts to calm down.

"His heart's racing," Brendan says quietly, as though he doesn't want to disturb the pup. "But he's doing well."

"Yeah." I can't take my eyes off the tiny animal.

"You're smiling. For the first time."

The corners of my mouth sink as though he's caught me doing something I shouldn't.

Again, Brendan pretends not to notice. "You should give him a name," he suggests. He's still sitting next to me, holding the pup to help him drink.

"No." I avoid his gaze and squeeze the bag gently to help the milk flow. "I can't name him if I know you might drown him."

"That's exactly why you should name him." He sounds like he genuinely means it.

"Why?"

"You want him to die without having a name?"

173

"Names just make it harder. Names bind you to things. Names give them meaning."

"If he doesn't have a name, that means he isn't important."

The remark gives me pause. Somehow it doesn't seem like something Brendan the Kidnapper would say. I watch the pup suckle on the baggie, propped upright in Brendan's grip.

"Maybe not necessarily 'Princess,'" Brendan adds.

"So he's a 'he' for sure?"

Brendan nods.

The bag is nearly empty now, and the pup's eyes fall shut. In slow motion, Brendan puts him back into the pullover, and I tuck him in.

"How do you know so much about wolves?" I ask, even though I don't actually want to talk to him.

"I spent a few summers out in the wilderness. Some of it I read, but a lot of things you can only learn from experience."

I probably don't want to know what drives a person to start living all alone out in nature. It probably has to do with his past. "Do you think he'll make it?" I ask instead. At that exact moment, the little wolf starts retching.

"Dammit." Brendan picks him up so he won't choke. "Hopefully he doesn't have roundworms."

The pup spits up the milk with a wheezing cough. It spills over Brendan's hands and drips onto the floor. He's a pitiful sight, hanging there in Brendan's grasp, lethargic and limp, closer to death than life.

"I think there's probably no point." Brendan pets the wolf pup's head. "He's already too weak to keep milk down."

"Maybe we gave him too much," I protest. "He just can't drink that much at once."

Brendan shakes his head, pressing his lips. "Sorry. I don't think this little guy's going to live."

"You're not giving him a chance!" Tears suddenly spring to my eyes. "You don't even want to try!"

"I just don't want him to suffer."

"But *I'm* suffering, and you don't care about that. You haven't drowned *me* in the lake yet."

Brendan flinches; his eyes darken. "That's different," he snarls at me furiously.

"No, it isn't. Give him a chance! Please!" My lips are trembling. I don't know why I'm so desperate for the little wolf to make it. Maybe because then I won't be so alone. Because I'll have someone to talk to, even if he doesn't understand me.

"Lou..." Brendan regards me attentively for a moment, and then looks down at the tiny, miserable bundle.

"Please, let's just try! I'll feed him every hour if I have to. A few drops each time. He can sleep in my bed, and I'll carry him around and keep him warm."

"Maybe I should get sick one of these days, too..." Brendan puts in dryly and then hoists the pup to eye level. "What do you think, big fella?"

"Bren! Please!"

He sighs deeply. "Okay. We'll try it for one day. But if he's not doing any better after that, I'm going to put him out of his misery."

"Three days!" I counter. "One isn't enough."

Brendan puts the pup into my arms again and washes his hands. "Two. And you give him a name."

I scratch the pup's ears. "Grey," I blurt out.

Brendan turns and raises an eyebrow. "Grey? Why Grey?"

I lean in and bury my nose in the pup's fine, fluffy fur. "It's the name of a story my brother wrote for me." I don't know why I'm revealing that information to Brendan. It seems wrong to tell him even more about me, when he already knows so much about my life. At the same time, though, it feels like I'm filling a need I didn't know I had until now. Maybe I'm building a bridge out of my loneliness. From me to him via Grey. Or maybe I'm telling him as a way of thanking him for giving Grey two days instead of just one.

When I look up, I find my eyes meeting Brendan's again.

"Jayden?" he asks quietly.

Of course he knows which of my brothers writes stories. I must have mentioned it in a Facebook post, or else he found it out for himself by spying on my brothers. If he went that far.

I merely nod.

"Okay, Grey it is," Brendan declares. Then he explains how to

175

prepare the milk. Only water from the plastic bottles, he warns me, because the tap water is chlorinated.

"I'll start keeping the propane on all the time," he says. "I've been turning it off whenever I leave you here by yourself."

"Why?" Grey falls asleep again, nestled against my hand. I hope he kept down a little of the milk.

"In case there was a gas leak, or there was a problem with the stove. If the gas got out, it would be dangerous in here... and for everything around the camper, of course. I didn't want to risk you getting hurt."

"So what are you going to do now?"

Brendan looks at Grey, and his eyes fill with something I can't quite identify. Longing? Sadness? A specific memory? As usual, when he starts talking, the feeling is gone again. He never allows himself to show his other face. "If you really want to feed him every hour, you'll have to use the stove," he says. "Which means I can't turn off the gas." He points to a small, white box at the base of one of the kitchen cupboards. "That's a propane gas detector. Gas is heavier than air, which is why it's not on the ceiling like a smoke detector. If there's a gas leak, it'll go off, and then you have to get out of the camper immediately."

I lift my shackled wrist demonstratively. "I'm not going to get far."

"I suppose I can stop putting out traps for the next couple days. And if we save water, I won't have to keep fetching more."

"Or you could leave the chains off for two days, right?" I force myself to smile. It's like biting into a lemon. Sour and painful, as if my own muscles are trying to go on strike.

"So you can run away again the first chance you get, and put yourself in danger?" He shakes his head firmly. "No, thanks."

"You'll just have to trust me. The way I trust you to not hurt me." *Dammit, Lou, smile!*

"My trust is earned. I don't just give it out." He leans casually against the counter, but his expression remains hard.

"Then give me a chance to prove myself. No chains for two days." I tilt my head, trying to remember how cute I thought he was back at the visitors' center, and to look at him the way I did then. "How else are you going to find out whether I'm trustworthy?"

Nothing about his expression changes. "You're not fighting fair. And you know it."

"What's fair, anyway?" I hate the way my voice is cracking. This conversation is wearing me out more than I expected, even though it's just words, just a bunch of plain old words strung together.

Brendan turns away and opens a cupboard above the sink, mumbling to himself the way he always does when he's searching for something specific. After a while, he reaches into the back corner, which I hadn't managed to get at, and pulls out a couple of small bells.

"What are you going to do with those?" I arch an eyebrow. "Tie them around my neck like a dog?"

Brendan's face remains stiff. "Something like that." He leans toward the cupboard again and withdraws a pack of cable ties. "The bells will tell me where you are at all times, so you can walk around outside—they'll keep you safe from bears. I was planning on doing it this way from the beginning, but you were more difficult than I expected..." A thin smile plays on his lips.

I briefly picture myself punching him square in the face, but I manage to make myself calm down. "So you're going to put the bells on me and then I don't have to wear the chain?"

He nods. "We'll try it this way for the next two days. Not at night, obviously."

"What if I have to feed Grey at night?"

"While I'm awake, that's no problem. Otherwise I can chain you in the kitchen."

"Good idea," I say a shade too cheerily, and get a cynical smile in response.

Even so, it's still a victory. My first victory. And his first mistake.

THIRTEEN

I pour some lukewarm milk into a sandwich bag and tie it at the top. It's well after midnight... maybe four or five in the morning, I don't know. I'm starting to realize how short the nights are in Canada—the sun doesn't properly set until almost ten, and it rises again maybe five hours later. A half-moon peeks out overhead between the treetops, pale in the thin strip of visible sky, which is already beginning to turn a soft orange. Luckily tonight isn't as cold as most nights, because Brendan's got the side door and all the windows wide open, probably to air out the stench of wolf and puke. Now the whole camper smells like rosin and spruce needles. It sort of reminds me of the sage ointment Jayden and I had to use when we had coughs.

Baggie in hand, I walk back to my bed. I've built a little hollow for Grey, with a towel underneath him and the blanket rolled up in a ring around him, like an igloo without a roof. Whenever he's awake, he whimpers so pitifully that I wish I could keep him snuggled against my body so he'll know he isn't alone... but I can't, because I need both hands to get these milk baggies ready for him.

He needs to gain weight. I know it's selfish, but I want him to stay here with me. It's the thing I want second-most in the world. After my freedom.

Carefully, I hold the baggie to his mouth, and he starts suckling immediately. I let him have a bit more this time—I started him on ten gulps, and I'm increasing it gradually. So far, he's kept everything down.

My arms jingle as I squeeze the milk through the tiny opening for Grey. Brendan threaded some small bells onto cable ties, like pearls on a string, and then put one cable tie around each of my wrists, so I sound like a court jester every time I move. It's still nice to be free of the chains, though. Now that Brendan's taken them off, I can truly appreciate how obnoxious they were. Now I don't have to watch out to make sure I don't trip on them or get caught on stuff. Not to mention the whole constant, burning awareness of being chained up, of being a prisoner.

Grey keeps suckling on the empty bag, kicking against the blanket with his tiny paws, maybe hoping it will stimulate the flow of more milk. He's so small. Carefully, I unroll the blanket and lie down next to him, nestling my head against his so that he can feel my hair. When I was little and my dad was still alive, I found a kitten underneath some sagebrush, probably barely two months old, and somehow I managed to convince Dad to let me keep it. Every night when I went to bed, the kitten would snuggle in by my hair and purr, probably because my hair reminded it of its mother's fur. If Brendan hadn't cut my hair, I'd be able to cover Grey in it now.

I draw him closer and cover him gently with my hand, scritching his thin pelt. "It's okay, Grey," I whisper in the most comforting tone I can manage. "I'll make sure he doesn't drown you. He wants you to make it too, I know it. Even if he doesn't say so."

Grey doesn't start whimpering again. Maybe he's fallen asleep.

I allow myself to shut my eyes for a minute, too. The egg timer Brendan gave me is going to go off in an hour, and then I'll have to do the whole thing again, put the kettle back on and mix some more milk. I turn over what I just said about Brendan in my mind. Deep down, I think I genuinely believe it. *Good people do good things*, he said earlier. He found Grey and brought him home. He could have simply left Grey in the wilderness, knowing some other animal would eventually eat him, but he brought him here. Either to raise him, or to put him out of his misery. I think he probably would have done the same thing if he'd been out here alone. He just does what he thinks he needs to do. He didn't cut my hair to be cruel; he did it because he was trying to make me less afraid. Although I'm not all that convinced by the argument that a guy wouldn't chop off a girl's hair if he was planning on having his way with her, I do buy that he was doing it as more of a symbolic gesture. Weirdly, it didn't even make me mad when he did it, because I *did* buy his explanation—and I actually *was* less afraid afterward. As much as I hate to, I have to admit that not everything he does is completely terrible.

Grey burrows his head deeper into my hair, and his tiny muzzle nudges my ear.

"It's okay, Grey, I'm here," I whisper, and the bells jingle as I adjust my hand. Grey's breathing is even, and he seems to be keeping the milk down again this time. He's going to pull through.

I keep my eyes closed, but I can't sleep. A whiff of cigarette smoke wafts in through the open window, along with the sound of the campfire crackling. Every once in a while, I hear Brendan put another log on. I listen closely for the howling wolves we've heard on so many other nights, but tonight they're silent. I wonder whether Grey's mother was part of that pack, or if her pack was just her and her mate and Grey's siblings, which is what Brendan thinks. I feel Grey's warmth against my ear and cheek, and for the first time in weeks, I don't feel quite so alone. I even manage to doze off, and when the timer goes off, I startle upright.

"You can sleep a while longer," I hear Brendan say. "I'll put the kettle on." I blink sleepily at him and then at Grey, who's awake because I moved and is turning his little head back and forth, searching for me. Immediately, I lie down beside him again and snuggle my hair against his head.

"Tomorrow, I'll cut up a bedsheet and make a sling so you can carry him like a baby," Brendan says. When I hear the words "cut up," I remember the scissors in the overhead cabinet.

I nod, but inside, I make myself a promise: I'm going to nurse Grey back to health and pretend like I'm coming to terms with this whole situation. Grey will even help me with that, because I actually do feel better when he's around. And while I'm taking care of Grey, I'm going to work out a new escape plan, a super well-thought-out one that will work. I just have to get Brendan to stop putting the chains on me. For good, I mean. I can't run right away, of course; I have to wait it out, to make him trust me more and more.

I pet Grey softly. "But first you have to live," I murmur quietly to him.

When Grey's two-day reprieve is up, Brendan takes the scale out of the kitchen cupboard. I'm so anxious I accidentally bite the inside of my own cheek.

"Put him on," Brendan orders, his expression perfectly neutral. His lips are thin and hard, his eyes impossible to read.

My hands shake as I place the bundle of fur that will someday be a wolf onto the tray. Grey drank plenty of milk, but he had some mild diarrhea, too. Now I'm afraid he's lost too much water, or that he'll stop keeping the milk down.

"You need to let go of him, Louisa."

It's so hard to take my hands away. I feel like I'm abandoning Grey when he needs me.

Brendan pushes the button on the side of the scale. His eyebrows drift upward, and I detect a hint of a smile on his face. "He's gained eight ounces," he says, sounding relieved. "That's really good."

"It is?" I ask in a trembling voice. I'm not letting myself get my hopes up. Apparently, I'm getting to be a real pro at that, because now I genuinely can't believe I'm hearing good news.

Brendan nods, and I see the rigid mask fall away from his face.

"So you're not going to drown him?" I reach for Grey, but Brendan gets there first, picks him up, and puts him in my arms.

"No. I think he's turned a corner. Now all we can do is hope he keeps gaining." His eyes shift from me to Grey. "You should probably go on feeding him frequently for a few more days. Every two hours, maybe. I'll help if you want—I can do part of the night shift."

I blink, sleepy but relieved. I've barely slept in two days, and I'm only now realizing how much my bones ache. "Sounds good," I say, forcing myself to keep my tone breezy. "It'd be great to get a few hours of sleep in a row again."

Brendan regards me quizzically—surprised by the ease in my voice, maybe. "Okay, I'll take the second half of the night, then."

Should I mention the chain? Is it too soon to ask for that? Will he get suspicious? Maybe I should be patient about that.

"Do you want to eat outside with me tonight?" Brendan asks as he puts the scale back in the bottom cupboard. "We could drink to Grey's will to live." He straightens up and turns his gaze to me.

My stomach does a flip-flop, and I feel the blood draining from my face. Maybe hearing me use a friendly tone of voice makes him think he's going to get lucky. Or is he expecting gratitude because of Grey?

"Hey, Lou." He pulls on a too-long strand of my hair—not hard, but not gently, either. "It's just eating and drinking a toast. Maybe laughing a little. That's all."

"Eating and toasting," I echo, forcing myself to concentrate on not clutching Grey too tightly. "Okay. If you promise not to put anything in my drink."

Brendan's expression darkens immediately. "I thought we were past that."

"And I thought you weren't going to touch me," I say in a tight voice.

He holds up his hands in a placating gesture, palms out. "Sorry, I was just joking. And it was only your hair."

"Bad joke."

"I agree. I shouldn't have provoked you."

We lapse into silence for a while.

"So what do you think about this evening?" Brendan asks, sounding for all the world like a boy trying to get a date.

"Only if you don't put the chain on me," I blurt out before I can stop myself. "Um, I mean... because it's been two days, and... you said two days..." So much for patience. I'll have to do better than this when it comes to my escape plan.

Brendan shrugs almost nonchalantly. "I was planning to start leaving them off during the day anyway. At least while Grey's going to need to be fed. After that, we'll see."

FOURTEEN

I'm pretty much only focused on Grey until afternoon, though that doesn't keep me from asking myself a few basic questions. What supplies will I need in order to escape into the wilderness, and how do I collect them without Brendan noticing? I wish I could sit down and make a list, but I'm afraid Brendan would find it. Maybe I could put it in my closet, tuck it in among the newspaper articles. Brendan's never looked in there. Why would he? On the other hand, do I know for sure that he doesn't check up on me? He may have rummaged through there while I was in the bathroom or something. Then I have another idea: I could carry the list around with me, since he's promised not to touch me.

I peek outside through the open side door. Brendan's not far from the camper, gathering tinder for the fire. He prefers dry birch bark when he can find it, but there's nothing in this area but spruce, pine, and a couple of larches. I doubt he's about to go down to the lakeshore and leave me here by myself for that long.

I look down at Grey, who just finished some milk and is slumbering peacefully in the "baby sling" Brendan fashioned from an old sheet. Moving as cautiously as I can, I open one of the kitchen drawers. Plastic forks, knives, and spoons that Brendan washes and reuses, plus a couple of dull butter knives and a can opener that's not particularly sharp. No pens, no pencils. I'm pretty sure I've already gone through every drawer in here and haven't found anything usable, but this is also the first time I've gone looking for a pen. I open the next drawer: sandwich baggies, trash bags, spices, kitchen rags. I hesitate. Brendan probably doesn't count the sandwich bags, and I'm going to have to keep my escape supplies somewhere. But where do I put the bag? Under the mattress? But what if Grey pees on it again and Brendan wants to re-make it?

I pull out a baggie, close the drawer, and stuff the baggie into the wardrobe underneath the newspaper articles. My fingers brush the dry paper. I'll need to make the list somewhere. As if on autopilot, I slide the bottom article out from the pile. I folded it so that the article itself is on the inside. Carefully, very carefully, I tear a small strip off the edge. It'll have to do. I can only take a few essentials with me, just what I'll need to survive in the wilderness. And what I absolutely cannot do is think about all the things that could go wrong. I don't have any idea where I am. I'm not even sure how many miles it is back to the main road Brendan turned off from. Plus, I've never been alone in the forest. If I get lost, I'll probably freeze to death or die of thirst or... No, if I start seriously thinking about potential what-ifs, I'll lose my nerve.

I fold the scrap of paper and stick it into my jeans pocket. Then I stand at the wardrobe uncertainly, still holding the rest of the article. I don't know why, but something forces me to unfold the page. Ethan stares back at me. *STILL MISSING*, it reads underneath in giant letters, and beneath that, *Louisa's brother holding out hope.*

I don't bother with the article itself—I just stare at Ethan's face. His heartbreakingly thin face, his sunken cheeks, the dark rings under his reddened eyes. He's lost at least twenty pounds. His skin looks as thin as vellum that might tear the next time he moves. And he looks like he'll never be able to laugh again, never crack another smile.

Tears blur my vision, and I'm almost glad of it. Ethan looks so haggard—almost like worrying about me is literally eating him up inside. Like it's too much for him to handle. Like life is too much for him.

That's when, for the first time ever, I really and truly understand how much he's already been through in life. First he lost Mom, then Dad. No wonder he was always so strict and hardly let me do anything: losing both of them made him vulnerable. He was terrified of losing someone else he loved. And then, out of nowhere, that nightmare became a reality. And from what I know of Ethan, he'll even blame himself. He insisted that I come camping with them. It's probably tearing him apart, thinking about how nothing would have happened to me if he'd just let me go to modeling camp with Ava and Madison instead. But he doesn't know how obsessed Brendan is with me. Brendan would have gotten me anywhere.

I tenderly run my hand over his printed face. All the horrible things I said to him about Mom and Dad seem a thousand times worse to me now. God, I must have hurt him so much.

"I'm coming back to you," I whisper hoarsely, blinking the tears away. "You're not going to lose me. I promise. I'll find a way back to you."

I fold the newspaper clipping without reading it and stick it back underneath the folded stack of pants. Then I stand on the bed, still cradling Grey in the sling, and forage through the overhead cabinet where Brendan put the "girl stuff." I'm pretty sure I saw tampons and pads and even makeup in there, the one time that I went through that cabinet. I've never used any of it, though—I didn't get my period this month, probably thanks to the stress, and makeup was pretty much the last thing on my mind. But now I rummage through the toiletries: pink and yellow nail polish, extra bottles of orange-blossom shower gel, blonde shampoo. Finally, I find some sky-blue eyeliner, brand-new, nice and sharp. I stick it in my pants pocket along with the bit of paper, and then carry Grey down from the bed with me.

I take a quick peek through the window. Brendan's still traipsing along the tree line with a bucket. I pull out the eyeliner and the thin paper strip again, and use the wall as a writing surface —carefully, so I won't smush Grey between my body and the wall. I write down everything that comes to mind:

Lighter
Birch bark
Water – bottle?
Food – cookies?

Warm clothes
Rain protection
Hiking boots/wear
Scissors/knife
Rope

I pause. There's no way I'll be able to hide all of that from Brendan. I'll have to have the warm clothes and the boots on already. I won't be able to carry a bunch of water bottles, either, so I should probably bring one empty bottle and refill it from the creek... or put creek water in a sandwich baggie, like we do with Grey. That would be the best. But is that water drinkable? I need to find out. And how do I know I'll keep finding water along the way? The rough forest road runs in a different direction than the water—but then again, I can't keep going parallel to the road anyway, because that's the direction Brendan will expect I've gone. He'll probably be driving up and down that road looking for me. So wouldn't following the water make more sense? It has to lead somewhere, and then I'm not just wandering aimlessly. That's probably the best plan.

I peek outside again. I don't see Brendan anymore—and I hear him walking directly beside the camper. Hastily, I tuck the eyeliner and the paper away.

"Hey, Lou," Brendan calls inside. "What do you want to eat tonight?"

I don't care, I'm about to say, but catch myself in time. "Spaghetti with tomatoes and pine nuts," I call out loudly. My heart's pounding in my throat. Please, God, let him not have seen me! How would he have, though?

"*Excuse* me?" My response seems to have surprised Brendan so much that now he's coming up the stairs into the RV. I hope I wasn't laying it on too thick. "Did I miss something?" He's in the hallway, peering back at me? Fine droplets of sweat gleam on his forehead, and the corners of his otherwise-stern mouth are turned up in a smile that actually reaches his eyes.

"I just thought maybe," I mumble, avoiding his intense gaze. "I'm getting sick of grilled stuff."

Brendan laughs. It sounds genuine this time. "Okay. If you help."

By evening, I've fed Grey a bunch more times, and I swear he's bigger than he was this morning. When I tell Brendan that, he merely grins in reply. Only later do I realize why. He probably wasn't smiling about what I said so much as about the fact that I spoke to him on my own initiative.

Later, he goes with me to the lake so that I can wash Grey's baby sling. He peed in it again, and it soaked through the towels I put down inside it. As I wash the cloth carefully, trying to keep the rest of the sling dry, Grey lies on Brendan's lap and watches me with his clear blue eyes. Brendan's sitting on the tree trunk by the shore, scritching Grey's ears. The pup looks perfectly content. He probably thinks we're his parents.

"If he keeps gaining weight, we'll be able to switch him to solid food soon," Brendan says thoughtfully. "Normally, once the pups reach eight to ten weeks, the parents feed them regurgitated meat."

I stop working the soft soap into the cloth and give him a sidelong glance. "If you think I'm going to puke bits of rabbit up for Grey, you've got another think coming," I say. "But you go right on ahead."

"Maybe I will!" Brendan takes a pack of cigarettes out of the breast pocket of his black linen shirt. The top two buttons are undone, revealing his smooth, tanned skin and a hint of his collarbone. Somehow everything about him is perfect, if there's such a thing as dark perfection. He regards me, squinting. Here in the pale daylight, between the trees and the water shimmering in the sun, his eyes glisten with that deep intensity, that strange mixture of strength and vulnerability, the way they did at the visitors' center. My stomach tenses up.

What if he hadn't kidnapped me? What if he'd just invited me out for a drink and then brought me home to my brothers?

His eyes never leave my face as he sticks a cigarette into his mouth with one elegant motion and then removes his lighter from his pants pocket—carefully, so he won't startle Grey.

I need that, I realize, and that thought drives the others from my mind. The lighter is the first and most important item on my escape list. Brendan is always talking about how essential fire is in the wilderness, even though we have the camper to protect us while we sleep. Not long after we got here, he told me about a group of hikers that got hopelessly lost in this part of Canada. One night, their fire died for some inexplicable reason, and they all froze to death.

At first, I thought Brendan was only trying to scare me, but now I believe he was telling the truth. We must be awfully far north, based on how early the sun rises and how late it sets. It has something to do with the Arctic Circle, if I remember my geography lessons correctly.

I gaze at the lighter as though hypnotized. "What are you going to do when you run out of cigarettes?" I blurt out. "Or lighter fluid?"

Brendan's face twists into that strange smile again. "I can also start a fire with two rocks, don't worry. But I brought plenty of extra lighter fluid, too. And as far as the cigarettes go..."

I can't meet his eyes any longer. I turn my attention back to the cloth in my hands.

"Don't you mean, 'When will you need to go to a grocery store?'"

I hear the lighter flare up, and the first cloud of cigarette smoke envelops me. "The smoke isn't good for Grey," I say in what I hope is a disparaging tone.

"He's not going to get lung cancer," Brendan replies dryly. "Wolves don't live that long."

I dunk the soapy cloth into the lake and swish it around. Maybe I should keep the conversation on the grocery store—at least then he won't start wondering if I'm planning to run off through the wilderness. Whatever I do, I have to make sure he doesn't suspect I might try to escape again. At any rate, now I know that he usually carries his lighter in his pants pocket, and that he makes sure it doesn't run out of fluid. I might be able to steal it while he's asleep. It shouldn't be a problem if my chain is long enough. And if he notices it's missing, he might assume he just dropped it somewhere. Maybe.

"So when will you need to go to a grocery store?" I ask casually, looking over at him. If this escape plan doesn't work out, that will be my next best chance.

Brendan takes what seems like an extra-long drag on his cigarette. "Never, if I put my mind to it."

"What?"

He must see the horror written all over my face, because his eyes turn another shade darker. "We have meat and wild herbs. Spruce needles for tea... raspberries, blueberries, rosehips... And not far from here, there's a wild meadow with edible berries you've probably never even heard of. In the winter, we won't need a freezer for the meat, because it'll be cold enough outside. And you can even eat the bast layer of some trees—that's the moist layer between the wood and the bark. Did you know that?"

Nope, but thanks for the tip, in case I'm ever in danger of starving while I'm running away from you!

"But what about toilet paper, soap, and pads?" I ask weakly.

"You can substitute cloth and natural products. People haven't always lived in this much luxury, you know."

"And water?"

Brendan points toward the lake. "Freshwater. There's plenty of it around here."

I keep my eyes on the cloth as I wring it out. "So you mean we can drink from the creek and stuff?"

"I've done it."

"We won't get sick?"

"There could be bacteria in it, but if it makes you feel better, we can boil it first. And I brought tons of disinfection tabs."

"Oh? I hadn't noticed." I go on wringing out the cloth. My stomach is twisting in knots. He's so perfect. And I'm so naive and confused about my escape plan.

I don't think Brendan senses how nervous I am. "We haven't had to use them yet. I still have gallons and gallons of water in the storage hatch."

I stand up, knot the sling, and slip it on again, arranging it so that the wet spot is against my back, between my shoulder blades. "Can I have Grey?"

Brendan stands as well, holding a cigarette in one hand and the wolf in the other. Grey hangs there in his hands, a helpless little bundle of life. "Sure."

I carefully transfer Grey back into the sling. He wriggles around, which is a good sign—he was mostly apathetic before. Eventually, he lands on his back with his short legs waving in the air clumsily. I flip him onto his stomach so he'll be comfortable, and then gather up my courage, preparing for what I'm about to say.

"I know where you found me." My voice is firm, and this time I hold his gaze.

Something like insecurity flickers on his face, but only for a moment, and then his usual superiority returns in full force. "Did you figure it out from the photos in the newspaper?"

I nod.

"Good." His tone is almost admiring, and for the first time he looks at me like I'm an equal, or at least like I'm someone he needs to take seriously, instead of just the cute, colorful butterfly flapping around helplessly in a cage, dependent on his kindness.

"I don't want to talk about that," I say. I don't even want to think about how he stalked me, how maybe he was looking at my pictures and touching himself, thinking about how my body would feel underneath his. I don't want any deep insights into his sick thought processes. But there's one thing I do need to know.

"How long did you spend preparing to kidnap me? When did you decide that you were really going to do it?" I'm amazed that my voice is steady. Maybe I'll understand him a little better once I know when and how he decided to kidnap me. If I want to get away from him, I have to know what makes him tick. It suddenly strikes me that I've barely given that any thought before, and it might be the key to my escape.

He regards me for a long time, seemingly trying to decide how to respond. "I wanted to have you. All to myself. Forever. Once I made up my mind about that, I started preparing. I estimated how much of everything I need for an average summer in the wilderness. And then I multiplied that by... a number you wouldn't like. And I added in everything girls need, plus what we'll need in winter. I'll probably realize over the next few months that there's something missing—but if I had to go pick it up after the fact, it wouldn't be the end of the world."

"And when did you decide to kidnap me?" His single-minded focus is starting to unnerve me after all.

"You suddenly disappeared from the Internet. It was like you'd left me. I couldn't allow that."

"My brother made me deactivate my Facebook account." As I say it, I suddenly understand what he meant weeks ago. *So I don't lose you again.* "You wouldn't have kidnapped me if you'd kept on seeing me on Facebook?" I wrap my hands around the outside of the sling to cradle the wolf-bundle.

Brendan takes a step toward me, and all at once, there's something threatening about him again. There's something in him that I don't understand, something dark. The thing that emerged the night of the thunderstorm. And I probably need to figure it out if I'm going to have a chance against him. Right now, though, it just terrifies me. I scoot away; twigs brush against my cheeks, and suddenly I feel a tree trunk at my back. My heart is racing.

"D-don't come any closer, please," I stammer in a thin voice.

He stops immediately, even steps back a few feet. Sunlight gleams on his dark hair. His expression softens so much that I can barely believe it's still Brendan. "I wouldn't put it quite that way," he says to answer my question. "I got the idea long before that, for a totally different reason."

"What... reason?" My voice is shaking.

"I'm obviously not going to tell you now, when you're already practically hyperventilating." He nods toward the camper. "We should go back and make dinner. If you still want to, I mean."

I lift Grey up inside the sling and press him close. "Yeah," I whisper. *But I don't want to, I have to.*

The walk back to the camper is unusually quiet. After a minute, I realize that only one of the many bells on my wrist is jingling. As Brendan pushes his way in front of me, I take a closer look at the cable-tie bracelet. The bells are full of water, and apparently it's keeping them from making noise. I can barely believe my luck. Now I know that I can not only drink the creek water, I can use it to escape silently. Discreetly, I release Grey and shake my arms a little at a time, so that the water will gradually run out of the bells before Brendan notices they're stopped up.

. . .

As Brendan puts the pasta water on to boil and I chop sun-dried tomatoes, my fear fades again, mostly because I'm keeping busy. Grey is crawling around in his pullover "nest" beside me, sniffing at the fleece. He's getting more animated by the hour. Every time I look at him, I have to smile. Brendan has noticed, too, and now he seems a lot more approachable.

"We still have to toast the pine nuts," he says.

"You want me to get them?" I ask in what I hope is a casual tone. I know they're underneath the camper.

Brendan raises an eyebrow suspiciously. "They're in a box in the storage hatch, right in front. The box says Kitchen 5 on it."

"Okay." I don't sound breathless, do I?

Brendan unhooks a key from his carabiner and hands it over as if it's the most natural thing in the world.

Without another word, I walk down the stairs and around the side of the camper. Past the *Travel America* logo. What if I just ran away now? It's late, the sun's already going down, the trees are like grey watchmen. I could dunk my wrist bells in the lake again and hide in the forest until Brendan comes out of his flashback. He'd go searching for me, but as soon as he left the area, I could come back and grab everything I needed, and then leave in a different direction.

It takes an inhuman amount of willpower to make myself unlock the rear hatch on the RV. *Not yet, Lou,* I tell myself as I open it. *Anyway, you're wearing flip-flops, how far do you think you'd get? Plus he might be watching you...*

I peer inside, reading the carton labels in the dim light. The one that says "Hunting" catches my eye immediately. It's near the back, all the way to the right, so I'd have to climb inside partway to get at it. On second thought, I've gotten more than enough new information for one day. Better not push my luck. This could be Brendan's way of testing me.

I open the box directly in front of me, which is labeled "Kitchen 5." Brendan must have reorganized everything in here, because the pine nuts were in a box near the back before. I know that because I remember the exact moment that he said he didn't have any fresh basil, but he had jars of garlic and pine nuts.

I discover gigantic quantities of flour, sugar, nuts, almonds, and trail mix. The smaller packets of pine nuts tumble around in between them. Where did Brendan get the money to buy all these supplies? What did he do for a living? Was he in college? Or did he pay for it with the money he won in that fight, the one where he killed his opponent? But he said that was three years ago. I haven't even been on Facebook that long. He must just have happened to have the money, then—he didn't go out and specifically earn it so that he could kidnap me.

I fish two packets of pine nuts from the box, close the hatch, and lock it.

When I turn to go, Brendan's face is right there, pale and ghostly in the semi-darkness.

"Took a while," he says quietly.

"I poked around in the box a little." I lift the pine nuts up demonstratively and then hand him the key. Hopefully he can't see how much I'm shaking.

"I just wanted to make sure you found the right box."

I walk past him, unbelievably relieved that I didn't try to run. I'm going to have to bide my time, get him to trust me more first.

We eat in silence—in the camper this time, because of all the black flies outside. Now I'm watching Brendan layer wood for the campfire and distribute tinder. I even help him for a few minutes, and once the first tongues of flame are flickering upward, he goes inside and returns with two beers.

He puts a can in my hand without asking, and then drops into his camping chair. I fed Grey before dinner. He fidgeted around in my lap as Brendan and I ate, but now he's asleep underneath a woolen blanket on my camping chair. Carefully, very carefully, I lift both blanket and furball, sit down in the chair, and settle Grey and the blanket across my lap.

Once I've opened the can, I slide my hand under the blanket and rest it on Grey. It's comforting. To him and me both.

"He does you good," Brendan says after a while. "Grey, I mean. You smile more often now."

I take a big gulp of beer. It tastes awful, dry and bitter, but I need the alcohol to loosen up. Ava and Madison and I have snuck a few hard lemonades or Lime-a-Ritas here and there, but I'm kind of a lightweight, so I have to make sure I only drink enough to relax, to work on getting him to trust me.

"He makes me feel less alone," I admit, sipping my beer. It's the truth.

"I can understand that." Brendan nods, and his face takes on that weird mysterious expression again. "I had a dog once. His name was Blackie."

"I guess he was black, then." I know it's a lame joke.

Brendan shakes his head. "He was a retriever mix, he was every color but black."

"So you were always kinda different, hm?" Even this small amount of alcohol is enough to make me bolder.

"How do you mean?" he asks, keeping his expression perfectly neutral.

I take another drink of beer, avoiding his eyes. "Um, I dunno, other people would have named him Goldie or Brownie or whatever. And other people would have asked me on a date, instead of kidnapping me... I assume you know I wouldn't have said no, right?"

"I wanted more than a date, though." His voice is gentle. I can almost hear him smiling.

But I don't want to live with you, I think, wishing I could say it aloud. If I want to find out more about him, though, I'll have to figure out who he is. My heart beats a shade faster as I ask my next question. "Why are you so afraid of being abandoned? How come you get flashbacks just from the thought of losing someone?"

Brendan stares at me, and I immediately regret asking. Maybe this is where he completely flips out and attacks me. *I'll kill you...* But he lowers his eyes, and his hands tense around the can. His hands that are capable of such terrible strength, it's like they've never known what tenderness is.

"I can't talk about it," he replies after a while, quietly but firmly.

A wave of something close to sympathy washes through me. I hate myself for it. For God's sake, he kidnapped me, I'm not about to start trying to see things from his point of view. "You can't, or you won't?" I ask.

His eyes are fixed on the pine needle-strewn ground. The fire crackles in the silence between us; now and then, a log bursts open in the flames with a loud crack-pop.

"Sometimes it's good to talk about things," I hear myself say. "It helps me a lot."

"I can't," he whispers, so quietly that at first I'm not sure if I imagined it. But then he speaks again, slightly louder this time. "I've tried so many times." He's still staring at the ground.

"Maybe you should start by just talking to yourself out loud about it," I suggest. "Without anyone else listening."

"Good idea, but it wouldn't work," he says with a smile so anguished, it's as if someone's whipping it out of him. "If I heard myself describing it all, it would be like I was raping myself, breaking every bone in my body, grinding myself into dust and ashes. I'd be nothing afterward."

I swallow. The things he's saying are hitting me hard, deep down where my tears are all waiting to burst out. I suddenly wish someone would come by and give him a hug, because I can't do it myself. Maybe that someone could fix him, and then he'd let me go. Maybe he really isn't such a bad guy, apart from kidnapping me.

I pet Grey, and it occurs to me that maybe Brendan ought to have him on his lap, warming him. The way he's sitting there now, surrounded by dark spruces, pale in the glow of the firelight, clutching the beer in his shaking hands, it's like there's a chill inside him that no warmth from outside could ever drive away. Like only an inner warmth could fill the emptiness at his core.

"When you say you'd be nothing…" I start cautiously, as though the words might literally break him. "Who… who are you now, Brendan?"

He lifts his head. "Someone who knows his strengths and weaknesses."

"So what are your strengths?" I think of Jayden. "If you could only name three, which would they be?"

"Determination, self-control, strength," he replies without hesitation.

"And your weaknesses?"

"The opposites of those."

I ponder. "So… indecision, helplessness, weakness?"

He nods.

"I don't think you know how my brothers described me, because I never posted about it on Facebook." I ignore his cynical smile, which has lost a lot of its usual superiority. "Ethan says I'm superficial, difficult, and don't use my head." I pause for a moment before continuing. "Jayden says I'm vivacious, insecure, and full of emotion. It's all the same, it's the light and shadow sides of the same character traits." I don't know where I'm getting this stuff. It's been locked away somewhere deep inside me.

"Maybe you're right." Brendan's gazing into the fire, the way he does so often. As though it's got the warmth he can't find inside himself. "But the shadows are always stronger than the light. When you turn on a light to drive the shadows away, all you do is feed them. It's like every glimmer of hope infuriates them... Isn't it weird how the things that are supposed to help you are what make it extra-clear how weak you are?"

I don't think anyone I know has ever been so honest with me, apart from maybe Jay. I'm not sure what to say, but I know I have to respond somehow. "Maybe the shadows aren't stronger," I muse. "Maybe the light just makes them easier to recognize, and what you see in them scares you, so you don't look. But maybe you should."

He smiles again, less anguished this time. More of a mixture of fascination and guilt. "You make it sound so easy. That's exactly why I wanted you, Lou. You're the light. You're like a sun. You were always so radiant in your pictures, like life was easy for you. You made it look like it could be easy for anyone, even for me. It was like you wanted to get everything you could out of life, without worrying about boundaries or limitations. You looked like you only expected the best in life."

I realize I'm more clinging to Grey than petting him. "You got all of that from my Facebook photos?"

"And the stuff you wrote."

"Wow, I really was the perfect victim," I remark bitterly. "I only expected the best of you, too."

"I'm sorry. I wasn't trying to take advantage of how you are... I mean, you're just... extraordinary, that's all."

"Never heard that one before."

"I'm surprised. I mean, you never knew your mom, and you lost your dad when you were young—sorry, yeah, I do know about that." He grins crookedly, as though stalking and kidnapping me is some cute little prank he pulled, but a moment later he's as serious as ever. "Other people would have complained about their terrible fate, having lost both of their parents. They'd have used it as an excuse every time they failed. You didn't, not once."

"I have my brothers. They're my family. I never wanted for anything."

"Yeah, because that's how you see things. Losing your parents never stopped you from jumping into life with both feet. You didn't waste time worrying about what you were missing."

"You're putting me in way too good a light. I wasn't missing anything. I grew up in a house full of love, everyone took care of me. You're wrong about me."

"Nah." He smiles and shakes his head. "I'm not. If there's anyone in the world who loves life, it's you."

I think about how dissatisfied I always was in Ash Springs, how much I hated being invisible to the rest of the world. It's like all of that happened in a different life, in another reality. The way I used to act suddenly strikes me as completely childish.

Even so, Brendan's not entirely wrong. I was never afraid to live, never afraid I might lose anyone. I always assumed the best about things, unlike Ethan who was worried about absolutely everything. Which is probably why I didn't understand him.

"We should stop talking about this for tonight," Brendan says, jolting me back to the present. "This is Grey's big day, right?" He points to my lap.

I nod, glad to change the subject.

"Why don't you tell me the story that you named him after?" Brendan suggests.

"You mean Jayden's story?" I take another large gulp of beer. The can's nearly empty.

He nods. In the bright light of the campfire, his eyes are black, glittering jewels. I've gotten closer to him tonight than ever. I like the idea of telling the story because I'll feel close to Jayden again, but it seems wrong to tell it to Brendan, the person who's keeping me away from my brothers. Then again, he's revealed a lot about himself tonight, if not anything concrete. And there's this faint voice in the back of my mind that says he did it so that I won't be as scared of his shadowy side, because he generally doesn't enjoy talking about himself at all.

"Okay," I finally make myself say before I can change my mind. "The name of the story is *Grey*, but it's about a Native American boy, not a wolf."

Brendan puts a cigarette between his lips and leans back with an expectant look on his face.

"I'm not really a very good storyteller," I add, "but this one I pretty much know by heart."

"I don't remember anyone ever telling me a story, so I don't think I'll notice if you do a good or bad job." He nods to me, and I spend a moment gathering my courage and strength and all the words I'm going to need for Jayden's story. Then I just start talking, picturing myself in the middle of the tale, with its magical scent in the air and its unique melody in my ears—I think that's about how Liam would put it.

"Once upon a time, many summers and winters before the ships of the white man brought death to the area around the Big Muddy River, a small tribe of Lakota lived near the river valley. It had lush forests of tall, white sycamores, thick-trunked oaks, and chestnuts as far as the eye could see. Every clearing was carpeted in red flowers, and in the autumns the trees glowed yellow and red like torches.

"The other Lakota had light-brown skin, but this particular boy was born grey, like, literally totally grey from head to toe. A pale grey, like ashes. His mother named him Delsin, which meant 'he is so.'"

"She didn't call him Grey, even though that's the name of the story?" Brendan breaks in.

I give him an admonishing frown, like a schoolteacher to a student. Blame the beer. "No. She knew that, looking how he did, he would never get a better name, so before the other children could start calling him Dead Skin or Grey Face, she picked Delsin, to show that she accepted him the way the Great Spirit had made him. Young Lakota were allowed to pick a new name for themselves after performing a heroic deed, but she was afraid that would never happen. Even when he was only five, his ashen skin made him seem like an old man. The girls were afraid of him and hid from him, and the boys excluded him and threw stones at him whenever he tried to play with them."

"This is a sad story," Brendan remarks.

I glance at him. He's listening with rapt attention. I realize how lonely he must have been as a child, if this is the first time anyone's ever told him a story. "When Delsin was six years old," I continue, "his mother died giving birth to his sister, so he had nobody left who loved him."

This is the first time I realize that Jayden wove part of his own story into this one. His—our—mom died giving birth to me, his sister.

"Delsin's father, the chief of the tribe, was ashamed of Delsin. He wanted to drown the baby at birth, but the medicine man foretold that it would bring great unhappiness to the tribe if the chief drowned his firstborn son like a deformed dog. But whenever the warriors of an allied tribe came over to plan attacks or negotiate trades, he would say to them, 'That is not my son. He was sent to us by the Great Spirit, and I must accept this fate and raise him.' But he never brought Delsin along on hunting or raiding parties, not even when Delsin had become a man and it became time for him to prove himself so that he could find his place in Lakota society. His sister, Alaska—which means 'where the sea breaks upon the shore'—avoided him as well, because she was afraid that the others would exclude her along with him, and then she would never find a man to take her into his wigwam.

"So Delsin was left by himself, and became a grey shadow that slipped from the village to the forest to the meadow lowlands unseen, like a ghost. His father put one bowl of beans in front of the wigwam for him each day. Delsin only crept inside at night to sleep, and rose long before his father so that he would not taint his sight, as the chief always said.

"Eventually, even Delsin began to believe that he was only a shadow, a grey shadow. Since the Lakota refused to speak to him, he went deep into the forest and began talking to the plants and animals. And the sunny days grew longer and longer, and one evening, he simply didn't return to the campsite beside the Big Muddy River. He was living by himself, but he was not alone—he spoke to the oaks and the sycamores, to the owls and the deer. He even spoke to the moon and the stars, because he had so much to tell, so many things he had heard and seen among the Lakota, but never understood. Beneath the great night sky, he spread out all of his stories, across the green-grey hilltops on the far side of the woods, and his words rose up and wove into the firmament like pictures. The moon he called 'yellow friend in the black ocean'; the stars he gave shimmering names that seemed to twinkle in his mouth when he spoke them."

"Like what?" Brendan asks.

"I asked Jayden the same question," I respond with a genuine smile. "He said he knew the names, but he couldn't say them or write them, because they were too beautiful, and if he tried, their letters would shatter like glass. For Delsin, the stars he named were droplets of silver that the Great Spirit had daubed into the sky. And sometimes, in his most secret dreams, he wished his skin was the color of the stars. Silver, rather than grey."

I look at Brendan. "When Jayden first told me this story, I hated him for not telling me the names."

Brendan laughs. A strange feeling creeps over me, and the longer I look at him, the stronger it gets. It's completely out of place here, fluttering like a butterfly under glass. It wants to fly off, but not necessarily to freedom. Whatever the feeling is, it horrifies me so much that I immediately push it back into the furthest recesses of my mind.

"When the animals came to him," I continue, "he gave them names according to their temperament. And after spending many, many winters living among them and talking to them, he suddenly found he could speak their language as well. It must have been an amazing morning for Delsin—imagine how he woke up and realized he understood the whispers in the forest around him! For Delsin, it was as though he'd awakened in a brand-new world. He ate nuts with the squirrels, he sang with the birds and the grasshoppers, he walked with the deer. And deep inside himself, he heard a voice saying, *This is how you are. This is your place.* Here, nobody laughed at him, nobody stared at him. All the animals spoke to him. At night, he listened to the music of the stars, watched his yellow friend the moon, and thanked the Great Spirit for finally giving him a home."

202

"Is that the end?" Brendan asks when I pause. He's like a kid—his eyes are even shining. I know I shouldn't be, but I'm moved at how simple little things are enough to make his eyes light up with joy.

I shake my head no. "The story's not over. Like I said, many winters and summers passed."

Brendan leans back again in his chair.

"Delsin could have been happy, but after a while, he started longing for a partner. He wandered back to his tribe's summer campsite, but kept himself hidden in the bushes. It seemed that everyone had forgotten about him completely. Nobody mentioned him, nobody used his name. His father and sister happily went about their day.

"Head hanging, he snuck back toward the forest, but then he came to the small stream, a tributary of the Big Muddy River. Several girls were there, fetching buckets of fresh water. Delsin froze as if he'd been turned to stone. He spent several days hiding in the bushes, but none of them noticed him. One of them was especially beautiful. She always came later than the others, but stayed longer. Her name was Istu, which meant sugar. Everything about her was sweet, from her small, full mouth to her smooth, black hair to her perfectly formed breasts that looked like they would fit right into Delsin's hands. After spending several days almost in a trance, he returned to the forest. He forgot the moon and the stars and the animals, and he wished he was not Delsin, more than he had ever wished for anything. He wished he were different, wished he had a name that was worthy of Istu. But he knew with every fiber of his being that that day would never come. He withdrew into the forest, grieving for something he would never have, and became very angry with the Great Spirit. The animals came to comfort him, but he sent them away in a rage. He told the moon they were no longer friends, and then he was all alone again. A grey, lonely shadow, just like before.

"But one cold morning, the call of an owl roused him. The owl was screeching about a massive army of warriors coming from the north, preparing to attack the Lakota. When Delsin heard that, his heart was filled with terror. He thought of Istu's sweet lips and her soft breasts. He hurried off, and a pair of does followed him, telling him about the enemy's plans, which they had heard during the night. The enemy tribe was going to surround the village, and then raze it to the ground in a single, terrible strike. They were going to steal the food the tribe had stocked for the winter, and they were only going to leave the unmarried girls alive.

"When Delsin heard that, he was furious, and he ran even faster. He traveled for three days and three nights. When he reached his old village, none of the others believed his story. They circled around him, shoving him and laughing at him. His father's friend, Istu's father, even proposed killing him, believing that Delsin had returned to bring a curse upon their people. He suggested that perhaps Delsin himself had revealed their location to the enemy out of revenge, because they had shut him out. But his daughter, Istu, stepped in front of Delsin and protected him from her father with outstretched arms.

"In that moment, Delsin knew that Istu's name was about more than just her sweet lips. She managed to persuade the Lakota to listen to Delsin. His father, the chief, demanded that he prove he could talk to animals, so Delsin spoke to a lame horse, and discovered that it was limping because it had stepped on a stone and developed an infected sore on its hoof—but the stone was too small to be visible from the outside.

"The Lakota were astounded. Delsin demonstrated his talent several more times, and the tribe was filled with respect, because none of them had ever learned to converse with animals. They began to set traps for the enemy, and brought their winter stock elsewhere to keep it safe. The women and children were brought to a neighboring tribe, whose young, able-bodied fighters joined the Lakota's own warriors. And thus the enemy arrived to find the village empty—and themselves surrounded.

"Not a single Lakota died that day, but the enemy warriors fell. It was a miracle.

"That evening, as the few remaining leaves on the trees glowed even redder than usual in the setting autumn sun, Delsin's father fell to his knees at his son's feet. 'I always denied that you were my son,' he said in a heavy voice. 'And I was right. I am not worthy to be your father. A man like you comes from the Great Spirit. Today, you saved our tribe. Without you, our people would have perished.' When he said that, the rest of the tribe sank to their knees as well, and bowed their heads.

"'From now on,' Delsin's father said, 'you will no longer be Delsin, Son of the Great Spirit, but Silver. For what is grey? Grey is silver that does not shine. And today you were radiant, Silver. Every person here saw it.'

"Tears sprang to Delsin's eyes, and he was not ashamed of it. He drew his father back to his feet and said loudly, 'My name is Delsin: He Is So. If I were not so, I would never have learned the language of the animals, and you would have perished, don't you see? I could only save you because I am so. My mother chose this name well.'

"And so Delsin kept his name. One month later, he took Istu for his wife beside the shore of the Big Muddy River, which today is called the Missouri. Istu, whose breasts and lips were sweet, but her heart was the sweetest of all."

With that, I end the story. The fire crackles between us, and in the distance I can hear the rushing waterfall. The pack of wolves we heard the first evening howls somewhere deep in the forest, so far away that it's only a notion of a sound.

Jayden said once that every story should leave behind a stillness, a moment of contemplation. Maybe that's what makes us both fall silent. Grey, on the other hand, suddenly springs to life on my lap underneath the blanket. He sniffs my hand and starts licking it like he's expecting milk to come out.

"Nothing in there, Grey," I say and giggle because his nose is tickling my fingers.

"You can stay there with him, I'll get the milk." Brendan stands up. He regards me for a moment, the story echoing in his dark eyes like a curtain of dreams. He hesitates.

"What?" I ask.

"Grey is silver that doesn't shine. It's the same, like the light and shadow sides of the same thing. Is that why you told me that story?"

"I told you that story because you wanted to hear it," I reply in astonishment. "If I'd been telling the story in order to make something specific happen, I'd have put in a part about Delsin kidnapping Istu."

"How would the story have ended then?"

Grey's suckling on my thumb, and I can feel his baby teeth, not sharp enough to hurt. "I don't know. That would have depended on Delsin."

Brendan raises an eyebrow, but doesn't reply. Then he takes the beer can from me and goes into the camper. Dishes clatter—he's probably washing them while he waits for the kettle to boil.

Suddenly, a piercing alarm echoes through the forest. It's so loud that I almost fall out of my chair.

"God fucking dammit!" I hear Brendan snap.

"What?" I call. Grey whimpers.

Through the open side door, I see Brendan reach toward the ceiling and shut the alarm off. "Just the smoke alarm!" Brendan laughs in relief. "For a second I thought it was the propane gas alarm."

"What would you have done then?" I ask loud enough that he can hear me. He said something about that once.

"I'd have had to turn the gas off, and you would have had to get yourself somewhere safe."

I sit there for a while, gradually realizing what he just said. *You would have had to get yourself somewhere safe...* what does he mean? "So where is that gas canister? I mean, in case the alarm goes off and you're not there?"

"It's in a compartment on the far side of the camper, about level with the side door. But don't go messing with it, or you might blow us both up."

Now he almost sounds like Ethan! My heart starts beating slightly faster. Not because he thinks I'm inept, but because for the first time, I finally have an idea for how I might be able to escape. Once I realize that it might actually work, I immediately feel completely calm—but there's also a heaviness in my chest, and I'm not sure why. I think about the feeling I got earlier when Brendan laughed. I try to call it up again, but I've buried it too deep, it's out of reach. Probably just as well. I definitely can't let myself get pangs of conscience over this. He made his bed, he can lie in it. If he hadn't kidnapped me, I wouldn't have to leave him. It's all his fault.

206

Even so, that butterfly under the glass bell jar keeps circling through my head—and part of me feels completely, totally empty.

Grey wriggles around on my lap, which is a nice distraction.

"You'll have to be there for him when I'm gone," I whisper and lift the blanket a few inches. Grey is still sucking and biting on my finger, kicking the inside of my hand with his little paws as if to say, *I'm hungry, right this second, don't go acting like anything else is more important.*

I have to smile. "Be there for him the way you've been there for me."

FIFTEEN

More time passes. The moon waxes and then wanes again. During the day, the air gets so hot that the heat shimmers between the trees. Even the chipmunks are only making their appearances in the cool of the morning and the evening, always hoping to snag a few crumbs.

Something's changed between me and Brendan. Not long ago, I started noticing changes in the forest itself, like how the needles on the trees were getting darker and the willow herb was shooting up. But those are just signs that it's midsummer; Nature's got that under control. The changes between me and Brendan are harder to pinpoint. He's still the kidnapper and I'm still the kidnapping victim, obviously. I wear the bell-bracelets during the day, and the handcuffs with the chain at night. The power dynamics around here are as clear as ever. And sometimes I still get scared of his dark side, still panic at the thought of him losing control of the shadow inside him, the way he did that night of the thunderstorm.

But those moments are fewer and further between now. Maybe I'm starting to accept him as he really is: not good, but maybe not pure evil through and through, either.

I've realized I sneak glances at him a lot when I think he won't notice. I look at his slim, sinewy body, at how the belt with the hunting knife fits around his narrow hips, at the pale scar on the back of his left hand, the same side as the leather armband with the silver coin. The day before yesterday, as we were piling up campfire logs, I finally caught a glimpse of the design on the coin. It's a bird with two different wings: one has normal feathers, the other branches out like a tree. I didn't get a proper look at it, because I didn't want to ask Brendan to show it to me. He wears the armband all the time, so it must be really important to him, like the charms on my pendant are to me. I wear the pendant constantly, even when I sleep or shower, and when it gets in the way during the day, I stick it under my shirt. Maybe Brendan associates the coin with some similarly painful memory. Maybe it has to do with the darkness in him, with his fear of abandonment.

Part of me thinks that I shouldn't care who or what made him into the person he is now, that I should go on hating him as much as I did in the beginning. I'm trying to, but for some reason it's not working anymore. If my escape plan works, I'm not even sure if I'll press charges. If I do, it will probably only be out of fear that he might get his clutches on me again.

But then there's this new, trembling part of me that wishes Brendan hadn't kidnapped me. That things between us had gone how they did with Delsin and Istu. Part of me wants to like him, to trust him... but no, he's my kidnapper, and obviously you have to hate your kidnapper. My escape plan is the only reason for me to have anything to do with him at all. I have to understand him better in order to outfox him.

I don't know why everything is suddenly so confusing. I'm probably letting his emotions influence me more than they should. Maybe I even pity him, as sick as that sounds. The logical part of my brain tells me it's wrong to feel anything but contempt for him, but I still can't quite shake it off. Sometimes I'm glad when I have another reason to be mad at him. Because he refuses to tell me what day it is or where we are, for example. I have no sense of time out here in the wilderness. It's like some kind of parallel universe— time, the forest, Brendan, everything. Like I'm living a life adjacent to real life, and I just have to find the portal to take me back to my old life.

I've started collecting spruce needles to help me keep track of the days. I could kick myself for not starting sooner. I'm dying to know what day it is, or at least what month. Otherwise I'm afraid I'll completely lose my grip on reality.

Brendan put *Hero of the Week* on a few days ago—reception was better this time—and I listened closely, waiting for them to announce the calendar week. "Ladies and gentlemen, that was Hero of the Week 30," or whatever. That's how David O'Dell always finishes every show. But Brendan shut off the TV before that tall blonde woman had finished talking, so I didn't get to hear that last, crucial sentence.

Later, I asked Brendan what the date was, but all he said was that time wasn't important anymore.

He's right, as far as day-to-day life in the wilderness goes. Every day is pretty much the same as every other. But I can sense how fast time is passing. I see it in the phases of the moon, and in Grey, who's getting bigger every day and now follows us, tumbling and bounding, when we fetch water or wash clothes. And I see it in my hair, too. It's growing steadily, though still not down to my shoulders yet. If hair really grows half an inch per month, it'll be winter before it's shoulder-length again. Brendan says winter lasts six months here, and spring and fall are short. Maybe it's just the approach of fall that's making me so nervous. Wherever we are in Canada, it's far enough north that it gets down near freezing at night. The days are getting shorter; the midday heat takes a long time to develop and then fades quickly, long before twilight.

Which means I don't have much time left to escape.

When I open my eyes this morning, the air is already scented with browning pancakes and fresh coffee. The spot by my head where Grey always sleeps is empty. I sit up and lean to the side, peering out. Brendan's sitting on the bench. He's wearing the hoodie he had on the day he kidnapped me. Same black cargo pants, too. Grey's on his lap, drinking his first helping of milk for the day. He doesn't have to be fed as often anymore, and now Brendan's the one who prepares his morning meals. I sit there quietly for a moment, studying Brendan's face. His dark-brown hair is up in a short pony-tail, and I can tell he's smiling. Faintly. Other people might not even recognize that it's a smile, but I know it is. When I realize how well I already know him, I try to make myself avert my eyes, but I can't. There's something about that smile that makes me sad and happy at the same time. I feel a dark, despairing flutter deep inside me, like some small, winged creature struggling to free itself from a drop of amber.

"Hey!" Brendan lifts his head and looks at me.

I startle, and the fluttering stops, as though the moth has folded its wings. It's still sitting there, though, trapped by something that won't let it out. I rub my face, pretend to be sleepy so Brendan won't notice how confused I am.

Without another word, he tosses me the key to the handcuffs. Every morning, he sets them on the table beside him so that he doesn't have to go through the whole process of unhooking them from his carabiner. He hasn't actually said so, but I think he does it so that I'll be free faster.

I unlock the chain and unwrap the neck scarf around my wrist. As I walk toward the bathroom, I inspect my hands and arms closely so that I won't keep staring at him. The wounds are all healed now; the last of the bruises has faded.

Once I've shut the door behind me, I start doing knee bends, as far down as the tight space will allow. Physical exertion seems to be a good way of driving away what's left of that fluttery feeling.

I feel more life returning to my body with each passing day, and since I'm eating regularly now, I think I'm almost as healthy again as I was before he kidnapped me. But I know I'm not in good enough shape to survive alone in the wilderness for days on end, even though I take every chance I get to move around: I help Brendan with whatever work needs to be done, run around the camper with Grey, and do gymnastics while Brendan's sitting by the campfire in the evening, drawing pictures he doesn't show me.

I decide to do more knee bends than usual today, but I stop at twenty-five so that Brendan won't wonder what's taking so long. If he discovers that I'm exercising, he might draw the right conclusions about why.

Still slightly out of breath, I wash my face with the blue soap, and then study it in the mirror. Still thin, but not as pale anymore. I look older than I did just a few weeks ago. I venture a smile, and it scares me—the face in the mirror is a complete stranger, and the smile looks fake, as fake as Brendan's laugh. Thinking about him makes me think of the feeling I got earlier, and I pluck at a stray strand of hair, suddenly deeply insecure about myself. For the first time, it actually bothers me that my hair is like this, a shock of blonde sticking out in weird directions. I haven't cared one way or another about my appearance, but all at once, I really want to look in the mirror and feel pretty again.

I open the door. "Do you have a pair of scissors I can use?" I call out.

"For what?" Brendan sounds surprised.

"I want to even out my hair."

"Check the closet."

What?

It takes me several seconds to process this new information. My fingers are suddenly quivering in excitement. The last time I looked through the shelves in here was just a few days ago—searching for stuff I might need when I escape, as usual. I grabbed a couple Band-Aids and stuck them in the plastic baggie I've hidden among my clothes. I couldn't quite work up the courage to steal an entire gauze bandage—I'll have to wait on that until a few hours before I'm planning to leave.

Now, when I open the closet, I see the scissors right away, sitting there on the bottom shelf.

As I snip my hair, I wonder whether this means Brendan trusts me now, or whether he's testing me. The urge to hide the scissors under my clothes is overwhelming, but obviously I can't do that. I scoop up the trimmed ends and toss them into the pedal wastebasket, and notice that the sink isn't draining properly. The tank needs to be emptied. Brendan's normally the one to do that, because I was too weak to carry full buckets to the creek. Today, though, I feel like I could do it. Anyway, that would give me a chance to scope out the area surrounding the creek unnoticed.

"The grey-water tank is full," I tell him immediately as I sit down on the bench with a cup of coffee.

"I know. There's standing water in the sink, too." Brendan reaches across the table to pass me Grey, whose little wolf's tongue immediately runs across my entire face, making me giggle. I set him on my lap.

"Looks good. Your hair, I mean."

"All I did was trim the ends." I wait for my shoulders to tense up the way they usually do when he comments on my appearance, but it doesn't happen. I don't know what to make of that, but I decide I'd better get back to my original plan rather than dwelling on it. I try to smile, hoping it looks more real than the one I did in the mirror earlier. "Want me to empty the tank later?" It comes out maybe a touch too sugary, and the smile might be overly sweet, too.

A suspicious shadow flickers across Brendan's face, though it could just be because I've never offered before. After hesitating for a long moment, he nods slowly. "I'll show you which levers to pull."

"I could carry the buckets to the creek, too. I think I'm strong enough." I give him an innocent look.

"Alone?"

I shrug like it's no big deal either way.

"Give them an inch, they take a mile," he says with a taunting smirk and rises to his feet. "Did you put the scissors back, or are you going to stab me in the neck with them later?"

"I put them back. You can check if you don't believe me." The scissors were a test. Of course they were.

One corner of Brendan's mouth twitches upward. "I will later... if you let me live that long."

As I eat, he threads the bells onto a new cable tie, the way he does every morning. I can feel him watching me as he does it. I keep glancing up at him, but then looking away just as quickly, like his gaze burns my eyes. There's that feeling again, the feeling of something inside me trying to break free, like millions of golden moths underneath a bell jar. Their wings are light, so light, but they can't get out. I don't know what the hell is wrong with me. Cheeks burning, I force myself to keep my eyes on my pancake.

"Done," he says after a few minutes.

Confused as I am, I still extend my wrist automatically—the usual routine—and he pulls the cable tie gently, like he's putting a piece of jewelry on me. When his hand brushes mine, my stomach tenses in shock. Not from the touch itself, but from the faint puff of air that seems to explode on my skin, tingling. I just sit there for a few seconds, so confused I'm almost light-headed. I can't look at him, even though I can tell he's waiting for me to. Instead, I pet Grey, who's still lying in my lap.

"Lou?"

"What?"

"Stop running."

My heart nearly stops. The golden feeling inside me collapses, leaving a strange darkness in its wake. "I'm not trying to escape," I lie, but my voice sounds too squeaky.

A moment later, his hand is underneath my chin, and he's lifting my head, forcing me to look at him. "That's not what I mean," he says, sounding tense.

I'm not sure if I'm relieved or horrified by his answer. His eyes are large and wide, the pupils flooding out over the brown. I stare into them, letting the waves crash over me, giant tsunamis dragging me under. *Do you want this?*

All I'd have to say is *yes* and he would kiss me. Then right and wrong would officially be switched around forever.

My heartbeat is thundering through my head. Hundreds of wings are beating inside me like a sea of fans, but I still don't have enough air to breathe.

"You said you... weren't going to touch me... not like this..." I whisper, sounding frightened. Frightened of my own feelings, not of his.

He withdraws his hand, but I can still feel the pressure of his fingers, the echo of his touch. It was neither gentle nor hard, but my chin is still burning like it's on fire.

I take a deep breath and force myself to keep eating breakfast as though everything is normal, even though every cell in my body is in chaos. I can't make heads or tails of what I feel or why I feel it or anything. It's one big tangled mess.

But there's one thing I do know: I need to get away from here before whatever this feeling is gets any stronger.

I stay sitting there, clutching Grey in my hands, and I don't start breathing normally again until Brendan goes outside.

I make myself a mental deadline. Three days. I can't wait longer than that. I can do without most of the things on my list. The only thing I definitely need is the lighter. The scissors can take the place of the knife. They're pretty sharp. I've got the Band-Aids, and I can get gauze. I tell myself that I don't *only* need to escape because of Brendan—I mostly need to get going while it's still summer. But deep down, I know that the thing I'm most afraid of is that dark, frantic fluttering inside me. I've never been so terrified of a feeling.

Involuntarily, I clench my fists, though there's nothing specific for me to fight against. A few weeks ago, I'd have punched Brendan in the face if I'd gotten the chance, if I'd been strong enough. Now I've run out of hate. I don't even feel contempt for him. I'm desperately searching for reasons to see him as a monster, but he's just not. When I think about him, all I get is that fluttery butterflies-under-glass sensation. Warm, golden, terrifyingly strong.

Abruptly, my thoughts turn to Ethan, to his haggard face. To him sitting at home worrying day and night. Maybe I really am a bad person, because otherwise I wouldn't feel this way. I'm trembling inside. This time, I'm not going to disappoint Ethan. I'm going to find a way back to him, no matter what it takes.

Half an hour later, I'm freshly showered, and I've changed out of the jogging pants and T-shirt, into the yellow blouse and a pair of jeans. I wrap a thick sweater around my hips just in case, and put on my hiking boots.

When I get outside, Brendan's already kneeling near the side door, in front of the open hatch containing the grey-water and black-water tanks.

He's all business—nothing about his expression is anything like how he looked at the table earlier—so I pretend it didn't happen right along with him. I set Grey on the ground between us, feigning nonchalance. Grey immediately begins chewing on Brendan's boot laces.

"Hey, you!" Brendan nudges him away, but Grey wants to play, so he sinks his teeth into one of Brendan's cargo pants pockets. Brendan sighs, plucks Grey off, and growls at him. Whimpering, Grey tucks his tail between his legs and jumps over to me.

"We need to start training him," Brendan says, nodding in the wolf's direction. "Otherwise, he'll start thinking he's the alpha."

An odd thought, as small as Grey is. "Can we actually keep him?"

Brendan gives me a sharper-than-usual look, and I wonder if it has anything to do with what happened earlier. "Of course, why wouldn't we?" he says then with a shrug, and sounds perfectly casual. "Wolves act more or less like dogs when they grow up around humans."

"Won't he want to go back someday? He can hear the other wolves in the forest, too..."

"It's a possibility, though I'm not sure whether the pack would accept him. Maybe one day he'll disappear into the woods and won't come back."

I have to force myself not to stare at Brendan constantly. What does he think about what happened earlier? Does he think I have feelings for him? And if so, what did I do that made him think that? Is it the way we're living together here, the way I'm acting cooperative? How can he know something I'm not even sure about myself? I'm pretty sure the only reason I feel like this is because I'm so lonely. I mean, basically, I just feel sorry for him. I've stopped hating him. Maybe I even like him a little bit. And I'm reacting to him this way because he's the only human being for miles and miles. It's not unheard of—lots of kidnapping victims fall in love with their kidnappers. I heard that years ago, back in Ash Springs. But I'm not in love with him, not really. It's pity, I think. Maybe a mix.

I'm so deep in thought that I only catch half of Brendan's explanation, so it startles me when he says, "Okay, go ahead!" and points to the silver pipe, which he's put a bucket underneath.

I blink at the two grey levers at the end of the pipe. Crap. I don't want to admit to Brendan that I missed the most important part because I was too busy brooding over how I feel about him. I'm guessing the grey water has to be emptied more often than the black water, so the lever is further forward because that's the one that gets used more often. As I'm reaching for the lever, Grey leaps in and sinks his tiny teeth into Brendan's pants pocket. Brendan shakes him off, cursing, and accidentally knocks the bucket over just as I pull on the lever.

And then a lot of things happen at once. A dark gurgling noise comes out of the pipe, followed immediately by a horrible stench.

"Fuck!" Brendan shouts, and a second later, brown sludge starts shooting straight at us. It spreads across Brendan's lap, spraying in every direction, and when he tries to leap out of the way, he catapults Grey backwards in a high arc. The wolf whines so pitifully that I can't help jumping in to rescue him from the spray, even though it means taking a direct hit straight to the back. Grimacing, I roll onto my side and set Grey on my stomach. A river of piss, crap, chemical tabs, and who knows what flows past my head, and I have to suppress a wave of nausea. It's worse than the time we had a butyric acid leak in chemistry class. I may puke. Brendan's already started, or at least it looks that way—he's kneeling on the ground a few feet away, spitting something out. Maybe he got that stuff in his mouth. It's so gross I don't want to move a muscle, for fear of spreading the sludge any more. Cautiously, I lift my head and look at Grey. His fur is soaking wet—he's completely covered. It's a pathetic sight. At first he just sits there, like he's not sure what to do with himself. Finally, he settles on doing what he does best, which is whimpering and hoping someone comes to his rescue.

"That was... goddamnit!... the wrong lever," Brendan wheezes after a while, sounding furious.

"Sorry." My whole body seizes up. Is he going to have another one of his attacks now? On top of everything?

Brendan props himself against his hands and curves his back like a cat. "You have poop in your hair," he manages to choke out. "Looks... funny!" Dark-brown sludge is dripping from his head and running down his cheeks. He wipes it away, checks his hand, and then bursts out laughing. He laughs and laughs like this is all the funniest thing in the world. Occasionally, the laughter turns to retching, so the overall effect is a mashup of a coyote howling and a plugged drain.

"You don't even want to know how you look," I retort once he's calmed down. Fat flies are already swarming around us, and the stench is everywhere. I glance over at the pipe, which is barely dripping now.

"Last one to the lake's a rotten egg!" Brendan suddenly cries, scrambling to his feet, and runs off. I stand up and trot after him, clutching Grey. We tear through the trees, stamping on ferns and jumping over roots, and finally scramble past the rotted tree trunk. Brendan leaps straight in without a second thought. He dips underwater for a moment and then emerges, snorting. "Fucking cold!" he exclaims before diving down again.

I set Grey in the ferns near the water's edge and struggle to kick my shoes off. "Be right there!" I promise and start wading slowly into the lake, picking my way across the mixture of sand and gravel at the bottom. It's really not that deep, but better safe than sorry. I can barely even dog-paddle—hell, Grey can probably swim better than I can. I plop into a sitting position, and then get on my hands and knees and slowly sink back. It's viciously cold. I dunk my head into the icy water a few times to rinse the worst of it out of my hair, and then start scrubbing the rest of my body with my hands. After a couple of minutes, my teeth are chattering. When I stand up, my wet clothes are clinging to me, but obviously I have to keep them on. Brendan's ripped his hoodie off, and his shirt is drifting toward the stream, but I barely notice it because I'm too busy being hypnotized by the sight of Brendan's sinewy back. I already knew he had a tattoo, but I'd only ever seen it in the dim light of the camper, and I thought it was a dragon or some other bad-boy thing, but now I see that it's the same design from the silver coin. The bird itself stretches across one of his shoulders. Its right wing is covered in dark feathers, and the left is made up of white tree limbs that extend over the bird's head as black branches, with fine, dark twigs spreading as far as Brendan's neck, so it's kind of a mix between a wing and a treetop.

Something fascinates me about the tattoo. I don't know if it's the design itself, or the combination of black and white on his smooth skin, or what. The limbs could be roots, I realize. Like a heaven-and-earth thing. My fingers twitch with the desire to touch Brendan, to trace the path of the branches up to his neck.

"Lou? Are you deaf?"

"What?" I shake my head, dazed. Brendan's turned around and is giving me a quizzical stare. What the hell was I just thinking? I must be completely batshit crazy. How can you use your head when you've already lost your mind?

"You can wash Grey back there near the waterfall if you want. There's one spot where the water is a little warmer."

"Oh, okay. Sure!" Still horrified at myself, I trudge back and pick up Grey, who's standing on the flat shore now, dunking his furry head in the water. Holding him as far away from me as possible, I wade over to the waterfall.

Brendan's calling to me, but the waterfall's so loud that I can barely hear him.

He shouts it louder now. "Left! Further left!"

Fine droplets of water spray my face and body as I maneuver through the spray, with Grey hanging limply in my grasp like a smelly, miserable lump. I take another step to the left and feel a warmer current against my calves, so that's where I dunk Grey into the water, just far enough that his head is still poking out. He whimpers and shivers, completely dumbfounded that I would subject him to this torture, mere minutes after he nearly drowned in a puddle of liquid waste. I scrub his small head clean with one hand and then lift him to cuddle him. Before heading back, I give the waterfall beside me a quick once-over. Here, up close, I can see the rock wall behind it. There's at least three or four feet of space between the waterfall and the rock. Freezing mountain water runs down the stone in steady rivulets, so it's worn completely smooth, like yellowish-brown marble with black pockets here and there.

Then I get an idea. I turn to look at Brendan. He's wading toward the stream, dragging his soaked hoodie behind him. I take another step to the left. There's a niche in the rock wall, barely big enough to hide in, and it's completely invisible from the other side of the rushing waterfall. My heart skips a beat. If I can distract Brendan with a fake propane-gas alarm, he'll want me to get far away from the camper. He'll go around to the back of the camper to turn the gas off, and I'll make a break for the lake and hide here behind the waterfall. Eventually, he'll start wondering if I've run off. Maybe I'll manage to leave a false trail. He'll go looking for me, and then the flashbacks will hit him, and I'll have plenty of time to go back and get everything I need in order to escape.

And then I'll leave.

I get butterflies in my stomach when I realize that it might seriously work. They rise into my chest, the way they did earlier when Brendan was gazing at me so intently.

I look in his direction again. He waves at me with the hoodie and laughs. His eyes are twinkling. He looks happy. Maybe his plan might actually have worked. Maybe I really am his medicine, his light, his sun, whatever it is he's expecting of me.

The butterflies turn into a dead weight that drags my legs down, like I'm wading through cement. The realization that I might be helping him gives me pangs in my chest. Knowing how miserable he'll be when I'm gone makes me feel like a traitor. Like I'm destroying something. Destroying *him*.

Grey starts wriggling and kicking, which brings me back to the here and now. I shake my head energetically. I don't owe Brendan anything. Not a damn thing. And I want to go home. I want to be back with my brothers.

Still... part of me wishes Brendan would come with me.

SIXTEEN

T he clearing Brendan's parked the camper in is an absolute furnace. The shirt I changed into in order to clean up the wastewater pool is sticking to my back, and I'm so thirsty I feel like I've been squeezed like a lemon. After a while, Brendan disappears into the camper and returns with a bottle of water, which we take turns drinking from.

When I wipe the sweat from my forehead, the back of my hand comes away with several squished mosquitos on it. I wrinkle my nose and rub them off on my jeans, and then glance over at the ground near the drainage pipe. An armada of blowflies is roosting there, despite our best efforts to carry the contaminated dirt away with shovels and then cover everything with fresh earth. I know I shouldn't care whether the cleanup works or not, since I'm not going to be here much longer, but I still help as diligently as if the situation actually affected me. And I know why I'm so eager, too. It's not to lull Brendan into a sense of security, to make him think I'm not planning on trying to escape. It's because I feel bad about abandoning him.

After we finish shoveling another load of fresh, dry dirt into the bucket and shaking it out over the smelly spot, Brendan pulls the camper forward a little so that we're not right next to the worst of it. Then he drains the grey-water tank, and we carry the buckets to the stream together, bathed in sweat and heat and the stench that's still seeping from our pores.

Later, in the shower, I lather up beyond recognition, twice, three times, over and over. Grey is in here with me, and he gets the same treatment, but against all expectations, he doesn't seem to mind the suds and the warm water at all.

Before taking his turn in the bathroom, Brendan shackles me as usual, of course. And he takes his time in there, of course.

It's already afternoon by the time I start hanging our wet clothes, and he opens a giant can of chili con carne. The air is getting cooler already. A soft breeze rustles through the treetops, carrying the scent of spruce and resin, which is a real blessing after that stench. I keep letting my eyes drift to Brendan without meaning to. He's wearing grey cargo pants and a dark-brown T-shirt that brings out his hair and eyes. To the outside world, we would probably look like a happy couple on a survival trip. Grey frolics between us, spraying us with fine droplets whenever he shakes himself off. He's like a sheepdog puppy, bounding from Brendan to me and back again, tumbling around and between my legs so that I'm constantly stumbling over him and losing my flip-flops.

This time, I land on a sharp stone and curse loudly. Spraining my ankle right before I escape would totally be the cherry on top of everything. I probably should have left my hiking boots on, but they're soaking wet, so they're sitting in a sunny spot near the camper to dry.

I reach into the wash bucket to hang Brendan's wet cargo pants on the line, but then I stop and sneak a quick glance in his direction. He pours the can of chili into a pot and hangs the pot on the hook of the tripod thing he cobbled together yesterday. Logs and tinder are already layered neatly underneath. Cooking over an open fire is his newest mission. He thinks it'll help us save propane so we don't run low during the winter.

I slip behind the tree I've knotted one end of the clothesline around. It doesn't hide me completely, but it's enough to let me slide my hand discreetly into the top left pocket of Brendan's pants —which is where I saw him put the lighter not long ago. Maybe he forgot it in there, amid all the chaos? I feel something hard against my fingertips. Cool metal. A rectangular shape. My heart hammers in my throat as I close my fist tightly around the small object and pull it out. It's Brendan's Zippo! Does it still work? I can't try it, because he's only about fifteen feet away.

"Hey, Lou, are those my pants?" he calls at that exact moment. "Throw the lighter here, would you? I wonder if it survived the dunking..."

I freeze. My hand cramps around the metal, making the bells on the cable tie jingle. A dozen possibilities go through my mind. I could drop it and hope he doesn't see it, and then retrieve it later. I could give it to him and lose this opportunity. I could put it in my pocket.

"Lou? Earth to Lou!" The impatient note in Brendan's voice makes me act immediately: I slip the lighter into my shorts pocket. I'm light-headed with fear. If he finds it on me, he'll get suspicious. He'll want to know why I took it from him. And if I can't come up with a good excuse quickly, he'll put two and two together. He might even go search my closet and find the plastic baggies and the bandages.

I still can't make myself respond. I see he's coming toward me, watch him approach as though through a haze of fog. If he starts doubting me, he'll start using the chains again.

"I... I don't see it." I hold up the pants, mostly to have something to do with my hands. "Maybe you... lost it in the lake? Or while you were washing off?" Please, God, don't let him see how badly my hands are shaking.

"Hm!" Brendan takes the pants and starts rummaging through the pockets, but his eyes are fixed on me. Dammit, what if he sees the outline of the lighter in my pocket? Instinctively, I tug my white ruffled blouse down an inch. "That sucks!" After thoroughly inspecting the pants, Brendan tosses them over the clothesline.

"Did you only have the one?" My voice sounds shrill and frightened to me.

"Of course not," he snaps as if it's a completely stupid question. "But that was the only gas lighter." He gives me a once-over. "Are you cold or something?"

"I don't feel so good," I reply evasively.

"Maybe you're getting sick. Your whole body's shaking, Lou." His lips are pressed together, and his eyes are narrowed to scythes. He takes a step toward me, so he's right there beside me. "I'm only

225

going to ask this once, and I expect you to be honest. Did you take the lighter, yes or no?"

"No!" I squeak.

He presses his lips even more tightly, until they're as white as chalk. "Okay." His voice is dark with fury. I *know* he knows, I'm sure of it, but now there's no going back.

"Can I go in?" I ask quietly.

"I told you, quit asking permission to do every single goddamn thing! It's sickening." His expression turns masklike. "As if I'm some kind of monster that never lets you do anything!"

Hopefully he's not going to have one of his attacks now, just because he thinks I'm trying to go behind his back somehow.

I slide past him, keeping a safe distance, terrified that he'll suddenly grab me, throw me to the ground and choke me... or whatever. The tightrope I have to walk in his presence is suddenly clearer than ever. How could I have forgotten?

As I walk up the stairs, I glance back at him over my shoulder. He's standing in exactly the same place, watching me. A chill runs down my back, and I curse the lighter in my pocket. Once I'm out of sight, I wrack my brain feverishly, trying to think of a good place to hide it. He promised not to touch me anymore, but he never said anything about my closets or cabinets. But I don't want to carry it around with me, in case his idea of not-touching-anymore doesn't include the occasional pat down search. Dammit, where? I look outside again. Brendan's coming toward the RV with long strides, still scowling. Grey's following him, but further away than usual— no doubt he senses Brendan's anger. At the last minute, I throw myself onto the bed and pull the blanket all the way to my chin.

I hold my breath when Brendan comes in, and shift around so I can watch him. He barely deigns to glance in my direction as he stalks to the cupboard above the side door, unlocks it, and removes a pack of matches. After that, he plucks out a small, brown bottle and sticks it into his pocket. A heavy sensation spreads through my stomach. Were those the knockout drops?

He looks at me again, his eyes inky black and cheerless, like I've ruined everything. Then he slams the cupboard shut and stomps back out toward the fire.

He left the cupboard unlocked.

Is he actually trying to set a trap for me that obviously?

I straighten up and draw the lighter out of my pocket. If only I could just leave right now! Cautiously, I flick it. Nothing happens. I feel like hammering my head against the wall in frustration. I try again. Click. Nothing. Tears spring to my eyes. I risked his fury for nothing. Now I bet he's going to put those drops in my food tonight and I'll wake up in the box again. That's probably how he'll punish me for lying. I burrow deeper in the blanket to shield myself against the icy terror inside me. But if he wanted to put me in the box, he wouldn't need to use drugs. He could simply knock me out cold. Then again, he has an especially unhealthy relationship with the word pain—maybe he doesn't want to hurt me physically.

I don't know what to do. Finally, I walk to the window and watch as Brendan stokes the fire and stirs the contents of the pot. Grey smells the meat, and he's slinking around Brendan and the fire in progressively smaller circles. Lately he's started acting like a starving tiger around anything that smells even remotely edible.

All at once, it hits me how much of a problem Grey is. He'll be able to track my scent for miles! When I leave, I'll have to make sure Grey is asleep. But I can't exactly give him knockout drops, can I? Is that why Brendan left the cupboard open? To trick me into stealing knockout drops so that he can catch me in the act?

Does he really think that far ahead?

I peek out. Flames are flickering upward, licking at the pot. Brendan's just standing there, staring into the fire. He's going to react to the thing with the lighter somehow. I'm sure of it. He always reacts. To everything. And I know he didn't believe me—otherwise he wouldn't have gotten so mad. He won't even care whether the lighter still works or not. What would I do with it anyway? Set the camper on fire and burn all of our supplies? How would I do that without him seeing me? Even if he's somehow figured out that I want it to help me survive in the wilderness, I'd have to get past him first. No, the only thing he cares about is that I lied. I broke his trust.

I hold my hand away from the window so he won't see me testing it again. This time, I manage to coax out a flame. It's small and weak, but hopefully the thing has enough fluid in it for a day or two.

It'll work. It *has* to!

Suddenly, there's nothing but chaos in my head. I have to get away before Brendan can react to me breaking his trust. He's probably out there trying to decide what he needs to do in order to control me. No doubt he'll do whatever he thinks will be most effective, regardless of how miserable it makes me.

Your tears won't help you. Tears never help. Not with me.

I haven't forgotten he said that. How could I?

As if in a trance, I go over to my closet and pull on a pair of jeans and a greenish-grey sweatshirt, and I pluck a pair of socks from the floor. Then I shove the plastic baggie with the bandages and the lighter into my underwear. I slip into the bathroom to grab the scissors and a few rolls of gauze. I stuff the gauze into the kangaroo pocket of my hoodie, and tuck the scissors into my back pocket, which is covered by the sweatshirt.

I set the tea kettle on the stove as I walk past the kitchen unit, and then go outside. Brendan's standing with his back to me, stirring the chili. The wind is whipping his hair in every direction. It might be a good idea to get a proper meal in before I take off. Then again, I don't trust Brendan any further than I can throw him, especially not now that I know he took the knockout drops out. And didn't even bother to hide it.

"I'm gonna make Grey's milk," I call to him and grab my hiking boots, which are sitting several feet from the campfire.

Brendan mutters something I don't catch.

It's probably just as well that he's so angry—it makes leaving that much easier when I can see this other side of him. Fear can be paralyzing, but it's also a good motivator.

I trudge into the camper on stiff legs and then hurriedly change into my hiking boots before rummaging through the drawers as fast as I can. Four granola bars, a package of hazelnuts, and a couple of cookies land in the kangaroo pocket, along with a couple of sandwich baggies. I don't have a knife, I don't have a rope, I don't have any protection from the rain, but I have to go before it's too late.

My heart is pounding wildly. This absolutely can't go wrong, because otherwise I won't get another chance to escape until spring, and I can't do that to Ethan. So I have to pull myself together. No mistakes. My gaze darts to the cabinet Brendan usually keeps locked. Maybe it would be easier to steal some of those sleeping pills and sneak them into Brendan's chili or something? No, no. I have no idea what's in those bottles or how to dose them. I might accidentally kill him. Anyway, he obviously left that cabinet open on purpose to tempt me. He must think I'm ridiculously naive.

He may have a phone hidden up there, though. Maybe I could call somebody. *Right, I'm sure the reception around here is fantastic. And seriously, do you really think he'd have been dumb enough to leave the cabinet open if he had a phone hidden in there?*

A gust of wind blows through the camper, and a loose sheet of paper spirals out of the cabinet and lands at my feet. I can't help it —I pick it up and flip it over to look at it.

I can see that it's one of Brendan's bleak drawings, but I'm not immediately sure what it's supposed to be a drawing of... I blink a few times, clearing my vision, but it doesn't help. It's the perspective, it's like nothing I've ever seen. I'm looking at something dark and solid from underneath, something that's threatening to crush me. My stomach twists at the very sight of it, and I sink down onto the bench. I think about what Jayden once said about art. A good story is like a good piece of music, he said. There's always a pattern to it, an interplay of light and shadows, woven together like a delicate web. Anybody can read a story or hear music or look at a painting and interpret it for themselves—the art itself is just the cocoon that the butterflies emerge from. Jayden called those patterns subconscious dreams, or else the deeply buried dream of life, because he thought that one sounded better.

But Brendan's drawing is different. There's no light in it, not even a hint of it. The sheer weight of the darkness is enough to crush the viewer. There's no pattern here, it's just a place of absolute torture, entirely outside the rational world. Stagnation. Death. It reminds me of the box... it could be a lid. When I look more closely, I see a fine wood grain in the structure, and the sides seem to slant downward.

My hand flies to my throat when I see it. It's a coffin lid, seen from underneath.

Shreds of memory tumble through my head, as if on the wind.

I'm nothing. Nobody can love me. I should be dead. Buried in the ground, in the darkness... I'm nothing... That's exactly why I wanted you,

Lou. You're the light. You're like a sun. You were always so radiant in your pictures, like life was easy for you...

He thinks I'm his salvation. That's why I'm here. It's never been so clear to me as it is right now. I remember what he said about the glass coffin. How perfectly that described the feeling. But in reality, he's the one who's still buried. Which is why he loves the light, his light... me.

I feel even sicker. Is this picture supposed to be a symbolic expression of how he's feeling, or did he actually experience it? I think maybe it really happened to him, because I remember the look he gave me when I asked if he was going to lock me in the box again. Like he shared my fear of the belly of the monster.

With shaking fingers, I set the drawing on the table, dazed with the horror that the drawing triggers within me. The insane part of me that likes Brendan wants to run to him and throw my arms around him, to hold him and comfort him. To tell him that the light can be everywhere if he can learn to stop seeing the world through the shadows of his past.

I stand up and take a deep breath, out longer than in, to drive away the veil of darkness. I have to go. Sympathizing with Brendan won't help him. No one and nothing can help him, apart from a good psychiatrist. Wanting to heal him is pointless. I have to forget about the way his eyes twinkle so mysteriously, about how I see my own desires reflected in them. I have to forget that he's a guy and I'm a girl. I have to forget that he's the shadow and I'm the light... that we could complete one another if we wanted to.

I have to do it now, or I'll never do it at all. I have everything I need. Not wanting to appear suspicious, I call out for Grey, and he hops up the stairs right away on his clumsy, awkward legs.

I pet him softly, and then lift him to my face and press my nose against the top of his head. "I'll miss you, Grey, honey," I whisper. I still don't know how I'm going to shake him off my trail later. I'll have to improvise that part as I go along. My only hope is if he loses my scent in the lake. Brendan might take that as a sign that I'm running through the creek, so I may have to abandon my plan to run alongside it. Right now, I couldn't care less, as long as I escape in the first place.

Carefully, not wanting to draw any attention, I kneel on the floor and hold the lighter directly underneath the propane detector. I'm glad I won't have to turn on all the stove burners, because that really would be risky. One spark and the camper would go up in a supernova. I set my jaw in determination and click the lighter, and a small flame flickers to life.

It's not even three seconds before the alarm goes off—a monotone, piercing beeping noise that vibrates my eardrums painfully. I leap to my feet and crank the stove burner underneath the tea kettle as high as it will go. That way Brendan will assume it was a leak.

Grey's already bolted outside, terrified by the racket. Through the mirror above the sink, I see Brendan running toward the camper. His anger seems to have melted away; his face is as white as a sheet. "Get out, get out now!" he shouts when I appear at the side door, trying to look confused. "Is anything still on in there?" Despite his promise, he grabs my arm and wrenches me outside with such force that I stumble down the stairs.

"The s-stove," I stammer. I don't even have to fake being scared.

"Okay." Brendan nods curtly. "Go over there," he says, pointing to the spruces separating the campfire area from the lake. "All the way to the right. I want to be able to see you from here." He pushes me toward the tree line and then disappears behind the camper.

I run to the place he pointed at, frantically trying to figure out how to get away from there. My only shot will be the moment when he turns off the gas, because he'll have to concentrate on that. I picture it being like defusing a bomb, but I suppose it's a lot simpler than that.

"Where's Grey?" I call to him, but the alarm is so loud that he might not hear me. Damn, the noise is perfect—it drowns out the bells and my movements through the underbrush. "Grey?" I pretend to keep calling out for him, even though I see him right there behind a straggly bush, sniffing around at something that may have once been a mouse.

I turn to look at Brendan. He's hooking the hatch open so he can get at the gas canister more easily. He casts a fleeting glance in my direction, but I can tell he's not really focused on me. My heart is pounding. "Grey?" I shout, loud enough that surely Brendan will hear me and start tramping across the ferns and roots like a stork. My mind is racing. He won't risk coming after me until he's turned the oven off. If I know one thing, it's that he'll be sure he can still catch up to me easily.

I take another step. He already can't see me anymore.

"Grey?" I yell so loudly that the wolf jumps in alarm. Blood is rushing in my ears, racing through my body like a storm. My legs are tingling with the adrenaline flooding through my system. I can't wait any longer.

CHAPTER
SEVENTEEN

Branches whip across my face, scratching my cheeks. I stumble over a gnarled root, catch myself in time, but it costs me precious seconds. The eyelets on the hiking boots keep snagging on ferns, and I can feel myself leaving a telltale trail through the greenery leading from the forest to the lake. I don't turn around until I reach the shore. The trees are so thick that I can't see anything anyway.

I can still hear the alarm from here. Beep-beep-beep. Echoing as loudly as my thundering heart. My idea of hiding behind the waterfall until Brendan wanders into the forest suddenly strikes me as idiotic. What if he finds me back there and flips out? In a moment of blind desperation, I dunk the bells on my wrists into the water, and then tuck my sweatshirt over them. At least I still remembered to do that! I glance to my left and right, not sure what to do next. Grey's probably still busy with that dead mouse, but he'll smell me, and Brendan will know to take advantage of that. Where should I go? This is the most terrified I've ever been in my life, except for the time I spent in the box and the moment Brendan pressed that cloth against my face. Tears spring to my eyes.

Running straight into the creek is most likely my only option, because of Grey. Once Grey loses my scent, Brendan will figure out which direction I must have gone, but hopefully I'll have enough of a head start.

I wade through the shallow water as quickly as I can, toward

235

the spot where the water has worn the sharply angled creek bed into the ground. Icy water laps around my calves, soaking my socks and the hem of my jeans. Doesn't matter. Nothing matters. I can dry my stuff later if I can just get out of here. I jump from one large rock to the next, across the transition from the lake to the creek.

Clenching my jaw, more from cold than fear, I try to keep my balance on the slippery stones, but it's practically impossible. It's not the moist, grey-green moss or the thick algae blanketing the rocks—it's just the fact that I can't tell which of them are stuck firmly into the creek bed and which are loose, ready to roll away as soon as I step clumsily onto them. Keeping my balance requires both hands, and I can already tell I'm moving much too slowly. Brendan doesn't have to cover his tracks, and I picture him hastening alongside the creek, bounding toward me like a wolf, like a hunter... grabbing me, shouting at me... or worse...

I stop, breathless. Something's different. The air is still. The splashing water is so loud it nearly tears me apart inside. Brendan's shut the alarm off. He's inside the camper!

Oh, God, not already! I don't think I've made it three hundred feet yet. Panicked, I clamber over a couple of boulders and onto the shore, and against all reason, I continue along the embankment, through the jungle of tall grass, ferns, and weeds separating the forest and the creek. Waist-high stinging nettles brush my hands, making my fingers burn, so I veer closer to the creek as I run, slipping on wet roots and the old, damp leaves of the few birch trees.

"Louisa!" Brendan's voice thunders through the trees like he's trying to slam me to the ground with it. "Come back!"

I stop, frozen in terror. Where is he? I glance back over my shoulder, but I don't see him anywhere. I'm not good at judging distances, but I think I probably have almost a quarter-mile head start now.

I listen for a few seconds, catching my breath.

"Louisa! Come! Back! Now!"

Hearing his enraged voice is enough to kill my hopes. Like I never really had a chance. In the distance, I hear Grey howling, which I've never heard him do. Can he sense that I'm leaving him forever? Maybe it's that mournful, accusatory sound that drives me onward. I start running again, but slower so that I can keep going longer. I'm just now starting to realize how steeply the ground drops off. I hear Brendan yelling again. *Louisa! Louisa! Louisa!* Raw and wild. *Louisa!* Completely out of his mind. He shouts things I don't understand, because he's so furious he's confusing his words, barely getting them out. Is he already having a flashback?

After a while, he stops, leaving behind the same eerie silence as before, after the alarm stopped beeping. Since Brendan isn't shouting anymore, I can't tell if he's coming this way or going in a different direction. I don't know which is worse: hearing him, or hearing only the silent forest. He could pop up behind me at any second—I know how quietly he can move when he wants to. Like a predatory cat, lulling his prey into a sense of security until the very last second. The thought terrifies me so much that I find myself glancing over my shoulder every ten steps or so, but I don't see anything, don't hear anything. This ragged breathing is giving me a terrible stitch, and pressing both hands against my side it is the only way I can keep running. I comfort myself with the knowledge that, if and when Brendan has his flashback, he probably won't be able to move silently anymore.

Once I've made it another half-mile or so along the shore, I risk venturing into the creek again. The water is breathtakingly cold, probably barely above freezing. My toes are completely numb after a minute or two, but I know I need to keep going for another half-mile at least so that Grey will lose my trail. I lift my feet extra-high with every step, trying to picture the fire I'm going to build tonight. A small, hot fire that will warm me up and dry me off. I imagine it crackling and popping, picture myself curled up beside it like a hedgehog. After a while, I don't even notice the cold anymore. Either I'm too focused on not slipping as I do this stork-running thing, or my feet are frozen solid.

After several minutes, the ground flattens out, and the water stretches out to either side, like an animal that suddenly has more room. Two smaller streams feed into it on my right. The bed is mostly gravel now, with only the occasional smooth boulder dividing the current, rippling the water into white waves. The creek is as broad as our Road to Nowhere back home. I come to a halt—my right side hurts so badly that I can barely breathe—and cast a fleeting glance across the green valley the creek is extending into.

Pale late-afternoon light scatters on the surface of the water, giving it a matte silver gleam that seems otherworldly amid the dark conifers towering into the heavens on either side. If I weren't so scared and out of breath, I might even stop and enjoy the view. I grit my teeth and try to start running again, but there's just no way.

I wade to shore, sucking in deep lungfuls of the fresh, moist air, and plunge my burning hands into the water to cool them. The sleeves of the sweatshirt are immediately soaked through. As I push them up, the cable tie full of bells catches my eye. My silencing trick has been working well this whole time, but I don't want to rely on it. I fish the scissors from my pants pocket, and then sit down on a moss-covered stone to cut the band. The cable tie material is tough, though, and although the scissors are sharp, they're fairly small. I keep sawing and filing away at the band, listening tensely for sudden noises as I work, but all I hear besides the rushing water are a couple of birds. Once in a while, a breeze rustles through the treetops and knocks a pine cone to the ground with a muted thud—or occasionally a crack when the pine cone lands on a pile of dead wood. I jump every single time, thinking it's Brendan, and then breathe a sigh of relief a moment later.

I just can't wrap my head around the fact that I've gotten away from him this easily. There's no way, is there? I know I'm free, but the rush of euphoria hasn't hit me yet.

Once I've finally managed to slice through the cable tie, I use a rock to sink the bells into the creek bed. When I straighten up, I spot a path winding into the bushes on the other side of the water.

My heart starts beating wildly. I don't dare get my hopes up that much, right? *A trail*! I can barely believe my luck, and immediately I start bounding through the creek like a lunatic, churning the water. Where there's a trail, there will be hikers. Canada may be isolated in parts, but that also makes it a nature-freak paradise.

But when I peer more closely at the line of trampled grass, a thick lump of disappointment forms in my stomach. It's hoof tracks, not footprints. Probably a game trail for deer or caribou.

I keep moving, slowly realizing how alone I actually am if I've gotten away from Brendan. My only companions out here are the wild animals that I assume are already eyeing me from a safe distance, wondering what to make of me. Black bears. Grizzlies.

Wolves. Elk. Male elk are supposedly even more dangerous than bears. I squint around, scanning the area, but practically anything could be hiding in the thick vegetation lining both sides of the creek here. I know I should be singing loudly so I won't surprise the bears, but that would obviously make it ten times easier for Brendan to track me.

I'm so absorbed in my surroundings that I don't notice how much stronger the current around my calves has gotten until it's nearly too late. I freeze in place for a moment, and then bound hurriedly to shore. I glance up and down the silvery surface of the water. The creek was perfectly flat this whole time, barely knee-deep, and it hadn't occurred to me that it might change. The ground still isn't sloped too steeply, but I still have to be careful—what if it suddenly drops off and I get swept away by the current? Ethan once told me that even experienced swimmers sometimes drown in mountain creeks. I decide to stay close to the shore, near the willow herb, nettles, and swamp grass.

There's a rushing sound in the distance, and it gets louder with every step I take. The air is heavy with cold moisture that clings to my clothes like a second, clammy skin. I squint, trying to make out what's up ahead, but the dark spruce branches hanging nearly to the ground make it impossible to see more than ten feet in any direction. I follow a bend in the creek, and all at once, it seems to end in mid-air. The rushing swells until it drowns out the sound of birdsong.

The bad feeling in my gut intensifies. It must be a waterfall, and I can't tell how steeply it drops off yet. To be on the safe side, I get out of the water and approach through the forest. It takes forever to get to the spot, but then I discover just how much of a catastrophe this is: the creek drops straight down into a steep ravine. A couple of trees hang drunkenly over the rocks as though staring into the abyss. I'll never get down there, not without breaking every bone in my body.

Cautiously, I walk along the edge. Thirty or forty feet, at least, with sharp rocks poking threateningly out from the side of the grey mountain-monster. I follow the creek with my eyes, watch the water tumble into the depths of the ravine, where it feeds into a large river that winds through the valley.

Exhausted, I grab hold of one of the birches leaning out over the cliff, and clutch a thick, horizontal limb for support. My throat tightens in despair and frustration. I'm not getting any further. But I can't go back, no way, not in a million years. Brendan's somewhere in the forest, searching for me.

Just as I've made up my mind to keep moving along the edge of the cliff until I reach a less-steep place to descend, I jump at the sound of a cracking twig. My hands tense around the tree limb. That wasn't a pine cone falling on dead wood. Heart racing, I turn around. And turn to ice.

Brendan's at the edge of the forest, maybe thirty feet away. Against the backdrop of dark spruces, his face is almost ethereally pale. His expression is calm and solemn, but the fire in his eyes singes me. That disconnect between outward composure and inner rage is what terrifies me more than anything. It's as if his two faces are fighting inside him, and there's no telling yet which one has the upper hand.

"Bren..." I gasp for breath, horrified. I want to say something to calm him down, but terror devours the words.

"End of the line!" He comes closer. Stoically. One step. Two steps. "The property ends here, at this ravine. You can run as far as you want along this cliff, you'll never reach the valley."

The information hits me with such force that I nearly black out. He knew from the beginning that I didn't have the slightest chance of escaping in this direction. It's only then that I spot the path behind him and realize just how stupid I was. He's been setting traps in this area for weeks. He knows the whole area and every game trail in it. All he had to do was pick one. I bet he even beat me here, and he's been sitting around waiting for me to arrive. Bile rises in my throat.

"Come here, don't make it any worse for yourself."

That's when I see the chain and the handcuffs in his left hand.

I retreat, clutching the limb of the birch tree, but the ground is loose. A couple of rocks roll away and tumble into the depths of the ravine.

"Watch out!" Brendan exclaims in alarm, and my heart does a terrified leap in my chest. Immediately, I clamber up the tree, which is growing almost horizontally over the ravine.

"One more step and I'll jump!" I warn him, and I'm so desperate I actually believe my own ears.

Brendan stops. "I'm not trying to scare you, Lou," he says, but it sounds mechanical, like a phrase he's memorized in case of emergency. Every muscle in his body is tense. "I'm not going to hurt you. I've told you that a hundred times, and it's not going to change. Not even now." His black T-shirt is so wet with sweat, it looks like he's just emerged from a swimming pool. "Come on, Lou. You know what will happen."

"No!" I shake my head frantically. "I don't want to be chained up like a prisoner again." Were those feelings I had for him ever real? How could I possibly be attracted to someone I'm so deathly afraid of? They must not be real, they must be a product of my own loneliness.

"It was my fault," Brendan says, jolting me back to the present. "I shouldn't have made it so easy for you." I must be giving him a look of confusion, because he hurries on to his next thought. "As soon as I realized that you'd taken my lighter, I knew you were plotting something. I should have reacted immediately." His smile is so tortured, I think it may kill me. "Now it's too late. I'm going to bring you back, and you'll start hating me again."

He may be right, I realize with a pang in my chest. The feelings I have toward him, wherever they are and wherever they've come from, might not survive tonight. I may end up hating him forever after this.

"Why didn't you search me if you were so sure?" I ask defiantly.

He closes his eyes for a moment and shakes his head in impatience, like he doesn't have time for these silly explanations. "I promised you I wouldn't touch you. How could I have—"

"So you left the cabinet open instead. To test me."

"No." He reaches into his bag and pulls out the small, brown bottle. "That was carelessness. I was pissed off, and I felt a flashback coming on. Anyway, there's nothing else in there that would have helped you get away from me." He gazes at the brown glass as though lost in thought.

"What's that for?" I can't go forward, can't go back. I'm caught in a trap, like one of his rabbits. My throat starts burning. It doesn't matter what I think about him, what I feel for him—I might be

241

about to lose all of it. Then things will go back to the way they were at first.

"I'm going to put you to sleep so that I don't have to drag you back by force. For your sake."

His honesty is like a slap in the face. The good intentions behind it are a punch in the stomach. How can he claim I'm his "light" and then do these things to me?

To buy myself some time, I straddle the tree limb that stretches over the ravine like an extension of the boulder. I'm absolutely positive about one thing: I am not leaving this tree of my own free will.

"I'd rather jump than let you force more of that shit down my throat!" I snap furiously and scoot slightly away, so that I'm over the ravine. I think I may be about to have a nervous breakdown.

"Lou, come down from there, right now!" It's definitely a command, not a request, but I hear a note of fear in it, too.

I slide out a little further, as if to prove to myself that I'm serious. My feet are dangling in the air; the wind whips my hair in every direction. "Go away!" My shoulders are shaking.

"Lou." Brendan's voice drops to a whisper, so tender it makes me want to scream. "I'm not trying to make you suffer. I know how much you miss your brothers. If I'd known how bad this would be for you, I..."

"You'd have kidnapped some other girl?" I shout, cutting him off. "We've been over this."

He shakes his head. "I only ever wanted you, and you know why. Which is also why I don't think you're going to throw yourself off of there. You love life too much."

A flood of tears streams down my face. "You took my life away from me. You *stole* it."

Brendan stands there, thunderstruck. A look of pure suffering flickers on his face, which makes me remember that drawing of his that I found. I hate myself for empathizing with him, but I guess that's life. None of us can control how we feel about other people. We can lie to ourselves about it, suppress feelings we think are wrong, but at the end of the day, the truth is the truth.

Brendan slips the bottle back into his pocket before stretching a hand toward me, seeming to sense my contradictory emotions. "Don't do this, Lou... please..."

242

I stare down into the ravine. Raging waves, sharp rocks, nothingness. If I let myself fall, I'll either drown in the river or smash against the ground. Wheezing, I scoot out a bit further. My heart is fluttering in a way that's making me nauseated.

"Lou. I know you never wanted any of this. You're desperate, and you want to prove it to me, even willing to put yourself in danger just to make your point. But you know what? I get it." Brendan takes a couple steps back, and then walks a short distance along the cliff. For one terrifying moment, I think he's preparing to jump. *No, don't!* I nearly scream, but then I see that he's winding up for a throw. The chain and the handcuffs fly over the edge in a high arc.

"See?" he calls in my direction with a short, rueful laugh.

I'm going back and forth between despair, affection, and fear. I'm not sure which one is strongest. He slides the brown bottle out of his pocket again. It looks as though he's going to toss that as well, but then, abruptly, he sinks to his knees, and the bottle slips from his grasp. He clutches the ground with both hands, clawing at the dirt, digging his fingers into it. He's whispering something, but I can't make it out over the wind whistling in my ears.

But I can guess.

So dark, so dark … in the ground … why did you leave? Don't stop breathing. Don't stop breathing. Keep your hands still. Don't cry. Don't stop breathing...

"Bren?" I hear the high, frightened waver in my voice. *Please, don't flip out, not now!* "Bren!"

He looks in my direction, but without seeing me. From one minute to the next, he's miles away, or at least his mind is. Panic spreads through my chest. If he loses it now, he may try to pull me out of the tree using force, so he can hit me or choke me or I don't know what. We might both end up going over the cliff.

I wrack my brain desperately. I talked him through it on the night of the thunderstorm, but he was also safely chained up on level ground, not standing near the edge of a ravine. And sometimes the talking didn't even help anyway.

"Bren!" I call loudly. I have to get him to snap out of it before it sucks him in completely. "Bren? It's okay, you're here, with me, you're not anywhere else. Bren... it's me... Lou."

It'd work better if I went over and put my arms around him, but I don't dare come down from the tree, so I simply keep talking. "Bren, I don't know what terrible things happened to you in the past... but that's over now, okay? You're free, you're not locked up, you just have to see it."

He shakes his head vehemently, rocking back and forth.

"Bren... it's okay," I call. "You're not trapped."

"Lies!" he suddenly hisses. The rocking stops. "It's getting dark." He jumps to his feet and strides toward me, his face distorted with hate. Finally, he stops directly in front of the birch tree, barely five feet away. "That was you," he says hoarsely. "It's all your fault. Why did you leave? Why did you leave me alone with him?"

I cling desperately to the tree, praying that he won't try to climb up after me when he's in this state. "It wasn't me," I whisper with my dry throat, not sure if he's hearing me. "That was someone else. Brendan, I saw one of your drawings... you have to get help..."

"You never loved me!" he shouts, clenching his fists. "You went away and left me alone with him. Even though you knew exactly how he is! You knew! I *hate* you!" His eyes are shining with unshed tears, and every muscle in his body is so cramped, it's like rage and hatred are the only things holding it together.

I'm starting to get a faint idea of what happened to him. His mother must have left him and his father. Was his father the person who did those horrible things to him that he can't find words for?

Brendan braces himself against the trunk of the tree with one foot, and then grips the tree limb with one hand. "Come down from there! Now! I'm not going to let you disappear again!"

"Bren... please..."

"Come! Down! From! There!" he bellows.

I start crying again. I'm frozen in terror.

His expression changes, twists into a hateful sneer. "There you go, crying again. Didn't I tell you to quit sniveling like a little girl?" He kicks out at me as if he's trying to curb-stomp me or something. "I should stick you in a box and bury you underground—then you'd have a reason to cry!"

"Bren..." I whisper, weeping. "It's me, Lou. Lou, the girl you kidnapped. And yeah, I ran away, I wanted to leave you, but I don't hate you. In fact, part of me genuinely likes you."

He stops for a moment, as though having some kind of epiphany.

"Bren! Look at me, please."

The hateful expression vanishes from his face. One of his eyelids twitches.

It seems like I'm doing something right, so I keep talking. He's not going to remember any of this anyway.

"Okay, I admit, the part of me that, that likes you is obviously insane, completely batshit crazy, like those guys in New York City that surf on top of subway trains, but it's true. I don't get it either. It's the part of me that wishes you'd invited me back to your camper for a beer or whatever, and then kissed me. You were right, I shouldn't have run from it."

He stares at me, and I can actually see his eyes clearing up, becoming his again. "Louisa?" he asks, sounding confused, like he's just been beamed here from another planet. "What the hell are you doing up there?"

A flood of relieved tears streams down my face. "Sitting in a tree, being scared to death." It comes out in a wavery whisper.

A faint smile flickers across his tense face. "I was out, wasn't I?"

I nod and feel the tension beginning to drain from my body. "Totally."

"It's too dangerous." He retreats behind the tree, glancing around, and then gestures with the bottle. "Come down here, please..."

I'm still dazed with fear. A gust of wind billows my sweatshirt outward. I clutch the tree tightly with my knees, digging my nails into the flaking bark. "I'm not drinking that!"

"It takes effect almost immediately. I tinkered with it for a long time to get the perfect mixture." Brendan takes another step back, and then another. "It was supposed to be for you, so it won't have as strong an effect on me... I mean, I weigh more than you do."

Now I'm officially lost. "On you?"

Brendan puts the small bottle to his lips and drains it in one go. He grimaces like he's swallowing a raw egg. "I wasn't planning on taking it myself, but I figure it's the only way to get you out of that goddamn tree. I don't know when I'm going to have another attack... what if I decide to try and yank you down from there? Or you get scared of the way I'm acting and lose your balance..." He disappears into the darkness of the forest. I can't hear what he's saying anymore.

Is he trying to trick me into coming down? I stay where I am for a few moments, trying to ignore the frosty wind caressing my soaked pant legs.

"Bren?" My stomach knots like a rope. Brendan's nowhere in sight. No, that wasn't a trick. He couldn't have known I was going to climb the tree. Carefully, I slide back from the ravine until I'm standing on solid ground again. I shiver as I trot after Brendan into the forest, and discover him sitting a safe distance from the cliff. He's leaning back against a tree, ghostly pale. I stop about five feet away, as close as I dare get.

"You shouldn't run, too... dangerous," he slurs when he sees me, wiping his hands across his sweaty face. "Plus I'll find you either way." That stuff must be starting to work already. What the hell did he just drink? His eyelids flutter. "It'll get way too cold at night, you'll freeze to death."

"I have your lighter," I whisper hoarsely, because I can't think of anything better to say.

He smiles weakly. "You'll set the whole forest on fire, and then I'll know where you are anyway... if you survive." He closes his eyes, and his head drops to one side. He seems vulnerable—and looks much younger to me than he ever has.

"Lou?"

"Yeah?" I finally muster the courage to approach him, though my legs nearly give out as I kneel beside him.

"Storm... tonight... stay..." He's breathing more shallowly now. "Don't go... too dangerous..." As he drifts off, his torso tips to one side. I grab him by the shoulders, but he's too heavy, and he ends up collapsing in a strangely contorted heap. I adjust his legs so he'll be more comfortable. If I had the chain now, I'd be able to use it on him instead. Was that why he threw it into the ravine first? Because he already knew he was going to drug himself?

I spend a moment studying Brendan's face more closely than I've ever done. Without the frown lines and the bitter expression, he looks so peaceful, so still. I notice several little details for the first time: the shallow dimple on his chin, the way his eyebrows are slightly thicker near the outer edges. My gaze comes to rest on his unyielding lips, and I find myself wondering whether he's ever kissed a girl, whether he's ever said "I love you" to anyone. Whether there was another girl before me, one who first made him happy, and then left him. My stomach twists a little at the thought. Conflicting emotions well up within me, taking over against my will. I can't let them. I can't look at him and wonder how it would feel to have his arms around me, imagine what it would be like if he came over and, instead of chaining me up, ran his fingers across my cheek. Seeing him lying here, totally defenseless, suddenly makes it easy to picture those things. He made that concoction for me, but then he drank it himself so he wouldn't put me in danger. I'm not sure what that means. Actually, I don't know anything about anything anymore, apart from that I don't want to leave him out here by himself. I dig for my hatred and rage, but find only doubt, pain, and fear. Almost as if in a trance, I brush a stray hair out of his face. I expected it to be rough, but it's as soft as silk.

"Lou..." he murmurs indistinctly.

I jump back, startled, and nearly lose my balance. What the hell am I doing? Sitting here, wasting the golden opportunity he's giving me? Sure, he advised me to stay, but we both know what I'm going to do.

Brendan sighs drowsily. "If you go... Grizzlies... don't stop... singing..."

If I kneel here watching him any longer it'll tear me apart. "See you!" I whisper, forcing myself to stand up, and forcing myself not to burst into tears all over again. "If there's really a storm coming tonight, I'd better get going!"

CHAPTER
EIGHTEEN

I've been running along the edge of the cliff for hours, trying to get the image of Brendan lying on the ground out of my mind. My sweatshirt is clinging to my sweaty back, though my teeth are chattering with the cold. I've been following the changes in the sky nervously. The puffy edges of the dark clouds are gleaming a deep orange—a clear sign that the sun's already low on the horizon. I need to get to the valley before it gets too dark to see. There must be a path somewhere along here, or at least a spot where it'll be less dangerous to climb down from.

I know I need to stay focused on where I'm going, but part of me is still back with Brendan. One minute I'm terrified he's going to find me, the next minute I'm wishing he would. Which is totally sick and twisted! How can I possibly wish he'd find me if I'm risking my life trying to get back home?

I stumble to a halt and clutch my temples with a scream. I have to quit thinking about him. I have to keep my mind on putting one foot in front of the other. I still have no idea where I'll be able to build a fire and rest for the night. I can't risk stopping up here in the forest, because Brendan might already be awake again, hunting me.

I break into an even faster run, glancing uneasily at the clouds. The last few ravens that had been circling over the cliffs sail away with the wind, and the darting chipmunks retreat into the underbrush. I'm starting to panic, especially because the temperature is dropping by the minute. I tug my sweatshirt down over my hands as I run, but it doesn't help. Soon my fingers are numb, my cheeks like ice. The wind howls darkly over the mountains, like a giant playing the flute. It gets so strong that I'm afraid to keep running along the cliff.

I look around, totally unsure what to do. I don't want to go back into the dense forest, which spreads out beside me like a lonely grave. No way, I can't go in there! Besides, the storm might make a branch fall on my head or something.

I wrap my arms around myself and move a few feet away from the cliff's edge. The wind tears at my clothes as if it's trying to rip them from my body. My eyes start to water, which blurs my vision. But the chill is the worst part. It crawls into me from underneath, reptilian, paralyzing my legs. The combination of cold and wind is making me clumsy. I trip over my own feet a couple of times and scrape my hands through the sweatshirt.

The temptation to sit and rest is growing steadily. Every time I pass a rock that might offer some shelter from the wind, I promise myself that I'll stop at the next one... but every time, I go right on running. Then I nearly tumble off the cliff and realize I can't keep ignoring the way I'm trembling with exhaustion. The next time I see a boulder, I collapse to the ground on the wind-protected side and curl into a ball. I know I can't let myself rest for too long without a fire—I don't want to risk falling asleep and freezing to death. But even if I can't make a fire, I can at least warm my hands for a minute. I pull the lighter out of my underwear and clench it tightly. It's wonderfully warm just from my body heat. I shield it with one hand as I hold it near my face and clumsily flick it. A yellow flame springs to life, but immediately goes out in the wind. I keep trying and trying until my thumb is black with soot. Frustrated, I shove the lighter into the kangaroo pouch of my hoodie, and struggle to my feet again.

Every bone in my body aches. I shouldn't have sat down. My legs are stiff; I can barely bend my knees. I wish to God I were home. Safe and warm.

Mechanically, I put one foot in front of the other. Left, right, left, right. Again and again. *Don't think. Run. Just a little further.* This is how soldiers must feel when they have to march through the night.

The temperature continues to drop. Something in my head

starts to shift, though I only half-notice at first. I start feeling like I'm falling asleep as I run. My mind drifts away, to a place where the sun always shines, where the sagebrush lines the monotone streets and a young man stands beneath an apple tree on one leg, doing the Crane.

I see a flat-roofed wooden house with an open door, and I follow the sound of a girl's bright, silvery laughter. It seems close, yet far away. I want to catch it, that laughter I hear. Catch it, and hold onto it forever. Implant it in my chest so I'll never lose it again. Then I know I wouldn't be as cold.

Wooden floorboards creak underneath the soles of my shoes as I walk down the hallway. The laughter is coming from the yard. Mesmerized, I step out onto the veranda and stop at the top of the stairs. A little girl in a white nightshirt is twirling on the dry ground, her blonde hair flying in the wind. She looks like she's pulling on something I can't see. Her turquoise eyes are as radiant as the cloudless sky above. She has everything, this girl does. Everything. A whole world. Including things I can't see. And she knows it. The realization sends a pang through my heart. She knows. I wonder when she forgot, wonder why life made her believe she didn't have enough. I wonder if she really did forget, or if she just can't remember, so she's looking for happiness in the wrong places. I wonder if—whether I go back or not—if I can ever be that girl again, or if I've lost her forever.

My heart is suddenly burning with longing. I pick up the pace. I just need to run fast enough to catch up to the girl. I need to get home. A couple of times, I think I spy a flash of something near the cliff, a glimpse of her white nightshirt, a strand of blonde hair. I stretch my arms out, trying to catch her so that I can laugh again, so that I can be warm again.

Is this how Brendan felt when he made his plan to kidnap me? Was his heart burning like this, with such violent heat that he couldn't take it anymore?

The thought makes me trip again. Instinctively, I reach out for something to catch myself on, but there's nothing there. I fly forward. The darkness encircles me, envelops me, blurs the boundaries between up and down. It happens so fast that I don't even have time to scream. Before I fully understand that I'm falling, my back slams against something hard, and a red star of pain explodes in my head. I can't breathe. My body slides down something smooth. Deeper and deeper. I open and close my hands, trying to grab hold of something, but it's futile.

The last thing I'm aware of is the pain, the pain in my ankle overwhelming my senses. Then the world sinks into an ocean of huge, black waves.

When I open my eyes again, the dark sky is spinning. My head is pounding. I lie still for a while as my memory returns, reliving the fall in slow motion.

I'm afraid to move. What if I'm seriously injured? I do a mental inventory. Arms, legs, hands, feet, all shivering. Which is good, because it means I'm not paralyzed.

With great effort, I struggle into a sitting position, and my stomach immediately rebels. I spit greenish-white liquid out onto the rocks. I feel like death. I don't think I can stand up. Now I notice the sharp, biting wind whipping my hair in all directions. Dazed, I try to get my bearings. To my left is the river I saw from above; three boulders the size of suitcases are jutting out of the water nearby. The steep slope is to my right. I'm sitting on a narrow strip of gravel. It's too dark to see to the top, but I still know that I'm super lucky to have survived the fall.

I wipe my face with shaky hands, and water drips from the sleeves of my sweatshirt. Only then do I realize that I'm completely soaked. I look around in confusion. The gravel is wet. There's water running down from the rock cascades into the grass at the foot of the steep slope. I spot a granola bar floating in a puddle of rain-water and mud.

My heart skips a beat. I try to reach into the kangaroo pocket of the hoodie, but my fingers seem to have other ideas. It takes me three tries to get them under control. Clumsily, I pull out a crushed cookie and a smashed granola bar. The rest is gone. I reach around to touch my back pocket and breathe a sigh of relief—the scissors are still there. But the lighter? That was in the kangaroo pocket. I fumble through the pocket one more time. Nothing.

I groan and start searching frantically, but it's nowhere nearby, either. It must be at the top somewhere, stuck among the rocks. Helpless, frightened, furious tears spring to my eyes at the realization. Why, why didn't I stick it back in my underwear? How could I be so dumb? I could smack myself.

I lean toward the puddle and fish out the granola bar. I know I should eat and drink, but I can't. I sit there for a few moments, staring out at nothing, wishing I could just burst into tears and wait for someone to come along and comfort me. But the only person who can find me here is Brendan.

With grim determination, I use the boulder beside me to hoist myself to a standing position. A wave of dizziness washes over me immediately, and I stumble to the side. A sharp pain stabs my ankle like a bread knife. Dammit! I take a few deep breaths, waiting for the pain to subside. Then I try again. Left, right—no, ouch, hop— left. It hurts so badly that I really do start crying, but I wipe my face impatiently and keep on hobbling, even though I feel like my ankle is one giant mass of splinters. Well, at least now I'm not going to fall asleep. I've heard of people walking for miles with a broken leg because they were determined not to die. And my ankle might not actually be broken. It could be just a sprain. I grit my teeth and wince. *Don't think about it!*

After what feels like an eternity, I reach a place where the river widens. The water is shallower here; countless boulders dot the middle. It's more of a mountain stream than a river. If I can cross it, I might find help on the other side. Besides, Brendan will never suspect I'm over there—crossing a river during a storm when you can't swim is completely insane. But right now, it's probably my only shot at shaking Brendan off my trail.

When I get to the shore, I find a piece of driftwood as long as my arm, swearing to myself that I'll turn back if the water reaches to my hips. Then I put a foot into the water and nearly abandon the plan immediately. Cold, so cold. I glance back through the darkness, toward the cliff. If I fell down there and lived, Brendan can probably climb down. And he will climb down, if he has even an inkling that I might somehow have landed near here.

Pressing my lips together, I feel my way across the riverbed with the driftwood, while also using it as a crutch. Left... right.... left. Everything is still here, except for the rushing of the river. The surface is like the skin of a slithering animal, dark and eerie. It takes every ounce of willpower I have to fight back the fear that suddenly, unexpectedly bubbles within me.

I'm at about the middle of the river when the waves reach my thighs. The current's so strong I'm afraid I'll lose my footing. A moment later, it tears the driftwood from my hand, and I nearly fall. Panic washes over me. I try to keep my breathing steady, but one thought has pushed its way in front of the others: I'm going to get pulled under and killed. My body is trembling so hard it's starting to cramp. I'm losing control.

Shh, Lou, calm down, please, please calm down.

Left. Right. Good, that's it!

The inner monologue helps me make it a few more feet, but just as I'm about to reach the far shore, my knees give out, and I fall into the water, stomach-first. It knocks the wind out of me for a few seconds. I instinctively clutch a nearby boulder, shaking so violently that I can't stand up. With the last of my strength, I heave myself forward using my forearms. My heart is pounding in my chest, raw and leaden, like I've just finished a marathon. I'm cursing, bawling, tasting the salty tears streaming down my cheeks.

Somehow, I manage to wriggle out of the water, and I curl into a ball on the gravel along the shore. Within minutes, my clothes are frozen stiff. I don't want to stand up anymore. I'm too cold. I stare at the gravel, mesmerized. Maybe if I lie here long enough, I'll turn to stone. At least then I won't feel anything anymore.

I close my eyes and listen to the howling wind. Rain starts pattering down on my face. I sink downward, in between the deepest layers of Antarctic ice, drenched in the waters of the South Pole...

I startle awake again, because the river's risen, and it's washing up around me. Woozily I stand up, swaying. My clothes are heavy with rain, seem to be dragging me back to the ground. I blink a few times. Directly beside me, there's a weathered wooden sign stuck in the ground. Private Property. No Trespassing. As soon as I've deciphered the message, it begins to blur and shift. I'm not sure whether that's good or bad, and I'm not really in any condition to think about it.

I stumble onward like a drunk person. My ankle isn't hurting as much now, and the uncontrollable shaking has stopped. I walk, fall, straighten up, walk on. Again and again. Somehow. After a while, I can barely see anything anymore, even though my eyes are open. I hear laughter from somewhere. The girl in the white nightshirt is nearby, dancing dreamily in the rain, arms floating. Her laughter is like a melody...

Don't forget to sing, I suddenly hear Brendan warn me. I'm not sure why I'm remembering that *now*, but maybe it'll help me stay awake. I rummage through what's left of my mind for a song, and can only come up with one, a lullaby Ethan patiently sang me night after night when I was small. I can see him sitting there on the edge of the bed, sweaty and exhausted from another long day at work.

"Hush, little baby, don't... say a word..." My voice cracks, but the memory washes over me with unrelenting warmth. I keep moving, I'm not sure how. Maybe it doesn't matter. Everything's spinning. I fall. Driftwood bores into my palms. "I'm gonna buy you... a mockingbird." I stagger to my feet. The sky flickers into its own negative, turns white, white like the girl's nightshirt. Have I finally found her? Am I home? It can't be much further, because everything hurts so much. I want to fall asleep in someone's arms, rest from this boundless exhaustion, this misery weighing so heavily on my heart. "And if that mockingbird... don't sing..." I collapse. Lying on the gravel, I try to remember the rest of the verse, but I can't think of the words. I crawl a few more feet, but my elbows buckle like broken matches.

And then I fall one last time—into the deep, black arms of oblivion. I feel myself slide down into it and settle gently onto the dry lawn on the other side. Reddish-yellow sunlight dances on my closed eyelids. When I open my eyes again, I see the pink rhinoceros, nudging me in the shoulder with its horn like it wants to play.

"Hey!" I lie there stroking its leathery, sun-warmed skin. "There you are. Have you been waiting for me here this whole time?" I turn my head and see all of my brothers standing on the veranda. A wave of pure joy envelops me, and then everything goes dark.

Arms embrace me. Strong, unyielding arms that lift me up. I feel myself being carried, and then being set down again a few moments later. I'm lying on something soft and warm. Oh, God, it's so warm that I want to cry. I can finally sleep. I sigh contentedly, but then I feel hands tearing at my sweatshirt. I hear the seams ripping, feel the wet material being peeled from my body. I don't know what's happening. I want to defend myself, but I'm as limp as a puppet. My legs are lifted, my shoes removed, my jeans and underwear jerked down from my hips. Everything happens quickly, in an eerie silence punctuated only by an occasional mumbled curse. I gather my strength, hoping I can draw attention to myself somehow, but all that comes out is a hint of a whimper. Some familiar sound is coming from nearby, either pattering rain or a crackling fire, I'm not sure... and next to me, I'm pretty sure I hear someone undressing, a zipper going down. Then the arms reach for me again, turn me onto my side, and draw me in like tentacles, against a body. And there's nothing I can do about it. Warm, unfamiliar skin presses against my back, my legs. *No,* I want to plead, but I can't get a sound out. A hundred horrible images flash through my head. I muster up absolutely inhuman strength and wriggle a few inches away, but the arms immediately pull me back with gentle force.

"I know you don't like it, but there's no other way." The voice is right against my ear, soft but stern.

Brendan!

Dim memories wash over me. He's found me. I didn't make it. A chaotic mix of emotions churns inside me. Despair, yes. Fear, yes. But also relief. Enormous relief. I know I should be more upset about the fact that he's found me, but the last remaining glimmer of my rational mind knows that he saved my life. Even so, I scoot away from him again. Too close! Much too close! I can feel him everywhere.

"Shh, calm down." He lays a leg on top of me and crosses my limp arms in front of my chest, enveloping me completely. "Relax!"

Oh, God, how? I'm naked! And he doesn't seem to be wearing much, either. I want to protest, but I'm too weak.

"You nearly died of hypothermia. Another hour and you wouldn't have made it."

Darkness and warmth encircle me like the steam from a hot bath. Wouldn't it be nice to let myself drift off, here in the warmth? Wherever this is?

Something rough but soft licks my face, straight across my mouth.

"Grey, leave her alone," I hear Brendan say in a scolding tone. He straightens up and does something, and the licking stops, but now I feel soft fur on my bare stomach. "You can keep her warm, that's okay."

I let out a dry sob when I hear his familiar yowl.

Brendan pulls me closer, so that my back is completely against his chest. "It's okay, Lou," he whispers. "Everything's okay. I found you. Nothing bad's happened to you." He sounds like he's fighting back emotions, maybe even tears. "I'm not trying to grope you here, I won't do anything to you. I'm warming you up, that's all."

I blink a few times before finally managing to keep my eyes open. He's still got his arms wrapped around mine. My nose bumps against something soft, and suddenly I realize that we're in a sleeping bag together. I tilt my head back and peek past the edge of the material. A massive, brilliant fire is flickering not ten feet away. I feel its steady heat on my forehead, on the tip of my nose and my eyelids. It's so wonderful that it brings tears to my eyes. I turn to glance upward and see that there's a tarp or something over us. Maybe a tent. I close my eyes in exhaustion.

"Bren," I murmur. My tongue is heavy. "Thanks. Thanks for saving me..." The words don't come anywhere near expressing the depth of what I feel.

He inhales more deeply. Once, twice, a third time.

"No problem, Lou," he whispers back.

I don't know why, but something about the way he's holding me suddenly makes me happy in a weird, disturbing way. It feels like he'll never let me go. Which is also the thing I'm most afraid of. Maybe I'm simply grateful for the sense of safety, for the knowledge that I'm not going to freeze to death, that I'm getting a second chance. Yeah, that must be it. I feel my tense muscles relax in his warmth, feel myself settle into his arms. I'm tingling from head to toe, like my whole body is smiling. It's just that sense of safety. I'm sure of it. And he's holding me so tightly that I wouldn't be able to get away from him even if I wanted to. He'd never let me go, end of story. It's not my fault.

It's still dark when I awaken. I'm trembling again, and my teeth are chattering, but Brendan tells me it's a good sign.

The next time I wake up, it's because the warmth against my back is suddenly gone. Grey is still curled up against my stomach, but I don't feel his fur against my skin anymore. I pat my torso and realize that Brendan's put a shirt on me. I rotate my head and see him by the fire, putting on another log.

"Bren?" I murmur sleepily.

"Lou!" He looks up in surprise. His eyes gleam in the light of the fire. "How do you feel?"

"Frozen."

He laughs. The sound practically bubbles out of him, so happy and vivacious that it makes me feel even warmer. "Are you in pain?"

I take a mental inventory. Tentatively, I move my foot. The shooting pain promptly returns. "My ankle," I croak. I'm still too weak to carry on a proper conversation.

He nods. "I saw. It's bright blue, swollen. I'll bandage it later."

"How did you find me?" This whole thing seems like a dream.

He smiles, suddenly bashful, as if hearing more admiration in my tone than I do. He tucks his hair behind his ears uncertainly. "Grey found you."

I close my eyes, because it's exhausting to keep them open. "But... the rocks..."

Whatever Brendan's doing, it involves something that clatters like steel or iron. "Grey found the spot where you went down. Did you fall?"

I just nod.

"You must have had a legion of guardian angels watching over you. I rappelled down with Grey. He didn't enjoy it one bit. Peed all over my pants."

The mental image makes me smile, and I open my eyes again to watch him. He's stirring a pot, which is sitting in the fire atop some kind of stone platform. For a moment, I really believe that the feelings I'm having aren't wrong. That being drawn to him, for whatever reason, doesn't make me a bad person.

"Grey lost your scent at the river, so I figured that's where you crossed." He lifts the pot and carries it over to sit beside me. He's wearing a dark down jacket and lined boots. "I made you some oatmeal. It's no culinary masterpiece, but it'll do the job."

"I can't eat."

"You have to," he replies gently, pulling me into a sitting position. Grey whines as he tumbles off of me, but then crawls out of the warm burrow and goes outside.

Brendan sets the pot on the ground and shoves something behind my back to prop me up. "Just a couple bites, then I'll let you sleep again." He dunks a wooden spoon into the pot, and I open my mouth and let him feed me like a wolf mother feeding a pup. The oatmeal tastes like cardboard, but right now it's the most delicious thing I've ever eaten. Maybe it's because of the concerned look on Brendan's face, how careful he's being with me. The first spoonful also makes me realize that I'm starving.

Much too soon, he sets the pot aside. "That's enough, otherwise you won't keep it down." He holds a cup to my lips. "Peppermint tea." With his help, I drink half the mug, and then he cautiously settles me back down onto the ground. "Get some more rest."

I curl up inside the sleeping bag, warmed through and through. Nearby, I hear Brendan working on something. I haven't even asked him where we are, or how he got all of this stuff here. And I haven't asked him what happens next, either. I don't want to ask, because everything still feels too nice. For a few more hours, I don't have to do anything but focus on the moment and enjoy the warmth, without worrying about what happens when we get back. Right at this moment, we're just Lou and Bren, a boy who saved a girl from freezing to death.

But there's one thing I can't wait to ask. "Bren... the drops, were they... bad?"

The working noises stop. "I'm okay."

"You sound tired, though."

"Of course I'm tired. But not from the drops. Now go to sleep already, or you'll find out what they're like." A couple more clanking sounds, then silence. "I was joking about that."

"I know." Contentment spreads through me, and it isn't long before sleep overtakes me in a massive, unstoppable wave.

When I open my eyes again, the sky is a brilliant blue, dotted with pale-yellow and pink clouds. The fresh, clear scent of spruce needles is in the air, and the air seems to be starting to warm. I lift my head and rotate it to the right. Brendan is kneeling in front of a dark-green backpack, rummaging through it. He smiles briefly when he notices that I'm awake, but goes right on doing whatever it is he's doing. Grey, on the other hand, bounds over and licks my face happily, barking and howling.

I straighten up, blinking sleepily. Those questions I didn't ask last night are lurking at the edge of my mind, but even now, I'm not quite ready to think about the end of our story. I think my rational brain understands that it would overwhelm me, and as I look around, I actually manage to push the questions to the back of my mind.

We're still by the pale-green river, but in a much broader part of the valley. The mountains are further apart, standing majestically at the horizon, their peaks veiled by pink clouds as though they were well-kept secrets. The gravel along the riverbanks has given way to a carpet of grey-green weeds and silvery grass framed by short conifers. Everything seems untouched here, frozen in time for eternity, like this part of nature has never heard of the other, louder world.

"It's a special kind of peace and quiet, isn't it?" Brendan must have been watching me take in the scenery. "Out here, it's as if nothing and no one can hurt you."

I nod, realizing all over again how terribly hurt he must have been if he thinks he's only safe when completely isolated from other humans. "Where are we?"

He merely smiles and takes a pair of jeans and a sweater out of his backpack.

"Bren. Where are we?"

"Somewhere in Canada." He tosses me the clothes. "Put those on, and then we'll take care of your foot. Oh… right, sorry, I forgot to bring dry underwear."

I'm just glad he brought me clothes at all. Even so, it annoys me that he refuses to tell me where we are. Carefully, half-hidden by the sleeping bag, I wriggle into the pants, and then peel off the dark-blue fleece jacket so I can tug on the oversized beige sweater. A chill shoots through my limbs, and I'm relieved when I finally get the jacket on again.

I peer around at my immediate surroundings. There's a neatly rolled tarp beside the sleeping bag; long pieces of driftwood have been sunk vertically into the gravel, and just beyond my feet are several large rocks about the same height as the driftwood. So it was a tarp Brendan put up, not a tent. I glance over at him. Now he's kneeling near the fire, extinguishing it with dirt and stones. I discover the pot I ate from last night, dangling from the backpack by a cord, sparkling clean.

"How did you get all this stuff?" I ask.

He scatters a few more handfuls of earth onto the embers. "When I woke up, you were gone," he says in a slightly accusatory tone. "I knew you wouldn't survive out there by yourself. Your escape plan was pure insanity!" He reaches for a bowl sitting near the campfire and hands it to me. "You should eat before we go. It's still warm. And there's more tea in the Thermos."

I take the spoon out of the bowl of oatmeal and start shoveling the creamy mass into my mouth like a starving person. I wonder if he's mad. He hasn't mentioned it yet, but maybe it was just to spare me the worst when I was half-dead. He might put the chain on me as soon as I finish eating.

There could be another possibility, though. I realize I can't ignore the question any longer. I'd never thought I'd ever find a way to change his mind, to get him to agree to let me go. But when he drank that knockout potion of his in order to protect me, it gave me a tiny glimmer of hope. I've been ignoring it, but it's still there, in my subconscious.

I glance discreetly at Brendan. He's squatting beside me, regarding me attentively, as if trying to figure out what I'm thinking about.

"I went back to the camper and got Grey," he finally says in response to my question from earlier.

"But how did you find me the first time? By the cliff, I mean?"

"I figured you'd follow the creek. No shortage of drinking water, and you're guaranteed not to go in circles." He picks up the tarp and ties it to the outside of the backpack. "When you ran away from the cliff, I went back for Grey so that he could find you. I knew there was a storm coming…"

"So you just packed everything a person needs to survive and started searching…"

"Killer of the Unprepared."

"What?"

"That's what they call death by hypothermia. Happens to a few tourists up here every year. Wind, rain, and temperatures under forty are the perfect conditions." Bren narrows his eyes. "What were you thinking? Stumbling through the wilderness at night, and then crossing the river… I thought you couldn't swim!" He shakes his head in disbelief.

"I can't," I reply quietly. "But what choice did I have?"

He rubs his face like he's trying to wipe an emotion away before it can build. "None, I guess. Apparently I'm more frightening than death." His voice sounds hard, but there's a defiant note in there, too. He goes on packing. "I fed Grey already. I'll just bandage your foot and then I'll bring you back."

A hard knot forms in the pit of my stomach as reality sinks its claws into me, and all of the thoughts I was trying to suppress come flooding back into my head at the same time. "Back?" I ask hoarsely. "Back where?"

He stops short. "To the camper, where else?" He avoids my eyes as he says it.

"Oh, of course," I mumble. There's a boulder on my chest. I feel tears start to form in my eyes, but I quickly swallow them. How could I have thought for a single moment that he might understand what it means to care about another person? If he really, truly liked me, he'd let me go. If he actually loved me, if I were actually the most important thing in the world to him, he would know that he can't keep me imprisoned without destroying me. He's obsessed with me, that's all. It doesn't matter how much or how little I care about him. He's never going to let me go. Never. Never. Never.

"Lou?"

The sudden gentleness of his voice burns. Why doesn't he understand what he's doing? How can he whisper my name so lovingly while he's being so terribly cruel? My cheeks are wet with the tears I was trying so hard to hold back.

"You thought the fact that I drank that stuff meant things would change, hm?"

I nod. There's no point in pretending around him.

"I'm sorry." He sounds so genuine, it makes me want to scream. "I wish I could let you go. I wish I could do it in order to prove to you how much you mean to me."

"Just do it, then!"

"I can't."

"M-maybe... maybe someday?"

"I drank that stuff because I was a danger to you. I was in the middle of a flashback, and anything was better than hurting you. At that moment, even losing you would have been better than knowing that I'd done something to you, or that you'd fallen to your death because of me."

"Maybe someday? Bren... please, just tell me... someday? Maybe? Someday?"

He smiles sadly, but doesn't reply, and I don't have the courage to repeat the question. I'm too scared to hear the no.

Silently, Brendan takes the gauze out of the backpack, then kneels in front of me and bandages my ankle. His fingers are strong and warm on my skin, and I have an urge to grab his hand and hold it there, so that I can feel human touch again. I know that what I probably ought to do is punch him and spit at him, but after last night, I know how much I long to be held. I miss Jay pinching my side affectionately, I miss Liam and Avery's hugs, I even miss Ethan's admonishing hand on my shoulder. I miss everything. And if I ever get back home, I'll never contradict Ethan again, I'll come home on time every night and do all my math homework. I wonder why it is that I'm only realizing how precious those things were now, after I've lost them. The little things. Watching TV together, eating dinner together, laughing together on the veranda...

"All right, there you go." Brendan tapes the bandage in place and looks at me. His face is blurry through my tears. My shoulders are shaking. After a while, I feel his hand on my cheek. Soft and rough. Hot and cold. Bitter and sweet. He wipes the streaked tears from my face, as if it will erase my pain. *Oh, God, please tell me you're going to let me go. Just say it already!*

"Maybe could mean never, and someday could be in ten years. So... okay, Lou. Maybe someday. Maybe someday. But don't ever ask me about it again."

I take a deep breath and burst out sobbing in the same moment. I press my lips together tightly, but it doesn't help. I suddenly have a lot more crying to do.

I'm clinging to Brendan's back like a monkey, arms wrapped tightly around his neck. My sweatshirt is sticking to his sweaty T-shirt, but he's forbidden me from taking it off, to make sure I get properly warmed one more time. He's got the backpack full of our stuff slung across his stomach, and once in a while he even puts Grey on top of it, so that only his head is peeking out. I'm not sure how he can take a single step carrying this much weight. We've been at this for hours; the sun's already past its zenith, but Brendan hasn't allowed himself a single break, just keeps right on going at a merciless tempo, not making any concessions to my throbbing head. At some point, I slump forward and rest my cheek against my upper arm. Brendan's hair tickles my ear, sending tingles down my spine. Part of me's completely exhausted. And I don't mean only physically, though there's not an inch of my body that doesn't hurt after this torturous experience. It's something to do with Brendan. I don't have the strength to fight my feelings for him anymore. And I definitely don't want to start wondering whether what he said earlier was a real promise, or whether he was trying to make me feel better. I can't, I absolutely can't deal with any of it. The fact that I have feelings for him despite everything he's doing to me is so completely insane that just thinking about the massive, gaping hole between those two extremes makes me want to throw in the towel.

I let my mind drift unmoored, settle into the warmth of Brendan's body and his even stride, and watch the landscape change. The gravel gradually gives way to sand, and lush yellow and violet flowers soon emerge amid the grey-green weeds and silvery grass. Fluffy, white umbels of yarrow bloom at the edge of the forest, and grey birds are fluttering around everywhere in search of mosquitos and dragonflies. Beside us, on the river that's gradually turning into a dark-blue lake, a group of loons is following us like they're trying to figure out where we're going. Brendan said he knew a spot where we could cross the water and get to the top again, but it would take days to get there. I hope it takes forever, because beneath this endless sky, I feel weirdly free—its sheer vastness almost makes all of my troubles seem less significant by comparison.

When we finally stop to rest, I'm relieved to hear Brendan say that he didn't make it as far as he was hoping to. He sets me down, and I watch him spread out the sleeping bag and collect wood for the campfire. He doesn't find enough driftwood nearby, so he disappears into the forest, and I don't see or hear him for a long time. He leaves me there with an old can filled with rocks so that I can make noise and scare bears away. It doesn't seem to occur to him that I might run off again. Well, of course it doesn't—he's faster than I am, especially now that I'm injured so badly that I can barely walk.

Later, he whittles himself a birchwood spear and uses it to catch salmon in the shallows, which he roasts over the open fire for us.

I'm starting to feel more like myself again, both physically and mentally, as though I was frozen to the depths of my soul and I'm beginning to thaw again. Brendan gives me his thick down jacket to wear and helps me onto the sleeping bag before sitting in the sand beside me.

The salmon's delicious. We eat in silence, and then just sit there for a while. The night air is as soft and cool as silk, and the full moon overhead casts a dreamy, silvery light over the mountains and treetops. Its perfect reflection sits atop the water, a huge, gleaming diamond flanked by an army of stars. The sight of the moon and the chirping cicadas fill me with the deep sense of peace and contentment I've been yearning for. I can feel myself relaxing. Everything is fine, I don't need to be afraid of anything, not of Brendan, not of my feelings. Not out here. The millions of twinkling lights, both in the lake and in the sky, make me believe in something bigger. Maybe it was my destiny that Brendan kidnapped me. Maybe a higher power brought us together, a power I can't possibly fight against.

With the down jacket draped across my shoulders, I limp to the water and carefully ease myself into a sitting position on the gravel. My gaze sweeps across the lake, to the silent, solemn forest on the far side. After a while, Brendan comes over and sits next to me. I draw my knees in and regard the rocks along the shore, frosted in green moss. My feet, in Brendan's oversized socks, look like foreign objects beside them.

"This is your land, right?" I look at him.

He nods, surprised. "How'd you figure that out?"

"I saw a sign. Private property, no trespassing." I've been wondering all day why I didn't realize it until I saw that wooden sign. It explains why Brendan wasn't the least bit worried that someone might see us at the waterfall, like a tourist or whoever.

"Legally, it doesn't belong to me." Brendan toys idly with a rock. "I'm the leaseholder." He nods toward the see. "That's why I'm allowed to hunt and fish here. Otherwise it'd be illegal—environmental protection and so on."

"So you rented this whole area? How much land are we talking about here?"

"I forget the exact size. I know the boundaries, that's all I care about."

A memory flashes through my mind. I see me and Brendan standing by the camper in that mysterious evening light, right before he knocked me out. "When you said you spent the whole summer traveling... you were always here, on this land of yours?"

He nods.

"How many summers?"

"Three."

I think back to a conversation that feels like it happened a thousand years ago, even though it probably hasn't been very long at all. "You've been coming here since you accidentally killed that guy."

He gives me a serious look. "You're quick."

269

"I don't have much else to think about when I'm not trying to plot an escape."

He doesn't acknowledge the last part. He just crosses his legs and rests his elbows on them. His face takes on a distant look. "I guess I wanted to get away. To leave everything behind. To forget everything."

I regard him thoughtfully from the side. "What do you mean, 'everything'?" This time I'm not asking so I can understand him better. I'm asking because I find it interesting. I find him interesting.

"Fights. Life in the slums."

I swallow. "You're from the slums?"

He raises his eyes and casts a melancholy glance in my direction. "Not originally. I fled to the slums. And then, yeah, I lived there for a couple years."

I'm not sure what to say to that. If he was fleeing *to* the slums, the place he was coming *from* must have been hell. "So where are you from, then?" I ask cautiously.

"Los Angeles. I was twelve when I finally managed to run away from home. I'd tried a bunch of times, but the police kept finding me. Eventually, I realized I'd be safer in the slums, because not even the cops wanted to go there."

"Safe in the slums?" I shake my head. "That's as crazy as crossing a river when you can't swim."

"I see the parallel, yeah." His short, strangely painful laugh shatters the stillness of the night. We lapse into silence again, and I go back to staring out at the moon reflected in the lake. A group of ducks swims past, a safe distance from the shore.

It takes me a minute to screw up the courage to ask my next question. "So what were those fights, exactly? Were they always for money?"

He nods. "A fight scout discovered me."

"A what?"

"They sort of spy on street fights and stuff to pick out the strongest guys and recruit them for the underground fighting circuit. There's a lot of money in it. Tons of money." He picks up a handful of gravel and starts tossing it into the water, piece by piece. "It's different from regular MMA. There are no rules, except that you can't use weapons. Which is why it's illegal—there are no limits. People bet massive amounts of money... and only the winner decides what happens to the loser."

I furrow my brow, baffled. "What do you mean? What happens to them?"

Brendan grimaces. "You mean besides the risk of getting killed in the fight?"

I nod silently. I'm still trying to work this new information into my understanding of Brendan. Fleeing into the slums, that's nuts, right? As nuts as testing knockout drops on yourself!

"There are a few popular traditions..." He glances at me and then away. "Trust me, you don't want to know."

I decide not to push it. "Have you ever lost?"

He rubs his face. "No," he says quietly.

"Never?" I raise an eyebrow in disbelief.

"Never."

"Which is why you could afford to lease this land."

"It's illegal money. I've got a guy who washes it for me."

"Oh..."

His eyes darken when he looks at me. "I'm not a good person. I told you."

I hold his gaze. "Have you ever decided to make something terrible happen to a guy after you beat him in a fight?"

"Never. I swear."

"Must have been awful, living that way," I remark softly.

He shakes his head. "Not for me. Violence and poverty, they were both better than what I'd been living in."

For the first time, I start thinking it might actually be better not to stir up his traumatic past. I try not to let it show how much this story is affecting me, because from what I know of him, pity is the last thing he wants. "So you quit once you had enough money, I guess?" I ask, making an effort to sound composed.

Brendan nods. "When I was eighteen, I rented myself a proper apartment. But I would have kept on living that life if that... incident hadn't happened. That was when I realized what I was doing." He sighs deeply. "I never wanted to kill anyone else, but I didn't care one way or the other about my own life."

"You didn't care about your own life?" I echo, not sure why I'm surprised to hear it after everything else I've learned about him.

271

"I had nothing to live for." He stares at the shimmering surface of the lake. "Maybe that was why I was so good. Fighting didn't scare me at all. I risked everything, every time. Death was always an acceptable option. I never really came out of the darkness... until I found you."

He turns his face toward me. The deep sadness in his expression is like nothing I've ever known in my own life. I wish I could erase all of that for him, so that he can break free of his past. Suddenly, I want to know everything. Everything about him, and everything about him and me.

"When was that?" I hasten to ask before he can decide he's revealed enough about himself. I can't let him slip away from me now.

"About a year ago." He smiles, like he's glad to hear the question, not scared like I'd have expected. He picks up another handful of gravel and closes his fist around it, as if it were memories he was clinging to. "Three years ago, I moved out of my apartment and bought the camper. I just drove off, all I cared about was getting away, and I had enough money to make it happen. After a month, I landed here, and I stayed the whole summer."

"What about in winter?"

"I spent the first two winters in a small town, and last winter here. There's an old log cabin on the property, right by the lake. It's small, but it's enough to survive."

"Why didn't you bring me there?"

He smiles again. "I'm going to."

I swallow hard, glancing down at the fistful of gravel in his hand.

"It's too cold to live in the camper in winter," he adds. "You asked about that a while ago, remember?"

"Yeah, of course." Back when I found the supplies.

"It's right by the lake, you can only get there on foot. It's pretty far away, even more isolated than here. I spent four months there last winter."

I can hardly begin to imagine what kind of life that was. "Had you already found me then?"

"I had a laptop. The Internet connection was pretty bad—I only got a couple of hours a day, and the generator kept going on the fritz from the cold. But winter here was an absolute paradise. I sat there thinking about how I'd show it to you one day."

I picture Brendan sitting alone in a snow-covered cottage, looking at my summer photos. The thought doesn't scare me to death the way it used to.

"When the lake by the cabin freezes, you can hear it singing itself to sleep. For days on end, these haunting melodies fill the cove—like whale song, like a giant blowing across glass bottles. And then these high, crystalline glass-harp tones... and noises like enormous water droplets falling onto the floor of a cave. And the fog is an army of ghosts dancing across the ice in time to the music, and the wolves howl in the background."

"Sounds pretty," I grudgingly admit. "And kind of spooky."

Brendan's expression turns dreamy. "Around the winter solstice, the sun is so low in the sky that it casts shadows two hundred feet long, turning the twinkling ice crystals to ruby-red glitter dust. And when the first snow falls, it reflects the moon and the stars and lights up the night." He looks at me again, and I can't help imagining him, tall and dark, walking across a frozen white sea, his endless black shadow trailing behind him like coattails. "This place gave me peace and security. Up here, I could breathe again, I finally stopped having nightmares every time I went to sleep. But I was also alone."

I take the hand he's clutching the gravel in, holding it between both of my own. "Didn't you ever have friends? Or a girl you liked?"

"Relationships leave you vulnerable to abandonment. I can't stand being abandoned, so I put up walls."

"But you don't have them up around me?" I open his fingers, and the gravel tumbles to the ground. His empty hand lies there stiffly between mine like a dead man's, like maybe he's afraid to move it.

"No," he whispers.

"Why not?" I whisper back.

"Because I made sure you can't leave me, so I don't have to protect myself as much. The minute I saw you, everything was different. It was like I could see things through your eyes... life and stuff, I mean. You were a ray of sunshine in a dark cave." He takes a deep breath and tries to clench his hand into a fist, but I hold it tight to keep him from doing it. "If I could go back, I'd do everything differently." He swallows hard, returning the pressure of my fingers. "I wouldn't kidnap you, I wouldn't drug you... I wouldn't touch you... but it's too late, I can't go back. I don't want to lose you. Especially not now that I've gotten to know you. At first I just hoped you could make me happy. Now I know you do."

I want to cry. This is all too much for me. Brendan and his story. Brendan and the singing ice. Brendan and me. It's like I'm being torn in two. Half of me is pulling Brendan in, the other half is pushing him away. But the truth is, I don't want to push him away anymore. I want to pull him toward me, to feel the way my heart races when he puts his arms around me and holds me close. I want to know how those unrelenting lips feel on mine, what his tongue tastes like. I want him to press me down onto the sand on my back, so that I don't see or hear anything but him. I want him to fill every inch of me and never stop.

But he promised not to touch me, so if I want him, I have to take the first step. And I can't. The divide between us feels way too wide to jump across. Because if I jump, there's no going back. Everything will change, and I'm not sure I'm ready for that.

I watch him from the side as he stares toward a point in the distance. Looking at him, I feel something like homesickness, but I'm not sure why.

"Bren." I release his hand gently. "I don't think you're a bad person."

He gazes at me. His eyes are as lonely as the land around us.

"Besides kidnapping me, I mean."

He smiles, but it's not a smile of agreement. It's a smile that could also be tears. At that moment, I realize that I believe him. If he could do it all over, he wouldn't kidnap me, he would ask me out.

Later that evening, he carries the backpack into the woods and hangs it in a tree so the scent of our food won't draw any bears. After that, he sets up his own bed for the night, next to my sleeping bag. As much as I'm longing for him, I'm also relieved that he doesn't join me in the sleeping bag, because I'm way too agitated to handle that kind of physical closeness. Either he senses it, or he's just keeping his promise about not touching me. Even Grey leaves me in peace tonight, and settles down near the fire beside Bren.

I lie there wide awake for a long time, watching the countless stars pulse above me—the entire sky is flickering with their light, creating a magical dimension between light and darkness. The longer I spend looking at it, the more lost I feel. I'm not sure what to feel anymore, what's right.

"Lou?" Brendan suddenly whispers. "You still awake?"

"Yeah."

"You always wanted something to happen, right?"

My pulse immediately begins racing. "How do you mean?" I ask, already starting to suspect the answer. I keep my eyes fixed on the stars.

"I told you once that there was a second reason why I kidnapped you." He pauses. "You wanted something to tear you out of your life and lift you up into the air like an eagle. You wanted something to turn you inside out, leaving you a completely different person, unrecognizable. You wanted something to make your heart light up... isn't that about how you put it?"

I can't respond. The seconds tick by. I lie there, stiff as a board, waiting for the stars to come crashing down onto me.

"I just wanted you to know that, Lou."

And I want to laugh and cry and scream all at the same time, but I don't do any of those. I can't move.

Suddenly, a gleaming red veil flutters across the sky, like a goddess's scarf, curling and billowing as though drifting on some invisible wind. The stars abruptly disappear.

"Northern lights," Brendan says quietly. He sits up, but I stay lying there, I can't help it. I stare up at the sky, hypnotized, watching a sea of fiery red light gather around us, illuminating everything. The edges of the sea tremble, and tendrils of it break free and soar away like phoenixes. I get goose bumps down my back, not from the cold this time. Soon the sea above us shifts into a series of deep-red bands, arching as far as the eye can see. Near the horizon, a pale-pink fog swims over the mountaintops; green light flows into the swirling red, which is gradually turning to deep

275

violet. I'm breathless with awe. I've never seen anything so magnificent, so beautiful. The patterns transform again and again, bathing everything in shimmering hues for minutes on end. Finally, different-colored rays spread in every direction; the violet dissipates, leaving behind the pale, clear green. It flits across the sky like a gentle, dreamy whisper, and then wafts away.

My heart is pounding. It's like I've had a spell cast on me. The stars reappear. I look over at Brendan, who's standing at the lakeshore, head tilted way back. The magical display we've just witnessed almost feels like some kind of sign. I look up again.

You wanted something to happen...

Light and darkness blur together overhead. Maybe right and wrong aren't as far apart as I always thought. Maybe they really are simply two sides of the same coin. Otherwise, how would what Brendan did feel so right and so wrong at the same time?

When I wake up the next morning, everything's still. I feel the cool air on my cheeks, and I sit up, yawning. Grey immediately comes bounding over with a joyful yelp, and I scritch his furry ears absentmindedly as I think about last night, about the northern lights and about all the things Brendan and I said. I'm still slightly dazed, but it's a nice feeling, one I wouldn't mind holding onto for a while. Still lost in thought, I glance over at Brendan. He's lying on his side with his face buried in the crook of his elbow, seemingly still asleep. I don't want to wake him... after all, he's the one who has to carry me the entire day.

Silently, I stand up, grab the pot, and hobble to the lake to fetch water. My ankle stings with every step I take, but it's better than it was yesterday. I kneel at the shore, where tendrils of fog are billowing up from the smooth surface of the water, enveloping the sky in the same otherworldly magic that I sense inside myself. The mountains are glowing a hazy orange red, like the ridge on the back of a burning dragon. The image makes me think of one of Jayden's old stories. I dip the pot into the water, wondering what my brothers are up to right now. Is Avery making scrambled eggs this morning? Is Ethan reading the paper? Is Liam balancing underneath the apple tree again, while Jayden hammers away at his computer keyboard? A strange pain wells up within me, but it's totally different from how it was at the beginning, almost like a beautiful piece of jewelry behind glass. Have they gotten over losing me, or was it too much for one of them to bear? Are they back to their old routines yet? I'm not sure why I'm thinking about them now, of all times. Maybe because I feel so estranged from them right now, as though they were characters in a story. Like that girl whose deepest desire was to turn some potatoes blue so she could get into some stupid club. I can barely remember that girl. I do remember the little girl in the white nightshirt, though. It feels like she and I have a lot more in common.

I reach for my pendant, but even before my hand closes around emptiness, I know I've lost it. It's somewhere in the wilderness, amid the nettles and the willow herb.

Despite this dreamy feeling I have, tears still spring to my eyes —partly from the loss itself, partly because I didn't even notice it until now, which strikes me as a kind of betrayal. Is having feelings for Brendan making me care less about my brothers? No, of course not. I love each one of them as much as ever, and until two days ago, I wanted nothing in the world more than to get back home... except so much has happened in the meantime. Not just that I nearly froze to death, either. It's like I'm a totally different person inside. Which makes it seem like a whole lot more time has passed.

I scoop the pot out of the water and stand up, blinking back tears. When I get a chance, I decide, I'm going to have to ask Brendan if I can let my brothers know I'm alive. That would make a lot of things so much easier to bear. I don't know why I never thought of it before.

Just as I'm about to leave, I spot a mother elk and two calves on the opposite shore of the lake. My heart starts pounding nervously, despite the fact that I know they can't do anything to me. She's looking straight at me as she plucks at a single willow tree to break off a thin twig. Chewing, she sizes me up as if trying to decide whether I could pose a potential threat to her babies.

The moment she lets me out of her sight, Grey comes barreling up from behind me, making a ridiculous racket—barking, yelping, yowling, somewhere between wolf and dog noises. Immediately, Brendan jumps to his feet and hurries over after him.

"Mama elk and two calves," I tell him, even though he's got two perfectly good eyes.

"Hm." He knits his brow thoughtfully, but doesn't look at me. "I wonder if we should start keeping Grey on a leash. Don't want him scaring the animals."

"But wolves belong in the wilderness," I retort, watching the elk retreat into the thicket.

"Exactly." Brendan trudges off, and then it hits me: he's afraid that Grey will leave us.

The sun rises and sets, rises and sets. My sense of time is officially gone for good. It might be September already. Maybe school has already started again in Ash Springs, except without me. I wonder if Ava and Madison still think about me. Or Elizabeth and Emma. Out here, all of that seems a million miles away. The only real things here are me, Brendan, Grey, the river, the trees, and the huge, clear sky.

A tender intimacy is developing between me and Brendan, along with something I can't quite put into words. It's everywhere, between the things we say and the things we don't. It's in the looks we exchange and the glances we steal, in the accidental touches and the necessary ones. It's in the air around us, and even when we sleep, it floats over us like a finely spun web, like a dream catcher. It's huge and powerful, but infinitely vulnerable as well. One wrong word, one badly phrased remark, and it could evaporate. It reminds me of Grey, the boy in Jayden's story, and the names he gave the stars. Speak them aloud, and they'll shatter like glass.

By the time we stop to rest today, it's already late afternoon. We've found a perfect spot to camp: a tiny cove by the lake, just big enough for a campfire and a spot to bed down, framed by a semi-circle of dark spruces, slim birches, and one gigantic weeping willow whose silvery-green branches dip into the water as though they're drinking.

Brendan's already built a crackling fire out of a few rotting branches, and I'm boiling our drinking water over it while he searches the forest for more firewood. Once I've fed Grey, he bounds off after Brendan. I can hear the two of them poking through the underbrush. Brendan says something to Grey, who replies with a single bark.

While I wait, I explore our campsite a bit, and discover a couple of raspberry bushes beside the willow tree. Raspberry leaves make good tea—Brendan showed me that yesterday—so I bring a cloth bag over to the bush and start carefully picking leaves, along with the occasional berry.

I need to hurry. The sky is already bathed in the embers of the setting sun, trailing a veil of small, dark clouds.

I'm so deep in thought that I barely register the soft splashing in the distance. Must be from that group of loons. At the back of my mind, I realize that it sounds different, more rhythmic. But there are so many other water birds I don't even know... or it could be otters.

As I'm gathering the cloth bag at the top to knot it closed, I hear voices.

At first, I think I must have imagined them, but then the water washes another swell of chatter and laughter over to me.

I freeze mid-motion. My whole body goes numb, and the bag slips from my hands. Now I understand what that rhythmic splashing is: oars hitting the water and being lifted out again. My mind is completely blank for several seconds, although I finally manage to remember how to move. I take two or three mechanical steps toward the shore, until I'm just behind the hanging willow branches.

They're still far away, gliding with the current through the dark-blue water. Three canoes, two men in each. They're not speaking my language—Germans, maybe?—but I bet they'd understand "Help" and "Kidnapped."

I open my mouth to shout, but nothing comes out. Several seconds pass. Now they're almost next to me, but they haven't spotted me yet. My mind is racing; everything's crashing in on me at once. Here I am, I want to call. I even picture each syllable in my head. But I remain silent, watching one part of myself wrestle with another. They're strong-looking guys, and there are six of them. I'm sure they would be able to overpower Brendan, no matter how strong of a fighter he is. Images flicker through my head for a fraction of a second: Brendan hog-tied on the ground, Brendan lying helpless in the canoe, Brendan on trial. Brendan in a cell. Locked up alone in the dark. *So dark...* My feet get icy, and I realize I'm standing in the water. The sound of the men's jovial laughter drifts across the lake again, and one of the canoes rocks back and forth. Silently, I sidle around the hanging willow branches, moving along with the boats. Now I see new images in my mind: Ethan's haggard face, the grief in his eyes. I feel his broken heart like it's my own. My chest is burning now, and the pressure in my lungs is building and building, because I'm holding my breath so desperately. I have to scream. Right now.

Help! I press a hand tightly over my mouth to stifle the yell rising in my throat. No matter what I do, I'm a traitor. I'm going to hurt someone either way. My heart is racing; the blood is rushing in my ears. This might be my very last chance to change things. Maybe could mean never and someday could be in ten years.

You promised Ethan!

I take a step forward, letting my hand drop. *Scream*, I beg myself, but I don't. I can't. I just stand there. My eyes are burning. *Do it already!*

Then a hand clamps over my mouth. Hard. I'm being dragged behind the willow again, watching the branches part on either side of me like the loose strings on a beaded curtain.

"Not. One. Sound." Brendan's voice is rough against my ear. He's holding me so tightly that I can't move, and for a minute I'm back in the past, reliving the moment he put the chloroformed rag to my face. Instinctively, I start wriggling, kicking water up around us. I bite my lip and taste blood.

"Stop," he whispers, tightening his grip. He's not really hurting me, but something still shatters inside me. I quit resisting, realizing it's pointless to even try. I'll never have a chance against him. Nothing will ever change. He's my kidnapper, I'm his hostage. How could I have possibly seen it any differently? Tears burn in my throat, heavy and hot, but I don't want to cry. I could have screamed, I could have ended all of this. I knew how he was. Is. But I didn't want to ruin this thing between us, and now he's hurt me more deeply than anyone ever has.

Far in the distance, I can barely make out the splashing and the soft confusion of voices, but soon the landscape swallows it all. The silence returns like a living creature back from a prowl, but Brendan still doesn't release me.

Time slows to a crawl, stretching on and on. Time enough for me to truly understand what I've done, or haven't done. Time enough for me to realize that I may have officially thrown my whole life away. But here's the crazy thing: it doesn't feel like I have.

When Brendan finally lets me go and my feet are firmly planted on the lake bed again, it's like waking up from a surreal dream. Now anything could happen. Anything at all.

Cautiously, I put some distance between us, not turning to face him until I'm several paces away. He's standing there in his cargo pants and that dark sweatshirt, hands balled into fists. There's a tortured expression on his ghostly-pale face, like someone's just beaten him up and he's trying not to let on how much pain he's in.

"You didn't have to do that," I say in a shaky voice.

"Afraid I did," he whispers weakly.

"Did *not*!" I shout with such force that he actually flinches. "I wouldn't have screamed." As helpless as he looks, my first instinct is to punch him in the face, to hurt him the way he's hurting me. "If I'd wanted to, I'd have done it," I blurt out. "I had plenty of time before you yanked me away like I was just the goddamn prey you're so obsessed with."

He stares at me for several long seconds, eyes widening. "You wouldn't have screamed?" he echoes. "I don't understand... why? I mean... that was your chance... wasn't it?" He shakes his head, looking dazed. "Lou," he says in a pleading tone, like a guy who's stumbled onto another planet and doesn't know the rules. "Why not?"

I want to hit him because he doesn't realize how important he is to me, because he doesn't get that I did this for him. I want to burst into tears because he didn't give me a chance to prove it. He probably has no idea how hard that was for me just now. For his sake, I've decided never to eat Avery's scrambled eggs again, never to study with Ethan again, never to bug Liam again while he's standing on one leg looking all solemn. For his sake, I've decided I'll never read another one of Jayden's stories. For his sake, my brothers will go on suffering, and that tears my heart to shreds.

I stare at him, speechless.

Brendan presses his lips together. It looks like tears are about to start rolling down his cheeks any minute. "I screwed everything up again..." He takes a step toward me. "When I heard them... I thought they were going to take you away from me. There were six of them." He stops and covers his face with his hands. "I thought that was it, I was going to lose you forever... why didn't you call for help? I don't get it... Lou... why not?"

I can see how hard his hands are shaking. Only now do I truly understand how vulnerable he really is. His past is etched so deeply into his soul that he can't get it out on his own. He's a moth with charred wings, flapping around in the net of his past, twisting and turning and making everything worse for himself. He doesn't have the strength to fight it anymore, because he's been doing it his whole life. The truth is that he's weak and I'm strong.

That realization is probably what allows me to approach him now, even in all my despair. I've just chosen him over everything else, and I can't start questioning that decision based on how he's reacting to this situation. This whole experience has simply shown us who we are and how we are. It's shown me how much power our pasts have over us, whether we love our pasts or hate them.

I take another step toward him. "You want to know why I didn't call for help?" It comes out sounding more confrontational than I feel.

He nods, lowering his hands.

I'm standing right in front of him, and I risk a smile despite my grief, or maybe because of it. I know that if I don't jump now, I'll never do it, and then I may as well have screamed. All of my fears and doubts flare up one more time, and the terror I've always felt in his presence returns with such force that my knees turn to rubber, going so weak that I'm afraid I may lose my footing, and I know Brendan's the only person who can take my fears away from me. By holding me.

I take the final step, wrap my arms around his neck, and rest my head on his chest. My entire body is shaking. For a few moments, he stands there, frozen, but then I feel his arms encircle my waist cautiously, almost like he's not sure how to do it, or like he's afraid he might accidentally break me. I don't know how long we stand there, holding each other, trembling and overwhelmed. I can feel his heart racing through his shirt, and his ragged breath ruffles my hair. My emotions are a confused jumble, but the fear fades away until all I feel are Brendan's arms around me. Careful. Tender. Comforting. Only now do I realize how badly I wished this would happen. It feels the way I always thought it would feel the moment I came home again. I let my tears flow.

After a while, I raise my head to look at him. "Do you know why now?" I ask with a soft sob.

In response, he pulls me in close, holding me so tightly that no power on Earth could ever separate our bodies. I gasp and lay my hands on his cheeks. His lips brush my forehead, my eyelids, the tip of my nose, and then find my mouth. A hot-and-cold shiver races through me. I kiss him back, realizing I'm losing myself. I've made the jump, there's no turning back now, not ever. I taste his lips, feel his tongue sliding softly into my mouth. I'm falling and flying at the same time. My legs give out; he lifts me up, and I wrap them around his hips, running my hands through his hair and pressing myself even more tightly against him. I want to feel him all over, I want him to fill me completely, I want him inside me.

We break off for a moment, gasping for air. Our eyes meet, and his are full of such longing that it almost breaks my heart. I can't believe this is the same Brendan I first met. I can't believe any of this.

I'm not sure how, but somehow we land on the small patch of sand at the foot of the willow, surrounded by its hanging branches. He's lying on top of me, kissing me, while his hand steals underneath my shirt and strokes my breast.

Suddenly, he stops. "Maybe... maybe we should wait..." he murmurs, giving me a look that's tender and searching, yet full of desire. It's flickering in his eyes like flames, though he's making an effort to hide it. "Maybe after everything that happened, you're too confused to know what you want."

"No," I whisper. "No... I'm not confused. I'm just sad because I can't have everything."

A look of realization forms on his face, and he tries to move away, but I pull him down to me and kiss him before he can protest. He tastes so good, like salt and dirt and fresh sweat, mingled with the sadness that always seems to surround him. I never want to let him go again. I feel his hesitation, but I take it away from him by sucking on his tongue, circling it until he can't hold back any longer, until his desire mirrors mine.

Soon he pulls away to remove his shirt, and then slides mine over my head. Our pants follow.

When I feel his skin against mine, I want to scream with joy. And with pain. All of this is like a rush of a hundred million different colors. His lips on my collarbone, on my stomach, further down, much further down. His fingers in my hair, on my breasts gleaming with sweat, between my legs. My hands, discovering every inch of him. My whole world is standing still. Rain patters down somewhere in the background, but we're safely protected by the canopy of the willow; only the sand beneath us is damp. We barely notice. We don't feel the cold, we only feel each other. We forget everything, even who we are.

When I open my legs for him and take him inside me, a sharp pain jolts me out of the reverie. I gasp, and he stops, horrified. "Lou? Everything okay?" His hot breath on my sweaty face. "Does it hurt?"

"It's okay," I assure him, breathless, gazing into his eyes. "It'll pass in a minute."

He waits a moment longer before starting to move again, never taking his eyes off me. His face is right over mine. His eyes are full of astonishment, like he can't believe he's allowed to experience something so beautiful.

I slide my arms underneath his so that I can hold him as tightly as I can. The pain is ebbing. We move together, and it's like I'm melting in his hands, beneath his body. I feel him through and through, I feel things I never dreamed possible, I feel like I can never let go of him no matter what happens.

Then, without separating our bodies, he rolls onto his back and pulls me on top.

"Your turn," he whispers, breathing hard, and smiles at me.

I prop my hands to either side of him and regard him from above: the way his mussed hair falls on the sand, damp with rain and sweat; the glow on his face; his hard mouth, now soft; the angle of his collarbone. Our eyes meet again, and I'm suddenly bashful, not sure what to do.

He runs a gentle hand through my hair. "Don't worry," he says, "it comes naturally." He presses his hands against my shoulders to take some of my weight. His lower body flexes upward.

I start moving instinctively, lifting my hips and letting them slide down again. Again and again. I feel the beat deep within me, like we're musical instruments playing the same song. My blood courses through my veins. Drums pound in my ears, full and heavy. Brendan's breathing in ragged gasps. He clutches my hips, thrusting into me, again and again. Everything is on fire, I don't think I can take it. His nails dig into my butt, trying to hold me down, but that's impossible. The drumming gets louder, faster and faster. I get faster and faster. Brendan gasps. My legs start to tremble. My vision blurs to a deep-blue night. Something explodes inside me, quaking in a new and unfamiliar place. Bright stars race toward me; I fly through them. I hear Brendan shout, and an electric current pulses through me, flooding me so sweetly that I gasp and whimper almost like I'm in pain. Everything spins and spins and spins.

I collapse against Brendan's damp chest with a muted cry. He wraps his arms around me, breathing hard. His heartbeat thunders through me, filling me like we're one body. He stays inside me as that dizzying feeling subsides, leaving in its wake a sweet, heavy exhaustion where only Brendan and I exist in the world.

We spend a long time lying there in silence, as if words might take the magic out of what we've just experienced—like one of those moments of reflection that follow a fantastic story. After an eternity, we finally separate, because the night air is chilly despite our body heat, and walk toward the fire hand in hand. We slip into the sleeping bag together, somehow incapable of not holding each other, like our bodies understand more about love than our minds.

After a while, before I'm fully aware of it, Brendan's lying on top of me again.

"You're so beautiful, Lou," he whispers in a voice so full of tenderness, it's like he's been saving it up for this one moment. "I can finally tell you that without scaring you." His lips brush mine. "I wish I could just stay right here forever. This place, this night."

I stroke his cheek. "Same here," I whisper.

"Lou?"

"Yeah?"

"I'm afraid no matter what I say, I'm going to ruin everything. It feels like this is a dream, and as soon as I say one wrong thing, I'll wake up from it."

I can sense his anxiety—a reflection of my own. But right now, at this moment, I can't imagine he's even capable of hurting me ever again.

"If you don't know what to say, you could just kiss me instead," I suggest, giggling.

Brendan holds me tightly. His pupils are so huge that I can't see any brown in them at all. "But if I start kissing you, I'll want you again. And that would probably hurt you... twice in a row..."

I draw his head down to mine. "If by 'hurting' me you mean what you did with me earlier, I'll allow it."

And then we do it again, so gently and tenderly this time that it spares my body but pains my soul.

When I wake up the next morning, we're lying the way we did that night that Brendan warmed me up: his body behind mine, his arms curled protectively around me. My limbs are heavier than usual, which is probably from last night, but I don't think my scratchy throat has anything to do with it.

I snuggle against him more closely, and he holds me tighter with a contented sigh. I wish I could just lie here with him forever, but Brendan wants to get an early start, because he wants to cover a lot of ground today.

It's barely dawn as we wriggle out of the sleeping bag and get dressed, and then do everything we usually do, except today we do them together. We're both afraid to talk, so we trust our bodies instead. It's like the rest of the magic is still hanging in the air, and we're clinging to it with all of our strength. We only say as much as we absolutely have to, we smile at each other whenever our eyes meet, we hold hands as often as our activities will allow. But then there are moments I catch Brendan staring out at nothing, probably brooding over the same questions I am. As much as I hate to admit it, I know that decisions will need to be made. What happens when we get back to the camper? Will he keep on chaining me to the wall night after night, or will he start trusting me? And if he doesn't trust me, how will I react? Will I react the same way I did under the willow tree, when I told myself I can't regret my choice based on his reactions?

The more time passes, the longer I spend on Brendan's back, the more agitated I become. I'm wondering if I'll always love him. If I'll always be able to love him, or if eventually my rational mind will butt in and remind me of how much I've given up for him. At one especially anxious moment, I even wonder if I've just automatically fallen in love with my captor the way a lot of kidnapping victims do.

I'm getting uncomfortably hot, and all this thinking is starting to hurt my head.

"You're shivering." Brendan stops abruptly and glances back at me over his shoulder. "Are you cold?"

"A l-little," I stammer, suddenly realizing how wretched I feel. Talking makes my throat hurt like I've eaten too much sour candy.

Brendan carefully slides me to the ground. When he lets go so that he can get a better look at me, my legs turn to Jell-O and I stumble to one side. He quickly grabs me under one arm, using his free hand to touch my forehead. "You're burning up," he says. "You've got a fever."

"N-now what?" My teeth are chattering. I barely register that Brendan's setting me down somewhere and wrapping me in his warm, fluffy jacket. Then he pours some raspberry leaf tea from a Thermos into a cup and hands it to me to drink.

"Warmer now?" He sounds worried.

I nod. It's so nice of him to take care of me like this. When he treats me with this much kindness and talks to me in that gentle tone, all of my questions seem to disappear.

"You're still shivering, though." He gives me a stern look.

"No worries. Your back keeps me warm."

He furrows his brow skeptically. "I don't have anything with me for fevers. You think you can handle going another mile or two?"

I force myself to smile. "Sure."

Once I'm on his back again, I rest my head against his cheek. It's nice and cool, and leaning my head against it feels so good. "You think this thing, with us, it'll last forever?" I must really be out of it if I'm asking these kinds of questions.

Brendan stops dead in his tracks. "Of course. Why do you ask?"

"I dunno. Just scared..."

"Scared of what?" Now there's a mistrustful note in his voice.

"Of everything," I reply evasively. "Of us, of the future... of what will happen..."

He takes a deep breath. "Lou... I love you. There's nothing to be afraid of... I thought you knew that."

"Okay," I sigh shakily.

"Really okay?"

"Yeah."

He starts walking again, and then points across the water. "Up there is the spot where we can cross to the other side. The lake turns back into a river again."

"Bren?"

"Lou?"

"If we're going to be together forever, we can live a normal life, can't we?" I wrap my arms more tightly around his neck and nestle against his back, as if it will help prove that I'm serious. I don't think I can actually picture what I've just suggested. What would it be like, living with him in Ash Springs? Or in a big city—New York, maybe? The thought has never occurred to me until now. Maybe someday we really could go back to my town and tell my brothers we eloped or something. The idea makes me dizzier than I already am. If we could make that happen...

In my feverish state, I only notice that he's stopped walking because I start to miss the rhythmic rocking motion. His shoulders are as hard as granite; his whole body is tense, even his arms, which are securing my thighs like ropes.

"I can't live a normal life, Louisa," he declares in a firm voice.

It's like getting thrown into ice-cold water. "But..."

"No buts. You know what happens to me during flashbacks, right?"

"But I'm not going to leave you." I'm still holding him tightly. "That means we can go somewhere together."

"No," he replies, sounding impatient. "It happens when I'm around a bunch of people. Did I tell you about the guy I beat unconscious during a flashback?"

"Yeah, once. Early on, after the thunderstorm."

"The only reason he didn't call the cops was because I paid him more money than he would have gotten from suing me. The regular world is full of triggers."

"You lived in the slums, weren't there triggers there?"

Brendan snorts in contempt. "Everything about them was one giant trigger, but that doesn't matter now. If I'd had flashbacks there, I doubt anyone would have noticed."

I'm not entirely sure where this conversation is going. I probably should have just shut my mouth, but now I can't help asking more questions, even though my head is pounding. "So the flash-backs didn't start immediately after... after whatever it was?"

"No."

Danger! Thin ice!

"When did they start?"

"When I was fighting for money. Years later. I thought I'd gotten past it all, like I could go on living without constantly thinking about it." He laughs bitterly. "Sometimes one word was enough. Or a bright light. Malls were terrible—too many stimuli. A certain perfume, the way someone walked or talked..."

"I can do the shopping," I murmur quietly, but I already know there's no point talking about it any further. Especially not now. Besides, I'm way too exhausted. My brain is being boiled to mush as we speak. "Bren?" I ask quietly.

"Lou?"

"Do you think maybe they'll get better someday?"

He sighs in resignation. "Maybe. Someday."

"Bren?"

"What now?" he asks in exasperation.

I press my face into his hair. "I love you too."

I hear him swallow hard, and then he releases one of my legs so that he can pull my head close to his. "Oh, God, Lou..." he whispers hoarsely. "You're always surprising me. I want to make you as happy as you deserve."

"Bren?"

"Yeah?"

"Maybe we should talk less and hold each other more?"

"Maybe you should stop talking entirely and get better first," he suggests and heaves me up again.

"Good idea." I close my eyes and let the gentle rocking of his steps lull me. When I'm so close to his body like this, I feel safe. Close to his body like this, my doubts fall silent.

I drift through the next few days like a ghost. I can't help Brendan at all anymore—I just sit there vegetating, bundled up like the Michelin Man, watching him set up camp. He makes leg compresses for me using cool river water, gives me plenty of tea and vitamins, but I get sicker and sicker, until Grey's howling sounds like it's coming through cotton and Brendan's gentle murmuring is so distant that I don't catch it at all. His words dance around inside me somewhere. I sleep a lot, even when I'm on Brendan's back, to the point that he finally ties our torsos together with a rope, because I can't hold on any longer and I keep tipping backward.

Once, I wake up and realize it's already dark, but Brendan still hasn't stopped to make camp. I'm shivering as violently as I did the night I fell into the water. I want to tell him I need a break, but for some reason I can't form sentences anymore. An indistinct mish-mash of noises comes out of my mouth, but Brendan seems to understand them.

"It's okay, Lou. We're almost there. I know it's cold and you're shivering, but I need to give you the antibiotics tonight. Your fever's too high."

"Antibiotics?" I don't understand what he's saying. Everything is liquid somehow, like I'm swimming.

"One more hour, two at the most. I know we need to get a fire going, but I can do it."

My forehead sinks against his shoulder. "Maybe someday, maybe never, maybe in ten years," I murmur, though I have no idea why.

The first few days back at the camper are like being in a vacuum. I alternate between shivering and sweating; Brendan's constantly hovering nearby, but I barely notice how he's giving me medicine, changing my leg compresses or feeding me soup until I start feeling better. I allow myself to enjoy having him take care of me, and pretend I'm back home with him there.

On the fourth day after our return, he makes me spaghetti with sun-dried tomatoes and pine nuts; the following night, he fixes practically everything else I like, though I can't eat more than a few spoonfuls at a time. He carries me to the bench and messes with the TV until I can watch *Hero of the Week*.

One evening, as I'm sitting on the bench wrapped in my blanket, watching him wash dishes, I realize how tired he looks. The shadows beneath his cheekbones are as thick as beams, and the skin underneath his eyes is reddened. He was unusually silent at dinner, too. Not that we've been talking much lately, but he usually tries to make me laugh. Today, though, he just asked how my food was and told me Grey chewed a hole in his favorite sweatshirt. That was it.

"Are you okay?" I ask as he sets a plate by the sink to dry.

He turns all the way around and smiles at me, but it doesn't reach his eyes. "Sure. Why do you ask?"

"You're so pale. I hope you're not coming down with the same thing I have."

Even though he's not finished with the dishes, he comes over and sits on the other side. "I don't think I *can* catch what you have," he replies, reaching across the table to lace his fingers with mine.

"Why not?" I don't like the look he's giving me at all. He looks like he's about to carry someone to their grave.

He doesn't reply, and for a moment we just sit there holding hands. I'd like to know what his emergency plan is. What if one of us gets seriously ill and he doesn't have any medication?

I study his face, trying to read it, but all I see is that tiredness. When he finally replies, it's in his voice, too. "I can't give you what you really need. There's no medicine for that. I think the only reason you're sick is because you're unhappy. It weakened your immune system... and then escaping into the cold..." He stands up and walks to the cupboard that he used to keep locked. He removes a brightly colored object. My heart leaps.

It's my pendant with the charms my brothers gave me. My umbilical cord to the world.

"I found it on the cliff." Brendan shifts from one foot to the other, suddenly uncertain. "Caught on a rock. I... I dunno, I wanted to wait to give it back until I'd fixed it for you." He holds it toward me, and I grab it with trembling fingers. "Seemed like it was important to you... you never took it off."

"Oh, Bren... thanks..." It comes out in a toneless whisper. I spread the chain out on the table in front of me, arranging it so that each of the charms is visible. I run my index finger over Ethan's silver cross, Avery's red heart, Liam's Buddha hand, and Jayden's turquoise disk.

Brendan sits across from me again. "Those are from your brothers." It's not a question.

I nod anyway, but can't manage to say anything in reply.

"Do you want to tell me about them?" He gives me an encouraging smile.

A single tear rolls down my face. He catches it with one finger, and then strokes my cheek. Now his expression is solemn, almost reverent. He probably thinks that if I talk about the people I miss, I'll feel better afterward. Maybe because I once told him that it helps to say things out loud.

I take the chain and put it around my neck. It feels like part of my heart is complete again, a part that's been hurting so badly since the night I saw the canoes that I've had it buried deep inside myself.

The desire to talk about home is overwhelming, so I pick up the chain like it's a life preserver and force myself to just start speaking. In a halting voice, I talk about the sacrifices Ethan made for the family, his fear of losing me, the burden he bore for us all. I tell Bren about Avery's way of mediating between us and keeping the family in balance. I describe Liam, who never felt like he belonged because he was too young to be one of the adults in the house and too old to be one of the kids, which is probably why he went to India—he felt like there was no place for him at home. I'm surprised at how clear all of that suddenly seems from a distance. I tell him about how smart Jayden is, how passionate he is about understanding every-thing, and how reserved he is around other people. And then I tell him about the little girl in the white nightshirt who chased invisible rhinoceroses and never wanted to live anywhere but that wooden house in Ash Springs.

When I stop talking, I'm crying. Maybe I've been crying this whole time.

Brendan strokes my hands, which are still clutching the neck-lace. He looks even worse than he did earlier.

"You're acting so weird today," I say, hoarse from crying. "What's wrong?"

"I dunno." He takes my head in his hands and kisses my fore-head tenderly before standing up and walking out.

I watch the door shut behind him. He seems lost in a strange way. But he has me, doesn't he? No, he has more. He has my love. Which was what he always wanted.

"Do you understand him?" I ask Grey, who's dozing beside me on the bench, but of course his only response is to lick my fingers happily.

Shaking my head, I get to my feet and finish the dishes. When-ever I have to stop and rest against the counter because my legs are threatening to give out, my gaze shifts outside, to Brendan sitting by the fire smoking. He's staring into the flames, the way he used to do all the time. Once or twice, I see him toying with his armband.

I snuggle up in the warm blanket again, follow Brendan out into the night, and then simply take a seat on his lap. He wraps his arms around me, but his embrace feels different. More cautious, more withdrawn, almost like there's something in between us that I don't know about.

"Is the charm on your armband a memento, too?" I ask after we've been sitting in silence for a while.

"It belonged to my mother." He clears his throat elaborately.

"Do you want to talk about her?"

"No." There's an edge to his voice I haven't heard in a while.

"You said she abandoned you," I say anyway.

He jerks like I've just punched him in the gut.

"And yet you still have that coin, and you even had that symbol tattooed on your back."

Now he lets out a pained groan and covers his face with his hands. "Please, don't, Lou."

"Bren, look at me." I gently pull his hands away. When I look into his eyes, they're huge and wide and full of all the terrible things he must have gone through. "I want to help you. One day you're going to have to talk about it. You've got to."

He stiffens. "I don't *have* to do anything."

"Otherwise we'll never be able to have a normal life together. I'll always be scared of you. Part of me will always be afraid of the other Brendan, you know?"

He stares through me like I'm invisible. "I never told you about my mom. How do you know I think she abandoned me?"

I try to hold his gaze with my own, but he's trapped in the darkness. "You talk about the past during your flashbacks," I finally admit. "You play different roles."

His whole body freezes.

"Hasn't anyone ever told you that?"

"No."

I slip my arms around his neck. "I guess I know more about you than you realize. You told me you couldn't talk about those days, but when you're stuck in your memories, that's exactly what you do." I hadn't planned on telling him any of this, but maybe it's better if he knows. "You have to talk about it. Maybe then the flashbacks will stop."

"Is that why you did it?" His voice is suddenly so icy and dark that a chill runs down my spine.

"Did what?"

"Loved me. Was it out of pity?" He jumps up, half-shoving me off his lap, which is all it takes since I tumble over in fright anyway.

I stumble a few feet away and can't help laughing because everything he's saying is so ridiculous. "Where did you get the idea...."

He stares at me, narrowing his eyes to slits. "Was it out of pity? Yes or no?"

"N-no, no! Of course not..." I stammer, realizing he's dead serious. My heart starts beating wildly—whether in fear, shock, or bewilderment, I'm not sure. I shake my head. "You think the only reason I didn't yell for those canoers was because I pitied the guy who kidnapped me? Do you seriously think that would be enough for me to want to sacrifice my whole life? Pity?"

He walks to the fire, stands there with folded arms. Suddenly, he doesn't look sick anymore at all. He's wearing that mask of rage and bitterness again. "Maybe you would have shouted for them, how can I know for sure?" he asks in the voice of a stranger.

I'm frozen in pain and devastation. "Stop it," I plead in a choked whisper.

"Maybe I got there right in time, and you took advantage of the situation. Slept with me to prove to me that you love me."

I'm trying to figure out what's going on here, but I just don't understand. How can he say these things after what we shared? How can he take that magical night under the willow and twist it around so that it was just some cheap game I was playing? How can he accuse me of faking my feelings when I'm laying myself bare to him, making myself completely vulnerable? Doesn't he know how much it cost me to admit all of this to myself? Doesn't he know that it feels like my soul has suddenly become a piece of raw, exposed skin?

"I wasn't trying to prove anything to you!" I hiss. Rage starts bubbling to the surface through my shock. "I had nothing to prove to you because I *love* you! But if you keep talking like this, I'll probably end up regretting it."

"Oh, yeah, I regret a lot of things, too." He glowers down at me with a frightening expression on his face. "How could I have believed for even one second that you meant any of it? What were

299

you hoping to get out of those theatrics? Were you going to appeal to my guilty conscience eventually? Tell me I can't go on keeping you prisoner since we're so close? That if I truly love you, I'll set you free?"

The light from the fire flickers across his features, making him look as terrifying as he does during his flashbacks.

"I... I can't believe you really think I would do that." I think I'm about to have a nervous breakdown. My brain can't keep up with all of this. "Do you seriously think I would go as far as to sleep with you... just so you would think I love you?"

He gives me a contemptuous scowl, shrugging his shoulders. "Maybe you genuinely thought you could heal me if you pretended to be into me. But it was never about me, it was about your freedom."

I'm freezing cold, shivering violently. This whole conversation is so wrong. "You... you must really, really hate me to say those things about me." I reach for my necklace and clutch it so hard that the charms bore into the palm of my hand. "I don't get you. All I said was that I know more about you than you realize. You had an attack during that thunderstorm. Even back then, you told me more than I think you would have otherwise. And I still hated you afterward anyway. Those two things have nothing to do with each other."

I look at him, at the way he's standing there, cold and hostile. I don't know where the Brendan who believed in me and my love has gone. He can't have just disappeared. I screw up my courage, walk over to him, and force myself to smile as I grip his shoulder, like maybe it'll pull him out of this confused rage. "Bren, please, surely you don't seriously believe that."

He shudders at my touch like he's afraid I'm trying to poison him. "Quit it, Louisa." He jerks to the side.

I'm so desperate to get through to him, I want to pound my fists against his chest. Not screaming is taking an absolutely inhuman amount of self-control. I take a couple of long, deep breaths. "Brendan. Listen to me. This is crazy! I didn't fall in love with you because your dad buried you in the ground somewhere," I say, shaking my head. Only when I hear him inhale sharply do I realize what I just said.

He's pale now. His eyes are dark graves. "Stop that! Now!"

"Bren, I love you! And of course I'm unbelievably sorry about what happened to you. And yeah, I *do* wish I were the one who could heal you, but unfortunately, love alone isn't going to do it." I reach for him again, but he retreats again like I'm a monster. "The things that happened to you, all the love in the world wouldn't heal them. When you left that cupboard open, I saw one of the pictures you drew. I told you that once already, but you were in a flashback, so you probably don't remember. Let's go to a psychologist and start fresh..."

"Sure, bring me to a psychologist so that you have a chance to escape!" he shrieks, completely out of his head. "You don't want me! You just want to leave!"

"*That's not true*!" I scream right back at him. "I gave up everything for you! My whole *life*. But apparently that isn't worth anything to you. You know what? I wish I *had* called for help at the river! I wish I'd at least *wanted* to call for help! I wish I was at home, instead of with you!"

He hunches his back as though bracing himself against a whipping. Then he stands there motionless for seconds on end, staring at me. When he speaks again, his voice is completely emotionless. "I'm so glad I saw through you in time."

The words are a maelstrom whirling through my head. A wave of dizziness washes over me. "What do you mean, *in time*?"

The corners of his mouth twist downward in scorn. I've never seen him this way. "I'm such an idiot! I wanted to let you go." He says it softly, but so cuttingly that each word is a needle in my heart. "No kidding, I've been considering it since we got back here. Wait, before that—since you told me you loved me." He grips his forehead and lets out a short laugh, then shakes his head in disbelief. "But it was all a lie."

He was thinking about letting me go! I can't believe it. Surely he's not serious. He's just saying that to hurt me. My head is one giant mass of chaos. But then I suddenly remember the weird way he was behaving earlier. He was acting so lonely, like he'd already lost me. The realization makes a violent sob bubble up in my throat. "You were going to let me leave?" I whisper. "You thought about it?" I take a step toward him, but he moves away again.

"Doesn't matter," he says decisively. He's as unapproachable as he was in the beginning. "I changed my mind."

I press my fist to my mouth to suppress my crying, but it won't stop, it just won't stop. I don't want to cry, though, because he'll think I'm crying over having lost my chance to leave... and I'm not, I'm crying because of him. Because he doesn't see how much I love him. He's so sick that he's denying the truth. He thinks he doesn't deserve love. And it's only now that I understand how real and true and genuine his love is. I know what letting me go would cost him. Knowing that he even considered it hurts so much that I want to die.

I stretch out a hand in his direction. "Bren... please... you can't think that about me..."

"You should go inside," he says coldly. "You're not quite healthy yet." Abruptly, like a marionette taking orders from the spirit world, he sets into motion and grabs the arm I'm still reaching for him with. "Come on."

He pushes me along in front of him. *Travel America* blurs into a red-and-blue ocean before he jerks me up the steps. "Brendan, please, snap out of this..." In the hallway, I stumble over the blanket, but he catches me and shoves me onto the bed.

He walks away stiffly to retrieve a chain and a handcuff. "Give me your wrist."

I hold out my arm. I can't see anything anymore through the tears. I hear the lock click into place, and then I hear him stomp away and slam the door to the outside. Every inch of me hurts. It's like I've lost everything—Brendan, my brothers, my freedom, all of it. I roll onto my side and draw my knees in. My whole body is wracked with sobs. I don't want to feel anything anymore. If there were knockout drops sitting around in here, I would drink the whole bottle.

An ear-splitting shriek shatters the night, chilling me to the bone. I'm totally confused for a few seconds before I realize that I must have nodded off from grief and exhaustion. At first I'm not sure whether the scream was real or part of my dream. But I wasn't dreaming, was I?

I jerk into a sitting position and peer out the window. The fire is still going, but Brendan's disappeared from view. I press my nose to the pane, trying to get a closer look, but then another scream pierces the air. It sounds dark and evil, like a wild animal discovering that it's chained up. Grey starts growling. I scoot to the center of the bed and peer into the hallway. Grey's standing at the side door with his ears back, snarling. Shudders of terror run down my spine. I'm not sure if those are human or animal noises.

"Here, Grey!" I whisper, patting the blanket with my hand. My gaze shifts to my wrist.

The chain is gone!

Brendan must have taken it off while I was asleep! Even as frightened as I am, the realization gives me a tiny glimmer of hope, but I'm way too anxious to figure out what this means. I tiptoe forward, leaving the light off, and peek through the window above the sink. Nothing's changed. The campfire casts a bright glow across the grassy area in front of the spruces. I scoot across the bench to peer out the window on the opposite side. Darkness and trees. Nothing else.

Grey's still growling at the door.

"Shh, calm down," I murmur as reassuringly as I can, and then scoot back toward the hallway. Is the door locked? Another wave of goose bumps runs over my arms. If Brendan's out there having a flashback, it'd probably be better if I made sure he didn't come in, regardless of what he thinks about me now. Cautiously, I slip toward the door and fumble with the lock until it clicks shut. I breathe a sigh of relief—but then another realization hits me.

What if the thing out there isn't Brendan? What if it's actually an animal? A grizzly bear or a bull elk? Those don't generally care much about locked doors. What if Brendan needs help?

I stand there for a moment, trembling. Grey's fallen silent now, and I listen hard for more noises, but there's nothing out there.

Silently, I sneak to the driver's cab, one step at a time. The front window is the only one I haven't checked. I kneel between the armrests and peer out. The sky is raven black, which is why it's so dark out that I can barely see a thing. I let my eyes drift down to the treetops, and then to their slim trunks.

Nothing.

I go back to the door. I'm not sure what to do. I cast an uncertain glance at Grey, who jumps up on my legs excitedly. He's grown a lot, but he's still no bigger than a poodle. Next to a full-grown bear, he'd probably look like a stuffed animal, and his growling and yowling wouldn't be enough to scare anything bigger than a squirrel.

The next scream seems to rock the whole camper. It feels like the floor is shaking underneath my feet. The evil in it has given way to a mixture of horror and hopelessness. Grey starts whining, and I break out in a sweat. All at once, I know that it's Brendan. He needs help. He's never screamed like this. I'm sure he's trapped in his past, reliving those horrible moments again. I remember how I felt in that box. Alone in the dark, not sure if I'm dead or alive.

I have to get to him! Flashback or no flashback! I have to tell him that I love him and that he can't give up hope. He needs to know that I'm not leaving him, no matter what! He told me I was his light, his sun.

I unlock the door and walk down the steps. Icy night air swirls around me, but I'm only half aware of it. Without the screams, the night suddenly seems deathly still, even if it isn't. The fire is crackling nearby; an owl hoots somewhere in the distance. As I walk along the edge of the woods, the dry needles snap and crack beneath the soles of my shoes.

"Bren?" As confident as I was about this idea a minute ago, I'm absolutely terrified now. Darkness lies in the forest like death. I keep peeking between the trees—Bren can't have gone far. I circle the entire area, staying close to the dark conifers. Eventually, I get back to the fire. "Bren? Where are you?"

Suddenly, I hear a clinking sound. Something huge and dark is racing toward me. It throws itself at me, and I tumble to the ground. Pain shoots through my hands, through my ankle. Dust and dirt whirl around me.

"You filthy bastard son of a godless whore! I'll kill you!"

I roll onto my back. It takes me several seconds to take stock of the situation. Brendan's standing over me, secured to a tree by a long iron chain, the way he was the night of the thunderstorm. The handcuffs at the end are around his wrists.

"Bren." I'm afraid to scoot away, afraid of how he'll react. "Bren, it's me, Lou." My heart is beating in my throat. His eyes are blood-shot, full of a chilling madness.

"I'll kill you," he hisses through his teeth.

"No," I whisper shakily. "You won't. You love me."

"You left me. You went away... it was so dark... do you know what it was like down there, in the ground..."

"Yeah. I do." I need every ounce of my self-control to keep myself from bursting into frightened, empathetic tears. "Everything was quiet. You were alone. In every space between two heartbeats, you thought you'd died. And when you thought you were dead, you were still alone. Even when you were out again. You longed for your mother's arms, but she never came back."

"How could you leave me?" All at once, his face is as haggard as Ethan's was in that newspaper article.

It suddenly occurs to me that my brothers may believe the same thing about me that Brendan does about his mother. "M-maybe... maybe she didn't leave you," I stammer. "Something might have happened to her. Maybe someone kidnapped her. Or maybe the person who did those things to you also made sure that she couldn't find you. Or that she couldn't come back."

Brendan stares at me with wide eyes. His fists unclench in slow motion. He shakes his head, dazed. "Lou?" he whispers weakly. "What are you doing here?"

"Bren, thank God..." When I look at him, I almost burst into tears after all, this time in relief. Only now do I see the blood welling up beneath his iron shackles, running down his hands. "You're hurt," I exclaim in shock.

"Better me than you," he growls and jerks on the chain, which releases another rivulet of blood. "You need to get back inside, now."

"No." I clamber to my feet. For a moment, my vision blurs into a swirling mass of shadows and light. I wait for the dizzy spell to pass before stepping toward him. "Let me stay with you."

He hunches over and then starts screaming again a moment later, seemingly giving voice to all the tortures of his childhood at once. He's shivering uncontrollably, staggering back and forth.

I can't stand seeing him this way. It tears me apart, because I don't know how to help him. All I can do is stand there, paralyzed.

305

When it passes, he doesn't seem to know where he is anymore. I step closer again, but he stumbles away from me. Then I notice just how many chains he's linked together. He disappears into the strip of forest between the campfire and the lake, hiding from me in the darkness. I follow him and discover him between two trees. He's standing perfectly still, breathing in ragged gasps. I don't know what he's going to do next. Knock me to the ground? Beat me up? Try to kill me, maybe? I know it'd be better if I stayed out of reach, but I can't leave him out here by himself in the darkness.

"Brendan..." I push aside a branch that's in my way. We're barely an arm's length apart now. *Go on, Lou, get closer!*

I know that I'm going to have to take one more leap in order to get through to him. Just jump this one final chasm, and then everything will be okay. It has to be! I look at him. He's frozen, trapped inside his own head, but I'm not going to abandon him. *Closer. Get closer.* I feel the cold loneliness enveloping him. My knees are shaking. *Keep breathing. Let your bodies take over. Closer. There you go.*

With a gasp of fear, I encircle his waist with my arms and put my head on his chest. I'm expecting him to push me away, but it's as though he's been turned to stone. I close my eyes for a moment to put myself in total darkness. He's not seeing anything, either, though his eyes are open. I cling to him, trying to imagine what he's been through. Reality seems to blur, like we're becoming one spirit. Even though we're in the forest, we're locked in. Locked into our reality, locked into this moment. The walls inside him are so massive, they seem to surround us both. But they might be glass walls rather than stone, judging from how he described it once.

"I'm not leaving you by yourself, Bren," I murmur after a long time.

"You're crazy." I can sense that he wants to push me away, but for once he doesn't have the strength.

"I don't care if you kick me or hit me or whatever when you're out of your head. I'm not going anywhere. Push me away, I'll still be here." I hug him as tightly as I can.

He's trembling in my arms. "I can't let you do that."

"You don't have a choice. You said I was pretending, but you're wrong. I love you."

He lets out a cry of despair and buries his face in his hands. His chains clink as he lowers his hands again to look into my eyes. "I know, Lou," he whispers. "I know."

Tears of relief spring to my eyes. I can't get a single word out. He strokes my cheeks, making them wet with his blood and my tears.

"I really was thinking about letting you go," he says quietly. "I guess deep down I was trying to find a reason not to have to do it. So I wanted to believe you were faking it. I wanted to be mad at you."

More and more tears roll down my cheeks. I'm so unbelievably glad he doesn't believe that crap anymore.

"Hey, don't cry. Shh. Everything's okay. I'm sorry about what I said." He withdraws from my embrace, but then his face abruptly turns anxious. "You need to go! Hurry!"

"No, I'm staying! And the next time you think you're in that place you're so scared of, just imagine I'm there too."

"Lou..."

I fling my arms around him again. "Do it, please! Just try."

His muscles tense up. "What if it doesn't work? What if I attack you?"

I press my hands against his back tightly. "I'll stay anyway."

I feel his rib cage tighten, like he's trying to suppress the horrors inside him.

"Let it out," I whisper. "Scream, shout, go ahead, nobody will hear you. Except me. And I can take it. I'll be right here."

His arms close around me. His fingernails dig into my shoulder blades. Within seconds, rivers of sweat soak his entire shirt. And then he starts screaming. Dark, anguished sounds of pain and horror fill the entire forest. Something dashes away through the underbrush. A knot of fear forms in my chest. Bren's trembling so hard he loses his footing. He takes me with him. I don't know what I was expecting, but this is worse than anything I could have ever imagine. His screaming seems to envelop me in his terror. I can feel it on my skin, like frost. See it in my head as twisted images, the product of my own imagination: a dark grave, a coffin, hands pushing on the lid from the inside, but it's too heavy. It's so heavy, and everything's so terribly dark. *So dark. So deep in the ground. I can't breathe, I can't breathe. Mom? Where are you? Come back! Mom, come get me out! Mom, please, it's so dark!*

I try to catch my breath, and then realize that I can't breathe. Brendan's squeezing me so tightly that my ribs are pressing against my lungs, so my rib cage can't expand at all. Desperately, I brace my arms against his, trying to push him away, but he doesn't let go. I throw my head back. A high, whistling noise comes out of my mouth. Black stars flash in front of my eyes. *Bren*, I want to scream...

A moment later, he shoves me back, and I stumble off to the side. "Bren." I gulp air desperately, trying to meet his gaze.

He's standing right in front of me, staring down with a hate-filled expression. He takes one long step toward me. "I should kill you," he whispers in a terrifyingly soft voice. Before I can react, his hand is at my throat, and then he slams me against the nearest tree.

"Bren," I croak. "Don't." I try to wedge my fingers underneath his, but I can't.

He squeezes, crushing my throat. Fear courses through my veins. His eyes are pure ice. "You're nothing, you little bastard. Nothing. Dust and ashes. I could kill you and nobody would ever know. Nobody would ever miss you."

A whimper escapes my lips.

"I'm going to stick you in a coffin and bury you in the yard. But this time, I'm not going to dig you up again. You can shit your pants in there as much as you want, and die in your own filth, how does that sound?" He leans in toward me, fixing me with midnight-black eyes filled with contempt. "Answer me!"

"Bren... stop... you're... not... him..." The pressure on my throat cracks the words into choppy noises garbled with fear.

"Your pitiful whining isn't going to save your weak, sorry ass." His breath hits my face like fists. His fingers tighten around my throat even more.

Everything is spinning. I have to get through to him, but I don't know how. I can't think. "Bren..." I pull on his fingers, taste salt on my lips. "I love you... come back..."

He stiffens. His eyes seem like they're made of glass.

"Don't... leave me! Come... back!" The raw pain in my throat is getting worse with every word. "Please... come back..." Snot runs from my nose, mingling with my tears. "Brendan... please..."

His grip loosens, and his expression turns to one of confusion. "I'm here, Lou," he whispers, bewildered. Then he freezes, staring at his hand, which is still clutching my neck. Confusion gives way to shock, and then absolute agony. Slowly, he releases his fingers one by one, like he's afraid he might make a wrong move somehow.

My legs buckle immediately, and I collapse to my knees. I draw in a sharp breath, and a moment later, I feel him pulling me up again carefully. "Lou, say something, please..."

I cling to his upper arms and inhale cautiously as tears stream down my face. My throat still hurts like hell, but right now I don't care, because it's over. For now, it's finally over!

"Forgive me... Lou..." He mumbles something else that I don't catch, and wipes my tears away.

I blink until my vision clears, and then look up at him: his weary eyes, his hollow cheeks, the sweat beading on his forehead. I don't regret anything. "Wasn't so bad," I whisper, trying not to let on how much pain I'm still in, or how terrified I was. My own fear is nothing compared to what he experienced.

He shakes his head vehemently. "You're lying. You're shaking like crazy."

"I'm just cold."

"Lou. My hand was around your throat, and you're telling me it wasn't that bad?" He lifts my chin to inspect my neck. "Fuck," he hisses. "When I flip out, you can't be there. That's insane. You have to believe me."

"I believe you, but I'm doing it anyway." Somehow I manage to force out a smile. "Anyway, you're back, that's all that matters."

He rests his forehead against mine. "I'm not letting you put yourself in danger again."

"You have to." I punch him in the chest playfully. Even that one slight motion is enough to wear me out. "You're the one who chained yourself to a tree like a dog, not me."

He responds with an artificial laugh, but then turns serious again immediately. "Then at least let me carry you back to the fire." Without waiting for my reply, he scoops me into his arms. He's shaking more violently than I am, but he pretends nothing's wrong —except once, when he nearly trips over his own long iron chain, and curses.

When we reach the fire, he sets me on the ground, and then scoots in behind me, wrapping his arms and legs around me to form a warm, protective cage. I lean my head back against his chest and hold his forearms.

"Don't let me go ever again, Lou," he whispers. "Not ever."

"I won't," I whisper back and close my eyes.

After a few minutes, he strokes my hair. "Next time I have an attack, you keep your distance, okay?"

"Bren...."

"Promise me!" He says it so urgently, so desperately, that I nod reluctantly. I know he'd never forgive himself if he injured me, and I definitely don't want him feeling guilty. He's suffered enough already. And if I'm being honest with myself, I know he's right.

"I'm only going a few feet away, though," I say in a decisive tone. "And if you need me, I'll be there."

He doesn't respond. I turn halfway toward him, and almost immediately, his lips are on mine, soft and rough, hesitant and insistent. I taste blood and tears. Sadness and joy. He runs his hands down my head and then wraps his arms around my shoulders, pulling me closer. I'm falling into a bottomless pit, down, down. I never want it to stop. I never want to hit the ground. I want to keep falling, keep losing myself with him.

The sky is already full of dove-grey clouds when I finally retrieve the key to Brendan's restraints, which he left on the side-view mirror. Arm-in-arm, we return to the camper.

Grey puts on a welcoming ceremony like we've been gone for a week. This time, though, I can't give him the attention he wants—I just fall straight into bed. We've fought too many battles tonight.

I'm dimly aware that Brendan starts heating some milk for Grey, but then I'm out, fast asleep like a newborn baby.

TWENTY-THREE

I awaken to the hum of the generator and the sound of the coffee maker burbling on the counter. I blink, bleary-eyed, and sit up.

"Hey, sleepyhead." Brendan smiles at me. He's standing in the hall, toasting our last few frozen pancakes as though nothing unusual happened last night.

"Hey yourself." It hurts a little to talk, but other than that, everything seems okay. Well, my body feels like one big crisis zone, but for the first time, I'm not worried about it. Not after last night.

"What time is it?"

"Afternoon."

I slide out of bed and walk over to Brendan slowly. He's still wearing the same clothes as last night, but his hair's neatly combed and tied back in a short ponytail. I catch a glimpse of a gauze bandage underneath one sleeve of his hoodie, and there's a Band-Aid on his forehead.

He wraps his arms around me gently, and I lay my head on his chest. We spend a few minutes just standing there, silent except for the humming generator and the dripping coffee machine. Everything around us is the same, but things between us feel new—deeper, heavier, more solid. Not fragile like glass anymore. I know I'm not going to have to weigh each word to make sure it won't destroy our relationship. I nestle against him, as secure as a moth that's found a safe spot to hide. I never want to come out.

When the coffee maker stops running, we let go of one another. Brendan lifts my head with his fingers and peers at my neck. He doesn't say anything, but his eyes speak volumes. I slip into the bathroom and immediately notice five long, red marks on my skin. Instinctively, I run my fingertips over them. They're not too bad—they'll probably be gone in two or three days at the most. Brendan's words, on the other hand, I'll never forget. The things he went through are still echoing inside me like a dull pain. I was wrong. He's not weak, he's strong. Otherwise he couldn't possibly have survived all of that.

I splash some water on my face and comb my hair, and then go into the back room to put on fresh clothes: clean underwear, long jeans, my white blouse, and the pale-yellow scarf with the tiny multicolored hearts to hide Brendan's finger marks.

When I return to the front, Bren gestures to the set table with a smile. "Sit!" He switches the generator off. To my relief, he doesn't say anything about the scarf.

I slide onto the bench. "Why are the curtains drawn?" I ask. This is new. Even the ones dividing the main room from the driver's cab are shut.

"I wanted you to be able to sleep as long as possible. I mean, by the time we went to bed, the sun was already up." He smiles again, but this time he averts his gaze. "Plus I thought this would be more romantic."

"So you want to spend the rest of the day in here with me, hm?" I tease him, not taking my eyes off him. Why won't he look at me?

But then he does, with a wink. "I can think of a couple things I wouldn't mind doing with you..."

I wink back, but the weird feeling stays with me. Head propped on my hands, I regard the blue dishes with the little vanilla-colored roses. Something's different, even though everything's the same. Everything except the drawn curtains.

I glance around again, and then I realize what's bothering me. "Where's Grey?"

Brendan pours two cups of coffee and sets them on the table before stacking the pancakes on a plate. "He's in the passenger seat. Probably better if we let him rest, he was puking all morning."

"He threw up? Is he sick?"

Bren sits down beside me, and having him close calms me down. I'm not sure why exactly I need calming down. It's just this weird feeling. "Don't worry about it. Probably ate something bad in the woods. I'll have to start giving him meat soon, or who knows what half-rotten dead things he'll start finding to chew on."

I smile. "You want to do that regurgitating thing, knock yourself out. I'm still gonna pass." I lean against him affectionately and sip my coffee. For some reason I'm not hungry. After a while, I realize Brendan's not touching his food, either. The funny feeling in my stomach flares up again. "You didn't sleep at all, did you?" I glance at Brendan from the side. His face is positively ashen, and the whites of his eyes are shot through with fine red lines. "If you spent the whole morning mopping up wolf puke, you can't have slept."

"Yeah, you're right." He nods at the pancakes, the maple syrup, and the lemon cookies. "Eat something, Lou, please. You need your strength."

There's a note in his voice I can't quite place. It's not just his usual worry. There's something decisive in it, too. And pained. But maybe he's simply wrecked after the long night and the work-intensive morning.

I try to smile away the weird feeling in my stomach. "Well, you eat too, then."

"Okay."

The longer we spend chewing in silence, the more I get the sense that Brendan's keeping something from me. Once I've choked down half a pancake, I set the rest back on the plate. "What's wrong, Bren?"

He lowers his hand in slow motion, staring at the pancake as though it's the most interesting thing he's ever seen. I pluck it out of his fingers and slap it onto my own plate. "Tell me!"

"Okay." He reaches across the table to take my hands in his, squeezing them so hard that a sense of foreboding rises in my sore throat. "That day on the river, when you didn't call to those guys for help... you made a decision that was right for you in that moment. It may have actually been wrong, but it felt right at the time, I don't know."

"It's still right."

He smiles, but he looks so lost that I nearly burst into tears right then and there. "Maybe today it is. Maybe it is for you. But what about for your family? What about your brothers?"

I swallow hard. Deep down, I know he's got a point, but I don't want to hear it. Not after yesterday.

He grips my fingers even more tightly. "What if our relationship falls apart five years from now? Then I'll have stolen part of your life, kept you from going to college or starting a career. You'll hate me."

"I could never hate you," I choke out. I'm not sure what he's getting at, but whatever it is, it feels horribly wrong.

He takes our interlaced fingers and presses them to his own cheek. "I believe that you love me, Lou. Don't get me wrong. But what if you only love me because you were so lonely? What if it's just the kind of love that victims have for their kidnappers?"

I withdraw my hands from his. "What do you want to hear, Bren? How am I supposed to answer? I can't be sure about any of that. All I know is that I love you. I liked you the minute we met at the visitors' center. I could just as easily have fallen for you without… this."

He gives me a penetrating look. "I'm not sure if you're capable of making good choices right now, Lou. Which is why I decided to choose for you."

"Choose what? What do you want?" My voice breaks.

He presses his lips into a thin, white line, but the shimmering tears in his eyes are what scare me the most. "Maybe is yes, and someday is today." His lower lip trembles, and he bites down on it so hard that it starts bleeding.

It takes me a minute to figure out what he means. "You… want to… let me go? Today?" All at once, my throat is so tight that I can't breathe—even worse than yesterday. It's like I'm underwater, watching Brendan's words swim past me from beneath the surface of a lake. I can see his lips moving, but I can't understand what he's saying. None of this is really happening. I'm imagining the whole thing.

"Lou? Lou… are you hearing what I'm saying?"

I shake my head briefly and look up at Brendan, at his red eyes and his firmly set lips. I know he thinks he's doing what has to be done. But I also know it's wrong. "You can't just send me away," I blurt out. "I'm not going."

He stands up. My first instinct is to threaten to tell on him if he sends me away, but we both know I would never do that.

Without saying a thing, he draws back the divider curtain in front of the driver's cab. For a second, I think maybe I've lost my mind. I stare outside, paralyzed. No spruces, no pines, no birches. No forest at all. Just a huge, grey parking lot with a couple of beat-up, forgotten-looking station wagons. A blackbird hops across the asphalt and picks up something I don't see. Suddenly, I feel totally and completely lost.

"Bren..." I whisper. "How... I mean... what..." I can't form a coherent thought. Dazed, I get up and go to the window over the sink, and then open the curtain... revealing more cold, grey parking lot beneath a cold, grey sky. In the distance, I see a long, flat concrete building, and what look like human figures in front of it. It strikes me as unreal, not part of this world. Not part of mine, anyway.

"I spent the whole day driving. You... you were dead asleep, you had no idea. I wanted to surprise you."

My vision blurs. "Grey didn't eat anything bad," I say absently.

"He got carsick."

I turn to look at him. I want to scream at him, but then I see that he's covering his eyes with his hands. "Wh-why... Bren? I don't understand..."

He comes over and embraces me, holding me tight. He's shaking, and his heart is racing. "You don't know?"

"Yeah, I do." A tear runs down my cheek. "But why today already? Why now, after everything that happened yesterday?" Just the thought of leaving him makes me freak out, the same way that I freaked out in the beginning at the thought of being trapped with him forever.

"The question is, if not today, when?" He takes my face in his hands, caressing it with his eyes. His pupils are as big as they were that first day. "I'm afraid I'll change my mind if I don't let you go right away. Like, right now, you know?"

"*Now*?"

He runs a thumb across my cheek. "There's no other way."

"No..." Each word he says is another cruel blow to my unprotected soul. I can't just leave now, so totally unprepared, so totally alone.

He rests his forehead on mine. Oh, God, when he lets go of me, I'm going to shatter into a thousand tiny pieces, and nobody and nothing in the world will ever be able to put me back together. Including me. But I know that moment's coming. It's inevitable. Maybe this is how things have to end. Maybe it was meant to be like this.

"Lou." He's never spoken my name more tenderly. "Trust me. It's better this way. One day, you'll know that this was the right decision. Maybe not for today, but for all of the other days that come after it."

"What about you?" I ask in a strangled voice. "What happens when you have another flashback?"

"After tonight... I'll just imagine you're with me." He carefully releases me, and I really do shatter, even though I'm just standing there stiffly. A crack opens up inside me, and then a thousand more spider out from the first. It's like my soul is bursting. "You've done so much for me already, Lou. So much." His voice echoes along the cracks. I feel empty, hollowed out. "All I can do for you is let you go. And that's what I have to do. Because I love you."

He walks to the door and opens it wide. The air outside smells unfamiliar: concrete, trash, and people instead of spruce needles and wood. I still can't move. "You need to go before I change my mind." His voice sounds so lonely. So empty. And suddenly I understand how hard this must be for him, how much this is costing him. It's a hundred times harder for him than for me. I need to pull myself together for his sake, regardless of how I feel.

"I'll tell everyone I ran away," I say mechanically.

"Your brothers will hate you for that."

"Ethan, maybe."

"You can tell them the truth. The police will never find me."

It's not just fear of the police finding him, though. It's also the thought of what they would turn our story into. I couldn't possibly make Bren out to be a monster—I would always add that I fell in love with him. I picture myself in the police station. I can see the looks on the officers' faces now. *So you're saying he never raped you that whole time? Come on. You had sex with him willingly? Surely he must have threatened you. Consenting isn't the same as not fighting back, you know that, right?*

No. Listening to those questions would kill me. It would be like they were trying to destroy what Brendan and I had. I don't want reporters to turn this into a bunch of lurid stories. I don't want them pestering me to reveal everything I know about him. What Bren and I had together will stay our secret forever. It's too precious. And if that means Ethan hates me for supposedly running away, I'll just have to deal with it.

I gaze at Brendan, terrified of leaving him. I'm more afraid of this than I've ever been afraid of anything. But I have to be stronger than him now. I swallow my tears and my fear. I need to act strong for a few more minutes, that's all. Until I'm out of sight. "Where are we exactly?" I ask, trying to sound objective.

"We're in British Columbia." He reaches into the overhead cupboard and pulls down a backpack. "Money, food, fresh clothes, newspaper articles."

It hurts to see how well-prepared he is again.

He points through the door. "There's a mall and a bus stop about a quarter-mile that way. They have Greyhound lines to all the bigger cities, and you can transfer from there. I packed you a list of stations and departure times, I Googled them for you on the ol' Samsung."

"You have a cell phone?"

"I don't get any reception up there, Lou. Anyway, it's better if you don't hear anything from me for now."

"Right." Not crying is the hardest goddamn thing I've ever done.

He smiles. His eyes are full of tears. "You'll understand soon."

"Promise me something?" I gaze across the grey parking lot and can't possibly imagine what I'm going to do out there.

"Depends."

"Will you come back to Sequoia next year on June 25th? To the visitors' center?"

He gives me a blank look.

"That was the day you first kidnapped me."

319

He lets out a strange, short laugh. "I know that."

"If we still love each other then, we can spend the summer together," I say hurriedly. I need something to hold onto.

"I don't know if that's a good idea, Lou. It would be better for you to just forget me. And it would definitely be better for me to forget you."

"Think about it," I whisper. With that, I take the backpack from him and walk down the stairs. For one crazy moment, I wish he would grab my arm and haul me back inside, slam the door, and chain me up. I wait for a moment, but nothing happens. "Bye, Bren," I murmur without turning around. I don't want to hug him again, I don't want to kiss him again, I don't want to see Grey again. It would break my heart, and I can't let myself cry. I have to be strong for Brendan one last time, so I simply put one foot in front of the other. Right, left, right, left, again and again, the way I did the night I tried to run from him.

I can feel him watching me, sense him crying. In my mind, I hug him tightly. I keep my shoulders straight and my head held high, but inside I'm dying.

I'm vaguely aware that there are suddenly other people everywhere: chattering voices, rumbling car engines. The smell of exhaust, corn dogs, and French fries. It's like I've landed on a different planet. I look around, but I can't see anything. It's too much for me to take in any details. Too many people, too many voices, too much noise. A wave of fear wells up inside me, and I'm not sure why. A moment later, I bump into someone else.

"S'cuse me," I stammer quickly. I vaguely make out the shape of a woman.

She takes my upper arm gently. "Honey, are you okay? Do you need help?" The warmth in her voice sends everything crashing down. I feel my lips starting to tremble. But before I let myself fall apart completely, I have to know one thing.

"What day is today?"

"September 6th, honey. You're so pale, you don't look too good."

I stare through her, tugging unconsciously at a strand of hair. September 6th. I was only with Brendan for two and a half months.

It feels like it was a lot longer. Almost as an afterthought, I realize I'm seventeen now.

"Do you want to sit down?"

"I want to go home," I manage to get out, and then I burst into tears.

CHAPTER
TWENTY-FOUR

Something inside me is broken, but physically I'm still functioning. Still eating, still drinking, still breathing. Thanks to Brendan's list, I even manage to take the right buses. I spend the entire ride staring out the window, but his face is always looking back at me from out of the dark forests, above the snow-covered mountains, behind the green lakes. Is this the same route we took? How did he feel? How hard was it for him to lock me in the box after he'd experienced that same horror? Is that why he kept me drugged for so long?

I trace the raindrops running down the glass with one finger. There are so many things I still want to ask him, so many things I haven't told him yet. I might never get a chance to. I don't even know his last name or how old he is.

I'm so lost in thought that I go right on gazing out the window long after it gets dark. I catch a glimpse of my reflection. Weeks ago, I thought maybe I looked different than I used to, but now I realize that I look the same as ever, except with shorter hair and slightly thinner cheeks. The only problem is that I don't feel like myself at all. It's like someone else has taken over. What if my brothers notice? For one frightened moment, I wonder whether they'll believe the pack of lies I'm about to tell them.

I've decided to say that I ran off with two other girls I met at the park. I'm going to say we went to Canada, so that I won't have to invent too many details. One of the girls, Mia, will have to be some

323

wealthy stockbroker's daughter, because otherwise I won't be able to explain how we survived without doing anything criminal. Yeah, obviously she withdrew a ton of money before we met. I'm going to say that we wrote letters to our families so they wouldn't worry, but I guess mine must have gotten lost in the mail, which is why no other girls were reported missing. And then I'll say I don't want to talk about it, and hopefully they'll quit asking questions after a week or two.

I'm dreading those first couple of weeks. They're going to be like a mile-long bed of nails that I have to walk across barefoot and alone. Nobody will know my pain. Nobody will comfort me. Ethan will hate me; my brothers and friends won't understand what I'm going through. But I have to do it for Brendan, for the secret I have to bury deep inside myself, in the hopes that our time together isn't over yet. And if it is, then I just pray I won't ever forget it, that I won't wake up one day and realize that all of these thoughts and feelings and dreams have faded to nothing more than the smeared colors of the sky, the river, the spruces, and bodies entangled in the sand—like the kiss of a moth settling upon us, only to fly onward after one fleeting encounter.

I close my teary eyes and reach for my necklace, clutching the charms because they give me something to hold onto. Ethan's cross, Avery's heart, Liam's hand, Jayden's disk, another disk... there's another round charm on my necklace. I stop short. The tears spill over. I don't even have to look to know what's in my hand: a silver coin engraved with a bird with two different wings. Brendan must have slipped it onto my necklace sometime this morning. I bring it to my lips with trembling fingers and brush a kiss onto it, the goodbye kiss I never gave Brendan.

When I get off the bus in Ash Springs four days later, it's late in the evening. I feel completely drained. Cried out.

The first thing I'm aware of is the herby smell of sagebrush, and then the heat radiating from the dry, dusty ground. It's a strange feeling, neither familiar nor unfamiliar. I walk along the perfectly straight road, hoping nobody sees me. Once in a while, I raise my eyes to marvel at details I'm noticing for the first time: the rust-red roof of the little convenience store, the tall mailbox on the corner, in front of the house with the peeling window sills.

I turn onto the Road to Nowhere, and suddenly every cell in my body is tingling. Underneath my infinite longing for Brendan, under all the confusion and the mental exhaustion and everything, I feel something close to joy. This is home, this is where the people I love live. The people I've been missing so desperately.

Without consciously trying to, I start walking faster. I didn't call in advance, because I had no idea what to say to my brothers on the phone. Soon I'm running down the path... and then I see our house. My heart is beating heavily in my chest. The space underneath the apple tree is empty; the door is closed. I slow down, come to a stop, sweep my gaze across the yard. Everything's exactly the way it was, but it's as silent as a cemetery. My joy immediately turns to anxiety. What if something happened to them? What if...

The door flies open. "Lou?" Ethan suddenly appears on the doorstep like a ghost, staring at me with wide eyes, clutching a book in one hand with all his strength.

"Eth..." My voice falters. I can't believe he's really there. Or that I'm really here. Time stands still for several seconds. We simply stare at each other, each wondering whether the other is a figment of our imaginations. I've pictured coming home so many times, but nothing has prepared me for this moment. It's like someone's torn my heart out of my chest, but brought me back to life rather than killing me. It's joy and pain, homesickness and homecoming.

"Ethan," I whisper again.

The book he's holding slips from his hand. "Oh, God, Lou, oh my God!" he shouts and runs over to me. Not three seconds later, he's there, throwing his arms around me, clinging to me, pressing me to his chest. His shoulders are shaking—he's crying harder than I've ever seen another person cry. My heart knots painfully and swells with warmth at the same time. I'm so unbelievably happy. And so unbelievably sad. I wonder how it's possible for a person to feel so much joy and so much grief at the same time. I wonder whether human hearts are even built to hold this much emotion.

In the distance, I hear more shouts. I peek over Ethan's shoulder and spot Avery, Liam, and Jayden bounding down the stairs. It feels like a dream. Soon they're clustered around me in a circle, squeezing me half to death, only releasing me when I'm gasping for air. Then the four of them just stare at me like I'm a museum exhibit. Tears are running silently down Avery's face; Liam keeps stealthily wiping his eyes, and Jayden's bawling as openly as Ethan. He keeps putting his hand on my arm, touching my fingers, as though he can't believe I'm real.

After a while, they start talking all at once, but I can't get a word out. I'm too overwhelmed. Not just with joy at seeing them again, but with a deep gratitude that also makes me sad. Brendan was right. He made the right choice. For me. For my family. And I love him even more for it.

CHAPTER
TWENTY-FIVE

I set the table with our best dishes, the white ones with the silver rims that used to be Mom's. The turkey's in the oven, full of cornbread-and-nut stuffing, and the whole house smells like meat, sweet potatoes, and pumpkin pie. It's Thanksgiving. And I'm thankful for so many things. One of them is my period, which I got four weeks after returning home.

Two months have passed since the night I came back. Two months of me catching myself just standing there not sure what I was about to do next. Two months of doing things and then not remembering when or how I did them. Two months that have felt like half a century. And not one day, not one hour, not one second of those two months didn't involve me missing Brendan.

The first few weeks were the worst. It was bad enough having to scramble to fill in the huge gaps I didn't spot in my story—like how unlikely it was that three girls who all wanted to run away from home would randomly bump into each other at the Sequoia National Park visitors' center. Or why I didn't call as soon as I was all over the news. Or where exactly we traveled. I managed to find more or less plausible explanations for everything, but it was stressful.

Compared to Ethan's reaction, though, it was a walk in the park.

When he heard what I'd done, he slapped me for the first time in his life. He hasn't spoken to me since—except for during tutoring sessions, which he still gives me, but his voice is completely cold and I can sense his hostility in every gesture he makes. Avery's always trying to mediate between us, but his efforts have been in vain.

I take the orange napkins out of the cupboard with a sigh. He'll probably try to get us to kiss and make up again tonight. *Guys, it's Thanksgiving, can't you just get along already?* I already know it won't work. I hurt Ethan too deeply. And I deserved that slap. I feel so guilty. I could have saved him that final week or two of pain by calling for help at the river. And if Ethan knew I was kidnapped, he wouldn't be beating himself up about how strict he used to be. Avery tells me Ethan blames himself for this, at least mostly. But he's also doing everything the same way he always did—a leopard can't change his spots, as they say.

I fold the napkins into little flowers and set them on the plates. Maybe it'll be good for us to eat dinner all together tonight, whether Ethan's speaking to me or not. Liam's been spending more and more time on his own lately. His hair's nearly to his waist now, and he's woven pearls into his beard. He should probably spend more time living and less time meditating.

I frown at the table. Something's missing. Oh, right, the candles. I put them in the holders, but then I left them in the hallway. I want to make everything as beautiful as possible tonight, for Avery's sake. He's been in the kitchen cooking for us since this morning. Now he's finally slipped out to take a shower, and I know that when he gets out, he'll smell like Wild Ocean Dream, the blue soap.

I have to stop for a moment and get the trembling in my hands under control. That always happens whenever something reminds me of Brendan. I stand there for a few seconds, lost in my memories. For the hundredth time at least, I wonder why he went to the trouble of getting that soap and tracking down my whole wardrobe. It bugs me that I never asked. In retrospect, I think he must have done it so I would feel at home. He wanted everything to be the way it is here. I guess he should have kidnapped my brothers, too. The thought of the six of us crammed into a camper together actually makes me smile. I wonder what Brendan's doing right now? Playing with Grey, maybe?

"Hey, Lou." The bathroom door swings open, and my brother comes out, barefoot and smelling of soap. "Table set?"

"Of course. I just forgot these!" I grab the candles and force myself to smile. Maybe I should ask my brothers to change soaps. "Oh, and I think your pumpkin pie may be burning, Chef."

"Whaaat?" Avery raises his hands in the air theatrically and dashes into the kitchen. I know he's doing everything he can to cheer me up. I follow him, smiling, and stand in the doorway watching him. Ever since I started hearing snippets of Brendan's story, ever since I lost the things I took for granted, I've known what an amazing gift I have here. I know Ethan's the main reason we have it so good here, and I'm grateful for that, too... but the truth is, I miss my brother. I miss talking to him.

Once we've taken our seats around the table, where the piping-hot turkey is waiting on its serving tray, surrounded by roasted apples and glazed walnuts, Ethan rises from his chair with a solemn expression on his face. Being a devout Christian, he always wants to say a Thanksgiving prayer; Liam usually leaves the room until he's finished, and Jayden sits there pretending he's going to be sick. This year, though, everyone stays right where they are, listening attentively.

"Lord Jesus." Even Jayden's sitting in silence, looking toward the head of the table, where Ethan is standing in his best shirt and his freshly ironed pants. "Normally, this is the day we give thanks to you for allowing us to share in your bounty. You make sure that our table is always richly laid, that we have work and a place to sleep. But today, we want to thank you for a completely different reason. While Louisa was away, you protected her, day and night, hour after hour. You made sure that no harm came to her, and helped her find her way back to us, safe and healthy. Thank you for allowing us to sit at the same table today... and thank you for the strength you gave us to get through those difficult times." He swallows and looks over at me. I smile tentatively. "We want to thank you... for this second chance. And this time, I want to do better." His eyes are shimmering faintly as he adds, "Amen."

I stand up and hug him, and he holds me close. I'm lost for words all over again.

Jayden isn't, though. "Come on, you guys," he says, "there's a turkey waiting to be eaten here. Can you at least save the waterworks for later this time?"

Everyone laughs.

After dinner, Ethan and I break the wishbone, and I get the bigger piece, so I get to make a wish.

I think about Brendan, and about how much I want to see him again.

Everything's been so much easier since Ethan's started talking to me again. He says he noticed almost immediately how much I've changed. He saw how much I was studying and how much effort I was putting into the tutoring sessions, though I sometimes got exasperated with the material.

I'm not getting into trouble at school anymore, either, and I'm following all the rules he laid out before vacation. The weird thing is, they don't bother me in the slightest. I could care less about Hades in Love now.

Ava and Madison obviously thought it was totally cool that I ran away, while Emma and Elizabeth have been mostly eyeing me warily from a safe distance since they heard the story. The news spread through Ash Springs like wildfire; there was even an article in the paper about my return. One week later, two women came from Child Protective Services to ask me a bunch of questions about my brothers, and to ask my brothers a bunch of questions about me. They told us they'd be visiting us once a month from then on, and suggested I go to the school psychologist, but I haven't gone. I feel so terrible about this whole CPS thing—now everyone thinks Ethan is the bad guy. But I know who I'm doing this for. All I can do is emphasize again and again that this was nobody's fault but mine.

It's early December now, and it feels like time is going faster, because so many things are happening to distract me. Jayden's writing a new story about a girl who runs away from home, so obviously he has a million questions. Liam surprised us by showing up one day with a trimmed beard and short hair and announcing he'd converted to Christianity and was planning on getting baptized. School is all end-of-semester tests, all the time. I'm getting my first C+ in math. Avery and I are planning Christmas dinner together, plus I have to buy gifts, and once in a while I get together with Emma. I still feel out of place at school, but I'm managing to hide it. I laugh at the right moments, and I act like I'm listening, although my mind is somewhere in Canada.

And then it's Christmas. Liam and I set up a colorful blinking sled and reindeer underneath the apple tree, while Jayden and Avery hang a string of red-and-white candy-cane lights along the roof. The four of us laugh and mess around like kids; only Ethan watches with a slightly disapproving frown. He was against all these kitschy decorations, but after I got my C+ and Liam suddenly converted, he couldn't say no.

Avery takes Christmas Eve off, so we have time to start cooking for the 25th. We're going to serve cream of chestnut soup to start, and then roast goose with red cabbage and dumplings. For dessert, we're doing banana pudding with toasted marshmallows on top.

On the evening of the 24th, Avery and I are totally dead. I've got bits of dumpling dough and pureed chestnut sticking to the ends of my hair. As I'm rinsing it out in the sink, I realize that my hair's finally reached my shoulders again. I give my reflection a melancholy smile and feel a pang in my heart.

"Hey, Lou, hurry up!" Liam calls from the living room. "Hero of the Week's about to start!" I look at myself again. The new me doesn't feel like quite as much of a stranger anymore. Outside and inside match again somehow.

When I come into the living room, my brothers are already gathered around the TV. Even Jayden's here, since he finally finished that short story about the runaway girl earlier today. I squeeze onto the sofa between Ethan and Liam and pick up the bag of chips lying on the table. The second I get it open, Jayden walks over and grabs an enormous handful, then retreats to the Moroccan pouffe ottoman from Dad's wild years.

"I can't believe you still have room to eat anything." Avery blinks at me in amazement. "You ate half the dumpling dough."

"That was you, not me."

"Can you guys be quiet? I can't hear!"

"Jeez, Ethan, you must be crushing pretty hard on David O'Dell." Jayden sighs.

"Shut up."

There's a loud pop.

"Since when do you drink alcohol?" Avery asks Liam, who's putting a freshly opened bottle of beer to his lips.

"Since I became a Christian." Liam grins.

"You're drinking to forget, huh?"

"Be quiet already, Jay."

"Tell Lou to stop chewing so loudly, then."

"Lou, don't chew so loudly," Ethan says, sounding defeated. "Now, can we please listen to this? I think they said today's hero is from Canada..."

Everyone goes completely silent immediately. We all watch the images flicker across the screen: a steely blue sky; a wintery forest full of snow-covered pines, spruces, and larches; a single blackbird soaring above the treetops; a grey-green river. In the background, a mountain range rises majestically into the heavens.

I recognize everything. Of course it's not exactly the same area, but it looks just how that part of Canada would in winter. My mind wanders to the lake singing itself to sleep as it hibernates. I swallow my mouthful of chips with some difficulty.

"Today's Hero of the Week comes from the lonely Yukon Territory in Canada," I hear David O'Dell say. The once-shy moderator smiles confidently into the camera. "Some people think of the Yukon as a place for hermits and eccentrics, but the Great Frozen North is also a land of myth and mystery, of wisdom dating back thousands of years. The original inhabitants believed that the raven brought the sun each morning, and that bears had souls most similar to our own."

"Did you learn that on your trip, too?" Jayden crunches his chips way too loudly.

I don't respond. I go right on staring at the television, mesmerized.

"Today's guest may be a lone wolf of sorts, but he's definitely a hero as well. At the age of just twenty-two, he's already saved five lives. Please join me in welcoming Brendan Connor."

Brendan?

I barely register the euphoric applause as the hero steps through the door into the studio. My hand flies to my heart. Bren! No, that's impossible. I close my eyes and open them again. It's still Bren. He looks so familiar, in his old dark-brown cargo pants and his black

hoodie. It's like I just saw him yesterday, just touched him yesterday. My throat tightens, and my hands start shaking wildly. I'm
totally helpless against the pain and the longing ambushing me
from the shadows. A storm of bittersweet memories rolls over me.
Involuntarily, I crumple the bag of chips into a ball as I try and fail
to follow what the moderator's saying. I half-hear something about
Bren having saved a five-person family from a grizzly attack, but
mostly I'm focused on other things: the way he keeps shyly
averting his eyes, seemingly embarrassed at all this attention; the
way he's trying to get out of the blinding spotlight by stepping
further and further away from the moderator. Mentally, I tell him to
be strong, and I wonder if he knows I'm watching. Yeah, I'm sure
he knows, or at least he's hoping.

A strange feeling comes over me as I watch him and David
O'Dell. What if he doesn't want me anymore? What if, now that
he's Hero of the Week, hundreds of people start sending him offers
of marriage?

I'm squeezing the bag so hard that the chips are probably
crumbs.

"Jeez, he's got some balls," Jay snorts admiringly. "Yells at a
hungry bear to distract it, without first figuring out where he's
gonna escape to?"

"What would he have done if he hadn't made it up the tree?"
Liam adds. "Hallelujah!"

"And then he carries that dude for miles and miles through the
ice and snow so he won't bleed to death... Hey, Lou, throw the
chips over."

Mechanically, I stretch out my hand, and Jay takes the bag.

"The hell? They're totally smushed!"

I can't reply. I can't take my eyes off Brendan.

"So, Brendan," David O'Dell says, "among all of our many
Heroes of the Week, do you have a personal favorite that you think
ought to win Hero of the Year?"

"Not a hero, a heroine," he replies quietly, and then turns to
look into the camera for the first time. "She was never on this show,
but she did save my life."

David O'Dell beams. "A hero saved by someone else? Sounds
interesting. Who is she?"

The camera zooms in on Brendan's face, so that it fills the entire screen. I see his pupils dilating, flooding the brown of his eyes—like he's looking at me. Before I realize it, I'm clutching the silver coin on my necklace.

"A girl from Nevada. She showed me that I'm not quite as bad of a person as I always thought. She believed in me when I had stopped believing in myself." He clears his throat briefly. "She brought sunlight into to my darkness, and showed me that grey is really just silver that doesn't shine. And I want to thank her for that, because it's the only reason I'm here today."

I must have made some kind of noise, because I feel all of my brothers giving me sidelong glances. Jayden especially. I can hear him practically grinding the chips in his hand to flour. The cameraman zooms in even closer, probably sensing that this is the love story of the year. Bren's eyes are shimmering. I can only imagine how difficult this is for him.

"When we parted ways, she wanted me to make her a promise. At the time, I wasn't sure whether I could keep it, but today..." He swallows so hard that his Adam's apple bulges out. "I want her to know that I'm in therapy and... and that I'll be here waiting for her whenever she's ready to give me another chance."

The image on screen blurs into a wet veil. The pain of having lost him gives way to an immense feeling of joy and longing that hurts just as much, maybe more, but in a different way. He wants to try. He still wants me.

As if in a trance, I get up and walk to my room. I can't stay in there with my brothers, not right now. I throw myself on the bed, and through the closed door, I hear the moderator summarizing the past month.

The things Bren said about me wash through my head as the tears stream down my face. When I got home nearly four months ago, I knew that he'd made the right choice—for me. But now I understand that he made the right choice for us, too. Because now I know that my feelings are real. They're not Stockholm syndrome, they're not sick or abnormal. I would have fallen in love with him anyway; he just made it unnecessarily hard on himself by kidnapping me. I lie there for a while, staring at the ceiling, but all I can see are colors and mental snapshots of our summer together. I miss the forest and the scent of pine needles, I miss Grey and the cool morning air. The scent of firewood. I miss Bren. June is so far off.

The minute the closing credits music starts, Jay barges into my room without knocking, and slams the door shut behind him. "Grey is silver that doesn't shine?" He raises an eyebrow at me— curious, not angry. "A girl from Nevada?"

I straighten up, already trying to figure out how to talk my way out of this, but I can't come up with anything on the spot. "Jayden..."

"I never *did* buy that story about the two girls."

I stare at him in horror. There are still tears in my eyes, so I can only see his blurry outline. "Why not?"

"The answers you gave me... none of it really sounded like you." One corner of his mouth quirks upward. "Can I sit?"

"Sure." I pat the blanket invitingly.

He drops down beside me, then scoots back to the wall and puts his feet on the edge of the bed. "Okay, little sister. Who's Brendan Connor, and what did you do with him?"

Suddenly, it's all too much for me. I'm desperate to share my secret with someone else, to have someone else know what I went through, how terrified I was at first with Bren, and how that fear turned to trust and then love. I want to have someone nearby that I can cry to, someone who will understand me.

Weird—I never thought it would be Jayden. I always figured I'd end up telling Avery, many years from now. Then again, Jayden's the one who loves crazy stories.

"You can't tell anyone," I say now. "You have to swear."

"Hm." Jay regards me indecisively. "Did he do something bad? Or did you?"

"He did."

Jayden's expression darkens.

Hastily, I shake my head. "Not the way you think."

He doesn't look convinced.

"Really," I add emphatically.

His face relaxes again, and then he nods slowly. "Okay, I swear."

"And you have to promise me something else."

"What?"

"You have to drive me to Sequoia National Park on June 25th."

337

He gives me a baffled look.

"Without the others finding out. And then, once I'm gone, you can tell them everything. The whole truth."

"Lou, what are you talking about? What do you mean, when you're gone? I'm not driving you somewhere so you can disappear again. You're out of your mind."

"I just want the summer."

Jayden sighs. "I probably don't really want to hear this story, do I?"

I smile, and the question makes me think of Brendan. Under different circumstances, with different pasts, I bet Brendan and Jay would have gotten along great. I clasp Bren's silver coin.

"Is that from him?" Jay eyes it quizzically.

I nod and hold the charm out. "He has this design tattooed on his back, too. This coin used to belong to his mom."

"Cool."

"But sad, too." I let the pendant drop and take Jay's hand. I'm going to need it—otherwise I'll never find the words to describe everything that happened to me.

CHAPTER
TWENTY

I stuff my suitcase into the trunk of Liam's old wreck of a car. Jayden's already behind the wheel. Before I get in, I take one last look over my shoulder. Our house is only partly visible through all the sagebrush. It's five in the morning; the sun will be up in half an hour, but we'll be long gone by then.

I think about the three letters under my pillow—one to Ethan, one to Avery, and one to Liam. Jayden and I have agreed that he'll hand them out when he gets back and tell them the whole story.

It took me two months to convince Jayden not to take back his promise. "What if you want to leave and he won't let you?" he asked. "All over again? What if this whole thing is some big, elaborate ruse, like he kidnaps a girl once a year and keeps her there until she's in love with him?"

I asked myself that same question at first, but that was before New Year's Eve, when I saw Bren on TV.

I've got my phone with me to ease Jayden's mind, but I doubt I'll get reception anyway. He's also going to insist that Bren tell him the exact location of his property, so that he knows where to find me in case of emergency. "Somewhere in Canada" likely won't cut it.

I slide into the passenger seat, and Jayden drives away. We don't talk much on the road. After a while, he turns on the radio, and we both hum along. The distraction helps a little, but my head is still pure chaos. What if Bren doesn't show up? What if he stopped going to therapy? What if he's met some other girl? What if he shows up just to tell me that he'd rather not see me again? What if he wants a fresh start?

I don't know what I'd do then.

I roll down the window and stick my hand out. The silken Mojave Desert wind blows through my splayed fingers, tickling my skin and filling me with a crazy feeling of freedom and joy. No, he'll be there. I know it. I close my eyes and picture the way we made love on the sand beneath the willow tree, the way our bodies fit into one another—two halves forming a perfect whole. I remember his kisses, remember the sweet sensations flowing through me. I can't believe I was ever afraid those memories would fade.

By noon, we're barely halfway there, because a truck full of oranges tipped over on the street in front of us. I'm starting to get nervous that Bren will think I'm not coming. Maybe the waiting will be too much for him, and he'll leave early. I keep glancing at the clock, watching time slip away from me. Three in the afternoon already? Jay starts getting annoyed with me fidgeting around in my seat, constantly begging him to drive faster. Eventually he threatens to throw me out of the car and drive the rest of the way alone, so I force myself to be quiet until he finally, finally reaches the entrance to the national park. It's four o'clock now, but that visitor's center is somewhere in the middle of the park, at one of the highest points in the area. Why didn't we leave earlier? But it only took seven hours to get here last time, so 5 AM seemed like it would be plenty.

Liam's old Ford struggles up the serpentine roads, but soon the engine starts to smoke, and Jay pulls into a lay-by.

"Are you serious?" I moan, throwing the door open angrily and stomping around to the hood, which is steaming like a locomotive.

"We've gotta let it cool off for a second, Lou. Otherwise it'll break down." Jay gets out and starts checking the car over. "Not far now."

"We should have taken Ethan's car. The visitors' center's going to close."

"Nah, it's open late. It was dusk, don't you remember?" Jay gives me a pointed look from across the open hood.

How could I forget? Every second of that day is burned into my mind forever. I don't say that aloud, though.

By the time the engine has cooled off "for a second," it's five thirty. I'm near tears. The narrow street goes on forever, up and up... speed limit 15! After a hundred and thirty-seven more curves or so, smoke starts rising from the hood again. Jayden sets his jaw grimly and keeps pushing the car onward. If we take another break as long as the first one, we'll definitely be too late.

After what seems like a thousand years, I'm close to a nervous breakdown, and the engine isn't just smoking, it's also rattling... and then the Lodgepole sign finally comes into view. The car crawls across the line marking the boundaries of the parking lot. The visitors' center is directly ahead.

Hastily, I sweep my gaze across the lot. My hands are clammy. I only see a couple of vans and a station wagon.

Jayden parks the wheezing car directly in front of the visitors' center. "Do you want to go in alone?"

I just nod. My heart is hammering like crazy. What if Bren isn't here? I stay seated for a moment, taking deep breaths.

"Lou, before you go... there's something you probably ought to know." My brother regards me with a solemn expression on his face. "I wasn't sure if I was going to tell you or not, but it's probably better if you know."

"What?" I turn to face him, forcing myself to focus on him.

"You know how you showed me that coin you got from this Brendan guy?" He taps his hands against the steering wheel in agitation.

"What about it?"

"I decided to do some searching, and I ended up on this online artists' forum, and I found this crafts shop in Albuquerque..."

I give him a look of outrage. "You went searching for him online and didn't tell me?"

"When my sister asks me to bring her back to a guy who kidnapped her and kept her in a box for five days last year, it seems like the least I can do."

"Well, what did you find out?" This is giving me a bad feeling in the pit of my stomach. I turn to look at the entrance to the visitors' center.

"The shop belongs to an old friend of Brendan's mom's. I know because I drove out there one weekend to meet her." He pauses briefly. "I had to tell her a little bit about you, otherwise she wouldn't have told me anything."

"That's okay," I say, swallowing the lump in my throat. I can't believe he did all of this behind my back! Then again... I know how much I'm asking of him right now. "What did she say?"

"Not a whole lot. She designed that coin at Brendan's mom's request, and then she liked the motif, so she made a few more." His eyes bore into me. "Brendan's dad—well, stepdad, actually—it sounds like he was a total psycho, like, seriously sick in the head. He was a coffin-maker from Oklahoma, and he beat the crap out of Brendan's mom, really tortured her. When he discovered he wasn't Brendan's biological father, he apparently locked her in a coffin and threatened to bury her alive in the yard."

My heart is seizing up. So I was right about what happened to Brendan. I shift my gaze back to the entrance as Jayden continues.

"Brendan's mom escaped the first chance she had, and went to stay with her friend the jewelry designer. She went that same day to pick Brendan up from preschool, but he was already gone—I guess his stepdad found out she'd left, so he pulled Brendan out of school. She called him and told him she'd call the cops to help her get her son back, but he told her he'd kill Brendan if she tried, and then he simply disappeared. To L.A., I guess, if that's where Brendan told you he grew up. Anyway, Brendan's stepdad called his mom over and over again, reiterating the threat. He was a total sadist, using the son to make the wife miserable. She spent years searching for them, trying to get Brendan back, but no luck, obviously. Finally, I guess she died of a broken heart."

I swallow hard. So Brendan's mother really didn't abandon him. I can't even begin to imagine what that will mean to Brendan. I look at Jay. "Why are you only telling me this stuff now?"

He exhales slowly. "I wasn't sure if I should tell you at all. If this guy had wanted to know anything about his own past, he could have just as easily gone searching for it himself. Telling you means now you have to decide whether to tell him or not."

"He was probably afraid of what he might find out. He was trying to just forget the whole thing." I glance at the entrance yet again. I'm so scared that he's changed his mind.

"Do you think you'll tell him?" Jayden asks.

"Well, he has to show up first."

Jay's hand brushes mine. "Lou. Go inside and check. Maybe he's already in there, and he parked somewhere else."

So Jay's noticed, too. "Or he came in a different car?" I say, trying to reassure myself.

"Or that!"

"Okay. Back in a bit." I hop out of the car and shut the door behind me. For a moment, I just stand there, pondering Jay's story. In principle, it doesn't change much of anything. More than anything, it confirms what I'd already guessed. And of course Brendan needs to know this stuff about his mom... but maybe not immediately, I mean, I don't even know how he's doing yet.

Still standing beside the car, I cast a look around the parking lot. It's twilight already, just like it was last year. There's that same familiar scent of pine needles and smoke. I relive the moment I decided to walk to Brendan's camper with him. I feel the wind on my face, hear the trees rustling and Bren's keys jingling and the camping lanterns clacking in his hand. A hot-and-cold shiver runs down my back: joy, fear, nostalgia. For the hundredth time, I realize to my continued astonishment that I'm not sure when exactly I fell in love with Brendan, when trusting him suddenly turned into more. I take one more long, deep breath, letting it out slowly, and then step through the open glass door.

Warmth envelops me. Suddenly, it feels like it was just yesterday that I came in here searching for camping lanterns. The wood paneling, the shop, the information stands, they're all exactly the way I remember them. I stop at the clothing rack full of hoodies, lost in thought. I'm still too nervous to check the whole store, because I'm terrified to find out that I came all this way for nothing. *Please let him be here*, I pray silently. *Please, please let him be here, or if he's not here yet, let him come here.*

Without realizing it, I've wandered into the alcove with the camping gear. I reach for the bear spray. I bet it really does do something. He engineered that whole encounter with such finesse. I turn the can over in my hand, but the printed information on the back blurs in front of my eyes. He's not coming. I know it. If he's in therapy, working through the stuff Jay was telling me about, I'm sure his therapist has told him he shouldn't see me again. It might even make his old dangerous thought patterns come out again, and then he'll relapse, the way alcoholics do. And then maybe he'll have to kidnap another girl, just to get that confirmation of her love.

I bite my lips hard. I should go. There's no point in standing here torturing myself any longer. If he'd been planning on coming here, he'd be here by now. He'd have been waiting in the lot for me.

Dazed, I set the spray back on the shelf. It would have been too perfect if he'd arrived at this exact moment, stepped into this same alcove where we had our first conversation.

I raise my head and take a long look around the store. My heart is thumping hard in my chest. Brendan's tall, there's no way I wouldn't see him over the shelves, and the only other people in here are two guys in army-green caps and a couple of girls my age. Should I ask the guy running the register if he's seen Brendan? *Um, excuse me, did last year's Hero of the Week 52 come through here by chance? By the way, I'm that girl who disappeared in the park...*

It's seven thirty now. The visitors' center is closing in half an hour.

Eyes burning, I glance toward the information area, and then over to the other exit, the one leading to the showers. He's not there, either.

I try to fight back my disappointment, but it rolls over me like an avalanche. My whole body is numb, deadened. He didn't come. My memories will be all I have left of the time we spent together. When I said goodbye to him in that parking lot in British Columbia, it was goodbye forever. Why didn't I give him one more hug? Why didn't I kiss him? I turn a complete circle, still searching. I just don't want to believe it... but that doesn't change anything about the fact that he isn't here.

Finally, I give up once and for all. Head lowered to hide my tears, I start for the exit.

Suddenly, a piercing howl comes from the direction of the back entrance, followed by loud barking. Someone screams.

"Hey, mister, you can't bring a wolf—"

"Lou! Lou, wait!"

Bren! My heart skips a beat and then restarts at full gallop. A giant boulder rolls away from my soul, releasing thousands of golden butterflies that lift me into the air. He's here!

346

"If you don't take that wolf out of h—"

"—s'cuse me, so sorry about this—"

Before I've even finished turning around, Grey leaps up and knocks me to the floor. Then he clambers onto me and licks my face. I pull his head in and hug him, stroke his fur. Tears well up in my eyes again, this time tears of joy. I push Grey aside a little with one hand and sit up.

Brendan's standing there in cargo pants and a hoodie. His face is thin and solemn, but his eyes gleam from somewhere deep down, some light hidden away inside him.

"You came," he says quietly, helping me to my feet. He seems like he's barely managing to keep himself under control. I want to tell him it's okay to cry, but I know he doesn't want to hear that, so I just squeeze his fingers.

"You doubted I would?"

He smiles, and I can see the tension falling away from him more and more. "Been doubting it all day."

My lips are trembling. "I didn't think you'd be there. We got a flat tire, and a truck tipped over, and there were these stupid oranges all over the damn street..."

He laughs, but it sounds like it's masking a sob, one that releases the rest of his pent-up fear. "I arrived yesterday, actually. I've been here since this morning." He takes hold of Grey's collar and casts a reassuring glance at the man behind the counter. "I had Grey tied up out there earlier, but he got loose—I had to run and catch him." His pupils get huge, and I feel the time we spent apart melting away to nothing. His eyes are like a butterfly net, catching me for the second time in my life. There's so much I want to say to him, but we have the whole summer for that.

I walk over to him and slide my arms around his waist. "I never want to be away from you again, Bren. Never."

He presses me close, buries his face in my hair. "You won't have to, Lou. Promise."

And then we kiss, cautiously and tenderly like it's the first time. A tingling wave washes over my skin like bubbles of air, making me shiver. His lips feel the way they did under the willow tree: wild-gentle, bittersweet. They're joy and pain, the calm and the storm.

We stand there for a long moment, wrapped up in one another, until the guy at the cash register threatens to call the rangers if we don't take the wolf out of the store this minute.

When we reach the parking lot, Jayden is waiting by the car. He's trying to act casual, but I can tell he's eyeing Bren carefully, taking in as much information as he can. Finally, he gives me a long goodbye hug.

Before we leave, he turns to Brendan with a grim look on his face. "If you hurt her again, I'll kill you."

Bren just nods, taking my hand. Then he whistles to Grey, who's busy sniffing Liam's car. This time, the wolf trots over immediately. He's full-grown now, with icy grey fur that's nearly silver, and his blue eyes have turned a deep honey color.

"He stayed with you," I marvel. I really did think it was only a matter of time until Grey wandered into the forest and didn't come back.

Bren claps Grey on the back with his free hand. I can sense the deep connection between them. "We had a couple pretty serious fights before he finally understood who's in charge around here." He looks at me. "The camper's a little ways off," he adds almost apologetically. "They wouldn't let me park it here all day."

I just smile and start across the parking lot with him. I know we're going to be okay, even though it won't be easy to forget the past. I know that the light of the future will cast shadows, too.

Right now, though, it feels like the past and the future are one moment, intersecting here and now, between the light and the shadows—weightless, like spreading wings preparing to soar away. I look around. Reddish-gold rays of sunlight filter through the gathering blue-grey clouds, and the long, dark band of sequoias at the edge of the parking lot stretch far into the distance. It'll be pitch dark here soon.

It's just how it was back then. The first time.

Bren glances over at me, and the red sunlight dances in his eyes.

I remember the question I saw in those eyes a year ago, the one he was only asking me in his heart.

Do you want this?

I know the answer now.

348

~

SOON

Louisa and Brendan's story continues!

Is their love truly real or does it stem from an illusion and Lou's loneliness during the kidnapping? Does this love have a chance or will it shatter in the face of reality? And how does Ethan react to what Jayden has done?

Read the sequel:

- "Trapped Until The Darkest Of Night"

Find out more about Bren's childhood and what he went through the months before and after the abduction, and how he discovered Lou. Or continue with Lou and Bren's story a year after the abduction in

- "Trapped. Between Sky and Wind"
- "Trapped. Where Dreams Take us"

Subscribe to my newsletter to learn about promotions, competitions, and new novels:

www.milaolsenbooks.com/newsletter

(Coming soon!)

Author's Note

A few attentive readers have pointed out that the episodes Brendan experiences wouldn't fit the textbook definition of flashbacks. They're absolutely correct: Brendan calls them flashbacks because he doesn't know any better. His deep-seated psychological trauma has caused him to develop dissociative disorder. Book 2 of the series (*Trapped: Until the Darkest of Nights*), which is soon available in English, gives more details about this highly complex condition.

THANKS

More than anyone, I want to thank my family for being so patient with me. I don't know how many times I said I "just needed to rewrite something really quick" and then disappeared for hours on end. Special thanks as well to my editor, Anne Paulsen, for her creative work on my manuscript, and for her many valuable ideas and suggestions when it came to complicated, hard-to-read sentences. I'd also like to thank Katie Weber for her striking cover design—I had a lot of fun working together!

Thanks very much to my test readers, especially Judy Zweifel, who also did the final proofread.

Finally, I'd like to thank you, my readers. Thank you for giving Brendan and Louisa a chance. If you liked the book, I'd love it if you could leave a review and/or recommend it to others—and please check out my homepage or my Facebook page!

Subscribe to my newsletter to learn about promotions, competitions, and new novels:

www.milaolsenbooks.com/newsletter

Made in the USA
Monee, IL
14 January 2025